PRAISE

The Siren o

"Unflinching, tender, and moving, the delicately crafted *The Siren of Sussex* might just be my favorite work from Mimi Matthews; it certainly is one of my favorite historical romance reads this year."
—Evie Dunmore, *USA Today* bestselling author of *Portrait of a Scotsman*

"Lush, seductive, original—*The Siren of Sussex* drew me in from the first page, and wove its magic. A fresh, vibrant, brilliant Victorian romance, making it an unforgettable read."
—*New York Times* bestselling author Jane Porter

"A moving love story and a vivid recreation of Victorian life, *The Siren of Sussex* by Mimi Matthews is a treat of a book for the historical romance lover."
—Award-winning author Anna Campbell

"An exquisite historical romance that is so captivating I had to force myself not to gallop through it at a breakneck speed, wanting to savor the author's obvious care and delicate attention to detail. . . . A must-read for lovers of historical fiction."
—Meg Tilly, author of *The Runaway Heiress*

"Marvelously crafted, Evelyn and Ahmad's world is ripe with nuanced social perceptions and characters that winnow heart-deep. At times passionately intelligent and achingly vulnerable, *The Siren of Sussex* is destined to dazzle readers of Evie Dunmore and Harper St. George."
—Rachel McMillan, author of *The London Restoration* and *The Mozart Code*

ABOUT THE AUTHOR

USA Today bestselling author Mimi Matthews writes both historical non-fiction and award-winning proper Victorian romances. Her novels have received starred reviews in *Library Journal*, *Publishers Weekly* and *Kirkus Reviews*, and her articles have been featured on the *Victorian Web*, the *Journal of Victorian Culture*, and in syndication at *BUST* magazine. In her other life, Mimi is an attorney. She resides in California with her family, which includes a retired Andalusian dressage horse, a sheltie and two Siamese cats.

The Siren of Sussex

MIMI MATTHEWS

PENGUIN BOOKS

PENGUIN BOOKS

UK | USA | Canada | Ireland | Australia
India | New Zealand | South Africa

Penguin Books is part of the Penguin Random House group of companies
whose addresses can be found at global.penguinrandomhouse.com

First published in the United States of America by Berkley,
an imprint of Penguin Random House LLC 2022
First published in Great Britain by Penguin Books 2023
002

Book design by Daniel Brount
Printed and bound in Great Britain by Clays Ltd, Elcograf S.p.A.

The authorized representative in the EEA is Penguin Random House Ireland,
Morrison Chambers, 32 Nassau Street, Dublin D02 YH68

A CIP catalogue record for this book is available from the British Library

ISBN: 978–1–405–95827–1

www.greenpenguin.co.uk

Penguin Random House is committed to a
sustainable future for our business, our readers
and our planet. This book is made from Forest
Stewardship Council® certified paper.

For Centelleo

Who rides the best horse in the row? Who drives the most rampageous ponies? Whom do all the best girls ape in dress and deportment, and in equipage if they can; aye, and in talk, too? . . . Why, one of our "pretty horsebreakers."

—THE TIMES (LONDON), JANUARY 29, 1861

One

*E*velyn Maltravers entered the dimly lit shop in Conduit Street. A modest sign above the door proclaimed the names and trade of the proprietors: *Messrs. Doyle and Heppenstall, Tailors.* The interior of the shop was equally modest—a small showroom furnished with a pair of plump leather chairs, a trifold mirror, and a tall counter of polished mahogany. Gas wall sconces cast a diffuse glow over the fabric shelved behind it. Rolls of superfine cloth in subdued shades of black, brown, and blue.

It was a quarter to seven. Nearly closing time. The murmur of a deep male voice emanated from the back room, drifting out through the curtained door that separated it from the showroom.

Evelyn's pulse quickened. A tailor's shop was a masculine domain. One in which a lady's presence was as rare as it was unwelcome. But she didn't let that fact deter her. Stiffening her spine, she approached the counter and rang the bell.

The voice in the back room fell silent. Seconds later, a thin, white-haired gentleman emerged from behind the curtain. His eyes were rheumy, his back bent, as if he'd spent a lifetime hunched over a worktable.

"Can I help you, madam?" His voice was as reedy as his figure.

"Thank you, yes. I'd like to speak with Mr. Doyle, please."

"I am Mr. Doyle."

Her spirits sank. She'd been expecting a man of fashion. Of vision. Someone with magic in his fingers. But the elderly fellow who now stood before her looked neither fashionable nor particularly capable. His fingers were gnarled with age, his hands trembling as if he suffered from some manner of palsy.

A hopeful thought struck her. "And Mr. Heppenstall? Is he at liberty?"

"Mr. Heppenstall passed away last autumn."

"Oh." Her spirits once again plummeted. The deep voice behind the curtain must belong to a shop assistant or one of the cutters. Someone of no account.

"Is there something I can assist you with?" Mr. Doyle asked with a hint of impatience.

She reminded herself that appearances were often deceiving. It was certainly true in her own case. For all she knew, the elderly tailor might still be a veritable magician with a needle and thread. "I sincerely hope so. You see . . ." She pushed her delicate silver-framed spectacles more firmly up onto her nose. "You were recommended to me by a . . . a friend."

Not entirely the truth, but not strictly a lie, either.

His bushy white brows lifted. "A client of mine?"

"Indeed," she said. "I'd like to commission a riding habit."

He gave her bespectacled face and plainly clad figure a dubious look.

A wave of self-consciousness took her unawares.

Perhaps she should have ordered a new dress before calling? Something from a fashionable modiste that would have lent her a bit of countenance? Instead, she'd worn an unembellished skirt and caraco jacket. A sensible ensemble cut and sewn by the village seamstress in Combe Regis. No doubt it made her appear thoroughly countrified.

But it was too late to second-guess herself.

Countrified she may be at present, but she wouldn't be so for long.

"Everyone with the slightest claim to fashionable dress knows that tailors make the very best ladies' riding habits," she continued determinedly. "And I mean to have the best."

"Understandably so, but if you'll forgive me . . ." He paused. "We don't design apparel for bluestockings."

Evelyn failed to suppress a flinch. She wasn't wholly surprised by the charge. She'd been called a bluestocking before. A wallflower, too, and any number of other unoriginal epithets applied to young ladies who failed to conform. Mr. Doyle's words nevertheless hit her like a dash of cold water. "You've mistaken me, sir."

"I think not, ma'am. Might I direct you to Mr. Inglethorpe in Oxford Street? He does a steady trade in ladies' habits, and would have no qualms about accepting your custom." Bowing, Mr. Doyle moved to withdraw. "I bid you good evening."

She opened her mouth to argue, but he was gone behind the curtain before she could formulate her words. She was left standing in the empty shop, her gloved hands clasped tight in front of her.

It took an effort not to let the old tailor's words pierce her armor. She knew all too well what people saw when they looked at her—if they saw her at all. It was the very reason she'd settled on her plan. And she wasn't about to be thwarted now. Not by Mr. Doyle. Not by anyone.

She considered ringing the bell again. She hadn't come this far to be so easily rebuffed. But what good would it do to summon Mr. Doyle back? She couldn't very well force the man to accept her business. Unless . . .

She supposed she could offer to pay him a higher price.

According to Evelyn's sources, Miss Walters had paid thirteen pounds for her latest habit. Surely Evelyn could manage to scrape together a few shillings more?

Long seconds of indecision passed, marked by the heavy ticking of a wall clock. It counted down the minutes until she must return to her uncle's house in Bloomsbury.

No, she decided at last. She wouldn't bribe Mr. Doyle. She couldn't. It was a point of principle. Of personal pride. If he didn't think her worthy of one of his creations, she'd simply have to find another tailor. Someone with comparable skill and artistry.

If such a person existed.

Marshaling her emotions, she turned toward the door, only to be halted by the sound of a deep voice behind her.

"The shop closes at seven."

"Yes, I'm aware. I was just . . ." She glanced back. The words died on her lips.

A man stood behind the counter. A tall, powerfully built man, with rich copper-colored skin and hair as black as new coal. The harsh planes of his face were half-shadowed in the gaslight, making him look almost sinister.

Her mouth went dry.

So, this was the owner of the voice she'd heard behind the curtain. The voice that had made her heart beat faster. That was *still* making her heart beat faster.

She moistened her lips. "I was just leaving."

But she didn't go.

She was caught by his insolent gaze. It drifted over her, seeming to take an inventory of her entire person, from the top of her three-times-made-over felt hat to the hem of her brown poplin skirts.

Her breath stopped. Never in her life had a man looked at her thus. So bold and knowing. She had the unsettling sensation that he could see straight through the fabric of her clothes, all the way to the naked skin that lay beneath.

Heat rose in her cheeks. "Are you Mr. Doyle's assistant?"

His eyes met hers. They were as dark as his hair. Black and luminous, like obsidian glass.

Which wasn't possible, she knew. It must be a trick of the light.

"Something like that," he said, a wry undercurrent in his tone that was just shy of amusement.

Her embarrassment swiftly gave way to irritation. It was one thing to be insulted and dismissed by Mr. Doyle, but to be laughed at by one of the man's underlings was something else altogether. She fixed him with her most disapproving glare. "May I say, sir, that the service in this shop is execrable."

"You have a particular complaint?"

"I have." She returned to the counter, very much on her dignity. "You may tell your employer that just because a lady wears spectacles, and just because she's new to London and hasn't yet availed herself of a dressmaker, does *not* mean she's a bluestocking."

He was silent for a taut moment. "With respect, ma'am, a business has its reputation to consider."

"And I have mine to establish." She leaned over the counter. "I am *not* a bluestocking. I don't attend intellectual salons or meetings on rational dress. I don't secretly write novels or newspaper editorials. And I certainly don't dabble in scientific experiments. I have only two passions in life: horses and fashion. I'm well-equipped to cut a dash with the former, but I need Mr. Doyle's assistance with the latter."

"Even if what you say is true, Doyle would still be obliged to refuse you. His female clients exist in a different sphere—"

"He outfits the Pretty Horsebreakers," Evelyn interrupted. "Yes. I know. That's precisely why I've come to him."

The man's gaze became even more intent. "These 'Pretty Horsebreakers,' as you call them, are no ordinary women."

Her chin lifted a notch. "I know what they are." They were courtesans. Famously beautiful courtesans who were also the most fashionable and accomplished equestriennes to ever canter down Rotten Row. "And I'm determined to outshine them all."

"You?" He didn't laugh at her, thank goodness. He merely looked at her in that same assessing way, examining her as if she were some variety of strange creature he'd encountered unexpectedly. "Have you seen Miss Walters and her ilk?"

"Nearly every afternoon since I arrived in London. Their riding

skills are good, but not *that* good. Certainly not as good as my own."
Evelyn squared her shoulders. "Admittedly, they far surpass me in
terms of dress. But I mean to remedy that."

"With Mr. Doyle's help."

"With someone's help. Mr. Doyle isn't the only tailor in London."

He regarded her thoughtfully. "Why him?"

She'd have thought the answer was obvious. "Because his riding
costumes are beautiful. And because they make the ladies who wear
them beautiful, too. It's a sort of magic, I believe. To create clothing
that can do that for a person. That can transform them into something extraordinary." It was what she wanted for herself. A bit of Mr.
Doyle's magic to set her own fortunes on the right path. "But, as I say,
he's not the only tailor in town. I'm sure I can—"

"Where do you ride?" the man asked abruptly.

She blinked at him from behind the lenses of her spectacles. "I
beg your pardon?"

"You claim to be an excellent rider—the very best. Better even
than Miss Walters. Where is it that you exhibit your vast skill?"

Her lips compressed. "I wouldn't characterize it as an exhibition."

"Where?" he asked again.

"I haven't yet ridden in London. My horse only arrived this morning. I meant to wait until I had my new habit. That way . . ." She
stopped herself, aware of how calculating she must sound.

"You want to make an impression."

"Something like that." She tossed his own words back at him.

He didn't seem to mind. "Tomorrow morning, at sunrise, I'll be
taking the air along Rotten Row. Not many are about at that hour."

She stared at him. "You wish to see me ride?"

He looked steadily back at her.

And little by little the truth crept up on her. The confidence with
which he carried himself. The way he'd looked at her figure so know-
ingly. And the way he spoke, not in the grating, obsequious manner
of a shop assistant or a servant, but in a voice of authority.

"Who are you?" she asked.

"Ahmad Malik," he said. "I'm the habit-maker."

"*You?*" Hope surged anew. She took an involuntarily step forward, nearly stumbling over her own half boots. "But I was told that Mr. Doyle—"

"At present, Doyle's name is more palatable than my own."

Her brow creased. Malik was an Indian name, wasn't it? And yet, Mr. Malik didn't appear Indian. Not entirely. Indeed, he might have been from anywhere—India, Persia, Italy, or Spain. He might even have been of Romany extraction, like the travelers who sometimes passed through her village in Sussex. It was difficult to tell. He had no discernible accent. All one noticed—all *she'd* noticed—was that he was tall and dark and rather unnervingly handsome.

"But they *are* your designs?" she asked. "You cut them and sew them yourself?"

He inclined his head.

"And you might consider making one for me? If my horsemanship is up to snuff?"

"I can make no promises."

For the first time since Evelyn entered the shop, she knew that all would be well. Once he saw her ride—once he clapped eyes on Hephaestus—he would see she was worthy. More than worthy. "Tomorrow, then? At dawn?" She extended her gloved hand. "You won't be disappointed, Mr. Malik."

An odd expression passed over his face. As if she'd taken him off his guard. Surprised him in some way—or offended him. "You have the advantage of me."

Her confidence wavered. "I'm sorry. I—"

"I don't know your name."

"Oh, that." She instantly brightened, stretching her hand out still further. "Evelyn Maltravers."

"Miss Maltravers." His hand engulfed hers, large and strong. And—*good heavens.* She felt it everywhere. That warm, pulse-pounding contact. It resonated deep within her, the strangest sensation. Something both alarming and exhilarating. As if a jolt passed between them. The spark of something new. Something important.

Her gaze jerked to his, and she saw it there, reflected in his eyes. He felt it, too.

His black brows lowered. "It is *miss*, isn't it?"

She nodded mutely, heart thumping hard.

He gave her a searching look. And then he released her hand. "Tomorrow at dawn," he said. "Don't be late."

⸻⋗✦⋖⸻

Ahmad climbed the creaking stairs to the set of bachelor rooms he rented above the tea dealer's shop in King William Street. Far from the fashionable traffic of Mayfair, it was an undistinguished address in a neighborhood rife with warehouses and commercial enterprise. A place a man could lose himself among the bustling shoppers and the shouts of overzealous hawkers.

His door was located at the end of a narrow corridor. A soft strip of light glowed from beneath it. He heaved a weary sigh. He'd hoped to have a bit of privacy this evening to work on the dress he was making for Viscountess Heatherton.

It was the first of what promised to be many commissions for the season. A chance to see his creations displayed not by the courtesans of Rotten Row but by a high-ranking member of fashionable London society.

"Is that you, Ahmad?" Mira's faint voice rang out.

"Who else?" Unlocking the door with his key, he entered the sitting room to find his cousin occupied at the round wooden table in the corner. She was hand-stitching a length of point appliqué lace onto the bertha of Lady Heatherton's unfinished ice-blue muslin evening dress. He scowled at her. "What are you doing here?"

Mira glanced up from her sewing. At four and twenty, she was six years his junior. Like him, her hair was black, but where his eyes were dark, hers were a stunning shade of olive green. A testament to her mixed Pathan and English ancestry.

Her mother, Mumtaz, had been Ahmad's aunt, an Indian lady residing on the outskirts of Delhi. After the death of his own mother, Mumtaz had taken Ahmad in, treating him as her own. A good, kind woman, she'd succumbed to a sweating sickness in the summer of '46. On her deathbed, she'd made Mira's natural father—a British soldier—promise to take Mira back to England with him. Ahmad had accompanied them, vowing to watch over his cousin.

And he *had* watched over her.

Her father had died of drink not long after they'd arrived in London, leaving Mira alone and penniless on the streets of the East End. Her survival had been completely dependent on Ahmad. He'd done the best he could for her, but he'd been only fifteen, still just a child himself.

Together, he and Mira had experienced some of the worst the metropolis had to offer. But their luck had changed of late, and much of that due to the kindness of Mira's employers, solicitor Tom Finchley and his wife, Jenny. Mira acted as companion to Mrs. Finchley. Ahmad had worked for the Finchleys, too, until last year, when he'd finally been in a position to strike out on his own.

"Mrs. Finchley had no need of me today," Mira said. "I was perfectly free to call on you this afternoon."

"You've been here that long?"

"Since five o'clock."

Of course she had. The fire was lit, coals glowing cheerfully in the hearth. She'd tidied the room as well. Plumped the cushions on the threadbare sofa and straightened his heaps of books and half-finished sketches.

She held up the bodice of the lace-edged evening dress. "I've nearly finished this part of the trim."

Ahmad moved to the table to examine her work. "Very good."

She gave him a smug smile. "I thought so."

He chucked her under the chin. Over their long years together, he'd taught her nearly everything he knew about dressmaking.

In the beginning, it had been precious little.

He'd been apprenticed to a tailor in India, not a dressmaker. Working in the Chandni Chowk Bazaar in Delhi, he'd learned how to cut and stitch European-style shirts, coats, and trousers with efficiency and precision. But it wasn't the garments of British gentlemen that had inspired him. It was the gowns of the British ladies. The elegance of a fitted bodice, and the sensual sweep of a voluminous skirt.

"You shouldn't be here," he said.

Mira resumed her needlework. "And why not? Would you prefer spending your evening alone?" Her eyes briefly met his. "You *were* planning to be alone, weren't you?"

"None of your business, *bahan*." He removed his coat as he crossed the room, tossing it over the back of a chair. He stretched his arms wide. Sewing took a toll on a man's neck and back. And he'd been sewing too much lately, trying to fit in his orders for evening gowns along with those for riding habits.

It was all part of the plan. A necessary sacrifice that would bring him one step closer to opening his own dress shop.

He stifled a yawn.

"Were you at the tailor's all day today?" Mira asked.

"Most of it. Doyle had two orders for suits he needed finishing."

"And you had to complete them, did you?" Her disapproval was evident. "He believes you work for him."

Ahmad didn't. Not officially. He and the elderly tailor merely had an informal agreement, one they'd been adhering to since the autumn.

After Heppenstall's death, Doyle had been reluctant to continue on his own. He'd been equally reluctant to have an Indian for a partner.

With Finchley's help, a compromise had been made.

Ahmad would work from the shop, lending his skill to gentlemen's tailoring. In return, Doyle had agreed that, in one year's time, he would retire, and—in doing so—permit Ahmad to buy out his lease.

Six months had already passed since they'd made their bargain. Which meant that, in six months more, Doyle and Heppenstall's would he his. Ahmad already had the capital. All that was wanted was the clientele.

"And the rest of the day?" Mira asked.

"I spent the morning in Grosvenor Square, doing a fitting," he said.

"For Lady Heatherton?" Mira frowned. "I don't like her."

"You don't have to like her."

Viscountess Heatherton had indicated that she might consider becoming his patroness. She'd already ordered three evening gowns from him to start the season. And once the ladies of the *ton* saw his work, they'd be clamoring for dresses of their own.

"The way she looks at you," Mira said. "As if she wants to eat you."

He grimaced. "The less said about that the better."

Mira ignored him. "I suppose she asked you to measure her again."

She *had*, actually. And in her boudoir, too. As always, he'd ignored her flirtatious remarks and the familiar way she'd touched him. What choice did he have? At this stage, he needed a patroness. One who would show off his designs to the best effect, and to the best people.

Mira clucked her tongue. "Between her and your soiled doves, it's no wonder you're so tired all the time."

"My soiled doves," he scoffed.

"Aren't they? Those creatures who wear your riding habits?"

He loosened his cravat. "What do you know of them?"

"I read the papers. I see what people are saying about that Miss Walters person. They call her 'Incognita' or 'Anonyma,' but everyone knows who they mean."

"I expect they do," he said dryly.

Catherine Walters was the most famous courtesan in England. A skilled equestrienne, she'd taken society by storm, as much on the bridle path as in the ballroom. Her slim figure, enhanced by the dashing riding habits she wore, had made her a sight worth seeing by anyone frequenting Hyde Park. Every day, during the fashionable hour, people gathered along Rotten Row just to watch her pass.

After seeing one of his habits on Mrs. Finchley last season, Miss Walters had approached Ahmad with an order of her own. She'd commissioned one riding habit to start, and then another five upon completion of the first. It had been something of a sartorial coup. The best sort of advertising, considering the crowds she drew. Almost worth the cost he'd expended in time and materials.

Indeed, since Miss Walters had first worn one of his designs, two additional courtesans had ordered their riding habits from him as well. The Pretty Horsebreakers, the newspapers called them. Their style and skill were emulated by women from every strata of society.

"You may set your mind at ease," he said. "Miss Walters is selling up. She'll soon be leaving London."

Mira's brows lifted. "She's found a new protector?"

"I believe so. With any luck, he'll settle her bill before he spirits her away."

"Don't say she hasn't paid you yet?"

"Not for this season's order." In truth, Miss Walters had only just settled her bill for last year's habits. Like most fashionable ladies, she saw no issue with letting her accounts go unpaid for months at a time.

"How much does she owe?" Mira asked.

"A substantial sum."

"How substantial?"

"One hundred pounds." Ahmad felt a bit queasy to admit it. It was no small amount, especially to a man in his position. When Miss Walters hadn't paid, he'd been obliged to dip into his savings to cover expenses. The very money slated to open his dress shop.

"*One hundred pounds?*" Mira's face clouded with outrage. She received only thirty pounds a year in her position as a lady's companion, and that was considered a generous wage. "I knew you shouldn't have accepted an order from her. She has a reputation for leaving creditors in her wake. I read only yesterday that—"

"Does Mrs. Finchley know about your penchant for reading the scandal sheets?"

"Don't change the subject."

He squeezed her shoulder as he walked past her chair on the way to the cabinet where he kept his liquor. "Have you eaten?"

She nodded. "Have you?"

"Not yet." He withdrew a bottle of brandy and a single glass. "A drink," he said. "And then I'll see you into a hackney. I have an early day tomorrow."

"Lady Heatherton again?"

He shook his head. "A new client, potentially." Sitting down at the table, he told Mira about the peculiar young woman who had come into Doyle and Heppenstall's today.

"Another soiled dove?" Mira asked when he'd finished.

"I don't know," he said, frowning. "She spoke and acted like a lady, but . . ."

"But?"

"She didn't have a maid with her. And she didn't have a carriage waiting. I suspect she must have walked to the shop from the omnibus stop."

"Was she very beautiful?"

He stared into his glass of brandy. "Possibly."

It had been difficult to tell. What charms Miss Maltravers possessed—if any—had been well hidden.

Still, he'd caught glimpses of potential.

Her eyes, behind the lenses of her spectacles, had been a velvet-soft hazel, wide and doe-like, framed by impossibly long black lashes. And the hair curling from beneath her dowdy flat-brimmed hat had appeared a lustrous brown, threaded with strands of red and gold that glittered in the gaslight. Auburn hair. A great, thick mass of it, twisted into a singularly unflattering knot at her nape.

As for her figure, it had seemed well proportioned beneath the shroud of her loose-fitting caraco and skirt. She stood at least five and a half feet tall, a respectable height for a lady, with hints of a generous bosom.

All the rest, at this stage, was so much guesswork. He wouldn't know for certain until he'd seen her with her clothes off.

The prospect sent a rare flush of heat creeping up his neck.

Mira's eyes twinkled. "You couldn't tell? You must have thought her pretty enough to have agreed to make a habit for her."

"I haven't agreed to anything. I'm merely curious."

"Why?"

He shrugged. "She has possibilities."

"She's probably nothing more than one of those ladies who attempt to copy the courtesans' style."

Ahmad supposed that she might be. There were enough of them about these days. Even so, thus far, none of those young ladies had yet had the ingenuity to visit Doyle and Heppenstall's.

Until today.

Miss Maltravers had recognized that his designs were something out of the common way. *"Magic,"* she'd called them. He'd been ridiculously flattered.

"Or perhaps," Mira said, "she's looking to go into business for herself?"

"As a courtesan?" He thought it unlikely. And yet . . .

And yet the mere touch of her gloved hand had sent a startling shock of arousal through him. His breath had jammed up in his chest, and his blood had swiftly heated to a simmer.

He'd wondered, in that moment, what manner of strange creature she was, this frumpy female who had the power to beguile a man as surely as a siren.

To beguile *him*.

Good lord.

He'd spent his formative years working as a bullyboy at Mrs. Pritchard's gentlemen's establishment in Whitechapel. It had been the first job he'd found in England, the only one that had allowed him to keep Mira with him. There, he'd been surrounded by attractive women—outright professionals at their trade—and none of them had ever affected him as deeply as Miss Maltravers had. Certainly not by the mere touch of their hand.

If this was a sample of her erotic skill, she'd soon be as much in demand as Catherine Walters herself.

The prospect left a sour taste in his mouth. He downed another swallow of brandy.

"What else?" Mira asked.

He flashed her a questioning look over the rim of his glass.

"If not a lady or a courtesan, then what is she?"

"I don't know," he said. "But I mean to find out."

Two

$\mathcal{E}$velyn crept through the back door of her uncle's town house in Russell Square. Uncle Harris gave his staff a half day on Wednesdays and Sundays. It was how she'd managed to sneak away this evening unobserved. Still, one never knew when a stray maid or footman might be lurking about. It was best to be careful.

She ducked through the empty kitchen and tiptoed up the winding servants' staircase and down the dark third-floor hall that led to her bedchamber. Slipping silently inside her room, she shut the paneled door firmly behind her, sagging against it with a breath of relief.

It had been over half an hour since she'd left Doyle and Heppenstall's, and yet her stomach was still fluttering wildly. She felt rather like she had as a girl when encountering a particularly difficult fence during the annual hunt at Babbington Heath. There was a low throb of fear in her chest coupled with an overwhelming swell of giddy anticipation.

This jump will not beat me, she'd often thought.

And nor would London.

Lighting a lamp, she removed her soiled skirts and jacket. Having missed the omnibus in Bond Street, she'd been obliged to walk most of the way home. It was only a little more than a mile and a half. Not a great distance for one who was used to striding about the Sussex countryside. London, however, was far dirtier than Combe Regis. All the smoke and soot. It clouded the evening sky and blotted out the stars. Her hem and cuffs were filthy with it.

She washed her face and hands and changed into a faded blue day dress. It took but a moment longer to tidy her unruly hair and drape an old cashmere shawl round her shoulders. Having done so, she exited her room and made her way downstairs.

For her first season to be a success, she'd need more than a stylish habit or two. She'd need an entire wardrobe. Not refurbished hats and gowns, and not dresses made with drab fabric bought at a bargain. She required the best. And the best would cost money.

It was past time she broached the subject with Uncle Harris.

Located on the first floor, adjacent to the library, her uncle's study was his private domain. The door was always shut, a light glimmering from within at all hours of the night and day. He rarely emerged, and on those brief occasions when he did, he looked—or so it seemed to Evelyn—rather like a mole popping its head up out of its underground burrow to squint blindly into the sun.

"Remember," Aunt Nora had said before Evelyn departed Combe Regis, "my brother is a scholar. Nothing exists for him besides his work. You must take pains daily to remind him of your presence, else he'll forget you're there."

Evelyn had promised that she would, but since arriving in London last week, she'd found it far easier to leave her uncle to his own devices. She much preferred her independence. The same independence she exercised at home.

Unfortunately, there were some things for which Uncle Harris was necessary.

She rapped lightly at his study door.

"Who's that?"

"It's me, Uncle," she said, cracking open the door. "Evelyn."

Harris Fielding was seated behind an enormous, and very untidy, carved mahogany desk, the surface of which was covered with so many books and papers that her uncle himself could scarcely be seen. Only the top of his tasseled cap was visible.

"Evelyn?" He repeated her name as if he'd never heard it before. "Ah, yes. Diana's girl. Come in, come in."

Evelyn entered and came to stand in front of his desk.

Her mother, Diana, had been Uncle Harris's youngest sister. She'd died when Evelyn was but fifteen, a result of exhaustion, the village midwife had said. Too many children in too short a time, not all of them living. The final birth had done for her. Baby Isobel had lived, but Mama had slipped away, closing her eyes as if to rest for a moment only to never wake again.

Her death had been the start of all their problems.

She'd been their lodestar. Their ballast. Strong and pragmatic, setting the wisest course for all of their lives. Without her, things had swiftly fallen apart.

Naturally, Papa had been no help at all. Consumed by guilt, he'd consoled himself with travel, never remaining at home for more than a few days at a time. Evelyn and her sisters had been left in the care of Aunt Nora—Mama and Uncle Harris's spinster older sister. She was a dear, sweet lady, but not the cleverest of the family.

"I've missed dinner again, I realize," Uncle Harris said. "It's this dratted paper of mine for the Antiquarian Society. Won't write itself, you know."

"You needn't disturb yourself on my account," Evelyn replied. "I do very well on my own."

In fact, she'd only seen her uncle at dinner twice since her arrival last week. Even then, he'd left the table early, wandering out of the dining room and back to his study in a state of abstraction.

He peered up at her over the clutter on his desk. The light from the oil lamp glinted on the lenses of his half-moon spectacles. "You're settling in, I trust? Your room and so forth?"

"Thank you, yes. I'm quite comfortable."

"And that horse of yours?"

"He's settling in as well. My groom is looking after him."

"Good, good. Nora said you had a fellow. Groom, manservant, general dogsbody. What's the chap called?"

"Lewis," Evelyn said. He'd been her father's groom long before he'd become hers. Indeed, it was Lewis who had accompanied Hephaestus back to England as a two-year-old after Papa had died in Spain four years ago.

"And you've spoken to Mrs. Quick about obtaining a . . . what do you call it?"

"A lady's maid? Yes. She told me that I might use Agnes during my stay."

"Eh?"

"Agnes. One of your housemaids." Evelyn had already struck up a sort of understanding with the girl. Formerly employed in Mayfair, Agnes boasted a vast acquaintance with many of the servants in that neighborhood—including an upstairs maid working in the Park Street town house of Miss Catherine Walters. It was how Evelyn had learned where the famous courtesan bought her habits.

"Could never keep track of staff," Uncle Harris said distractedly. "I leave that to Mrs. Quick. She's a capital housekeeper. Always knows precisely what to do." He paused. "Is that all?"

"I'm afraid not. There's still the small matter of my clothing allowance for the season. I have a little money of my own set by, but Aunt Nora was hoping—"

"That I might contribute to the cause? Yes, yes. Quite right. She mentioned something to that effect." He rifled through the papers on his desk. "Had a letter from her just this morning, reminding me of the fact."

"Aunt Nora's written?" Evelyn stepped forward. "What did she say?"

"A great deal, as I recollect. Ah. Here it is." He raised a sheet of elegant pressed paper to the light. It was covered from edge to edge with Aunt Nora's familiar spidery scrawl. "I'm to see that you're clothed and shod, etc., etc. And to hire a maid for you, etc. Same requests she made in her last letter. Nora's a great one for repeating herself."

With a brother as absentminded as Uncle Harris, Evelyn didn't wonder. "Does she mention anything else?"

"She reminds me to write to Lady Arundell."

"You haven't written to her yet?" Evelyn failed to keep the exasperation from her voice.

Rosamond Deveril, Countess of Arundell, was an acquaintance of Uncle Harris's from the Antiquarian Society. A wealthy widow involved in all manner of charitable causes, she was best known for the lavish ball she hosted every spring. Uncle Harris never failed to mention it in the letters he wrote to Aunt Nora. According to him, the Arundell ball was the highlight of the season.

Evelyn had thought Uncle Harris had already approached his friend on her behalf. That Lady Arundell might, in fact, be on the verge of calling any day now to offer her assistance.

"Don't know why I would. Unless . . ." His brows beetled. "She's lately touting a school for girls in Wimbledon. Always on the hunt for teachers. Don't suppose Nora means you to take up the trade?"

"I should think not. I have no wish to be a teacher and no aptitude for the profession, either."

"Then what business can you have with her?"

Evelyn possessed herself in patience. It wasn't easy. Not with her entire future—and the entire future of her sisters—depending on her uncle's actions. "Aunt Nora hoped Lady Arundell might be persuaded to take me under her wing while I'm in town. That she might help to introduce me into society."

He gave a thoughtful grunt. "And I'm to convince her, am I?"

"You're to broach the subject, yes."

"Can't think you'll have much of a season this year, with or without her ladyship's support. What with the Prince Consort cocking up his toes. Bound to put a damper on things."

Evelyn couldn't argue the point. Prince Albert's death *was* rather inconvenient. He'd passed away in December, reportedly from typhoid fever. A tragedy for the Queen, and for the country, too. For a time, businesses had shut their doors and public entertainments had been canceled. Even now, three months later, some of the shops in London still had their windows swathed in black fabric.

But life must go on.

She had little choice but to make the best of the situation. "Nevertheless . . ."

"You require a sponsor."

"It needn't be anything formal." Evelyn desired a degree of independence during her visit. Still, she couldn't do it all on her own. "At the very least, Aunt Nora trusted you'd be able to secure an invitation for me to Lady Arundell's ball next month."

"Daresay I can. If Nora asks it." The letter remained poised in his hand. He stared at it in silence.

"Is that all she says?"

He harrumphed. "Tells me I'm to take care you don't go down the same road as your sister."

The reference to her older sister's disgrace brought a frown to Evelyn's lips. "There's no danger of that, sir."

He peered at her again, his gaze flicking over her person with a dismissive air. "Don't imagine there is."

Evelyn supposed she should take that as an insult. She wasn't as pretty as her older sister, a fact of which she was well aware.

Fenella had been the undisputed beauty of the family. The repository of everyone's hopes. Three years ago, Aunt Nora had expended the bulk of her savings to give Fenny a proper London season. A seemingly wise investment. If Fenny had made an illustrious match, she would have been in a position to bring out Evelyn, and their four younger sisters, too.

But Fenny hadn't won herself a wealthy husband.

Instead, she'd run off with Anthony Connaught, the rakehell son and heir of their neighbor, Sir William.

Babbington Heath, Sir William's estate, was located not far from Combe Regis. The Maltravers family had long been acquainted with Sir William and his sons. Evelyn had counted Anthony's younger brother, Stephen, as a friend. More than a friend. She'd often gone riding with him or stood up with him at village assemblies.

But no more.

The scandal had reverberated from London to Sussex. As a result, any thought Aunt Nora had had of bringing out Evelyn or her younger sisters had been set aside. Worse than that, Evelyn's own girlhood tendre for Stephen had crumbled to dust. Thrown back in her face by Stephen himself, who had believed that Fenny had trapped his brother—and that Evelyn had been trying to trap him.

Trap him. As if she were some desperate, grasping female! Her father may not have had great wealth or rank, but he'd been a gentleman and she was a gentleman's daughter. What did it matter that she lacked illustrious connections? That she didn't have a sizable dowry? She was still worthy of respect.

At least, that was how she felt *now*.

Three years ago, she hadn't been so rational. Only twenty at the time, she'd been crushed. Heartbroken. She still felt a twinge whenever she thought of it.

But there was no use in repining.

Fenny was gone, possibly forever. To the Continent, some said, to live with Anthony as his mistress. The fate of the Maltravers girls now rested on Evelyn's shoulders.

She was determined not to let her younger sisters down.

"A bad business," Uncle Harris said, folding away Aunt Nora's letter. "Thank heaven none of it can be laid at my door."

It was true. Fenny hadn't stayed with him during her season. She'd resided with friends—a fashionable society lady and her daughter. Aunt Nora had thought it more suitable. "What does my brother know about bringing a girl out?" she'd asked at the time. "Not a blessed thing."

Evelyn's own season was expected to proceed along vastly different lines. Not only was she lodging with her uncle in relative obscurity in Russell Square, she had her sister's scandal to contend with. *And* she had far less money at her disposal than Fenny had boasted. A sum only sufficient to see her outfitted—*frugally* outfitted—through August. If Evelyn wasn't in receipt of a proposal by then, she must return to Combe Regis in defeat.

Never.

She wasn't going to fail. Not if she had anything to say about it.

"Don't expect you've had any word from her?" Uncle Harris asked.

"None," Evelyn said. "Not since she left London."

"Pity. She might have made a creditable connection." He took on a bracing tone. "But looks aren't everything. Many a gentleman prefers a plain, levelheaded female."

"Even plain, levelheaded females must be fashionably attired for the season," Evelyn said. "One might argue it's an absolute imperative in their case, having so few other charms to recommend them."

Uncle Harris nodded his agreement. "Quite so. Nora said you were sensible."

"Did she? How gratifying."

He shot her a sharp look.

She instantly regretted her lapse. Now wasn't the time to bristle. She affected what she hoped was a properly submissive expression. "I've frequently been told that I favor my mother in that regard."

"High praise, to be sure," Uncle Harris said, mollified. "You may draw upon my bank for whatever you require—within reason, of course."

"Thank you, Uncle," she said. "You won't forget to speak with Lady Arundell about the ball?"

"I'll send a note round."

"Shall you write it now?" If he didn't, Evelyn had little hope of him writing it at all. "I don't mind waiting."

Uncle Harris was quiet for a moment. "May as well," he grumbled at last. "I'll get no peace otherwise."

—✦—

Later that evening, Evelyn sat at her own small desk in her bedroom, finishing the last of her letters home. She'd written one to Aunt Nora and one to each of her younger sisters: Augusta, Caroline, Elizabeth, and Isobel—fondly known as Gussie, Caro, Bette, and Izzy. They ranged in age from eight to eighteen, each of them a uniquely precious individual.

Gussie excelled at watercolors and needlepoint. Caro adored ghost stories and gothic novels. Bette was a hoyden, refusing to ride side-saddle and already spouting opinions about women's suffrage. And Izzy, the youngest, was—like Papa—a born adventurer.

"I shall follow your journey on the map," she'd announced on the day Evelyn had departed Combe Regis.

"And I shall look for you in the society pages," Gussie had added, giving Evelyn a fierce hug.

Her sisters had been almost as excited for Evelyn's London season as Evelyn was herself. And that's what she'd conveyed to them in her letters: excitement. The grandeur of the city, the thrill of riding in an omnibus, and the prospect of attending a ball.

All will be well. Though she never wrote the words, they were implied with every line. *You are safe. You are loved. I have things entirely under control.*

As she blotted the ink on the final missive, a knock sounded at her chamber door.

"It's me, miss." Agnes entered. She was wearing a black stuff dress, her mouse-brown hair combed back into a severe knot. "Will you be needing anything before I retire?"

"No, thank you. I'll be retiring soon myself." Evelyn glanced up. "How was your visit to your cousin?"

"Oh, she was all right. Only a bit tired, with the new baby and all. She was glad of the company." Agnes collected Evelyn's discarded skirts and jacket from the settee at the end of the four-poster bed. She examined the mud-stained hem and cuffs with a frown. "You didn't visit that tailor's shop?"

Evelyn tucked her finished letter into an envelope. "I did."

Agnes gave her a sharp look. "Alone?"

"I often do my shopping alone. Many young women do."

"Not ladies," Agnes said. "Not *proper* ladies, anyway."

"Possibly not, but it isn't as if anyone saw me. Doyle and Heppenstall's was quite empty, and no one on the street paid me any mind. They were too caught up in their own affairs."

"Yes, miss, but Mrs. Quick said as how I'm supposed to accompany you—"

"Not on your afternoon off, you aren't. Besides, I was quite safe." Evelyn sealed her envelope with a wafer. "I'll have a great deal more shopping to do in the days ahead. You may accompany me then."

This seemed to satisfy Agnes for the moment. She draped the soiled skirts and jacket over her arm. They'd need to be sponged and pressed before Evelyn could wear them again. "Did you place your order with Mr. Doyle?"

"Mr. Malik."

"Who?"

"He's the one who designs the riding habits, not Mr. Doyle or Mr. Heppenstall." As she put away her writing implements, Evelyn described her visit to the shop, telling the maid everything that had transpired there.

Well, almost everything.

She didn't mention how handsome Mr. Malik was. And she didn't say anything about how she'd felt when he'd looked at her, or when he'd touched her hand.

"You really told him you weren't a bluestocking?" Agnes's lips quivered in a smile.

It wasn't the most flattering reaction.

"And why should I admit to a label?" Evelyn demanded, nettled.

"First it's *wallflower*, then it's *bluestocking*, and then it's *old maid* or *spinster*. I don't wish to be filed away in a neat little category, labeled and dismissed by society as if I weren't a person full of mysterious complexities. I don't even know the full depth and breadth of what I am yet—or what I'm capable of. How can a man? How can anyone?"

Agnes looked doubtful.

"And yes," Evelyn added, "I'm fully aware that it's those very thoughts that put me squarely in the bluestocking column."

But that was no one's business but her own.

She wasn't in Combe Regis anymore. She was in London—a place where no one knew her from Adam. If she must be put in a column, it would be one of her own choosing. Not *wallflower* or *bluestocking*, but *horsewoman*.

It was Mama who had given her the idea. She'd always said that one must approach a problem from a position of strength.

Evelyn had thought of that advice countless times since first formulating her plan to come to London. She knew she wasn't likely to win a well-to-do husband in a ballroom or a drawing room. Unlike Fenny, she had no particular talent for dancing, music, or conversation. Her strength lay in riding. And it was on Rotten Row that she intended to wage her campaign.

"Will Mr. Malik do it, then?" Agnes asked. "Will he make you the same kind of habit he made for Miss Walters?"

"As to that . . . I don't know yet." Evelyn stood from her desk. "I expect I won't, not until after he sees me ride in the morning."

"I don't like it," Agnes said. "For him to set a test for you like that. What right has he to—"

"He's an artist, and a male one, at that. One must excuse his impertinence for the time being." Evelyn smiled faintly. "He'll soon learn."

Three

$\blacklozenge$

The following morning, Evelyn entered Rotten Row at a trot, her groom following close behind. Hephaestus's muscles were tense beneath her. He pranced and sidestepped, ready to jump straight up into the air at the slightest provocation.

He'd never before been to London, let alone Hyde Park. And the weather wasn't helping to calm him. It was foggy and drizzling, the sun breaking through the trees in cold ribbons of light that shone in her eyes. She was glad she wasn't wearing her spectacles. The glare would have been unbearable.

Lewis rode up beside her on his steady chestnut gelding. He was a stocky man past middle age, with a wealth of horse sense hidden behind his bland expression. "He's looking to bolt."

"He's fine," she said. "A little hot, but manageable. All he wants is a gallop to clear away the cobwebs."

There was time enough for it. Mr. Malik didn't appear to have arrived yet. She looked for him along the fence line, where people usually stopped to survey the passing parade of horses and riders, but it was as empty as the rest of the park.

Hephaestus arched his thick neck and flared his nostrils, snorting great clouds of steam. She soothed him with a scratch on his neck.

"You reckon you can bring him back down from a gallop?" Lewis asked.

Were it anyone else, Evelyn would have been offended at having her skill called into question. But Lewis had known her since she was a little girl. "Of course I can."

She shifted her weight very slightly in her sidesaddle and, tightening her reins, applied a subtle pressure with her seat and leg. Hephaestus sprang forward as if shot out of a cannon, half rearing as he surged into a ground-covering canter.

There was no one else around that she could see. No one who would object as she gave him his head and permitted him to lengthen his stride into a gallop.

The net veil on her hat whipped against her face, and the long skirts of her old black habit flapped back against Hephaestus's powerful flanks.

"Easy," she murmured. "Easy."

Hephaestus was a Spanish-bred Andalusian. The breed was known for its sensitive temperament and the smoothness of its gait. Papa had once said that a person could hold a cup of tea while cantering on an Andalusian and never spill a drop. It was an exaggeration, of course, but it was nearer to truth than fiction. Hephaestus's stride was as smooth as glass.

Evelyn's gloved hands were just firm enough on the reins to maintain contact. She didn't believe in riding heavy on a horse's mouth. Control should come from the seat. A difficulty in a sidesaddle, but not impossible. Not with a horse as responsive as her own.

She slowly brought him back down, first to a trot and then to a walk, praising his obedience with a pat on his shoulder. "That's better," she said to him.

It was then that she saw they weren't alone.

Another rider emerged from the trees ahead. A slim, raven-haired young lady mounted on an impossibly large black hunter. She held his reins loosely as he walked up the path, letting his head stretch free, as if cooling him off after a bout of rigorous exercise. Her groom rode not far behind her.

"Good morning," the young lady called out.

Evelyn raised a hand in reluctant greeting. She'd hoped to avoid other people this morning. Her first appearance in the park was meant to be something special, not a hurly-burly dawn gallop through the mud, clad in an old wool habit. She prayed the other rider would pass on.

But the young lady didn't oblige her. Quite the opposite. She slowed her mount to a halt, her wide gaze moving avidly over Hephaestus. "What a handsome stallion! Is he Spanish? He looks Spanish. Though I've never seen one that isn't gray."

"Blood bays aren't common in the breed," Evelyn said, "but they do appear from time to time." Their rarity made them all the more valuable. It was one of the reasons Papa had bought Hephaestus, spending far more on the purchase than he could afford.

"And you ride him in a snaffle? Extraordinary. I consider myself something of a horsewoman, and I'd never ride Cossack in anything but a Pelham. Not here in the park."

Evelyn smiled at the roundabout compliment. "Hephaestus has a soft mouth. I frequently ride him with a single rein."

"But he's a stallion!"

"A gentle stallion."

"Lady Anne rides a stallion, too. But Miss Hobhouse prefers a mare. She has a gray Thoroughbred cross at the moment. A beautiful creature—almost completely white. The three of us often ride together of a morning. It's more comfortable than the afternoons when everyone else is about." A frown marred the young lady's brow. "I haven't seen you here before. I'd remember if I had."

"This is my first outing. My groom delivered my horse to town only yesterday." Evelyn turned Hephaestus in a half circle. He was still tense with energy and could use another canter. "Forgive me, but I must walk on."

"By all means. You wouldn't wish him to take a chill." The young lady's horse fell in step beside them. "Are you here for the season?"

"I am," Evelyn admitted.

"As am I." The young lady paused, adding, "For the third time." Her blue eyes took on a rueful sparkle. "I'm Julia Wychwood."

"Evelyn Maltravers."

"Miss Maltravers." Miss Wychwood smiled at her. "I shan't importune you any longer. My ride is over and yours is just beginning." She turned her horse, diverging from the path. "I expect we'll meet again. I ride here so often at this time."

"I shall look forward to it," Evelyn said with genuine warmth.

Miss Wychwood saluted her as she rode off. "Good day to you!"

"Good day!" Evelyn called back.

What a strange girl. And a voluble one, too. Still, Evelyn was grateful to have met her. She hadn't any friends here in London. Not yet. Certainly none who shared her passion for riding. And Miss Wychwood looked as if she knew what she was about.

It was rare to encounter a truly good rider these days. So many were content to rely on brutal bits, martingales, and other punishing methods for keeping a horse under control.

Evelyn urged Hephaestus back into a trot, and then into a canter. His hooves pounded down the strip of tan. She kept him to the same gait for a long while, enjoying the easy, effortless motion of his powerful stride. The hoofbeats of Lewis's mount echoed a distance behind them.

As she rode, her gaze once again drifted to the rail. It was as empty as it had been when she'd arrived. Mr. Malik hadn't come. She'd just about resigned herself to the fact when, up ahead, a slight movement caught her attention.

Her eyes widened behind her veil.

Good gracious, it was *him*.

He stood in the shadow of an elm tree, hardly noticeable at first glance. But once she set eyes on him, there was no mistaking his presence. Dressed in an impeccably cut black coat and trousers, he looked both handsome and dangerous. Like a fallen angel, reluctantly come to earth.

Awareness crept into her veins, warm and shivery. She didn't know why. At three and twenty, she was no green girl. And it wasn't as if he'd been particularly nice to her. Even now, the way he looked at her . . . That darkling glance. Frowning and sullen. As if he were weighing her in the balance.

She rode up to him at a canter, bringing Hephaestus to a slow halt in front of the trees. He piaffed for several steps—an elevated trot in place—before coming to a standstill. "Mr. Malik," she said, a little breathless. "Good morning."

He bowed. "Miss Maltravers."

"Have you been here long?"

"Since you first entered Rotten Row."

Her mouth nearly fell open. "That long? But . . . I didn't see you."

"Why should you? You were riding."

"And you were watching? The whole time?"

"I was."

Frustration knotted her stomach. So far, she'd done nothing but gallop on the straightaway. It had required little skill on her part—or on Hephaestus's. Hardly the exhibition Mr. Malik would have been expecting. "I can ride a bit longer if you like," she said. "Put him through his paces. He's well schooled in dressage, and knows most of the movements of the haute école. I trained him myself."

"I've seen enough," Mr. Malik said.

Her heart sank.

Dash it all! It wasn't fair. To have her riding skill dismissed out of hand. Then again, when had anything in life ever been fair? Her plan could still succeed. She wouldn't permit his rejection to rob her of hope.

If it *was* a rejection.

He was still here, after all. That must mean something, surely.

"Well?" she asked. Her muscles tensed in anticipation.

"You're an accomplished horsewoman."

"I know that," Evelyn said impatiently. "What I mean is . . . have you decided if you're going to make me a habit?"

Mr. Malik's mouth ticked up at one corner. Too late, she realized the double meaning in her words. "Do you know, Miss Maltravers, I believe I am."

❖

Ahmad thrust his hands into his pockets as Miss Maltravers rode away.

She looked different on a horse. Elegant and confident. Entirely at her ease.

In truth, he'd never seen anything like her.

She hadn't been boasting when she'd said that she was a better rider than the Pretty Horsebreakers. From what he'd seen this morning, Miss Maltravers's skill as an equestrienne was beyond compare. Galloping down Rotten Row on that great Spanish stallion of hers—a horse that would have intimidated most men—she'd been at one with her mount. Thoroughly in control, while at the same time seeming to exert not one ounce of physical force.

Impressive, to be sure. But it was more than that.

There was an inherent grace to her riding. A feminine ebb and flow that had riveted his gaze. It was almost sensual, the way the lines of her body had been in harmony with every movement. Still and sure, with gentle hands and a quiet seat.

He'd watched her with growing awe, a tightness forming in his chest. Good lord. Did she realize how much potential she had? All it would take was the right dressmaker—the right hairdresser and corsetiere.

The right habit-maker.

Miss Walters had managed to snare a marquess as her protector. What was Miss Maltravers aiming for? A duke? A prince?

If she played her cards right, Ahmad didn't doubt that she could have whomever she wished.

Turning from the rail, he walked back the way he'd come, down the path toward the main entrance of the park. Raindrops fell intermittently, dampening the shoulders of his coat and the brim of his hat. He was too preoccupied to mind, already consumed by visions of the fabric he'd use—the color, texture, and cut.

At present, there was nothing resembling what he wanted at the tailor's shop. Miss Maltravers required something new. Something special.

Back on the main street, Ahmad hailed a hansom. "Phillotson's in Holborn Hill," he told the driver before climbing into the cab.

Phillotson's was one of four very good woolen warehouses in the city. Ahmad preferred it to the others purely because it was the largest. There were treasures to be found there if one had time enough to spare.

He didn't have time today. He was meant to be finishing Lady Heatherton's evening dress. She expected him to bring it to her in the morning for her final fitting. But his mind wasn't on Lady Heatherton.

His thoughts were full of Evelyn Maltravers.

That same evening, only minutes before Doyle and Heppenstall's closed and locked its doors for the night, Miss Maltravers entered the shop, accompanied by her maid.

Ahmad was in his shirtsleeves, a cloth measuring tape draped round his neck. He'd told her to come at closing time. He generally did his habit fittings after hours, when the cutters had retired to their rooms abovestairs and Doyle wasn't there to loom over his shoulder.

Miss Maltravers stopped just inside the doorway. Her bespectacled gaze flicked from his face to his waistcoat and white linen shirt and then back again. Clad in a shapeless afternoon dress, she looked nothing like the dazzling vision she'd presented on horseback. She appeared nervous, truth be told. Wide-eyed, with a flushed face and trembling hands.

He felt a bit trembly himself. The damnedest thing. It made him gruffer than usual. "You're wearing your spectacles."

Her hand went immediately to her face, pushing the offending article further up onto her nose. "Shouldn't I have?"

"You weren't this morning."

"I never do when I ride. I don't require them for distance. Only for close up. Reading and talking to people and so on. Without them, your face would be a blur, and so would any fabrics you show to me."

Outside, a rush of foot traffic passed in front of Doyle and Heppenstall's glass window—customers leaving shops as they closed, and shopkeepers and their clerks locking up and going home for the day. One of the passersby caught the attention of Miss Maltravers's maid.

"Oh, miss!" she cried. "That's Sally, from my old employer in Green Street. May I speak with her? I won't be a moment."

"Of course," Miss Maltravers said. "Take as long as you need."

The maid slipped out into the street, the door shutting behind her.

"A new hire?" Ahmad asked.

Miss Maltravers's mouth curved in a slight smile. "A parlor maid in my uncle's house."

Her uncle.

"I'm not permitted to go out unaccompanied during my stay," she explained. "Not in the normal course of things. Though I must say I do prefer my independence. At home, in my village, I'm used to shifting for myself."

He regarded her in silence for several long seconds. She was staying with an uncle. And she had a horse stabled here, and a groom along with him. And now, she had a maid as well. A full complement of respectability. "You're not, I take it, planning to set yourself up in Miss Walters's trade?"

The flush in Miss Maltravers's face briefly darkened to crimson. "No, indeed. Is that what you thought?"

"You wouldn't be the first," he said.

Every day in London, pretty young women arrived from the countryside, hoping to make better lives for themselves and their families. They were always welcomed into the oldest profession—sometimes tricked or trapped into it, by canny madams or brutish brothel-keepers.

Ahmad had known enough of the type while working at Mrs. Pritchard's. Among them, young women who could affect the speech and manner of a lady were much in demand. Many wealthy gentlemen preferred their mistresses to have a veneer of elegance. And those mistresses were well compensated for that quality, with town houses, servants, coaches and four, and monthly allowances greater than most people could earn in a year.

It was to that class that Miss Walters and the other Pretty Horse-breakers belonged.

Ahmad passed no judgment. He'd lived among working women for the better part of his life in London. Some were good and some bad, just as in every line of business. As for the morality of it, he had no fixed opinion. One did what one must to survive. Life was difficult enough without having to feel ashamed about it. Nevertheless . . .

On discovering that Miss Maltravers wasn't aspiring to be the next *grande horizontale*, he owned to a distinct sense of relief. He didn't know why. Her career choice was no concern of his.

"No," she said again. "I'm not interested in becoming a courtesan. But I do recognize the power the Horsebreakers hold. Their particular allure. It's that which I wish to emulate, not their profession."

"To what end?"

"Why . . . the obvious one, of course. To find a husband."

"Ah." The mundanity of her goal was vaguely disappointing. Though he didn't know what else he'd expected. Something grander? More ambitious? Something that would set the stars on fire?

"You disapprove?"

He shrugged. "Why should I?" A glance at the window revealed Miss Maltravers's maid still talking animatedly with her friend.

Miss Maltravers followed his gaze. "We needn't wait for Agnes. She's only here to oblige my uncle."

"As you wish." He pulled back the curtain that separated the showroom from the work- and fitting rooms and gestured for her to precede him. "After you."

She walked through, under his outstretched arm, leaving the faintest fragrance of orange blossoms in her wake.

His pulse jumped.

Stupid.

She was just a woman. One of the many who frequented Rotten Row attempting to ape Miss Walters and her fellows. Wealthy, spoiled young ladies with their expensive horses and their close-fitted riding costumes. Pale imitations of the courtesans, tiresome in their ordinariness.

But no. He was being unjust. And merely because Miss Maltravers provoked a reaction in him. The sight of her and the scent of her. The way she'd extended her hand to him yesterday, as if he were an equal. Addressing him not as a dark-skinned man beneath her notice, a servant to do her bidding, but as an artist—a person worthy of respect and admiration.

"It's a sort of magic, I believe," she'd said. *"To create clothing that can do that for a person. That can transform them into something extraordinary."*

He'd been thinking of that—of *her*—ever since leaving the park this morning. Seeing her ride had inspired him like nothing in recent memory. He'd spent half the afternoon sketching designs for her.

"Is no one else here?" she asked as he led her past the empty workroom.

"Not this evening, no." He showed her into a large gaslit fitting room. A cheval glass was arrayed in front of a raised platform. Bolts of cloth were stacked on a narrow table against the wall. And in the corner stood a wooden horse, equipped with an old leather sidesaddle.

Miss Maltravers gave it a wary glance.

He moved to block her view of the offending contraption. "Are you certain you don't need your maid to assist you?"

"I can undress myself." She slowly removed her hat. "How much should I—"

"Down to your chemise and drawers," he said briskly. "You can leave on your corset to begin with."

Her lashes lowered. She looked away from him with something like embarrassment.

"Call out when you're ready." With that, he withdrew, leaving her to her own devices.

Most tailors in the habit-making trade employed female fitting-room attendants. But that wasn't the way Ahmad worked. He did all of the pinning and measuring himself. It gave him a familiarity for what was required. That particular knowledge elevated his work. Or so he believed.

No one had yet complained.

Then again, his clients thus far had been courtesans and married women like Lady Heatherton. It was easier with them. They knew what was what and weren't likely to get the vapors the minute he applied his measuring tape to their scantily clad bodies.

Good God, he hoped Miss Maltravers wasn't going to swoon.

But minutes later, when she called him back again, he realized— much to his chagrin—that it was quite the reverse. As she stood before him in her faded white cotton underclothes and well-worn corset, it was he who felt a little light-headed.

So this was what her shapeless clothing had been hiding. A figure molded along the lines of a Venus. A full bosom and hips, with a narrow waist, long shapely legs, and daintily rounded arms. She was a delectable morsel of femininity. Lushly curved in all the right places. And yet there was strength in her. An athletic firmness to her limbs, and a healthful glow to her complexion.

She was arresting. And it wasn't only her figure, exposed to him for the first time. It was her face.

It looked different in the gaslight. Soft and vulnerable, with dark brows winging gracefully over her eyes, and delicately sculpted cheekbones casting a shadow along the elegant line of her jaw. Her nose was a touch overlarge, and very slightly aquiline—a haughty, almost bookish feature. It was balanced by the shape of her mouth.

And such a mouth.

Wide and generous and eminently kissable.

He swallowed hard.

"I confess, this is all very strange." She folded her arms over her bosom. "I've never been measured by a man before. In Combe Regis, the village dressmaker makes my habits." She cast an anxious look at the cheval glass. "It's fortunate I can't make out my reflection at this distance. I should be mortified to see myself in such a state."

"No need to be," he said. "I've seen hundreds of ladies in their knickers."

"You've never seen *me*, Mr. Malik."

He gave her a wry smile. "Point taken. Shall we acknowledge the awkwardness of it and agree to move past it? We'll be here all night otherwise."

She nodded. "That sounds reasonable." Her arms loosened from her chest to hang at her sides. "What now?"

"First things first." He offered her his hand.

She took it without hesitation.

And he felt it again—that same shock he'd felt when they'd shaken hands yesterday. Only this time, she wasn't wearing gloves.

Bloody hell.

Her skin was warm and silky soft, her hand surprisingly strong as it gripped his.

He assisted her up onto the platform. "All right?"

"Yes, thank you."

He stepped back, his gaze drifting over her figure with a practiced eye. Excitement simmered in his veins. "I trust you haven't fixed on any particular color or fabric?"

"Not especially. Why?" she asked. "Do you have some idea of what might suit me?"

"Several ideas."

"Different from the other habits you make?"

"In essentials, no. But in every other respect, yes."

She frowned. "I don't understand."

It seemed simple enough to him. Simpler still now that he'd seen her—*truly* seen her. "You wanted a riding habit that would transform you. I believe I can design something better. Something that will reveal who you really are."

She was silent a moment. And then she smiled. "I hesitate to ask what that might be. I've already been accused of being a bluestocking."

"Indeed, you hide it well. I didn't recognize it myself until I saw you ride this morning."

"Recognize what?"

"You're a singular beauty, Miss Maltravers. A diamond of the first water, I suspect. All you lack is the proper setting." Ahmad went to the table and retrieved the bolt of dark cloth he'd purchased at Phillotson's. "What do you think of this shade?" he asked, returning to her side.

She was staring at him, stunned. It took her a moment to register the fabric in his hand. When she did, her brows knit. "Black?"

"Not black." He came closer, moving into the halo of light cast from the wall sconce. "Look again."

She squinted down at the fabric through her spectacles. Her eyes widened. "It's green!"

"It is. A shade so dark it appears black, unless one views it in the sun." He tilted the bolt of cloth in the gaslight.

"My goodness," she breathed. "It shimmers."

"An illusion. The wool is woven so finely that it has a sheen to it." A luscious sheen, as elegant as it was seductive. He draped a length of the fabric over her shoulder. "May I?" he asked, reaching for her spectacles.

Her lashes fluttered. "Oh . . . yes. Of course."

He gently removed them from her face. Her eyes met his, a little shyly, catching the subtle color of the cloth, absorbing and reflecting it like twin jewels. A surge of satisfaction went through him. He turned her to face the glass. "Look at yourself."

A flush seeped from her throat into her face, turning her cheeks the shade of a damask rose petal. Her bosom rose and fell on an unsteady breath. "The color *is* very flattering."

An understatement.

It made her auburn hair glow with fiery warmth and her skin appear as creamy as unblemished ivory.

"*Very* flattering," he said. "And that's just the beginning."

She touched the fabric with her fingertips. "There's more? You begin to frighten me."

He returned her spectacles. "You prefer hiding?"

"I wasn't aware that I *was* hiding." She settled her spectacles back onto her nose. "I commissioned a habit from you, didn't I?"

"For a reason. You wanted a bit of my magic. And you can have it. All I ask is that you put yourself entirely in my hands."

She lifted her gaze to his. Her soft hazel eyes were thoughtful behind her spectacles. "Very well," she said at last. "I shall."

Four

⊰✦⊱

$\mathscr{E}$velyn stood still as a statue as Mr. Malik applied his cloth measuring tape to her waist, hips, and bust. Any embarrassment she felt at the intimacy of his touch was overshadowed by the memory of his words; phrases that still circled merrily in her dumbfounded brain.

"A singular beauty," he'd called her. *"A diamond of the first water."*

No one had ever called her anything resembling a beauty or thought of her as one, she was convinced. She didn't even think of herself in such terms.

It wasn't that she rated herself so meanly. It was only that she'd spent the majority of her life standing in Fenny's shadow. And Fenny was beautiful. The most beautiful young lady in Sussex. All refined feminine fragility, with a wilting figure and a laugh as delicate as a silver bell.

Evelyn had never been that. Had never wanted to be that. And there had been no need, not with Fenny around. Instead, Evelyn had developed into something else. An athlete. A sportswoman. An equestrienne to rival any man in Sussex. Or so she liked to think.

Not that she didn't love fashion.

She hadn't lied when she told Mr. Malik that it was one of her two passions in life. Indeed, her spirts always lifted at the sight of a gaily colored ribbon, a ruffled petticoat, or a newly trimmed hat.

All the same, she'd never aspired to be a great beauty, or to be acknowledged as one. She hadn't even realized how much she needed to hear the words until Mr. Malik had said them.

"A singular beauty."

He sank to his haunches in front of her, running his measuring tape from her hip to the floor.

In that brief moment when he wasn't looking, when his head was bowed and his attention fixed on ascertaining her measurements, she couldn't stop herself from blurting out: "Do you really think I'm beautiful?"

He glanced up at her, brows drawn together in a distracted frown.

She immediately regretted her question. Good heavens. Look at him! He was so heart-wrenchingly handsome it fairly took her breath away. And here she was in her knickers, with her hair a-tumble and her spectacles slipping on her nose, asking for reassurance about her appearance, of all things. Reassurance from him. A man who was as close to beautiful himself as any gentleman she'd ever seen.

"I'm not fishing for compliments," she added quickly. "It's only that . . . I've never been called beautiful in my life."

"No?" He stood in one fluid motion and went to the table in the corner. A notepad lay there, in which he'd been periodically jotting her measurements with the pencil he kept tucked behind one ear. He scratched down the latest figures.

"Not ever," she said. "It was my older sister who was the beautiful one, not me. She looked just like the plates in the ladies' magazines. An English rose, people used to call her."

"You've mistaken sameness for beauty."

"I beg your pardon?"

"Many do." He turned back to her, his gaze sweeping over her—speculative and assessing. "Sameness is comfortable. People like it because it reassures them. But it's nothing extraordinary. It's not true beauty. Not the kind that moves the soul."

She blinked. He wasn't saying that she was that kind of beauty, was he? Surely not. She opened her mouth to ask him—and she would have done, too, if Agnes hadn't chosen that precise moment to enter the fitting room.

"Beg your pardon, miss," she said, dropping an unpracticed curtsy. "The time got away from me." Her voice trailed off as she perceived the absence of a female fitting room attendant. Her apologetic expression transformed into one of blank incredulity.

"It's no matter." Evelyn looked to Mr. Malik. "We're nearly finished, aren't we?"

"Nearly." Mr. Malik's gaze swept over her again. He didn't seem at all affected by the arrival of her maid. His manner was just as it had been from the start, that of an artist examining his canvas. "You'll need a new corset."

Agnes sucked in a scandalized breath.

Evelyn ignored the sound. She was already in her underwear, and far past the point of schoolgirl blushes. "What's wrong with the one I have?"

He came to her in two strides, putting his large hands on her midriff as familiarly as if he were her physician.

Or her lover.

Her heart thudded so heavily she could scarcely catch her breath.

"It's too long here." His fingers skimmed down past her hips where her corset pinched tight into her flesh. "It should be elastic over the hips, with a shorter busk for ease of movement. And here." His hands moved to her waist. "The boning is inadequate. It does nothing at all to support your figure—or to emphasize it."

"I suppose I could lace it tighter," Evelyn suggested. "But not too tight. I can't have it squeezing the breath out of me. Not if I'm to ride with any degree of skill."

"I advise that you dispose of it altogether. It's not a matter of tight lacing. You need a corset that molds to your figure. There are better models available than this."

"Which do you recommend?"

"For the habit I design? You'll need riding stays." Returning to his notepad, he jotted something down.

Evelyn stared after him, her insides simmering. She could still feel the pressure of his hands on her waist, warm and strong. She wondered how his other female clients could submit to being measured by him with any degree of equanimity. Every touch was an intimate brand, scorching through the layers of her corset and the thin chemise beneath, all the way down to her skin.

"And for the rest of my gowns?" she asked, a little breathless.

"That depends on the gown. Have you engaged a modiste?"

"Not yet. I intended to visit Madame Elise tomorrow." According to Agnes, Madame Elise was presently the most sought-after dressmaker in London.

Mr. Malik shot her a dark glance over his shoulder. "I wouldn't advise it."

Agnes visibly stiffened. For an instant it looked as though she might say something out of turn.

Evelyn didn't give her a chance. "Why not?"

"You'd do better to go to Madame Lorraine in Bruton Street. She's not as famous as Madame Elise, but she'll see you're turned out in a manner that best suits your figure." He tore off the piece of notepaper he'd been writing on and handed it to her. "Her address, along with that of a good corsetiere."

Evelyn's gaze skimmed over the page as she took it. A third address was written beneath the first two. She looked up, meeting Mr. Malik's eyes. "Who is Monsieur Phillipe?"

"A hairdresser."

She fell silent. Insecurity bubbled within her. Was there nothing about her that was good enough as it was? But no. She wouldn't permit herself to be offended. She'd promised to put herself in his hands. Entirely in his hands. "I see." She folded the slip of paper and passed it to Agnes. "Is that all?"

"For the moment." He withdrew to the door, taking the bolt of dark green fabric along with him. "You may get dressed."

No sooner had he departed the fitting room than Agnes rushed to assist Evelyn down from the platform. "The cheek of the man," she said under her breath. "Alone in here with you, and with no girl to assist him. Who does he think he is? Why, he's not even English!"

Evelyn frowned. "What on earth does that signify?"

Agnes fetched Evelyn's folded bodice, skirts, and underpinnings from the chair in the corner. "You never know what those like him are up to, do you? And you in your knickers!"

"Really, Agnes." Evelyn flashed the maid a speaking glance as she stepped into her petticoats and crinoline. "Mr. Malik is accustomed to seeing ladies in their underclothes. He's a habit-maker, for heaven's sake."

"An Indian habit-maker," Agnes muttered, helping Evelyn into her skirts. "It's as I say, miss. Men like him—there's no telling what liberties he might have taken."

"Nonsense. He was a perfect gentleman." Evelyn knotted the ties of her skirts at her waist. "And you can't have been too concerned, else you wouldn't have lingered so long visiting your friend."

Agnes flushed. "You won't be mentioning that to Mrs. Quick, will you?"

"Of course not." Evelyn slipped her arms into the sleeves of her bodice. "I only mean to say that your instincts were right. Mr. Malik took no liberties. He was far more concerned with measurements and fabrics than he was with my poor self."

Agnes snorted. "That's not what I saw." She fastened the hooks that closed the front of Evelyn's bodice. "You should've seen how he stared at you when you weren't looking."

Evelyn's cheeks warmed. "Rubbish." Mr. Malik had no more interest in her than any other talented habit-maker would have in his client. "He's a visionary, that's all. He's determined that I look my best in the riding costume he designs."

Another snort.

"He is," Evelyn said firmly. "It's his reputation, too. And if he sees fit to recommend a new corset, and a particular modiste and hair-dresser, I intend to heed his advice."

⬥—✖—⬥

Ahmad followed Viscountess Heatherton's sour-faced lady's maid up the servants' stairs of her ladyship's town house in Grosvenor Square. He was never permitted to enter the residence by the front door. He came in through the kitchens, where he waited until he was summoned, all the while subjected to the suspicious glances of the scullery maid, cook, and every passing maid and footman.

It was only upon entering Lady Heatherton's lavishly appointed boudoir on the third floor that he began to be treated as something more than a common tradesman.

"Mr. Malik. At last." Mildred Lacey, Viscountess Heatherton, was a blond sylph of a lady, on the shady side of thirty, with a penchant for tight-lacing that made a bounty of her modest charms. She greeted him with a feline smile, clad in nothing more than a pale pink peignoir worn over her lace-trimmed chemise, French corset, and stockings. The sheer, gossamer fabric clung to her slender curves. "That will be all, Crebbs."

"Yes, my lady." Crebbs was an older woman, wiry and shrewd, with graying hair and a mouth bracketed by deep lines. She departed with a curtsy, shooting a warning glare in Ahmad's direction before she shut the door behind her.

Ahmad didn't know if Crebbs held him in such suspicion because of his sex, his class, or his race. All three, probably. A damning combination, as far as some were concerned.

But not Lady Heatherton.

To her jaded palate, the mixture was as potent as an exotic liqueur.

She approached him with that same lazily seductive smile. Her attention was riveted on his face. She showed no interest in the large white dress box in his arms. "As you see, I'm ready for you."

Ahmad set the box down on the gilded rose-silk settee, ignoring Lady Heatherton's advances. She was the kind of woman who relished flirtation. A product of her class, he supposed. Romantic entanglements were a game to ladies of the *ton*.

"The question is," Lady Heatherton continued, "are you ready for me?"

As she drew closer, he couldn't help but contrast her calculated manner with the frank openness of Evelyn Maltravers.

Lady Heatherton didn't fare well in the comparison.

Miss Maltravers bested her in every regard save one: Lady Heatherton was no untried country debutante. She was a lady who set the fashion. A lady whose wealth and patronage were necessary in order for Ahmad's own reputation to flourish.

One day, he'd have his own shop, staffed by a dozen seamstresses. Then, he'd have the luxury of making dresses for any lady who inspired him.

Ladies like Miss Maltravers.

Until then, he must choose his commissions with care.

Evening dresses and ball gowns were both time-consuming and expensive to make. And he had little time or money to spare at present. His hours were already stretched thin with his tailoring commitments—making riding habits and the occasional gentleman's suit. What time he had left could be spent on only one lady's gowns. The one best poised to help him achieve his goal.

That he didn't like her very much mattered not a whit.

"Your gown isn't quite finished yet," he said. "But all of the alterations from your last fitting have been made." He drew the dress from the box, holding it up so that the full ice-blue skirts swept the richly carpeted floor.

She ruffled the fabric with her fingers, temporarily diverted. "How plain it is."

Ahmad repressed a surge of annoyance. The evening gown wasn't plain. The delicate muslin was cut and sewn to fit the viscountess like a glove, every piece of costly lace positioned with calculated intention. "You must try it on to appreciate it."

"If you insist." She gave a delicate shrug, sending her peignoir slipping off her shoulders to slide down her arms. It dropped to the floor in a frothy puddle around her stockinged feet. "How many petticoats did you say it would require? And what sort of crinoline? You must help me into them, sir, since I have dismissed my maid."

"Shall I summon her back?"

Lady Heatherton's pale blue eyes flickered with irritation. "Don't be absurd. It's you I want, not stuffy old Crebbs." She gestured to a tall, lacquered wardrobe that stood against the wall opposite her silk-draped four-poster bed. "I've fresh underthings in there. Fetch them."

Ahmad saw no point in arguing. They'd been through this before. One of the many small power struggles in which the viscountess inevitably got her way.

And why shouldn't she? She was his customer. Practically his patroness. It didn't pay to refuse her.

That didn't mean he had to enjoy performing the little offices she required of him. He wasn't her plaything. Her bit of rough, as some fine ladies liked to call it. If he were, he wouldn't be half so obliging.

He'd come of age in a whorehouse, for God's sake. If she expected her advances to rattle him—to make him stammer and blush—she was in for a disappointment.

Retrieving her petticoats and crinoline from the wardrobe, he assisted her into them with a briskness that spoke more of impatience than intimacy. "Might I suggest that, in future, you have these on before I'm summoned?"

"And why should I when you're so accommodating?"

He bent his head to tie the tapes of her crinoline at her waist. "Because it would save us both a great deal of time."

Her fingers slid through his hair.

He stiffened at the sensation. There was nothing pleasurable about it. Her touch left him cold. Repulsed. The same way he'd felt as a boy when Mrs. Pritchard had taken such liberties.

He despised being handled.

"How thick it is," she murmured. "I've been longing to run my fingers through it."

Straightening, he drew back from her, well out of her reach. "Lady Heatherton—"

"Have I shocked you? Upon my word, I do believe I have. No wonder this gown you've made me is so demure and simple. It seems you've mistaken my character."

Like hell he had.

"Perhaps you should try it on," he suggested.

"I intend to. But first . . ." She beckoned to him with a crook of her finger. "Come. My corset needs tightening."

"It's tight enough."

"I insist." She turned, giving him her back. "You're stronger than Crebbs. I'd be a fool not to take advantage of you while you're here."

Clenching his jaw, Ahmad reluctantly did as she bid him. He didn't know why he should be so surprised by her behavior. Lady Heatherton was always skirting propriety. Always speaking in an overly familiar way, or brushing him lightly with her fingertips as he pinned and marked her garments. He was used to it.

As used to it as a man could become.

Even so, she'd never touched him as intimately as she had today. She was growing bolder.

"You're very strong." She gasped as he cinched her corset. "I remarked on it only recently to Lady Godwin. She visits a cobbler in South London on occasion. A shockingly good-looking specimen of a fellow. Makes lovely boots. He's quite strong as well. No doubt you know him."

"Should I?"

"He's an Indian, didn't I say?"

Ahmad gave another sharp tug on her laces before knotting them in place. "India is an exceedingly large country."

Lady Heatherton exhaled the breath she'd been holding. "Hmm." She sounded doubtful. "I couldn't say. I've never visited the colonies. After the mutiny, who would want to? The people seem the veriest savages. But not you." She flashed him a hooded glance. "You're quite tame, aren't you?"

Her words rankled. He supposed they were meant to. Another not-so-subtle expression of her dominance. In other circumstances he would have ignored her. He'd become adept at doing so with ladies of her ilk.

But not today.

This time, her words cut a little too deeply.

The Indians who had rebelled five years ago weren't mindless savages. They were an oppressed people—subjugated in their own land by colonizers who had no respect for India's history, for its traditions, or even for the religions of its native inhabitants. Indeed, the whole uprising had been sparked by a rumor that the cartridges used in British muskets were greased with both pig and beef fat.

Ahmad had left India as a boy. He had no religious beliefs to speak of, no more than he had any other claim to that part of his heritage. He could still comprehend the horror of such a thing. The offense to both Hindus and Muslims. The deep, unspeakable disrespect.

He didn't expect Lady Heatherton to understand.

"Your dress, my lady," he said evenly.

"Yes, yes. Bring it here. I never did see a man so single-minded." Her mouth screwed into a pout. "I begin to believe you don't notice me at all. You think of nothing but ladies' dresses."

"It's why you hired me."

"I hired you because I saw one of your gowns on that solicitor's wife—Mrs. Finchley—at the dinner for the Society for the Betterment of Orphans. She looked far better than she ought to."

Ahmad refrained from comment. He owed a great deal to Jenny Finchley. While employed as her manservant, he'd made her riding costumes and several of her gowns. Gowns that she wore to the occasional evening entertainment or to charitable functions, like the one Lady Heatherton had attended.

Unfortunately for him, Mrs. Finchley rarely moved in society. Indeed, she scarcely resided in London for more than a few months out of the year. The fact that Lady Heatherton had crossed paths with her was so much chance.

"It doesn't fall to a woman of her class to set the fashion. A solicitor's wife, of all people!" Lady Heatherton raised her arms above her head so Ahmad could slide the skirts of her evening dress over her shoulders and down to her waist. "I was never so unhappy with Madame Elise. To think, until then, I'd been content with her designs."

"I trust you'll be more than content with mine." He helped her into the bodice, fastening the delicate hooks at the back and settling the lace-trimmed neckline so it skimmed her bosom in line with the short, fluttering sleeves that brushed her upper arms.

It was an exceptionally lovely gown, made to enhance a lady's beauty instead of manufacturing it. Rather like a frame to a portrait. One should never overshadow the other.

Or so Ahmad believed.

No sooner had he arranged the last bit of lace than Lady Heatherton brushed his hands away and hurried to her looking glass.

"Why, this *is* rather pretty." She preened herself in front of the glass. "I look quite youthful, don't I? And yet it exposes far more of my bosom than my last evening dress."

"It's the coming fashion."

"You'll hear no objection from me on that score. Though it could do with more in the way of trimmings. There isn't a flounce or frill, nor a single ribbon bow. Nothing like the gowns my friends have ordered for the season."

"Lavish trimmings *are* popular at the moment," he conceded.

No thanks to Charles Worth.

The famed dressmaker's luxurious Parisian gowns, sold at his fashionable salon in the Rue de la Paix, were adorned with acres of expensive lace, glass beads, and silk bows and fringe. It was what Worth was known for. Garments as costly as they were coveted. His designs were copied by modistes from London to New York.

"But excess ruffles and ribbons don't flatter everyone." Ahmad straightened the finely sewn seams of her bodice. "This gown does far more to emphasize your figure than an evening dress weighted down with tinsel."

"Hmm. Perhaps it does. Though I wonder if it would be as flattering on an ugly lady? I imagine not. You see"—she turned to the right, gazing at herself over her shoulder—"it's my own beauty that draws the eye."

"I'm sure you're right," he said.

Lady Heatherton *was* an acknowledged beauty. More than that, she was regularly written about in the society pages.

A fact that Ahmad hoped would accrue to his benefit.

If she wore a new design to a ball or soiree, fashionable ladies would pay attention. Many of them would be quick to follow her lead.

"Of course I'm right." Glancing down at her skirts, a frown of disapproval etched her brow. "I shall trip on these."

"I've yet to hem them." He gestured toward the upholstered stool on which she usually stood when he made alterations. "If you please, my lady."

"Yes, but do be quick about it. I have engagements this afternoon and can't be troubled to stand about all morning." She extended an imperious hand.

Taking it, he assisted her up onto the stool.

And he felt nothing.

Nothing, save a deep desire to get on with things.

It wasn't anything like what he'd experienced when he'd clasped Miss Maltravers's hand. There was no warmth. No crackle of electricity. No quickening heartbeat or swiftly skipping pulse.

He was entirely unaffected.

Strange to think of it. Out of all the women he'd known—all the riding habits and dresses he'd made for courtesans and for the working girls at Mrs. Pritchard's establishment—it was a bluestocking who had finally moved him. A bespectacled bluestocking from Sussex, of all places.

But no. Not a bluestocking.

An equestrienne.

Smiling to himself, Ahmad knelt to pin Lady Heatherton's hem.

Five

❧❧

$\mathcal{E}$velyn drew off her gloves as she entered the hall of her uncle's town house in Russell Square. Agnes and one of the footmen trailed behind her, arms filled with boxes—the result of a morning shopping excursion in Bond Street.

"You may take them to my room," Evelyn said.

"Yes, miss." Agnes hurried the footman up the stairs. "Careful with those! Miss Maltravers don't want your grubby mitts crushing her linens."

Evelyn sighed. She'd spent all of yesterday visiting the names on the list Mr. Malik had given her. First the modiste, where she'd ordered a small selection of day dresses and afternoon gowns, and then the corsetiere, where she'd purchased two new corsets and a pair of short-boned riding stays.

This morning had been the draper's shop for gloves, parasols, and stockings, followed by the milliner, and—finally—the hairdresser.

Drawing out the long hatpin that secured it, she carefully removed her new leghorn hat and placed it on the hall table. A gilt-edged looking glass hung above it. She surveyed her reflection.

Like Mr. Malik, Monsieur Phillipe had been all business. The mustachioed little Frenchman had examined her this way and that, turning her head to all angles. And then, at last, he'd cut, wielding his scissors with all the decisiveness of a master.

Her hair was still long, falling well past her shoulder blades, but it was no longer an unruly mass of bushy curls. Now what curls she had appeared soft and glossy, gently framing her face in a flattering style.

And such a style!

He'd rolled her hair at the sides and wrapped it up at the back over a cushion to make a large roll at her nape. The whole of it was gleaming and thick, secured with an invisible hairnet and more than a dozen metal hairpins, and then lightly misted into place with a clear, liquid gum solution called bandoline.

Agnes had watched the process with keen attention, knowing she'd be required to replicate the coiffure in the days to come.

Evelyn smoothed back a stray curl with her hand. She still couldn't quite take it in. When paired with one of her new dresses from Madame Lorraine, she was beginning to feel like quite another person.

"Miss Maltravers."

Evelyn turned from the glass to find her uncle's housekeeper descending the stairs.

Mrs. Quick was an older woman of keen efficiency, as thin and sharp as a whittled branch. She wore a spotless starched cap over her iron-gray hair. "It's half past one."

"Is it?" Evelyn glanced at the long walnut-case clock that stood in the hall.

"Mr. Fielding informed me you would be receiving from one to three."

"Eventually. Once I've been introduced to people." In the meanwhile, Evelyn hadn't thought it necessary to make herself available for receiving hours, certainly not on a Saturday. "Why? Did someone call?"

"Lady Arundell and her daughter have come."

Evelyn stilled. "To see *me*?"

"And Mr. Fielding. Though at the moment, he's nowhere to be found."

"He's not in his study?"

"He's not in the house."

"Perhaps he's gone to the museum?" Evelyn suggested. He sometimes did. The British Museum was practically next door. An easy walking distance if he had a bit of research to do.

"He might have done." Mrs. Quick didn't appear overly concerned. No doubt she was accustomed to Uncle Harris's strange behavior. "I've put your guests in the drawing room and brought in the tea tray. If you'd care to join them?"

"Of course." Evelyn straightened the flounced skirts of her new silk gown. It had originally been made for someone else, a lady who hadn't wanted it. Madame Lorraine had altered it for Evelyn on the spot, insisting that the deep rose shade was complementary to her complexion. Evelyn had her doubts, but in matters of dress, she was resolved to defer to the experts.

She followed Mrs. Quick upstairs to the drawing room. Like the rest of Uncle Harris's house, it was well furnished, if not fashionably so. Heavy mahogany tables laden with bric-a-brac resided next to sofas and chairs upholstered in faded silk. Dark damask drapes framed the tall windows and well-worn carpets covered the expansive floor, the pile nearly threadbare in places.

Lady Arundell and her daughter were seated beside each other on a scroll-armed sofa near the fireplace. Flames flickered in the grate, casting a faint glow of warmth in a room that was, otherwise, cold and stale from disuse.

"Miss Maltravers, my lady," Mrs. Quick said by way of introduction.

Lady Arundell rose in a rustle of expensive fabric. She was a stately dark-haired woman, clad entirely in black crepe, with a slight double chin and a magnificent bosom. A carved stone cameo glinted at her pale white throat.

Evelyn curtsied. "Lady Arundell."

Lady Arundell inclined her head. "Miss Maltravers." She gestured to the young woman beside her. "My daughter, Lady Anne."

Lady Anne briefly emerged from her mother's shadow. She was wearing the same black crepe—and possessed of the same magnificent bosom. There the similarities ended. Lady Anne had a delicate frame, not a stately one, and her hair wasn't dark like her mother's. It was the color of spun gold, drawn back in a pair of jet combs.

"You don't look a thing like your uncle," Lady Arundell said after Mrs. Quick had withdrawn. "He's still not returned, I gather?"

"No, ma'am," Evelyn replied. "I'm sorry for the inconvenience."

"Never mind it. It's you I came to see. Fielding tells me I'm to have a hand in launching you." Lady Arundell withdrew a silver-filigree lorgnette from her reticule and held it up to her eyes. "Step forward, my girl. Let me see what I have to work with."

Evelyn's lips compressed. She didn't care to be commanded by anyone. She nevertheless crossed the room to join them. Being stubborn and contrary to those who might help her cause would achieve nothing. Better to be quiet and obliging.

At least, for now.

Coming to a halt in front of the low table that held the tea tray, she silently submitted to Lady Arundell's perusal.

Lady Anne resumed her seat, her hands folded neatly in her lap.

"You've been too much in the sun," Lady Arundell pronounced at last, lowering her lorgnette. "If you don't take care, you'll ruin your complexion."

"I do wear a hat whenever I—"

"And what about these spectacles of yours?" Lady Arundell plowed on. "Not becoming at all. They only serve to emphasize the unfortunate shape of your nose. Rather too aquiline for my taste. Never looks quite right on a younger gel."

This time, Evelyn absorbed the criticism without comment. It wasn't the first time someone had told her that her nose wasn't right, or that her spectacles were unflattering, and it surely wouldn't be the last. There was no point in taking it to heart.

Lady Arundell waved her lorgnette. "Get yourself one of these. You can wear it on a silk cord about your wrist. Use it on those occasions you wish to see clearly, and then slip it into your sleeve the remainder of the time."

"But I always wish to see clearly, ma'am." Evelyn sat down in her chair. "And as for my complexion—"

"I shall give you a recipe to whiten it." Lady Arundell settled back beside her daughter on the sofa. "Anne uses it nightly herself. Don't you, Anne?"

"Yes, Mama," Lady Anne replied. There was a starchy undercurrent in her voice at odds with her submissive demeanor.

Evelyn glanced at her, intrigued. For all that she deferred to her mother, Lady Anne didn't appear to be a shrinking violet. She exuded a visible confidence, evident in both her countenance and in her posture. One had the impression that, if she was in her mother's shadow, it was precisely because she chose to be there.

And her skin *was* quite flawless, now Evelyn looked at it. Rather like alabaster. A shade Evelyn had never achieved, or aspired to.

"Add to that a rotation of strawberry water, lemon juice, and Gowland's lotion," Lady Arundell went on. "That's what I recommend."

"I thank you for your advice." Evelyn poured out their tea. It was still hot, thank goodness. "Do you take milk, my lady? Or lemon?"

"Lemon, if you please," Lady Arundell replied. "And for Anne."

Evelyn passed them each one of the painted porcelain teacups Mrs. Quick had arranged on the tray. There was a plate of sugared biscuits, too. Lady Anne eyed them with a vague expression of longing. However, when Evelyn offered some to her, Lady Arundell declined for the both of them.

"We don't hold with sweets," she said. "Bad for the teeth and for the figure. A lady can't be too careful."

Evelyn returned the plate to the tray. After such a pronouncement, she could hardly take a biscuit for herself. She consoled herself with a sip of tea. "I hadn't considered."

"You haven't a mother to advise you. You must allow me to fill that office while you're in town."

Evelyn's fingers tightened reflexively around the handle of her teacup. She willed them to loosen. "You're too kind."

"Not a bit of it. Fielding and I are friends of old. It's the very least I can do for him." Lady Arundell drank her tea, continuing to examine Evelyn. "I didn't have the opportunity to meet your older sister during her come-out. We were away at the time, else I might have taken her in hand. She was a great beauty, I understand."

"People have always said so," Evelyn acknowledged.

"And you . . . Not very much like your sister, are you?"

"Not in that respect, ma'am," Evelyn said. "Nor in any other, I trust."

Lady Arundell's gaze narrowed. "Fielding tells me that you're a horsewoman, with a stallion or some such beast you've brought up from the country."

"Yes, ma'am. I intend to ride a great deal while I'm here."

"Pity. If marriage is your goal, you'd be wise to desist. Gentlemen don't like sporting girls, although they might pretend to. Anne can attest."

Lady Anne said not a word, but her eyes briefly met Evelyn's over the edge of her teacup. There was a glimmer of devilry in them.

"No fear," Lady Arundell went on. "We'll get you sorted in time for my ball. I'll consult Dmitri about how best to proceed."

"Who is—" Evelyn's question was arrested by the sound of a floorboard creaking in the hall. It was immediately followed by the reappearance of Mrs. Quick.

"Begging your pardon, miss," she addressed Evelyn from the drawing room doorway. "Mr. Fielding has returned. He says he'll be up directly."

"Has he gone to his study, Mrs. Quick?" Lady Arundell asked.

"He has, my lady."

Lady Arundell returned her teacup to the tea tray. "In that case"—she stood—"I shall go to him."

Evelyn moved to rise, but Lady Arundell waved both her and Lady Anne back to their seats.

"Finish your tea, girls. I'll return with him in a trice." With that, Lady Arundell sailed from the room, Mrs. Quick at her heels.

Lady Anne lowered her teacup to her lap. "You must forgive Mama.

She and Mr. Fielding share a passion for antiquities. She visits so often she's become accustomed to roaming free about the place."

"I don't mind it." Evelyn had no right to mind. This wasn't her home. "I'm only grateful she's agreed to help me."

"You truly have no one to sponsor your come-out?"

"Indeed, I have not. My aunt might have done, but she's remained with my little sisters in Sussex. I was obliged to come to London alone."

"How unfortunate."

"Not at all." Evelyn smiled. "I'm accustomed to managing things for myself."

Lady Anne shot a swift glance in the direction of the door before reaching for a biscuit. "Mama won't like to hear that. She's a great one for managing people. There's no one on earth who can change her opinion once it's been fixed. She takes no advice from anyone."

Evelyn took a biscuit for herself. "That can't be so. She mentioned consulting with someone named Dmitri."

"No one on earth, I said." Lady Anne finished her biscuit before explaining, "Dmitri isn't of this realm. He's Mama's familiar spirit."

Familiar spirit?

Evelyn gave her guest a blank look.

Lady Anne's mouth curved. "You *are* very countrified, aren't you? Haven't you any spiritualists in Sussex?"

"None that I've ever known." Evelyn had heard about them, of course. Her little sister Caro had a girlish passion for all things otherworldly. She was forever relating stories about séances that she'd read in the papers. Evelyn couldn't wait to write to her about today's events. Imagine, encountering a genuine spiritualist in Uncle Harris's drawing room!

"There are a great many spiritualists in London," Lady Anne said. "Mama's been involved with them ever since Papa died."

Evelyn was struck, all at once, by the significance of Lady Anne and her mother wearing so much black. The Earl of Arundell must have passed sometime in the last year. "Oh, I *am* sorry," she said. "Please accept my condolences on your loss."

Lady Anne helped herself to another biscuit. "What loss?"

"Why . . . the loss of your father. You *are* in mourning, aren't you?"

"Gracious, no. Not for my father at any rate. He died years ago."

"Then—"

"It's done at Mama's insistence. For Prince Albert."

"I see. Your mother knew the prince?"

"No, indeed. But she hopes to make his acquaintance very soon."

Evelyn didn't know what to say. Was Lady Anne in earnest? Or was she having a private laugh at Evelyn's expense? The very idea was enough to set Evelyn's back up. "You have me at a loss, I'm afraid."

Lady Anne's expression softened with sympathy. "I don't wonder. But you'd best acclimate yourself. Mama isn't the only devoted spiritualist hereabouts. Your uncle is as well. You must have realized."

Evelyn's teacup froze halfway to her mouth. "My uncle is a spiritualist?" She was dumbfounded. "But . . . I understood his passion lay with antiquities."

"Antiquities, yes," Lady Anne said. "The *Book of the Dead*, and so forth. Mama and Mr. Fielding are keen on finding evidence of spirit contact in ancient texts. Or rather, they *were* until very recently. The death of Prince Albert has lately consumed all of their energies. Mediums from here to America have been trying to make contact."

"Have they? My goodness."

Lady's Anne's sherry-brown eyes sparkled with sudden humor. "You really didn't know?"

"I thought my uncle merely absentminded. I'd no notion he kept company with spiritualists and like-minded people."

Aunt Nora had never hinted at the fact. Evelyn wondered if she knew. She'd always described Uncle Harris as a respected scholar. A bachelor recluse more concerned with his books and papers than with the welfare of his distant relations. He'd only agreed to host Evelyn because Aunt Nora had given him no other choice.

"Not altogether like-minded," Lady Anne said. "The difference being that while your uncle might be absent by nature, my mother is ever present. To be sure, there's only one activity in which she doesn't shadow my every step." She took a sip of her tea. "Is it true you enjoy riding?"

"Above all things. It's the chief pleasure of—" Evelyn broke off, suddenly recollecting her encounter with the young woman in the park. "Forgive me, but you wouldn't happen to be acquainted with a lady by the name of Miss Wychwood, would you?"

Lady Anne's face brightened. "You've met Julia?"

"Only once, three mornings ago. I encountered her in Rotten Row. She said that she often rides with you, and with another lady. Miss Hobhouse, I believe."

"Stella Hobhouse." Lady Anne nodded. "We frequently make up a threesome during the fashionable hour. Or we *did*, anyway. Julia prefers to ride at dawn this time of year. She never could stomach the laughs and whispers once the season commences."

Evelyn went still. "What laughs and whispers?"

"Some of the young gentlemen in town fancy themselves to be wits, and when they see the three of us trotting abreast down Rotten Row, they will call us all manner of silly names. Under their breath, naturally. They haven't the courage to tease us to our faces."

A flicker of unease went through Evelyn's frame. She hesitated to ask. "What names?"

"The three Fates. The three Furies. The spinsters three." Lady Anne grimaced. "We none of us have been very popular on the marriage mart."

Evelyn was appalled. "What has that to do with anything?"

"Nothing at all, so long as we keep to our places. But I never could resist giving an impertinent fellow the sharp side of my tongue. And Stella won't shrink from anyone, least of all an encroaching young jackanapes. As for Julia . . . her shyness has a power all its own."

Evelyn remembered the way Miss Wychwood had chattered with such animation. "She didn't appear shy to me."

"Ah, but the two of you were mounted. Julia is much more confident on horseback—as are we all." Lady Anne smiled wryly as she helped herself to another biscuit. "Pity one can't ride a horse into a ballroom."

Six

———✦———

$\mathcal{D}$oyle and Heppenstall's was closed on Sunday, a fact of which Ahmad took full advantage. Seated at one of the empty worktables in the back, he finished basting together the final pieces of Miss Maltravers's habit.

It wasn't his only commission. Neither was it the most pressing. He had Lady Heatherton's gowns to finish. She was expecting him to deliver the first on Wednesday morning. It was the gown she planned to wear to her first ball of the season—an event as important to Ahmad as it was to her.

Wasn't that his dream? To have his designs worn by the fashionable elite?

And yet, he'd spent most of the last several days working not on hemming Lady Heatherton's ice-blue evening gown, but on Evelyn Maltravers's riding costume.

He'd cut the fabric on Friday, from a pattern of his own devising. It was a variation of the last habit he'd made. One for the infamous Miss Walters.

But this habit was different.

Not only had he adjusted for Miss Maltravers's measurements, he'd shortened the jacket, widened the sleeves, and left ample room in the bodice and skirts for additional darts and seams.

It was a departure from the style he usually made. Something new, as functional as it was beautiful. A garment well suited to a lady like Miss Maltravers, and one he hoped she would favor.

He'd sent a note round yesterday informing her that he was ready to do her second fitting and asking if Sunday afternoon would be convenient. She'd responded almost immediately in the affirmative.

As he tied off his last stitch, he felt a throb of anticipation at the prospect of seeing her again.

Ridiculous.

He was a man of thirty, not some raw lad pining over his first woman.

It was because of the habit, that was all. He was anxious to see it on her. To fit it to her figure, pinning it into an approximation of its final style.

But even as he told himself that—even as he assured himself that there was nothing personal about his desire to see her again, to touch her and speak with her—he recognized the truth of his feelings.

Miss Maltravers hadn't merely inspired him. She'd aroused his interest.

A dangerous thing, curiosity. Especially when it came to English-women. He prided himself on the lack of it. The less one knew, the less one was tempted to get involved.

Things never ended well when one tangled with an English fe-male. There were too many differences. Too many inequities to account for. If he'd learned nothing else from his years at Mrs. Pritchard's, he'd learned that.

It didn't stop his pulse from leaping when a knock sounded at the front of the shop.

Setting aside his sewing, he walked into the empty showroom to unlock the door. Miss Maltravers was waiting on the other side of it. Alone.

"My maid has a half day off on Sunday," she explained as she entered the shop. She shook the raindrops from her drab wool cloak. It was drizzling outside. Had been ever since sunrise.

He shut the door behind her and slowly turned the lock. "You might have said so. You could have come another day."

"I didn't want to wait another minute."

Ahmad gazed down at her. Her face was framed by the hood of her cloak. "Your habit isn't finished yet."

"I know that."

"There's a final fitting after this one."

She smiled. "I know that, too. I still couldn't wait. I'm anxious to see how it's coming along."

He motioned for her to precede him through the back curtain that led into the gaslit fitting room. Once there, she drew back her hood. His heartbeat quickened. Her dark auburn hair was no longer a bushy cloud of curls around her face. It was sleek and elegant—the sides rolled back, and the length bound up in a beaded hairnet. "You've seen Monsieur Phillipe."

"I have. And Madame Lorraine as well." She unfasted her cloak. It slid from her shoulders, revealing the dress beneath—an overly flounced confection made in a shade of magenta so garishly bright it nearly burned his retinas.

Ahmad regarded her in mild horror.

Her face fell. "You don't like it?"

"Did you choose it?"

"No. It was part of an order for someone else. This and another dress. Madame Lorraine persuaded me to buy them so I'd have something to wear while I await the rest of my order. She said the colors were flattering."

"Blinding, more like it. What color is the other dress?"

"Rose."

He grimaced. "Worse and worse."

Miss Maltravers cast her gown a rueful glance. "Is it truly that bad?"

"You don't see it?"

"I confess, I did wonder." She draped her cloak over the wooden chair in the corner of the fitting room. "Neither gown is to my particular taste. But you said Madame Lorraine was better than Madame Elise, and that I—"

"Better than Madame Elise in most respects." Not in color selection, apparently. And not when it came to trimmings. The excessive flounces and frills did nothing to flatter Miss Maltravers's figure.

"In other words, dreadful." She looked at him. "What am I to do?"

He rubbed the side of his jaw. "Have you placed a large order?"

"Not very. Only a few dresses. And I haven't bought any of my evening dresses or ball gowns yet."

"Don't."

"Where else should I go? There isn't a great deal of time before my debut."

"You needn't go elsewhere. Madame Lorraine should be able to amend your order, provided she hasn't started cutting the fabric." Ahmad doubted she had. During the season, a London modiste prioritized orders from her most distinguished clients—ladies of wealth and rank. Miss Maltravers was neither. "I'll write up a list of suitable colors for you to give her."

Miss Maltravers was visibly relieved. "I'm obliged to you."

"Not at all," he said. "Do you need help undressing?"

A delicate blush suffused her cheeks. "The fastenings at the back are a little difficult to reach. If you wouldn't mind?"

"Turn around."

She promptly did as he asked. Her voice held a note of apology. "It's just the first five hooks."

He stepped up behind her. Close. So close, he could smell her orange blossom perfume, a faint whisper-soft fragrance that set his heart to thumping. He unfastened the first of the small metal hooks that secured the neck of her bodice. It was something he'd done countless times while making alterations—helping women to dress and undress—his assistance rendered with dispassionate efficiency. It was the veriest commonplace for a man of his trade. But this time . . .

This time he felt neither dispassionate nor particularly efficient.

There was something warmly seductive about being this close to Evelyn Maltravers. Something about her scent, and her posture. The way her neck was curved so elegantly before him, her bodice opening hook by hook to reveal the creamy expanse of bare skin just above the line of her lace-trimmed chemise. It was a soft, secret place. A place that beckoned to be touched. To be kissed.

Naturally, he took no such liberties.

He never had done, not even when altering gowns for the women at Mrs. Pritchard's. It was only the thought of it that plagued him now. The sort of thought that had never before entered his head while he was working, no matter how alluring his client.

Did she feel it, too?

If so, she gave no indication. Nothing save the ordinary blushes one might expect of a modest, respectable young lady being unclothed by a man.

"Perhaps this is something I should have mentioned," she said. "The importance of being able to dress and undress myself. Will the habit require the assistance of a lady's maid?"

"No." As he unfastened the final hooks, his fingers brushed against the silken thickness of her hair. A jolt of awareness went through him.

Damnation.

He backed away from her.

She cast him an uncertain look over her shoulder. "Is anything wrong?"

"Nothing." He cleared his throat. "Can you reach the rest yourself?"

"I believe so."

"Then I'll give you a moment of privacy." He withdrew, swiftly returning to the safety of his workroom.

━━━✖━━━

Evelyn slipped off her gown and stepped out of her crinoline and petticoats, folding each item meticulously before stacking it on the fitting room chair. Perhaps it would have been wiser to bring a maid. It would certainly have made undressing easier. Unfortunately, in this case, propriety had had to give way to expediency.

When it came to getting herself outfitted for the season, she hadn't a second to spare. One season, that was all that had been granted to her. A period of less than five months in which to make a suitable marriage. A brilliant marriage. One that would secure her future, and that of her sisters. And that season couldn't start—not for her—until she had her wardrobe in order.

She was already woefully behind schedule. And now she'd gone and purchased the wrong color gowns!

"Should I not wear shades of rose or magenta?" she asked when Mr. Malik returned.

His tall, broad-shouldered frame was clad in black wool trousers and a single-breasted waistcoat. He'd discarded his coat. The crisp white linen of his shirt stood in stark contrast to the healthy bronze of his skin. "Never."

"Oh." She hadn't expected him to answer so definitively. "Then what colors—" She stopped short at the sight of her new habit draped over his arm. "Goodness. Is that it?"

"The beginning of it." Mr. Malik set the unfinished garment down on the fitting room table. Turning back to her, he offered his hand.

She took it, her attention still fixed on the habit as she climbed up on the raised platform in front of the fitting room's cheval glass.

Shopping for gowns had been a pleasure—choosing patterns and fabrics and trimmings. But it was nothing to equal her excitement at the prospect of a new habit. Especially *this* habit. It was the linchpin of all of her plans.

"I suppose green is acceptable," she said.

"Not every shade of it. Not with your coloring." His eyes dropped to her riding stays.

Made of fine linen coutil, the modified corset was cut high over her hips, with a short busk and no shoulder straps to impede her movement. Just the style he'd prescribed.

He stilled to examine them.

Evelyn felt his quiet regard all the way down to her marrow. As if every brush of his gaze over her tightly bound bosom and midriff was a touch. A bold caress that heated her blood and tied her stomach in impossible knots.

She moistened her lips. "I trust you approve."

"Wholeheartedly. These will do nicely with my design. So long as you can breathe?"

She couldn't at the moment. Not very well. He was still holding her hand. Holding it as naturally as if he'd always done so. And she was letting him. Permitting what would otherwise have been an impertinence for the very same reason. Her hand fit so well in his grasp. As if it was made to be there.

Which it most certainly wasn't.

She slowly slipped her fingers from his. It was impossible for him not to notice. Impossible not to draw attention to the sheer awkwardness of it all.

A faint flush of red appeared on the strong column of his throat, just above the line of his black cravat. "I beg your pardon," he said stiffly.

"It was my fault. I—"

"You were distracted. As was I. Anticipation, no doubt."

Anticipation?

"You must be as anxious to see it on as I am." He moved back to the table to retrieve the first piece of her habit.

"Yes," she managed. "Most anxious."

"I must ask for your patience. For future orders, things will go quickly, but today, I must mark all four pieces."

"Four?" The dressmaker in Combe Regis had only ever made riding costumes that were three pieces: a skirt, a jacket, and the close-fitting riding trousers one wore underneath.

Mr. Malik seemed to read her mind. "I've added a silk petticoat, the same color as your habit."

"Why silk?"

He returned with her riding trousers. Made of a thin chamois leather, they were dyed the same dark green as her habit. "Silk won't bunch up under your skirts," he explained. "My design requires a smooth line, and no unnecessary bulk beneath."

"Oh. I hadn't thought of that." She usually just wore one of her everyday white cotton petticoats under her habit. The lumpiness of it had never been a concern. Not when riding in the country.

No wonder Mr. Malik's habits looked so dazzling on the Pretty Horsebreakers. He seemed to account for everything.

Crouching down in front of her, he moved to help her into her riding trousers. Evelyn was obliged to rest a hand on his shoulder to balance herself.

He had exceedingly muscular shoulders.

She briefly closed her eyes against the sensation. Good gracious. He might have been chiseled from granite.

He tugged the trousers up her legs and over her hips.

"They seem to fit nicely," she managed.

"Very well." He sounded pleased with himself. "They only want a few minor adjustments."

Taut moments followed, during which Evelyn reflected that having Mr. Malik pinning and marking her trousers provoked very different sensations than when her riding trousers were fitted by the village dressmaker in Combe Regis.

He took no liberties. His touch was brisk and efficient; nevertheless . . . it was everywhere. He marked adjustments to be made on her hips and rear, and even along her inner thigh.

She began to wonder if it was possible to spontaneously combust from repressed blushes. Indeed, by the time he'd finished, the two of them must have begged each other's pardons half a dozen times.

And it wasn't over.

The silk petticoat came next, and then the habit skirts.

Mr. Malik rose, sliding the waist-opening up over her hips. Their eyes met, and he gave her a sudden smile. It was as fleeting as it was sympathetic, seeming to acknowledge their mutual discomfort, even as it dismissed it. "We can't keep apologizing."

Her mouth trembled on a faint smile of her own. "No, indeed."

"A little familiarity can't be helped in these circumstances. I have to touch you."

"Of course you must." She cast about for something else she might say. Something to put an end to this strange intimacy developing between them. "Er, it hasn't much shape at this stage, has it? The skirt, I mean."

"It will have." He slid a pin through the partially open side seam, securing the fabric at her waist. "This part will take a bit longer. If you don't mind standing perfectly still?"

Evelyn nodded. How many times had she been required to stand motionless for the village seamstress? Or for Aunt Nora while she let out the seams of a hand-me-down dress? How many times, when fidgeting, had she been stabbed with an errant pin?

"I won't move," she promised.

And she didn't, for all the long, silent minutes that followed.

Mr. Malik alternately stood and knelt, pinning darts and seams and making marks on the fabric with the piece of tailor's chalk he kept in his waistcoat pocket.

"You asked about colors," he said at last. He was pinning the skirt fabric behind her, far out of her line of sight.

"Yes?"

"Shades of rose and mauve are never suitable for ladies with auburn hair."

"And not greens either, you said. Not all shades of green, anyway."

"Darker greens, like this one, will always suit you. Bottle greens and invisible greens. But steer clear of lighter shades—apple or moss. They'll drain the life out of your face." He folded the fabric of her skirt very slightly over the curve of her rear, securing it with another pin. "What colors do you wear at home?"

"Blue, mostly. Dark blues and grays." They were subdued, inoffensive hues, suitable to a young lady of her station—and her pocketbook. Colors that could withstand regular washing. She paused, expecting him to make a sound of approval. None was forthcoming. "Are those wrong, too?"

"Yes."

She huffed a short laugh. "What do you recommend, then? I can't always be wearing green."

Standing up from his work, he stepped back to look at her, his brow drawn into a contemplative frown. "Black will suit you. Indeed, it would be quite striking. Also, claret, stone gray, and shades of gold and amber. And white, of course. Not bright or blue-white, mind, but creamy white."

"Creamy white," she repeated. "Ivory, do you mean?"

He shook his head. "It's a lighter shade than ivory. Clearer, with a richness to it. A softness. Regrettably, I don't have a sample to show you. The shade would make a stunning ball gown for someone of your coloring."

"I thought only debutantes wore white."

"This is your first season, isn't it?"

"My first and my last," she said. "I'm three and twenty, Mr. Malik. Not a young girl. If I can't make a success of my time here . . ."

He regarded her in silence for a long moment. It was unnerving, that silence, fraught with a palpable tension. A part of her longed to fill it up. Anything to diminish this attraction she was having to him.

A tailor, of all people!

Not even a gentleman. Certainly not one who could see her family right.

Was she no better than Fenny at heart? Willing to throw her reputation to the wind for a handsome face and figure?

"It was my sister who was supposed to do all of this," she blurted out. "The clothes and the season—the husband hunting. And she did, three years ago. But she didn't finish the job." Evelyn cast a glance at herself in the glass. "She was much prettier than I am."

"So you've said."

"It's true. She had a dainty retroussé nose. And she didn't require spectacles. Not that she ever admitted."

"Is she dead?"

Her gaze jerked back to his. "*What?* No. Why would you ask that?"

"You speak of her as if she was. In the past tense."

Evelyn's mouth tugged into a frown. "Yes, I suppose I do." She ran a restless hand over the front of her skirt, narrowly avoiding being stabbed by a pin. "No. She isn't dead. She's simply gone. If you must know, she ran off with a man during her first season and caused a terrible scandal."

"I'm sorry to hear it."

"No more than I am. Had she done her duty, I'd never have been obliged to come to London, or to enact this reckless plan."

Mr. Malik's brows lifted a fraction.

Evelyn belatedly registered that she'd said too much.

"What plan?" he asked.

She bit her lower lip, worrying the plump flesh between her teeth. Her plan for the season wasn't a secret. Not entirely. And even if it was, why shouldn't she tell him? He was her ally, after a fashion.

"To make my debut in Rotten Row," she said.

"*That's* your plan?"

"Well . . . yes. I can hardly impress people in a ballroom."

"Even if that were true, which I take leave to doubt . . . young women don't make their debuts on horseback."

"Some do."

"Not ladies."

"Just because they haven't done yet doesn't mean it's impossible. I'm an excellent rider."

"You are," he said.

Her insides pooled with unexpected warmth. He'd acknowledged it so quickly, and with such matter-of-factness. As if there were no argument to be made against her skill. "Yes, well . . . My mother always told me that, in a difficult situation, one must proceed from a position of strength."

"Wise advice."

"I've always thought so. And when I saw the story in the paper—" She broke off, explaining, "My aunt takes the *Times*. At the end of last summer, they printed an article about the scarcity of husbands in London. It said that eligible gentlemen were avoiding the ballrooms— and the young ladies on the marriage mart—in favor of the Pretty Horsebreakers."

"And so, you thought . . . ?"

"I thought of a way I might find a husband."

"Proceeding from a position of strength."

"Exactly."

He picked up the jacket of her habit from the table and returned to her, holding it as she slipped her arms into the overlarge sleeves. "The Pretty Horsebreakers aren't offering themselves up for marriage. You do realize?"

"Yes, but it's not only courtesans who frequent Rotten Row. There are many respectable young ladies there who endeavor to ape their style. The papers report on that, too. How none of them measure up. But *I* can. At least, in so far as my riding. As for the rest, I knew I'd need a little assistance."

"Which is why you approached me."

Some of her confidence left her. It was impossible to tell what he was thinking. His face was void of expression, his attention focused more on pinning her bodice than it was on her. She wasn't convinced that he wasn't privately laughing at her. "Wearing one of your habits, I'm sure to make an impression."

"Undoubtedly." He lifted her arm.

She held it out of his way, sucking in her breath as he chalked a dart on the side of her bosom. "Rotten Row isn't the only place I'll be making an appearance," she said in a rush. "I've received an invitation to Lady Arundell's spring ball. That will be my official debut."

He flashed her an interested look. "The Earl of Arundell's widow?"

"My uncle counts her as a friend. She's offered to help introduce me into society."

"Does she know of your plan?"

"Indeed not. No one does." Evelyn's eyes met his. "No one except you."

Something flickered in the depths of his dark gaze. "I'm honored."

"You're necessary." It was the truth. She hadn't really believed her plan could succeed until she'd set eyes on his riding habits. "You have a great talent."

"You flatter me." He lowered her arm gently back to her side. "What do you think thus far? Is it to your liking?"

"It's hard to tell at this stage. The color is becoming, of course. Quite remarkably so. As for the rest of it . . ." She studied her reflection in the glass. A glow of warmth built within her.

The unfinished habit had only a vague shape to speak of, all chalk marks and metal pins, with no cuffs on the sleeves or buttons to close the jacket.

It didn't mar her appreciation.

She could already see the lines of it coming together, the way it seemed to enfold her figure in a lover's embrace, enhancing the curve of her waist and the swell of her bosom and hips. He was fitting it to her, molding it to her body as expertly as he'd done with the habits of the Pretty Horsebreakers.

Though it wasn't completely the same.

"The skirt isn't shaped like the one I saw Miss Walters wearing," she said. "It seems less full, somehow."

"It is. This is a different design." He adjusted the pinned folds of her skirt, smoothing it over her abdomen and hips. "I've gored the fabric to lie flatter at the front and the sides. It has the effect of pushing some of the fullness to the back."

Evelyn pivoted at the waist to get a better view of the fabric behind. "It's perilously close to a train."

"Indeed."

She cast him a questioning glance. "Is that the style now?"

Mr. Malik's face was set with resolve. "It will be."

Seven

✦

B y the time Ahmad emerged from the workroom at Doyle and Heppenstall's, it was half past six. Drawing his tall beaver hat down over his brow, he walked to Bond Street, where he hailed a hansom cab. "To Half Moon Street," he said, climbing in.

The jarvey slapped the reins, and the rangy chestnut trotted off in the direction of Piccadilly. Half Moon Street lay just off the main thoroughfare—an elegant, if not ostentatious, address, tucked away from the ordinary hustle and bustle of Mayfair.

Ahmad sank back onto the poorly padded seat of the cab. The straw on the floor was damp from the rain, and the interior reeked of cheap perfume. In better weather, he'd have walked to Mr. and Mrs. Finchleys' house. It was less than a mile away from the tailor's shop. But he'd already lingered too long. First, taking his time with Miss Maltravers, and then, after she'd gone, taking his time with the adjustments to her habit.

She'd left him feeling inspired, just as she had the last several times he'd seen her. He didn't fully understand it, this strange desire to help her achieve her potential. He was attracted to her; that much was clear. But it was something more than mere attraction. It was a variety of kinship. A mutual recognition that whispered to his soul.

And it *was* mutual.

He didn't know her as well as he might, but he knew enough of women to recognize the signs. It was present in the way she clasped his hand, and in the way her breath stuttered when he touched her. It was in the way she held his gaze, even as she blushed.

What courage she had. To enact this plan, coming to London and seeking him out all on her own. All because she'd seen his habits on the Pretty Horsebreakers.

"*I'm determined to outshine them all,*" she'd proclaimed the day she'd walked into Doyle and Heppenstall's.

Recalling it, his mouth ticked up into a smile.

He was still smiling when the hansom came to a halt in front of the Finchleys' town house. After paying his fare, Ahmad made his way past the front entrance to the black cast-iron fence that shielded the stairs to the back.

The servants' entrance.

Descending the damp stone steps, he rapped on the door. It was opened almost at once by Mrs. Jarrow, the Finchleys' dour cook-housekeeper.

Her flinty eyes narrowed. "It's you, is it?"

Ahmad removed his hat before entering the kitchen. A pot was boiling on the stove, and at the back of the room, a young kitchen maid in a white apron loaded steaming dishes into the dumbwaiter. "Have they already gone into dinner?"

"Near as can be. They're in the parlor. Your cousin's with them." Mrs. Jarrow returned to the stove, grunting under her breath, "Didn't reckon I'd have an extra mouth to feed this evening."

Ahmad crossed the kitchen to the servants' stairs, ignoring the muttered remarks.

Mrs. Jarrow and her husband had been employed by the Finchleys for years. They were a stern-faced married couple of middle age. A product of Mr. Finchley's charity, just as Ahmad and Mira had been. The only difference was that the Jarrows were English. While he and Mira were . . .

Not entirely English. Not entirely Indian, either.

The Jarrows had never wholly approved of their presence.

Nothing was ever said outright. That wasn't how civilized people operated. It was the sharp looks and the double-edged remarks. It was the lingering suspicion. As if his and Mira's ancestry was but the first step toward committing some manner of crime.

Or perhaps it *was* the crime.

The Jarrows wouldn't be the first to think so.

Ahmad ascended the stairs to the Finchleys' small parlor. It was a cozy room, furnished with an overstuffed chintz sofa and chairs, a tufted ottoman with tassel trim, and heavy tables on which stacks of books resided along with various trinkets the Finchleys had collected during their travels.

A fire of hot coals glowed cheerfully in the grate. Mira was seated in front of it, in company with her employers, Tom Finchley and his wife, Jenny.

"Ahmad!" Mira rose from her chair at the sight of him. She was wearing a simple gray silk dress, unadorned, though far from plain. It was a sophisticated design, with clean lines that flattered her figure. One of his own creations, complemented by delicate embroidery at the hem—Mira's contribution. She had an ineffable talent for needlework.

Finchley stood as well. He was a plain sort of gentleman in appearance. Of medium height and slim build, with hair that was a commonplace shade of brown, and eyes of a nondescript blue, hidden behind a pair of spectacles. An ordinary-looking fellow in every respect. Deceptively so.

The truth was, there was nothing ordinary about Tom Finchley. He was possessed of a ruthless legal mind. Indeed, at one time, he'd been considered the most formidable solicitor in London.

"This is a surprise," he said. "I trust nothing is amiss?"

"Nothing at all." Ahmad bowed. "Mrs. Finchley. Mira."

Mrs. Finchley greeted him from her place on the sofa. She was an attractive woman, and rather formidable, too, in her own right. Ahmad had first met her two years ago when she was still Jenny Holloway, a headstrong spinster determined to travel to India to find the missing Earl of Castleton—a distant cousin of hers, presumed dead after the rebellion. Finchley had hired Ahmad and Mira to accompany her.

And then, at the last minute, Finchley had decided to join them.

Together, they'd journeyed through France, and then on to Egypt and India, traveling as far as the hill stations of Darjeeling. It was there they'd found Lord Castleton, weak and injured but very much alive.

The whole adventure had given them a familiarity with each other that was more in keeping with a friendship than the relationship of masters and servants.

"Do sit down, Ahmad," Mrs. Finchley said. "My husband was just extolling the virtues of London during the season."

Finchley resumed his seat. "And my wife was reminding me of the beauties of summer in Devon."

"Not the least of which would be a chance to visit Lady Helena and Captain Thornhill." Mrs. Finchley smiled. "But I'll say no more on the subject. We've ample time to sort out our summer travel plans." She looked to Ahmad. "I hope you'll stay for dinner?"

Ahmad sat down in the empty chair next to Mira. The very mention of Lady Helena, sister to the Earl of Castleton, was enough to remind him of his predicament.

As if he could forget.

"I don't wish to be any trouble," he said.

"No trouble at all," Finchley replied. "It's been far too long since we all dined together."

"Indeed," Mrs. Finchley said. "It will be just like old times."

A moment later, Mr. Jarrow appeared in the parlor doorway to inform them that dinner was served, and the four of them repaired to the dining room.

Ahmad hadn't eaten a proper sit-down dinner in ages. He hadn't the time. Since striking out on his own, his evening meals, such as they were, had been bolted down in between cutting and piecing fabric and hand-stitching seams. Sometimes, when absorbed in his work, he forgot to eat altogether.

But not tonight.

There was spring soup, chicken cutlets, boiled leg of mutton with steamed vegetables, and a rhubarb tart to finish. A plain English meal, typical of Mrs. Jarrow. Ahmad ate every crumb on his plate. It wasn't until he was finished that Mr. Finchley finally pressed him on the reason for his visit.

"I need Mira," Ahmad said bluntly.

Mira froze in the act of wiping her mouth. "Me?" She lowered her napkin. "For what?"

"To assist me next week. I have too many orders at the moment. Three evening gowns, and several riding habits—almost all due within the next ten days. It's more than I can finish on my own."

Mrs. Finchley looked pleased. "But that's promising, isn't it? To be so busy during the early months of the season?"

Ahmad liked to think so. But there were no guarantees. Not when his initial outlay wasn't recouped until after an order was filled. Even then, among the upper classes, it was often the custom to delay payment for months at a time. Indeed, many fashionable members of society lived off credit, maintaining a lavish lifestyle even as the tradesmen they owed went bankrupt.

"It's early stages," he said. "But yes. So long as nothing goes wrong."

Mira pursed her lips. "Viscountess Heatherton hasn't paid him."

"I haven't delivered her gowns yet," Ahmad said. "Orders aren't paid in advance."

"And what of Miss Walters?" Mira asked. "Is her bill still outstanding?"

He privately cursed himself for having shared that bit of information with his cousin. "That's not what I came here to discuss," he said with growing impatience. "The fact is, I have orders—ample orders—and once Lady Heatherton wears one of my designs, I expect there'll

be more. In the meanwhile, I need assistance to finish her gowns—
and the habits commissioned by Miss Maltravers."

Mira gave him a puzzled look. "I thought she'd only ordered
the one?"

"Today she ordered two more." He'd all but encouraged her. If
Miss Maltravers planned to cut a dash in Rotten Row, she'd require
more than the one habit to do so.

"I intend to ride daily," she'd told him. *"It's why I came here."*

To find a husband. A well-to-do husband. One of the droves of
men who frequented Hyde Park, in fact. The ones who came to ogle
the Pretty Horsebreakers.

Ahmad felt vaguely irritated to think of it.

Foolish of him.

The whole point of the habit he'd designed for Miss Maltravers
was to make her an object of beauty, every stitch and seam placed to
draw attention to her charms. It was why she'd sought him out.

Finchley regarded Ahmad with interest. "Who is Miss Maltravers?"

Ahmad had seen that look before. The one that said Finchley was
inferring meaning where none existed. "A young lady from Sussex.
She's here for the season, making her debut."

"She wants a riding habit like the one Ahmad made for Miss
Walters," Mira said.

"Not quite the same." Ahmad crumpled his linen napkin next to
his plate. "The point is, I don't wish her to wait any longer than necessary. Which is why I need Mira. If you can spare her?"

"Certainly," Mrs. Finchley answered. "If it's what she wishes."

"I do wish it." Mira leaned forward in her chair. "When shall I start?"

"Tomorrow if you can," Ahmad said. "I only require the week."

"Is that all?" Mira's eager expression vanished.

Finchley exchanged a glance with his wife. An unspoken communication seemed to pass between them. The two of them stood,
practically in unison.

"Now that we have that settled," Mrs. Finchley said, taking her husband's arm, "we'll give you a bit of privacy."

"You may use my book room if you'd prefer," Mr. Finchley offered. "And please, do make free with the port."

Ahmad rose as the Finchleys exited the dining room. The door swung shut behind them, leaving him alone with Mira. She was oddly quiet. "Would you like a glass?" he asked her.

"Of port?"

"Why not?" He retrieved the decanter and two glasses from the mahogany sideboard. As a rule, ladies didn't drink port. It was a masculine libation, enjoyed after dinner, when gentlemen lingered at the table to talk among themselves, free from the constraints of female company.

"Because it's vile," she said.

"You've never tried it." Ahmad poured out their drinks. It was an old vintage by the look of it. The tawny liquid gleamed in the light of the crystal gasolier that hung overhead. He passed a glass to Mira. It was little more than a mouthful. "Here. Have a taste. It might make it easier."

Mira raised the glass to her nose and gave it a wary sniff. "Make what easier?"

"Whatever it is you have to say to me."

Her gaze snapped to his. Her green eyes were watchful, her mouth tugged into a sad little frown.

"I know you, *bahan*," he said.

Even if he didn't, the Finchleys couldn't have been more obvious. Their sudden withdrawal. Their eagerness to give Ahmad and Mira privacy. It wasn't exactly subtle.

He sat down next to her. "What's wrong?"

Mira stared at her drink. Taking a small sip, she grimaced, choked, and blurted out: "I'm missing you."

It wasn't what Ahmad had been expecting to hear. Not put quite so bluntly, and with so much rawness lurking beneath her words. A knot formed in his stomach. He couldn't think how to respond.

He supposed he knew that she missed him. It was why she was forever showing up at his rooms in what, he suspected, was a vain effort to re-create the closeness they'd shared at Mrs. Pritchard's. Then, it had been just the two of them in the same attic bedroom, their twin cots separated by a tattered Chinese screen.

Far from ideal.

Given a choice, he'd rather have found work somewhere respectable. Somewhere safe. Unfortunately, there had been no other option. Not if he and Mira were to stay together.

"Keep her out of sight during working hours," Mrs. Pritchard had commanded him on the day he and Mira had arrived. *"I don't want any of the gents getting any ideas."* She'd ushered them up the rickety stairs to their room. *"And I'll hear none of that gibberish you people like to talk. It puts the customers off. You'll speak English here or you'll keep your mouths shut."*

Ahmad had been but fifteen, and Mira little more than eight. She'd clutched weakly at his shabby wool coat, hiding her face against his sleeve. He remembered how he'd put a protective arm around her narrow shoulders.

That wasn't all he remembered.

There was the smell of the place, dank and sour with sweat and sex. And there was the sensation of Mrs. Pritchard running her fingers through his hair as he passed through the door.

Just as Lady Heatherton had.

"We've always been together," Mira said. "From the time we came to England. The same house, the same room. You were my whole world. And now you're gone—"

"I'm not gone," he said. "King William Street is only three miles from here."

"It may as well be one hundred miles."

"We still see each other. You visit often enough."

"Of course I do," she said, with something approaching bitterness. "I haven't any friends of my own. Not in Mayfair. And it isn't safe to be always traveling to the East End to see the friends I left behind at Mrs. Pritchard's."

"*What?*" He nearly spilled his drink.

A rare flash of defiance glinted in her gaze. "Did you think I could forget the life we left behind?"

"Yes, actually. I did." It took an effort not to lose his temper. "You have no cause to go back to that place. You're safe here. Far away from all that filth."

It was the one saving grace of all this: her life here with the Finchleys. The life of a lady's companion. A better existence than any he could ever give her. Here, in their house, she had the benefit of good food, clean air, and a warm bed. A sanctuary, far away from the squalor of the East End, and from the low characters who had patronized Mrs. Pritchard's.

"It wasn't filth," Mira said. "Not all of it."

"No, not all of it," he acknowledged. "Not us. And not some of the girls. As for Mrs. Pritchard and all the rest of them . . ." His gut twisted at the very thought of his cousin returning there. "Good God, Mira. How many times—"

"It doesn't matter."

"It matters. We didn't leave Mrs. Pritchard's on the best of terms." There had been a fight, and a resulting scandal. The threat of Ahmad being transported. "If not for Finchley's intervention—"

"I know, I know." The spark faded from Mira's eyes. "You're right. I shouldn't have gone. They were never my friends anyway. I realize that now. They only tolerated me because they were fond of you."

Fond.

The word left a sour taste in his mouth. Yes, Mrs. Pritchard had been fond of him. Exceedingly fond.

He downed a swallow of port. It burned his throat. "You don't know what you're talking about."

"I've never had true friends here. I know that much. I thought I had. One in particular. But the last of my letters has gone unanswered. It's time I faced the facts."

"Letters to whom?"

"It doesn't matter," she said again.

"It clearly does if it's upset you to this degree."

"I'm upset because I'm alone. Because I don't seem to belong anywhere."

Ahmad sighed. "You're shy, that's all. You always have been." Shy, and frail from an illness in her youth. The same sweating sickness that had claimed her mother's life. It had left Mira wan and weak as a child, depending on him for so much.

"I'm adrift," she replied.

Adrift.

It felt like an accusation. An indictment.

"What am I to say to that?" he asked.

"Nothing. I only thought you should know. It's why I'm so concerned about the state of your finances."

"*Our* finances," he corrected her. Some of the funds in his account were rightfully hers. Reward money they'd received for helping to find Lord Castleton, bestowed on them by a grateful Lady Helena. It was meant to go toward opening a dress salon.

And it would, when he had a reputation to support one.

"Our finances, then," she said. "Though I didn't do anything to earn that money. It was you who went about questioning people, not me."

"You helped enough," he replied grimly. The journey had put a strain on Mira's health, and the heat of Egypt and India had weakened her even further. She was no longer accustomed to extremes of temperature. It had taken months for her to regain her strength. "And you needn't worry," he said. "Our finances are in perfectly good order."

She took another grimacing sip of her drink. "You've been making withdrawals at the bank."

He gave her an alert look. "How did you—"

"I guessed. It wasn't difficult. What with Miss Walters owing you one hundred pounds, and the viscountess demanding the very finest of everything." Mira was silent a moment before asking, "How much have you taken out?"

"Only enough to cover expenses. Fabric and trimmings and the like."

"And Lady Heatherton intends to pay for it?"

"Eventually, after the gowns are delivered. It's not uncommon for ladies to take their time in settling their dressmaker's bill. You know that. It's a hazard of the trade." He liked it no better than she did.

"Yes, but . . ." Her fingers curled around her glass. "I'm depending on you opening a shop of your own. On coming to work with you. Helping you with your designs. Even keeping house for you."

He might have laughed if the subject wasn't such a sore one. "I haven't a house for you to keep."

"Not yet. But it won't be long before you'll see success. You must. My entire happiness depends upon it."

The knot in his stomach tightened. He already understood that Mira was depending on him. It didn't help to hear it. Not in those terms. He had enough pressing on him at the moment. "I thought you wanted to marry? To have a home of your own one day? You've often spoken of it."

She shrugged a shoulder. "I've grown up."

"Mira—"

"I mean it. When Mr. Doyle retires at the end of the summer, you must take over his lease and open your shop. You must make a place for me. Otherwise—"

"I'm doing everything I can," he said. "But I can't promise anything. The season hasn't even fully begun yet."

"You'll make a success of it. Once Lady Heatherton wears your gowns, everyone will see how good you are, and then—"

"It's not that simple. God, I wish it were." He leaned toward her. "Don't you understand, my dear? It isn't enough for a man like me to be good at what he does. It isn't even enough for him to be great. In order to succeed—to be accepted—he must be extraordinary. Better than the best. Better than Charles Worth, even. It's a different standard altogether."

"Because of our heritage."

"In short? Yes."

She bowed her head. "And just what *is* our heritage, exactly? We haven't any people. Any country. No family, save each other."

He felt a rush of sympathy for her.

In his younger days, he'd often felt as she did. A sense of being on the outside looking in, disconnected—nay, rejected—from the society in which they lived. British society.

Indian society had been no more welcoming.

On returning there two years ago, Ahmad had been equally out of place, as much a stranger as any Englishman. Mira had felt it, too. That lack of connection. The absence of a home. A people.

"We're not alone in that regard," he said.

"You aren't. You have a life outside of here. A purpose."

"I do," he acknowledged. "That doesn't mean it's been easy."

The shadow of British colonial rule was ever present in his life, evident in the very fabric he worked with and the sugar that sweetened his tea. A man could easily become consumed by the injustice of it all.

But Ahmad had never had that luxury, not with Mira counting on him.

In order to live and work among English people, he'd long ago had to negotiate an uneasy peace with himself. To find a way to reclaim the spoils of colonialism—all those Chinese silks and India muslins—and transform them into something beautiful. Something that was uniquely his.

It was a symbolic exercise, but a powerful one.

"Easy enough for you," Mira said. "You're a man. And one day you'll meet someone. You'll fall in love and marry and—"

"*Love?*" Ahmad was surprised into a humorless crack of laughter.

"How did we come to this subject? You know I've no interest in romance. All I want is to open a dress salon."

"And to be thought extraordinary," she said.

"My designs *are* extraordinary. I only need people to see them. The *right* people."

"The beau monde."

"Precisely." Thus far, no one who had worn his creations had any claim to that exalted sphere of fashionable society. Not even Lady Helena. Though she was the sister of an earl, she'd married humbly, and now lived a retired life with her husband and child in a remote abbey on the North Devon coast.

Mira's expression turned thoughtful. "You're relying on Viscountess Heatherton."

"She has a reputation for setting the fashion."

"That isn't the only reputation she has," Mira said ominously.

Ahmad knew that only too well, but he saw no reason that Mira should. "The gossip rags again?" He frowned at her. "Is this how you choose to occupy your time?"

"With reading? Yes. It's how I learn things about the world."

"From the scandal sheets."

"From all the papers. From books. And from listening to what people say when I go about with Mrs. Finchley. You may take my word on it. The viscountess isn't known for being a particularly nice woman."

Ahmad knew that, too. He downed the remainder of his port. "I can handle Lady Heatherton."

Eight

❖

$\mathcal{E}$velyn drew back the hood of her cloak as she entered the stables. Hephaestus's great bay head hung over the wooden door of his loose box, his long forelock sweeping down over his eyes in a heavy black veil. He greeted her with a soft nicker.

"Were you waiting for me?" Approaching him with outstretched hands, she cupped his head and pressed a kiss to his velvet-soft nose. "Beautiful boy. How are you this evening? Bored? Missing home?"

As she murmured to him, he nuzzled her face, lipping softly at her skin. His breath was warm and sweet, the long whiskers on his muzzle tickling her cheek.

She didn't fear him biting her. There was no malice in Hephaestus. Only the same affection for her that she bore for him. She ran her fingers through his tangled mane. "I'm homesick, too," she confessed in a whisper. "Terribly homesick."

"That you again, miss?" A man's voice broke through the darkness.

Evelyn nearly jumped out of her skin. "Good gracious, Lewis! You frightened me half to death. I thought you'd gone in to dinner?"

Lewis emerged from the gaslit shadows, an oily rag in one hand and a half-polished piece of harness in the other. "Had my meal down at the Seven Bells. Don't much care for the company at the house. No offense."

"None taken." Evelyn didn't much care for it, either. Not the company, but the lack of it. She'd eaten alone again this evening, waited on by a silent Mrs. Quick and an equally silent footman. Uncle Harris was dining at his club. He'd left the house in the early afternoon. Heaven knew when he'd return. "Is Hephaestus settling in all right?"

"He's not off his feed."

"I should think not. It would take more than a change of address to ruin his appetite. His stomach has always been in good order." She scratched Hephaestus behind the ears. "What about the rest of him?"

"He's restless. Pawing at the door of his box."

Restless.

So was she.

"He's longing for his paddock." She ran a hand over the stallion's silky neck. In Combe Regis, he spent the better part of his day roaming the fenced perimeter, rolling in the mud, or dozing under his favorite shade tree. Not a care in the world.

No. It was she who'd begun to worry, watching him grow from a homely colt into a big, magnificent beast—an eminently valuable piece of bloodstock. She'd always assumed that when she married Stephen Connaught, she'd take Hephaestus with her to her new home. That he'd be her riding horse, her much-doted-on pet, for decades to come.

More than that.

If she was married, Hephaestus could be put out to stud. It was what Papa had originally planned for the stallion. Evelyn had been powerless to arrange it on her own. Not because she didn't understand the particulars of horse breeding, but because unmarried ladies weren't meant to know about such matters. To involve herself in them would have been seen as dangerously eccentric—injurious not only to her reputation but to those of her younger sisters.

Yet another reason she'd hoped to marry Stephen.

All that was needed was for him to propose. He'd seemed to like her well enough. They'd been friends, hadn't they? It only wanted time. Another summer spent riding together, and then he'd have asked her.

Of course, that had all changed with Fenny's disappearance.

Now any thought of marrying Stephen Connaught was at an end.

Evelyn had set her mind to marrying someone else. Someone new. As much for her younger sisters' benefit as for her own. Not because she desired a fine house and fine clothing. Not because she longed for riches, or even because she desired children. But because a riding horse was expensive. Far too expensive for a family of rapidly dwindling fortunes. The sale of a stallion like Hephaestus could bring in a pretty penny.

Aunt Nora hadn't said anything. Not yet. But she would, and soon, if Evelyn didn't return from London with a proposal of marriage in hand.

"I'll take him for another gallop tomorrow," she said. "If you can have him ready at sunrise?"

Lewis bobbed his head.

The next morning, Evelyn left the house at dawn for her ride in Rotten Row. Hephaestus danced and pranced beneath her, tossing his head as they entered the park. She put him through his paces, just as she had the previous morning, riding him until his neck, shoulders, and flanks were damp with sweat.

No one else was about, save a few stragglers walking on the mist-covered grass. Working people, by the looks of them. As Evelyn rode, she kept an eye out for Julia Wychwood. But there was no sign of her, or her outsized black hunter. No riders at all to speak of.

Perhaps Miss Wychwood had resumed riding in the afternoons, during the fashionable hour, with Lady Anne and Miss Hobhouse?

The three Furies.

Evelyn smiled to think of it.

She'd rather be thought of as a Fury than a wallflower or a bluestocking. The Grecian Furies were formidable sisters. Women of justice—and vengeance.

The thought appealed to her.

Which only went to show that she was a bluestocking at heart.

Smile fading, she urged Hephaestus back into a trot as she exited the park, Lewis following close behind them.

She was going to have to work on making herself more agreeable, if for no other reason than to appeal to the eligible gentlemen she'd meet during the season. No man wanted to court an oddity. Gentlemen wanted ladies who were soft and sweet. Who would listen to them in awestruck silence, only opening their demure little mouths to agree with a man's ideas or to laugh at his feeble witticisms.

It wasn't her. It had never been her.

You don't have to change, she assured herself. *Not really. It's only a game. A game you must play for a very little while.*

Once she met a suitable gentleman, she could revert back to her true self. She'd do it in stages, little by little. Who knows? The gentleman in question might come to like her as she really was. Perhaps he might even fall in love with her.

An impossible dream.

She daren't give any weight to it. Such dreams only led to disappointment.

Better to be pragmatic. To stick to her plan. Marriage was a business, after all. Any gentleman of wealth and rank would say the same. She was resolved to view it as such. As for the rest of it . . .

She wouldn't dwell on the messy particulars. The intimacy that came at the end of a courtship and proposal. The kisses and embraces.

The wedding night.

And all to be endured with a stranger. Someone Evelyn would marry, not because she loved him, but because he was wealthy and powerful and able to help her family.

It was no small thing.

Returning to Russell Square, she washed and changed and repaired her hair. The day stretched empty ahead of her, no appointments or visitors to break up the monotony. She was still keeping herself to herself, hidden indoors, waiting for the moment she could properly make her debut.

Her final fitting with Mr. Malik was tomorrow morning. She had a whole day yet to get through. Feeling as restless as Hephaestus, she summoned Agnes to accompany her to Hatchards Bookshop.

"My uncle's taken the carriage," she said, slipping on her bonnet, gloves, and paletot, "but we can take an omnibus. It isn't too far."

Agnes didn't appear enthusiastic at the prospect.

The nearly two-mile ride—jolted to and fro against strangers inside a cramped omnibus—did nothing to improve her mood. When the pair of them were finally set down on Piccadilly Street, outside the famous bookshop, Agnes peered up at the front window with a frank look of distaste.

"You needn't come in if you don't want to," Evelyn said. There were benches in front of the shop, presently occupied by what looked to be the servants of other customers—a young girl in a black stuff dress and two tall footmen in livery. "You can wait here if you like."

"If you don't mind, miss?" Agnes exchanged a private glance with one of the footmen. "I never could see much use in books."

"Very well. I shan't be long." Evelyn entered the shop alone. She was at once assailed by the scent of fresh ink, paper, and new leather bindings. A delicious fragrance. She breathed it in, feeling at once both excited and oddly at peace.

For a reader, a bookshop was rather like a church.

A fanciful thought to be sure. Aunt Nora would call it sacrilege. But to Evelyn, it seemed an apt comparison.

She and her younger sisters loved reading. It was one of their only means of escape. Indeed, every dry dusty tome remaining in Papa's library was a passport to a different world. Volumes on Ancient Egypt, Rome, and Greece cluttered the shelves, along with collections of philosophical essays and treatises on the flora and fauna of distant lands. A testament to Papa's love of travel. The Maltravers girls had read them all at one time or another.

But books were a luxury.

It had been ages since Evelyn had bought a novel. If not for the small circulating library in Combe Regis, she'd have had to go without entirely. As it was, she'd missed out on Mr. Dickens's latest. The library hadn't had a copy of it to lend.

Which was why, on entering Hatchards, she wasted no time in inquiring after a copy of *Great Expectations*.

A busy clerk at the front counter directed her to a row of shelves against the wall. There, Mr. Dickens's works were neatly arrayed with works by other authors. She scanned their names on the spines—Jane Austen, Wilkie Collins, and Anthony Trollope. And something by George Eliot, too.

She was tempted. Very tempted.

But no.

She'd come for one book in particular. It was located on a shelf far above her head. Standing on her tiptoes, she stretched her hand up to reach it. Her gloved fingers barely brushed the gilt-stamped spine.

Botheration.

The clerk would have to fetch it for her. She was just about to summon him when a gentleman came to her aid. Evelyn felt his presence before she saw him—big and tall and masculine. His large, black-gloved hand reached up over her head to pluck the novel easily from the shelf.

"Allow me," he said.

Her heart thumped hard. Only two words, but she'd recognize that deep voice anywhere. Turning sharply, she found herself staring up into a pair of familiar obsidian eyes. "Mr. Malik."

He was dressed in an elegantly cut suit, his thick coal-black hair gleaming in the sunlight that poured through the leaded-glass windows of the shop. "Miss Maltravers." He offered her the book. "Is this the volume you wanted?"

"Yes. Thank you." She took it, clasping it to her breast. "What are you doing here?"

"The same as you, I expect."

"Forgive me. It's just . . . it seems so odd to see you outside of a fitting room." Indeed, gazing up at him, she couldn't help but recall the last time they'd met. She'd been in her knickers, and he'd been touching her with as much familiarity as a lover.

A faint smile edged his lips, as if he knew precisely what she was thinking. "Likewise."

Heat crept up her throat. Good heavens. He was just a tailor, that was all. Not a lover. Not even an eligible gentleman. She had to stop thinking of him in such terms.

It was his own fault. A habit-maker shouldn't be so terribly good-looking. It made one melt into a puddle of treacle whenever one saw him.

Whenever *she* saw him.

She moistened her lips. "You, ah, look very well."

What?

"And you . . ." His gaze dropped to her plain wool paletot and day dress. A frown notched his brows. "Is this something new?"

"Something old. I've only slipped out of my uncle's house to fetch this book. I'm still very much incognito."

"Not for long," he warned.

"No. Not for long." The prospect of her new habit lifted her spirits. "Are you shopping for a novel to read?"

"It isn't for me. It's for someone else. Why? Do you have any recommendations?"

"That depends on the person you're shopping for. What sort of stories does he enjoy?"

"She."

She.

A surge of disappointment dimmed Evelyn's smile. It occurred to her, quite suddenly, how little she knew about him.

Of course, he must have a sweetheart. Heaven's sake, he was probably married! Just because he didn't wear a wedding band didn't mean he didn't have a wife—and probably several children besides. It was none of her affair.

She turned back to the shelves. "In that case . . . What about a romance?"

"No romances," he said darkly.

"No?" Was he one of those stuffy men who disapproved of romance novels? Many did. Even so, she'd expected better of him. A man who designed clothing so beautifully shouldn't be averse to sentiment. "What about this one, then? *Silas Marner.* It only came out last year."

Mr. Malik drew it from the shelf. It was bound in brown cloth with gilt lettering on the spine. "What's it about?"

"An individual and his place in society. The hero of the story is a weaver. A man with no family to speak of, who keeps himself apart from his community."

"A bit too close to home." He returned the book to the shelf. "She needs something bright. Something to boost her spirits."

Evelyn wondered why. Was she ill? Melancholic? Had she had some sort of disappointment? "In that case"—she reached for a Jane Austen novel—"I recommend this one."

He took it from her, giving the title a dubious glance. *"Northanger Abbey."*

"It's Miss Austen's satire of a Gothic novel. A vastly entertaining read. It should take her mind off whatever it is that's troubling her."

Mr. Malik thumbed through the pages. His expression was doubtful.

"I confess," she said "there *is* a romance in the story, but it's witty rather than mawkish. I can't imagine she won't enjoy it."

"It's still a romance."

A cough sounded nearby, along with the thump of books being shoved back on a shelf. It was a reminder that she and Mr. Malik weren't alone. Far from it. The shop seemed to be growing busier.

Evelyn sunk her voice. "What does she have against romance?"

"Nothing," he replied, his tone equally low. "I just don't want her to get any ideas."

"Ideas about what?"

"About happily-ever-afters."

The wide swell of Evelyn's skirts brushed his leg. She belatedly realized that she'd drawn closer to him. That their conversation had taken on an air of intimacy. "You object to them?"

"I don't believe in fairy tales," he said.

She gave him an amused look. "Is that what they are?"

"In my experience."

"How illuminating."

"Is it?" He turned another page.

"Indeed. You're a cynic, Mr. Malik. I wouldn't have thought it."

"I'm a realist."

"Happily-ever-afters *are* real. For some people, at least. And even if they weren't . . . a little romance never hurt anyone."

His eyes lifted to hers. There was an expression in them that was hard to read. "You think not?"

Butterflies unfurled their wings in her stomach. The same feeling she'd had when she'd first touched his hand. A fluttering, breathless sensation. As if her corset had been laced too tightly. "No," she said. And then she thought of Fenny. "Not in a novel, anyway."

His mouth curled into the barest hint of a smile.

Once again, she had the unsettling sensation that he could read her mind. She took a step back from him. "I mustn't linger. My maid is waiting for me."

He closed the book, clutching it in his hand. "Thank you for your help."

"It was my pleasure. I hope your . . ." Wife? Sweetheart? "I hope she enjoys the story."

"My cousin."

Evelyn nearly stumbled in the process of taking another step backward. "I beg your pardon?"

"The book is for my cousin."

His words penetrated before she could school her features. She was certain an expression of relief passed over her face.

She was equally certain that he saw it.

Heaven only knew what he must think.

"Your cousin. Well, that's . . . that's splendid." *Splendid?* Evelyn's eyes closed against a swell of embarrassment. She was quite ready to disappear into a hole in the earth. She took another step back. "Please convey my regards."

His smile broadened. "I shall."

She didn't dare say another word. Good lord. He was amused by her. And not in a good way, either. No doubt he had countless ladies making fools of themselves over him.

Evelyn refused to be one of them.

Turning on her heel, she made for the front counter, where she hastily paid for her book, and then, with as much of her remaining dignity as she could muster, promptly fled the shop.

Nine

❧

"I can come with you," Mira offered. She was seated at the table in Ahmad's rooms above the tea dealer's shop, a needle and thread poised in her hand. She'd almost finished basting together the pieces of Miss Maltravers's second riding habit.

"I don't need you there," Ahmad said. "I need you here." He slipped on his coat. "The habit I'm fitting this morning is almost done. It's these habits that must be completed."

Mira resumed her sewing. She was a diligent worker, with a neat, even hand. Someone accustomed to stitching for hours. The occupation seemed to lift her spirits, as had the novel he'd given her. She'd been reading it during her breaks—when she deigned to take them.

"And Lady Heatherton's evening gown?" she asked. "You must deliver it tomorrow."

"I'll finish it when I get back." He pressed a kiss to Mira's cheek as he passed. "Keep the door locked."

He bounded down the stairs and out to the busy street below, where he hailed a hansom to take him to Doyle and Heppenstall's.

Miss Maltravers was due for her final fitting at ten o'clock. He'd have rather seen her in the evening, after the shop was closed. They'd have had more privacy. Something he'd never have imagined he would have wished for with any of his clients.

But time was of the essence.

The truth was, he'd taken on too much. Even with Mira assisting him, it was all he could do to stay on top of his work. To finish his commissions on time—without dropping his standards.

If business continued in this vein, perhaps he could hire another girl? It needn't wait until he had somewhere to put her. Many seamstresses worked out of their lodgings. He already knew the right one for the job. Becky Rawlins, formerly of Mrs. Pritchard's establishment, was a dab hand with a needle. He should know. He'd taught her himself.

"You've just missed Mr. Fillgrave," Doyle said when Ahmad arrived at the shop in Conduit Street. "He asked for you expressly."

"Did he?" Ahmad walked through to the back.

Doyle followed after him into the workroom. Two young men— Mr. Beamish and Mr. Pennyfeather—were busily engaged there, cutting and stitching the components of gentlemen's suits. "He placed an order for a new frock coat and trousers. He insisted that you be the one to make them."

Ahmad collected Miss Maltravers's habit from his worktable. He'd been at the shop until all hours last night finishing the last of the alterations. "How soon does he require it?"

"By next week. Earlier if you can contrive it." Doyle cast a frowning glance at the habit.

It wasn't the first time Ahmad had caught him examining his work.

The old tailor often lingered around Ahmad's worktable, watching him sew with that same look of scowling consideration. Once Ahmad had even discovered Doyle holding up one of his designs to the light of an oil lamp, his rheumy gaze inspecting every stitch and seam.

"I can't." Ahmad carried the habit to the fitting room, where he draped it over the table in preparation for Miss Maltravers's appointment. "I have more commissions than I can handle at the moment."

Doyle hovered at the door. "What am I to tell him? I've already taken the order."

"Tell him he'll have to wait," Ahmad said.

Doyle's lips thinned. He withdrew back to the workroom, muttering under his breath.

Ahmad paid no attention to him. Doyle wasn't his employer, no matter how much he might like to think so.

Returning to the showroom, Ahmad spent the next few minutes straightening the bolts of cloth on the shelves, waiting for the clock to strike ten.

Miss Maltravers arrived precisely on the hour, accompanied by her maid.

He felt a flash of disappointment.

Stupid of him.

Of course Miss Maltravers had her maid with her. What had he thought? That it would be just the two of them again, alone together in the fitting room? Not at this time of the day. Not unless they wanted to start a scandal.

"Good morning," Miss Maltravers said. "You did say ten, didn't you?"

"I did." He showed her into the fitting room. "Your habit is just there."

She went to it immediately, picking up the pieces to examine them. "Shall I change into it?"

"If you please. I'll return momentarily." He withdrew back to the workroom, where he paced, restlessly, until a decent amount of time had passed.

Beamish and Pennyfeather eyed him as they worked. Ahmad rarely interacted with them, not trusting them with his commissions. They didn't trust him, either, seeming to regard him with an equal measure of awe and contempt, never truly certain of his position in the hierarchy of the shop.

Ahmad saw no need to explain it to them. Glancing once more at the clock, he returned to the fitting room. Entering, he found Miss Maltravers standing in front of the cheval glass, staring at her reflection.

She was alone, her spectacles hanging loose in her hand.

His pulse quickened. "What's happened to your maid?"

"She's gone to fetch a package from the milliner." Miss Maltravers continued looking into the glass. She seemed transfixed.

Ahmad couldn't blame her. He took in the fit and drape of her dark green riding habit in one comprehensive glance.

Pride rose within him.

The habit was as flattering to her figure as he'd intended.

Slightly sprung over her hips, the jacket bodice was made with a blunt point in front and short basque behind, trimmed at the top with gilt buttons. Artfully placed darts lent a fullness to her bust, and the waist was gracefully curved, giving her a pronounced hourglass shape as the jacket gave way to the voluminous swell of her trailing bell-shaped skirts.

When combined with the singular loveliness of her face and the warm vibrance of her thick auburn hair, the finished picture was one of sensual elegance. Of a lady—undoubtedly a lady—but one of beauty, mystery, and bountiful charms.

Miss Maltravers turned faintly to the right to examine herself. A peculiar shimmer glinted in her wide, doe-like gaze.

A jolt of alarm went through him. Good lord, there were tears in her eyes. He moved toward her, only to stop short, uncertain what he should do. "You're upset."

"No. Not at all." She dashed a tear from her cheek. "Rather the opposite." A rueful smile curved her mouth. "You see, the day we met, I meant it when I said that I loved fashion. The problem is, it's never seemed to love me back. Not until this moment."

Understanding dawned. With it came a swell of affection for her so powerful that it closed Ahmad's throat. "Then you approve."

"It's perfect." She resumed looking at her reflection. "It's . . . it's beautiful."

He came to stand behind her. "*You're* beautiful."

A delicate flush tinted her cheeks. "If I appear that way, it's only because you've made me so."

"I'm not a magician."

"You *are*. I believe you must be able to turn lead into gold."

"It wasn't any kind of alchemy. You gave me a great deal to work with."

She looked at him in the glass, her eyes glistening. "Thank you for this, Mr. Malik. I knew you would amaze me."

His chest tightened. He felt the sudden urge to touch her. Not as a habit-maker but as a man. To cup her face in his hands and kiss her soft, voluptuous mouth.

Heat crept up his neck.

"Come," he said, "before you put me to the blush." Taking her arm, he guided her to the wooden horse that stood in the corner. "If I may?"

She nodded, her color heightening by a slight degree. Likely no one else would have noticed. But *he* did. He was painfully conscious of her, registering the subtle changes in her mood and breath as keenly as a tuning fork.

It wouldn't do. These burgeoning feelings, or whatever it was they were. It was one thing to be physically attracted to a customer. It was quite another to be developing some sort of tendre for her. Neither had ever happened to him before, but he was acutely aware that one was inherently more dangerous than the other.

He couldn't risk any missteps. Not now. Not with his whole future hanging in the balance.

And Mira's future, too.

She was depending on him to make a success of things. Which he couldn't do, not if he became entangled with some bluestocking Sussex equestrienne no one had ever heard of before.

It was time to refocus on his work, and *only* on his work.

Encircling Miss Maltravers's waist with his hands, he lifted her up onto the old sidesaddle that was strapped to the wooden horse.

She settled her leg over the pommel, exposing a brief glimpse of her dark silk petticoat and snug-fitting riding trousers. "Will this do? Or do you need me to—"

"You're fine." He arranged her skirt over her legs and down to her stirrup, and then stood back to study her.

Long seconds passed.

"I wonder what it is you see," she said, "when you look at me like that."

Her question jolted him. Their eyes met, and he very nearly answered her with unfiltered honesty. Possibilities. That's what he saw when he looked at her. Not only the possibilities she presented for his designs, but the possibilities of *her*. Of what she might mean to him if circumstances were different. If they were of the same race and class.

But possibilities were just that. Things that *might* be, not things that *were*. And right now, in this moment, Ahmad couldn't afford to dwell on fairy tales.

He forced himself to remain detached. Professional. "I'm not looking at you, Miss Maltravers," he said. "I'm looking at your habit."

His words felt very much like a setdown. If they were, Evelyn supposed she deserved it. She'd become too emotional when she'd seen herself in the looking glass. Even tearing up, for heaven's sake. No doubt she'd made Mr. Malik keenly uncomfortable. "Yes, I know," she said. "That's what I meant. That I wonder what it is you're looking for."

Mr. Malik's expression was inscrutable. Though, she thought she detected a flicker of emotion at the back of his dark eyes. As if he was relieved her question no longer strayed toward the personal.

"A habit skirt is longer than the skirt of a day dress, often by more than a quarter of a yard. I'm always conscious of how I use the fabric." Returning to her, he arranged the folds of her skirt. "It must fall gracefully around a rider, even at a gallop. And it shouldn't be so much material that she's unable to manage it."

"I can manage anything when I'm on Hephaestus," Evelyn said. "I'm more concerned with the appearance of the habit than its functionality."

Mr. Malik's mouth tilted up at one corner. "By the time I'm finished, you shall have both."

She sat still as his hands moved over her, adjusting not only her skirts, but the fit of her bodice and sleeves. "I always feel a little foolish," she confided, "sitting up on these wooden horses."

"Don't. It allows me to properly gauge the fit before I pin the hem. You don't wish your skirts to fall unevenly, do you? Or your jacket to bunch up at your waist or under your arms as you're riding?"

"No, indeed. I hope my new habit will look as handsome when I'm mounted as it does when I'm standing in front of the glass."

"More handsome." He straightened one of the gauntlet cuffs at the end of her sleeve. "I chose the color to flatter both you *and* your horse."

A smile sprang to her lips. "Did you?"

Mr. Malik withdrew from her to collect his pincushion and thread case from the fitting room table. "The bay stallion is the only horse you'll be riding this season, is he not?"

"He is. But I hadn't realized you'd taken it into account."

"Naturally. This shade of green wouldn't have been as flattering on a chestnut or a gray." Returning to her, Mr. Malik knelt and began to pin her hem.

Evelyn looked down at his bent head. Butterflies fluttered in her stomach. His thick black hair was as glossy as a raven's wing. Cut in the prevailing style, it was short above his ears and at his nape. His close-cropped sideburns were equally short, ending halfway beneath the harshly hewn lines of his cheekbones.

When she'd seen him in Hyde Park last week, she'd thought he resembled a fallen angel. She still thought so. It was something about his commanding height and strength. The brooding set to his mouth, and the equally brooding look in his eyes. It should have served as a warning. *Stay back. Don't come any closer.*

Instead, it inspired her curiosity.

"You know so very much about it all," she remarked.

"It's my business to know."

"Yes, but how did you learn it?"

He speared another pin through her unfinished hem.

"I suppose you were born with the talent," she said. "You must have been, to be so gifted."

"Sadly, no. I had to be taught like anyone else. Apprenticed to someone who rapped my knuckles and boxed my ears. In the beginning, I was a hopeless case."

"You were apprenticed to a habit-maker?"

"An old tailor in Delhi." He drew back to examine his work. Brow furrowing, he adjusted one of the pins.

"You *are* from India, then?"

He glanced up at her. "Hadn't you realized?"

"I suspected, but . . . I confess, it was hard to be sure. You don't look like the other Indian gentlemen I've seen since I came to London."

A smile edged his mouth. The same smile he'd given her when they'd parted at Hatchards. As if he was amused by her. "Have you seen so many?"

"A few," she said, on her dignity.

"Servants?"

She regretted bringing up the subject. It seemed he was teasing her. No doubt he thought her the veriest country bumpkin. "A footman," she answered at last. "He was dressed in crimson livery, following after his mistress in Bond Street."

"That would be Mrs. Perkins. A soldier's wife, lately returned from Calcutta." Mr. Malik resumed his work. "Some of the memsahibs like to bring back souvenirs."

Evelyn stilled. "Do you mean *people*?"

"You sound appalled."

"I *am* appalled. A person isn't a souvenir. You can't simply pluck someone out of their life and bring them to another country."

"No? How do you suppose I came to be here?"

She stared at him, shocked at the very idea of it. "That didn't happen to you, surely?"

The look of amusement faded from Mr. Malik's face. "No. It wasn't quite the same." He slowly folded the edge of her skirt before pinning it. "My cousin's father was a British soldier. When her mother died, he brought her to England. She was frail and sickly, little more than eight years old. He knew nothing about how to care for her. So . . . I came with them."

"To look after her?"

"As much as I could. I was but a child myself at the time."

Warmth curled in Evelyn's belly. She hadn't thought it possible to admire him more. "Is this the same cousin you bought the novel for at Hatchards?"

"The very same. She's enjoying it tremendously, by the way. She was grateful to you for the recommendation."

"You've told her about me?"

"Of course," he said, as if it were the most natural thing in the world.

And it was, Evelyn supposed. Indeed, it was quite a small thing, really. And yet, it felt significant somehow. His cousin was a part of his life. The same cousin he'd accompanied from India. The one he'd looked after for all of these years. "What about your own parents?" she asked. "They can't have approved of your leaving home so young."

He stopped pinning. "I had no parents."

"Do you mean to say that you were orphaned?"

"In a manner of speaking." He looked up at her. "My father was a British soldier, too. I never knew him. As for my mother . . ." A shadow darkened his face. "She died shortly after I was born."

Her heart swelled with sympathy. "I'm sorry," she said. "I lost my parents, too."

He gave her a dry smile, as fleeting as it was brittle. "It was a long time ago. But thank you."

She sensed she'd hit a nerve. That her questions had probed into something he never spoke of—never thought about. Something dark and painful. It hadn't been her intention. "I expect your tailor was grieved to lose you," she said lightly.

Her words had the desired effect.

Mr. Malik uttered a short laugh. "I'd wager not. I hadn't as much interest in stitching men's waistcoats as I had in designing ladies' gowns. Mr. Khan was glad to be rid of me."

"Is that when you learned to be a habit-maker? When you came to England?"

"Yes, though not formally." He seemed little inclined to elaborate.

"You don't have to tell me," she said. "I know it's none of my business."

He shrugged one broad shoulder. "It's no great secret." He pinned another section of her habit skirt. "When I arrived here, there was little employment to be had, save the kind that required brute strength. I was only fifteen, but already quite tall and strong. A woman encountered me as I sought work on the docks and offered me a position at a house she ran in the East End. She allowed me to bring my cousin with me—to share room and board. It was the only opportunity of its kind."

"She wanted you to sew?"

"No. She wanted me for the same reason the men at the docks did. For my size and strength. It was my job to throw out the men who misbehaved and to see that no one gained admittance who wasn't welcome." He was quiet again for several seconds. "A bullyboy, they call it. A chucker-out."

She'd never heard either phrase before. "I don't understand. What kind of place—"

"It was a house of ill repute, Miss Maltravers."

Her mouth nearly fell open. She dropped her voice. "A house for courtesans, do you mean?"

"Nothing so exalted as that. But yes. They were working women."

It was all she could do to keep her countenance. Great goodness. He'd worked in a brothel. And not only worked there. He'd lived there, too.

If he was embarrassed by the fact, he didn't show it. He merely continued pinning her skirt.

"They served as models for my early designs," he said. "If a hem tore, or a bodice needed taking in—or letting out—I'd see to it for them. Sometimes I'd make alterations. Little adjustments to improve the appearance of their gowns. In time, I could make their gowns over completely."

"You taught yourself all of this?"

He sank back on his haunches. "I had the basics from Mr. Khan, but as for the rest . . . yes. I suppose I did. Fortunately, there were enough women about at Mrs. Pritchard's establishment who didn't mind my practicing on them."

Evelyn bet they hadn't. "Did you, ah, practice very much?"

"Every free moment I had. My skills improved in time. And now, I am as you see me."

"A habit-maker at Doyle and Heppenstall's."

He smiled. "Something like that."

It was the same thing he'd said to her on the first occasion they'd met. A nonanswer, really. One that indicated he was unwilling to reveal anything more. Not to her, anyway.

She felt oddly deflated.

It served her right for asking so many questions.

Did she imagine she was the only woman to interact with him thus? She already knew about Miss Walters and the other Pretty Horsebreakers. He'd worked his magic for them just as he had for Evelyn. What were a few women more to the total?

A whole brothelful of women.

She adjusted her spectacles. "Have you finished the hem?"

"You'll need to dismount for the rest of it." He stood. "Let me help you down."

She unhooked her leg from the pommel. "I can do it myself."

"Not with a skirt full of pins you can't." He took her by the waist.

Their faces were almost level. A rare occurrence with a gentleman so tall. He bent his head, preparing to lift her, and as she leaned into his arms, her cheek brushed against his.

Oh my.

A tremor went through her. Or perhaps it went through him. It all happened so quickly she couldn't be certain. One moment she was turning her head to apologize and the next . . .

Her lips met his.

It was a kiss, however unintentional. A soft, tentative caress. Faintly lopsided. But a kiss all the same.

His hands tightened spasmodically around her. For an instant, his mouth softened under hers. And then—

Just as quickly as it had begun, it was over.

Drawing back from her lips, Mr. Malik lifted her from the saddle and set her gently onto the ground.

Her heart thumped as swiftly as the hoofbeats of a runaway horse. Good lord! What in the world had just happened?

But she knew what had happened.

She'd kissed Mr. Malik. And he'd kissed her back, hadn't he? *Hadn't he?*

A burning mortification rose within her. She waited for him to let her go. But he didn't. Not immediately.

He remained there, gazing down at her, his large, capable hands resting on the corseted curve of her waist. "Miss Maltravers," he began gruffly. "I—"

"Miss?" Agnes opened the door of the fitting room, a pink hatbox cradled in her arms. "I've brought your new riding hat from the milliners."

Mr. Malik and Evelyn broke apart so quickly that Evelyn stumbled. His hand shot out to catch her elbow. "All right?" he asked.

She looked up at him sharply. His face was a studied blank. And yet . . . there was a dull flush of red seeping across his cheekbones. The sight of it made her stomach perform a queer little somersault. "Yes, thank you. How clumsy I am."

Agnes glanced from Evelyn to Mr. Malik and back again. Her lips thinned. "Shall I take it out, miss?"

"Please do." Evelyn cleared her throat, making an effort to compose herself. "It's the hat I bought to complement my new habit," she explained to Mr. Malik. "I thought you might give me the benefit of your opinion."

He'd moved away from her. His hands were clasped behind his back. "Of course."

Agnes withdrew a stylish black felt hat from the box. It was trimmed with black and green feathers, and sported a dark green hatband with a bow at the front. She affixed it to Evelyn's head, securing it with a hatpin. "The milliner said she could add more feathers if you wanted."

Removing her spectacles, Evelyn inspected herself in the glass. She'd never seen such an elegant little riding hat in her life. It looked positively French. "What do you think, sir?"

Mr. Malik stepped forward. "I approve. But perhaps . . . more like this." He adjusted the hat so it tipped slightly forward, the curved edges dipping to frame Evelyn's face. "There." He curled one of the plumes to sit along the brim. "That's better. It will look charming when you wear it for your ride tomorrow."

She turned to him on an indrawn breath, temporarily forgetting about their kiss. "My habit will be ready tomorrow?"

"It will. I can have it delivered to you in the morning." He gestured toward the raised platform, his manner as businesslike as any respectable tradesman. "If you please. I have more pins to place before we're finished."

Evelyn permitted Agnes to help her up onto the platform. "And what about the others?" she asked. She'd ordered two more habits in different colors and styles. Mr. Malik was handling all of the particulars. She trusted him to make her look her best. After what he'd achieved with her green habit, she could only imagine how he might dazzle her next. "When shall I come for my first fitting?"

"Not until next week," he said.

Some of her excitement dimmed. A week seemed a very long way away. She'd grown accustomed to her time with him. The talks they'd had during her fittings, and the way he touched her, with such care and confidence.

And what about today?

What was it he'd been about to say to her before Agnes had interrupted them?

Evelyn prided herself on being practical. Nevertheless . . . Her mind conjured a dozen different sentiments he might have expressed to her, each more devastatingly romantic than the last.

What a moment to succumb to girlish daydreams!

It was bad enough that she'd accidentally kissed him. Now she was imagining that he felt something for her, too. That when he'd gazed down at her so intently, his hands circling her waist, he'd been about to declare himself.

Foolish.

She was on the cusp of realizing her ambition. Of solving all of her family's problems. She could think of nothing more ill-advised at this juncture than indulging in silly fantasies about the man who made her riding habits. It didn't matter that he was a genius with a needle and thread. Or that he was handsome and kind.

Or that he had the most sensual pair of lips in Christendom.

No, no, no. She gave herself an inward shake. It simply wouldn't do to fixate on him this way.

Better to keep her attention on her plans. On her official debut in Rotten Row.

"Next week, then," she said.

A great deal could happen in a week.

Ten

❧❧

The following morning, Ahmad packed Miss Maltravers's finished habit into a tissue paper–lined dress box and sent it off to Russell Square in custody of Doyle and Heppenstall's ginger-haired delivery boy.

Ahmad would rather have taken it to her himself, but after what had happened yesterday, he dared not risk it. Being around Evelyn Maltravers conjured too many emotions. It affected his composure. Made him think things he shouldn't. *Feel* things he shouldn't.

How couldn't he? By God, the two of them had kissed each other. And it *had* been a kiss. It didn't matter how inadvertently it had begun or how short its duration. What mattered was that her lips had clung to his, sweet and soft and trembling. A blazing heat had torn through him like wildfire. It had taken every ounce of his control to draw back from her.

And what about afterward?

He'd come dangerously close to saying something. He didn't know what. Some manner of foolish declaration, no doubt. He hadn't been thinking particularly clearly at the time.

It would do him good to have a week to cool off. A week without seeing her or talking to her. It was time to refocus his efforts on Viscountess Heatherton.

Unlike Miss Maltravers, Lady Heatherton demanded that her order be delivered in person. He'd finished her evening dress last night and boxed it up this morning. All that was left was to put it into her hands.

Arriving at the Heathertons' town house at half past eleven, he was met in the kitchens by her ladyship's maid, Crebbs.

"You'll mind your manners if you know what's good for you," she warned as she escorted him up the servants' stairs to Lady Heatherton's chamber. "My lady may think you good enough to dally with, but I see you for what you are."

"And what's that?" Ahmad inquired.

Crebbs only scowled. When they reached the viscountess's wood-paneled door, Crebbs opened it to admit him. "Mr. Mah-leeky, my lady."

Ahmad gave her a dry glance. English people were often inclined to make an exotic mincemeat of his name. In his experience, it was done as much as a sign of dominance as of genuine misunderstanding. Another way of illustrating that he was different—foreign, and thereby inferior.

In the beginning, it had grated. As a boy, he'd wanted so much to belong. Now he found such thinly veiled aggressions merely tedious. Tedious, and wholly unoriginal.

"Come in, sir," Lady Heatherton called out from her dressing room. "And Crebbs? See that we're not disturbed."

Crebbs's scowl deepened. "Yes, my lady." She stood by, glaring at Ahmad as he entered, and then she withdrew, shutting the door firmly behind her.

Ahmad came to a halt inside the door. The viscountess's boudoir was abnormally dark for this time of day. On his previous visits, the drapes had been opened. But not today. They were shut tight, blocking out the midmorning sunshine. What light existed was provided by a branch of candles on the mantel and a fire crackling in the grate below.

Across the room, the counterpane on her ladyship's four-poster bed had been pulled back invitingly. And on a table nearby, a cut-crystal decanter and two glasses stood at the ready.

A flicker of uneasiness went through him. It was followed by a feeling of grim resignation. Calling on Lady Heatherton was never a pleasant proposition. But today it appeared it was going to be even less so. "Your evening dress, my lady."

"Bring it to me." The viscountess emerged from her dressing room, clad in an embroidered silk wrap and—he suspected—little else. Her feet were bare, her blond hair hanging loose about her shoulders. She padded to the table by the bed and unstopped the crystal decanter.

Ahmad put the dress box down on the silk-covered settee. "Would you like me to take it out?"

"The dress?" She laughed softly to herself. "Yes. Why not?"

Removing the lid of the box, he liberated the gown from its tissue paper wrappings and held it up for her perusal. He was quite proud of how it had come out. It was simple and elegant. A masterwork of seams and stitchery, made to showcase her figure rather than to camouflage it in a sea of fabric and furbelows.

She cast it an absent glance. And then she looked again. An expression of appreciation briefly warmed her coldly beautiful face. "Splendid," she said. "I expected nothing less."

"I'm glad you approve." He draped the gown carefully over the tufted back of the settee. "Will you be trying it on today?"

"Not at the moment. I have other plans for us." She poured out two drinks. "Come. I insist you join me for a glass of brandy."

Ahmad stilled. Regarding her from across the candlelit room, he felt very much like a lone traveler who had reached a pivotal crossroads. An intersection he'd suspected was coming from the first time they'd met.

All that remained was to choose his path.

It would have been easy to accept her invitation. To drink with her, and thereby avoid souring their business relationship.

But he was no fool.

A drink wouldn't be the end of this. It would only be the beginning.

"I beg you would excuse me, ma'am," he said.

"I will *not* excuse you. My husband has gone to Berkshire for the remainder of the week, and I am completely at my leisure. You have no cause to refuse me."

Ahmad didn't move.

Her smile hardened. "You cannot claim you don't drink, for I have it on good authority that you do."

His brows lifted infinitesimally.

"Crebbs has been making inquiries. She's rather protective of me." Lady Heatherton crossed the room to join him, both glasses in her hands. She held one out to him. "I'm told you don't adhere to any of that religious nonsense that so many of your people insist upon. Indeed, Crebbs informs me that you once worked in the most scandalous place imaginable. It seems you have no scruples at all, outside of those attached to ladies' fashion."

He silently took the glass from her.

She brought her own glass to her lips and drank deeply. "I trust you haven't forgotten everything about your culture. Lady Godwin claims that Indian men are well versed in the art of love. You have sacred texts, don't you? Books with lewd figures drawn in them. It's all very titillating. And now that I know you've worked in a—"

He set down his drink, untouched, on a nearby table, next to an arrangement of flowers. The glass made an audible clink against the inlaid malachite.

Lady Heatherton broke off. "You're being very uncivil."

"If I am, I must beg your pardon."

She advanced upon him. "You must have known what I had in mind. I made no secret of my interest, and you took no great pains to disguise yours." Her hand lifted to touch his chest. "If it's my husband that concerns you—"

He backed out of her reach. "You've mistaken me."

Her hand fell to her side, fingers clenching into a fist. "I bloody well haven't. There's no mistaking the way you touched me. Do you expect me to believe that, through all these fittings, you've been thinking of nothing but sewing?"

"It's why you hired me." It was the same thing he'd told her countless times before. Reminding her that theirs was a business relationship, not a personal one. Certainly not a romantic one.

"I did hire you, didn't I?" Her eyes glittered. "Take care that you don't offend me."

Ahmad recognized a threat when he heard one.

His head told him to comply with her demands. To take her to bed; to provide the exotic diversion she was so desperately looking for. And why not? He needed Lady Heatherton's patronage. Needed it desperately.

But he couldn't bed her. He wouldn't.

She'd had enough of him already. The very best of him. She had his work.

"Your evening dress is the finest garment I've ever made, my lady," he said. "I trust it will make up for any offense I've given." He bowed and turned to leave.

"How dare you?" Her voice trailed after him. "I haven't dismissed you!"

He closed the door behind him, muffling her words.

There was nothing to be gained by remaining. To do so would only generate further ill will. No lady enjoyed being rejected. Not in such circumstances as this—not with candlelight, brandy, and a waiting bed.

He made his way down the hall to the servants' stairs, and thereby to the kitchens.

Crebbs was seated at the table having a cup of tea. She gawked at the sight of him, her mouth opening as if to speak.

Ahmad paid her no mind as he exited through the back door,

grateful for the fresh air and brilliant sunshine that greeted him on the street. He inhaled deeply.

"The finest garment I've ever made."

Even as he'd uttered the words, he'd known them to be a lie. Lady Heatherton's dress wasn't the finest garment he'd ever made. It was stunning, to be sure. Certain to make an impression on all who saw it. But he hadn't created it with his whole heart. Hadn't fashioned it into existence with the entirety of his soul.

Those pieces of himself had been reserved for someone else's garment.

Hyde Park in the afternoon bore no resemblance at all to Hyde Park at dawn. To be sure, once the fashionable hour commenced, Rotten Row became as busy as a city thoroughfare. Evelyn had known it would be so. During her visits to observe the Pretty Horsebreakers, she'd seen what a crush it was—riders mounted on expensive horse-flesh navigating amid open carriages and high-sprung sporting gigs containing the crème de la crème of polite society.

Hephaestus broke stride as they joined the fashionable throng. Evelyn was nervous, which made him nervous, too. She tightened her fingers on his double reins. He was in his Pelham bridle today. An added precaution. She couldn't allow for anything to go wrong.

"You mind he doesn't get his head," Lewis advised, riding along-side her. "A lot of mares nearby."

"I'll give him something else to think about." Deepening her seat, Evelyn stilled her hands and tightened her leg, urging Hephaestus into a passage—a slow, cadenced trot. Andalusians were bred for such elevated movements, and it was one he performed with great expres-sion, his hooves lifting high, suspending in the air for a beat before returning to the ground.

A gentleman on a chestnut hunter turned to watch her as she rode past him.

Evelyn's pulse skipped. She'd hoped to draw attention, as much for her horsemanship as for the design of her new habit. The dark green riding costume fit her like a custom-made kid glove, the artfully sewn bodice cut close to her figure, and the full skirts draping in a sensual sweep down her legs. The trimmings were no less sophisticated. Crisp linen undersleeves peeked from beneath her wide gauntlet cuffs, and the gilt buttons on her jacket glinted in the sun.

With her hair rolled into an invisible net and her chic little hat pinned atop her head, the dyed feathers fluttering in the faint afternoon breeze, she felt as dashing as a French fashion plate. Indeed, never in her life had she believed herself more beautiful, nor more powerful.

People were looking at her. *Staring* at her. She registered the weight of their regard, both men and women alike, as surely as if they'd touched her. It provoked a fleeting swell of self-consciousness. An impulse to pose, rather than ride. To worry over her posture, the tilt of her head, and whether or not she was smiling enough—or too much.

She refused to indulge such doubts.

Instead, she focused on her riding. She passaged Hephaestus around a barouche with a pair of toplofty ladies inside and past two gentlemen on horseback who looked as though they were on the hunt.

An open carriage rolled by, driven by a young man in company with a pretty young woman, and up ahead a golden-haired lady in a dark blue habit was mounted on an enormous pale-gold stallion with a flaxen mane and tail.

Evelyn recognized her at once. "Lady Anne. Good afternoon."

"Miss Maltravers." Lady Anne acknowledged Evelyn with an inclination of her head. "How do you do?"

"Very well, thank you. And you? I trust you're well?"

"I'm always well." Lady Anne guided her horse in step alongside Hephaestus. She appeared to be a competent rider, with a lovely seat and quiet hands.

"Your horse is very fine," Evelyn said. "And so well behaved."

"Saffron." Lady Anne leaned forward to scratch his shoulder. "He's nearly seventeen, and would rather sleep than put up with all of this nonsense." She gave Hephaestus an appreciative look. "Yours has a bit more fire. How old is he?"

"Six. Still quite young."

"He's turning a great many heads." Her gaze flicked to Evelyn. "Or perhaps it's you who's turning them. Is that a new habit?"

"It is. The habit-maker's boy delivered it only this morning."

"Which habit-maker? It can't be my man in Oxford Street. He'd never turn his hand to something so daring."

Evelyn hesitated. A part of her was reluctant to share Mr. Malik. Which was stupid, really. No doubt he'd appreciate the business. "His name is Mr. Malik. He's located in Conduit Street, at Doyle and Heppenstall's."

"The foreman?"

"I'm not entirely sure of his position," Evelyn admitted. "But this *is* his design."

"I shall make a note of it. Not that Mama would ever approve. She's quite set on my using Mr. Inglethorpe. He once made a skirt that broke away when she was thrown. She claims she'd have been dragged to death otherwise. In truth, it was just shoddy craftsmanship. But Mama believes what she wishes."

"I've not seen your mother since last she called."

"Haven't you? I know she's been back to Russell Square to see your uncle. The two of them are as thick as thieves planning the ball."

Evelyn gave Lady Anne a startled look. "What has my uncle to do with it?"

"Mama often solicits his input in the final weeks. There's no one she trusts more with occult matters. Excepting Dmitri, of course. He always takes a hand in planning Mama's entertainments." Lady Anne smiled, adding, "A noncorporeal hand."

Evelyn found nothing humorous about the situation "But the ball isn't anything of that nature, surely? I was under the impression it was a normal affair. A *grand* affair. One where a lady might meet suitable gentlemen during the season."

"Yes, quite. That reminds me," Lady Anne said suddenly, "have you ordered a gown yet?"

"Not yet. But if the—"

"Mama says I'm to accompany you to Madame Elise's salon tomorrow. She can run up something within a week if she's paid well enough, and you couldn't ask for anything better outside of Paris."

Evelyn exhaled. "That's all very well, but I hadn't reckoned this was going to be an occult ball. If the only men in attendance are spiritualists—"

"You needn't worry on that score," Lady Anne said. "There will be society gentlemen aplenty. It's a great whizz for some of them. And more are sure to attend now they've spied you. Only look at how Mr. Fillgrave is eyeing you. Or is it your stallion he's admiring? Take care he doesn't steal him out from under you. He has two Spanish mares he's looking to breed."

Evelyn turned her head sharply. "Which one is Mr. Fillgrave?"

"For pity's sake, don't be obvious. One mustn't be seen to show any interest in their impertinence." Lady Anne slowed Saffron. "He's there by the lamppost. The po-faced gentleman with the brown muttonchop side-whiskers."

Evelyn brought Hephaestus down to a walk, matching Saffron's long stride. She chanced a sidelong glance at Mr. Fillgrave's face as they passed him. His countenance wasn't very inspiring. "Is he considered a great catch?"

"Some might say so. Though not as great as Lord Milburn."

"Who—"

"The thin fellow on the rangy gray gelding. He's staring at you quite blatantly."

Evelyn pretended not to notice as she and Lady Anne rode by.

"He's another you should beware of," Lady Anne said. "He treats his horses abominably."

Evelyn was beginning to suspect that Lady Anne's knowledge of gentlemen tended more toward their stables than their suitability as husbands. "One wonders how he treats young ladies."

"Equally abominably. He's of that school of gentlemen who believe a teasing remark more effective than a compliment."

"There's a whole school of them?"

"If there is, Mr. Hartford is the proprietor of it." Lady Anne pointed her whip in the direction of an approaching gentleman driving a high-sprung sporting gig. Dressed in plaid trousers and a cloth sack coat, he was tall and well-made. Dashing, even, with a devilish quirk to his mouth. "That's him there. The swine."

Catching sight of Lady Anne, Mr. Hartford tipped his hat to her. "Greetings, fair Fury."

"Ignore him, Miss Maltravers," Lady Anne said. "There's nothing more trying than a rattle who imagines himself a wit."

Mr. Hartford only grinned. His gaze moved from Lady Anne to Evelyn. "Miss Maltravers is it? A horsewoman, too, I see."

Evelyn inclined her head as they passed him, uncertain whether a snub was entirely called for. She didn't know him, after all, and it was rather early to burn her bridges.

"Good day, ma'am," he called after her with exaggerated civility. "And to you, my lady. Give my regards to your sisters."

"Infuriating beast," Lady Anne muttered the moment they were out of earshot. "And no, I haven't any sisters. He's talking about Miss Wychwood and Miss Hobhouse. It was he who began all that foolishness about calling us the three Furies."

"Perhaps he thinks he's being funny?"

"You give him too much credit. He's the most provoking man I've ever met. Always nettling a person with his japes and gibes. Always assuming he knows what's best for them."

Evelyn cast Lady Anne a speculative glance. "It sounds as though you know him rather well."

"I know enough. He's too puffed up with consequence for his own good. Most of the younger gentlemen are during the season. They'd far rather ogle the Pretty Horsebreakers than pay court to respectable young ladies." Lady Anne's features tightened. "And there they are, like clockwork, drat them. Putting us all in the shade."

Evelyn couldn't help but look at them herself as she rode past. There were only two Horsebreakers today—a dark-haired courtesan and a brassy blond. One was perched atop a gleaming chestnut, the other mounted on a dappled gray. Both women wore formfitting black riding habits that emphasized their tightly corseted waists.

Had Mr. Malik designed them? Evelyn didn't think so. Though the women's riding costumes served to emphasize their assets, there was nothing truly special about them. They didn't possess the elegant sensuality of Evelyn's own habit, nor that elusive Parisian flair.

"I wish they'd refrain from riding at this hour," Lady Anne said crossly.

"You don't approve of them?"

"I don't approve of any females who diminish my friends' already-dwindling chances of matrimony."

Evelyn gave her a curious look. "What about your own chances?"

Anne shrugged. "Given the choice, I'd be content to remain a spinster."

"But you're taking part in the season, aren't you?"

"What else am I to do? Mama and I live in London nearly all the year round. I'd die of boredom if I didn't move about in society." She frowned. "No. It's Miss Wychwood and Miss Hobhouse's chances I worry for. They must find husbands this year. Yet how can they distinguish themselves with the Horsebreakers swanning about? See how the gentlemen stare at them? Like dogs outside a butcher's shop."

"We're not competing with the Horsebreakers," Evelyn said. "And even if we were . . . their riding isn't so impressive. Only look at the dreadful bit the chestnut is wearing. She has him entirely behind the vertical. And what about the gray? He's not engaging his hindquarters at all."

"Do you think men care about such things when a rider has bosoms like that? Or when she boasts a seventeen-inch waist?" Lady Anne huffed. "I suppose we must be thankful that Miss Walters isn't among them. It would be worse if she were. All the young men would be out in force."

Evelyn glanced back. Lady Anne was right. The famous Catherine Walters was nowhere to be seen. No doubt she was somewhere with her protector—a man rumored to be the Marquess of Hartington. "There must be some gentlemen who can resist their charms."

"No one between the ages of fifteen and fifty. If you're intent on marrying in your first season, you'd do better to look for an old gentleman in his dotage. They're kind enough. Almost fatherly. Or you could try a retired military man. Rumor has it that Captain Blunt is in town, seeking a new bride to raise his brood of illegitimate children."

"Captain Blunt?"

"The infamous Hero of the Crimea," Lady Anne said. "And the Earl of Gresham arrived only yesterday. He's on the lookout, too, I've heard. Newly widowed, and casting about for a fertile female to deliver him an heir."

Evelyn suppressed a grimace. Her prospects were starting to sound rather bleak. "Do you know everyone hereabouts? All the gentlemen?"

"Most of them." Lady Anne made a soft sound of reprimand as she tugged at Saffron's reins, narrowly preventing him from nipping Hephaestus's neck. "There's Mr. Phillips, riding with Mr. Edgeware, both perpetual bachelors, and hopeless wagerers at the track. That large man in the barouche is Sir Newton, a hunt-mad baronet from Hampshire, intent on marrying a fortune. And that gentleman . . .

Hmm. That's strange. I don't recognize him. Though he appears to recognize you."

Evelyn followed Lady Anne's gaze. A fair-haired man stood along the viewing rail. He was pale and slim and startlingly familiar.

A shiver traced down her spine.

Hephaestus felt it and responded, springing into another elevated trot.

"There's room ahead," Evelyn said hastily. "Shall we canter?" She didn't wait for Lady Anne to agree. A touch of her heel, and Hephaestus leapt forward.

Lady Anne kicked Saffron into a canter, swiftly catching up. "Who is he?" she asked. "Do you know him?"

"I do," Evelyn admitted. It was her former friend. The man who, up until three years ago, she'd believed she was going to marry. "His name is Stephen Connaught."

Eleven

❖

In Ahmad's experience, actions, no matter how well-intentioned, invariably had consequences. There would be a price to pay for rejecting the viscountess's advances. He'd been expecting it to be exacted ever since he'd left her town house and returned to Doyle and Heppenstall's.

The prospect left him distinctly uneasy. Leaning over his table in the shop's workroom, he was scarcely able to focus on cutting and basting the pattern he'd designed for Miss Maltravers's third riding habit. Not even the sumptuous Venetian cloth he'd chosen for her—a fine worsted fabric of rich mink brown—served to distract him.

It was the uncertainty of it all. The sense of impending disaster. He'd much rather know where he stood than be left waiting to find out. Once he knew, he could make a plan. Until then, he was stuck in limbo, dangling at the viscountess's pleasure.

It wasn't for long.

Not three hours later, as he was shelving a bolt of wool suiting fabric behind the showroom counter, the viscountess's lady's maid, Crebbs, entered the shop. She was clad in a dark cloak and bonnet and carrying a large dress box in her arms. The same dress box Ahmad had delivered that morning.

She dumped it unceremoniously onto the counter. "My mistress don't want this."

Ahmad had expected retaliation in some form or another. It didn't stop the reality of it from stinging like the very devil. Approaching the counter, he lifted the lid off the box, dropping a grim glance at the evening dress he'd spent so long perfecting. It had been shoved inside, left to crumple and crease amid the torn tissue paper. "She requires an alteration?"

"She don't want it," Crebbs said again. "And she's got no use for you anymore, either."

He might have known Lady Heatherton would react this way. She was angry, and very likely embarrassed.

But such emotions didn't last.

She was bound to cool off in a day or two. Then she'd remember how well his design had suited her and she'd want her dress back again. All it needed was time and patience.

"You may tell your mistress that I'll call on her tomorrow," he said. "When she's more herself."

"Oh, no you won't." Crebbs leaned halfway across the counter. Her foul breath gusted into his face. "Don't you understand English? You're not welcome at the house no more. My lady's left word with the butler and the footmen. If you so much as set foot on the property, they'll haul you up before the magistrate."

An icy chill seeped into Ahmad's veins. Empty as the threat may be, it couldn't be taken lightly. He'd been up before the magistrate before. Had very nearly lost his freedom. "On what charge?"

"Don't get cheeky with me, sir! I know all about you and your sort. You've no business with my mistress." Crebbs gave the dress box a hard shove. "And she won't be wearing this, or anything else you've made. If she wants an evening gown, she'll go to a proper dressmaker, not the likes of you."

"I see." He regarded Crebbs with studied impassivity. She wasn't the first aggressively offensive Englishwoman he'd dealt with, nor was she the worst. He'd learned self-control in hard school. Losing his temper was never an option. Even now. Even when she was destroying his future with every word.

And not only his.

"And what about her ladyship's bill?" he asked. "Will you be settling it?"

Crebbs laughed, as if the very idea of payment for his work was something too outlandish to contemplate. "My mistress won't give you a ha'penny," she said. "The nerve of you people! You don't know your place, is your problem. Best learn it before you find yourself in trouble."

Ahmad stood immobile as she exited the shop. She slammed the door behind her with such force that it rattled the panes of glass in the front windows. The sound jolted him from his stupor.

Good God.

He'd just lost his patroness. His one chance at making his name in fashionable society. And all because he'd been too proud—too damned particular—to give in to the lady's erotic demands.

And why hadn't he?

She wasn't an antidote. Not by any means. She was an attractive woman in her prime. As comely as any of her class. Would it have been so difficult to accommodate her? So distasteful? Principles were all well and good, but what was the point of them if they left one in this position? Out of a job. Out of options. And out of pocket several hundred pounds.

Doubts crowded his brain. If only he'd done as she asked. Kissed her. Slept with her just once. If only he'd behaved as she'd expected him to.

But he didn't have the luxury of second-guessing himself.

At this very moment, Mira was back at his rooms in King William Street, diligently working on the remainder of Lady

Heatherton's order. An order Ahmad could no longer expect to be paid for.

.He was going to have to tell her. And sooner rather than later.

❖

Mira stared at Ahmad, her needle and thread frozen in her hand. She was seated in an armchair near the sitting-room window in his rooms above the tea dealer's shop, her rosewood sewing box open on a table beside her. One of Lady Heatherton's evening gowns was spread over her lap. "What do you mean she returned the dress?"

"Just that. She had her maid bring it to Doyle and Heppenstall's." Ahmad plucked the needle and thread from Mira's fingers and dropped them into her sewing box. He closed the inlaid lid. "You can leave off your work on her others gowns. She won't be wanting those, either."

"*What?*"

"With luck, we can salvage them for someone else. Though I don't know who at the moment." He collected the evening dress from her lap. It was a glittering confection of mazarine silk with a half-finished application of glass beadwork on the bodice. "Pity. This one is nearly done."

"Wait." Mira stood to follow after him. "You're making no sense at all. Do you mean to say she didn't like the finished dress?"

"It's me she doesn't like." He opened a low wooden storage chest in the corner and lay the dress inside it. There would be time enough to pack it away properly. For now, it was enough that it was out of sight. The last thing he wanted was a reminder of Lady Heatherton.

His patroness, indeed.

A simmering anger grew within him. Anger directed not at her, but at himself.

He'd been so confident about his skill—so certain his designs would ultimately win the day—that he'd ignored every warning sign.

And there had been plenty.

He'd recognized them all. Lady Heatherton's mercurial moods. The fact that she fancied him. That she was growing bolder in her words and actions.

Had he truly believed that her interest would be limited to an infrequent touch? An occasional double entendre? He should have known she'd eventually expect something more from him. The fact that he didn't—or rather, that he *had*, but had chosen to overlook the danger— was enough to make him want to put his fist through the wall.

He'd been convinced that his work would be enough for her. That once she put on the evening dress he'd designed, all the rest of it would fade into the background, replaced by a sense of appreciation. Of awe. The same emotions Miss Maltravers had experienced when she'd put on her finished habit and looked at herself in the cheval glass.

"I knew you would amaze me."

Ahmad's heart clutched to think of her. Miss Maltravers. *Evelyn.* His own personal siren sent to tempt him.

"Why not?" Mira asked. "Did you quarrel with her?"

He raked his hand through his hair. "Something like that."

"Ahmad, stop." She caught his arm as he moved to walk past her. "Look at me. Tell me what's happened."

He reluctantly turned to face her. It didn't occur to him to lie. Mira was no worldly sophisticate. Neither was she a child. "Lady Heatherton made overtures to me today that I wasn't of a mind to accept. That's why she's returned the dress. Not because she didn't like it, but because I've hurt her pride."

Mira's expression hardened. "I *knew* it. I knew that's what she was after."

"Not very flattering to my skill as a dressmaker."

"I didn't mean—"

"She *did* admire the dress, you know. She was quite pleased with it, right up until the moment I rejected her advances."

"Naturally she admired it!" Mira burst out. "She'd have to be blind not to see how perfect it was for her. As for the rest of it . . . how *dare* she? What gives her the right—"

"Her rank. Her race. Any number of things." He gently extricated himself from Mira's grasp. "It's no use getting angry, *bahan*."

"I'm not angry," Mira said. "I'm livid. The fact that you're not—"

"I don't know what I am. Still in shock, probably." He gave his cousin a fleeting smile. There was no humor in it. "She's threatened me with the magistrate if I turn up at her house again."

Mira's jaw slackened. "She never."

"I'm rather relieved, actually. Better to have a clean break than to return to her, groveling for her custom. And who knows but that I might have done, given time enough to reflect on the matter. I'm out of pocket quite a bit on her account."

The color drained from Mira's face. "She won't pay for the dresses she ordered?"

"Not a ha'penny, according to her lady's maid."

Mira shook her head. "But she can't refuse to pay you. She simply can't. Not when you've spent so much money on her behalf."

"She can and she has. There's nothing for it."

"Of course there is. You must tell Mr. Finchley."

His brows snapped together. "Absolutely not."

"You *must*," she insisted. "He can do something about it. Instigate a lawsuit to recover your expenses or—"

"And how would that look?"

"It would be justice!"

"It would be the end of my career as a dressmaker. I can't hope to start a business by suing my customers. What would that do to my reputation?" Ahmad exhaled. "The fact is, Lady Heatherton's put me in a damnable position. I expect she knows it."

"What will you do?"

"I don't know." He paced to the window and back again. His mind was in a muddle; his muscles bunched with tension.

All of his plans were crumbling around him, and he had no recourse at all. No action he could take to resolve things with Lady Heatherton, and no other titled society darling waiting in the wings to wear his gowns. No one on whom he could display his skill to the eyes of the beau monde. Only courtesans. Pretty Horsebreakers.

Unless . . .

A spark of an idea flickered in his mind. A ludicrous notion, born more of desperation than good sense.

But no. It could never work.

Could it?

Ahmad's pulse accelerated. He looked at the clock on the mantel. It was a quarter past five o'clock. Fifteen whole minutes into the fashionable hour. There was still time if he hurried.

"What I need," he said at last, "is some fresh air to clear my head." He turned to Mira. "Will you join me for a walk in Hyde Park?"

"At this hour?" She wrinkled her nose. "It won't be very restful. Everyone in Mayfair will be out walking and riding. Even your Miss Maltravers, I don't doubt."

Ahmad fetched their coats. "I'm counting on it."

Twelve

❈

Riding home from the park, Evelyn narrowly missed the first crack of thunder.

It was a portent of worse weather to come.

The approaching evening brought heavy rains and dark clouds that blotted out the setting sun. It left a damp chill in Evelyn's heart and limbs. A feeling at odds with the sense of triumph she'd experienced as she'd entered Rotten Row on Hephaestus. The sense of beauty and power she'd felt until . . .

Until she'd seen *him*.

What in heaven's name was Stephen Connaught doing in town? He was a country gentleman, never setting foot outside Sussex, except for the handful of years when he'd gone away to university. He'd always professed to despise London.

"You'd never want to live there, would you?" he'd asked her once.

"Never," she'd answered. *"I'm happy in Combe Regis."*

"You're sensible," he'd said approvingly. *"Too sensible to indulge in a season in town. You'd never suit London society. And there's no use your going there just to be disappointed."*

Evelyn had been stung by his words. Hurt, and a trifle confused. Like much of what Stephen had said to her during the last year of their friendship, it had seemed to be an insult wrapped in a compliment. Words engineered to make her doubt her own value.

His silence had made her doubt herself even more.

After the scandal, he'd not only stopped speaking to her, but when they'd next encountered each other in the village, he'd given her the cut direct. Everyone had seen him do it. Everyone had known.

That had hurt worst of all.

Back in her room at Russell Square, Evelyn changed out of her habit and boots and into a comfortable dress and a pair of soft slippers. Wrapping an old cashmere shawl about herself, she repaired to the drawing room. It was less drafty there than her bedchamber, and warmer, too. The wall sconces were lit, and a fire blazed in the hearth.

Snuggling up in the cushioned window seat, she perused the society page of her uncle's daily paper in an effort to refocus her attention on the task at hand.

A futile enterprise.

Stephen was here, and with him all of the knowledge of Fenny's scandal. Who knew but that he might rake it all up again?

It was Evelyn's greatest fear. That her older sister's conduct would reach out from the past to, once more, spoil the prospects of the Maltravers family. It was bad enough that the scandal had hurt them three years ago. But to do so again, right when Evelyn was on the verge of making a success of things?

She couldn't stand to think of it.

Her younger sisters didn't deserve to have their futures thwarted. They had hopes and dreams of their own, some of which Evelyn knew and others she only guessed at.

Gussie was a gentle soul who craved a home and children. Caro wanted to write her own gothic novel someday. Bette had often mentioned the possibility of attending the Ladies College in Bedford Square. And Izzy longed for travel. To see Paris, Rome, and Constantinople.

What chance had they for any of that if Evelyn didn't succeed in her goal?

Resting her cheek against the rain-streaked glass, she made another vain attempt at reading the society page. She was still huddled there, nearly a half hour later, when Mrs. Quick appeared in the doorway.

"There's a tradesman come calling at the kitchen door, Miss Maltravers. He's asking to speak with you."

Evelyn lowered the paper. "With me? Whatever for?"

"He claims to be your habit-maker."

Evelyn's pulse jumped. Mr. Malik was here? She wasn't set to see him again until next week. She'd quite resigned herself to the fact.

"Shall I send him away?" Mrs. Quick asked.

"No, no. That won't be necessary." Setting aside the paper, Evelyn hastily rose from her seat. "I don't suppose my uncle's back from the museum?"

"Not yet."

"And Agnes? Has she returned?"

"No, miss. I wouldn't expect her back before eight o'clock."

Evelyn smoothed her faded gray dress. It was only Mr. Malik. They'd been alone together plenty of times in far more intimate circumstances than these. She didn't need her uncle to lend her countenance. And she certainly didn't require the presence of her maid.

But it wasn't her lack of a chaperone that made her hesitate. It was that kiss.

That kiss.

It had changed everything. And now—

"Miss Maltravers?"

Evelyn sighed. "Very well." She moved to stand in front of the fire. "You may show him in."

Mrs. Quick returned promptly. "Mr. Malik, miss."

Mr. Malik strode into the room. He was wearing a dark wool coat and trousers, his shoulders squared and his expression intent, looking for all the world like a man resolved to face down an implacable foe. He held a dented dress box in his arms. "Miss Maltravers." He bowed to her.

Evelyn's heart beat swiftly. "Mr. Malik. This is an unexpected pleasure." She turned to Mrs. Quick. "Thank you, Mrs. Quick. That will be all."

The housekeeper departed without so much as a look of curiosity.

Evelyn didn't wonder. Goodness only knew what sorts of bizarre things Mrs. Quick had witnessed while employed by Uncle Harris. A late-in-the-day call by an Indian habit-maker was likely the least of her concerns.

"Forgive the interruption," Mr. Malik said.

"You aren't interrupting anything." Evelyn's attention fell to the box he was carrying. "Is that my new habit?" She moved toward him, excitement briefly overshadowing her anxiety. "I thought it required another fitting?"

"It does. This isn't your habit. It's something else." He offered the box to her. "I can explain better once you've opened it."

She set the box down on the sofa, flashing him an uncertain glance as she lifted the lid and parted the cloud of tissue paper within. What she found inside fairly took her breath away. "Oh," she said softly. "Heavens."

It was an evening dress. A stunning confection of flawless silvery-blue muslin. She carefully withdrew it from the box, marveling at the shimmering spill of the skirts and the daring cut of the bodice. A fall of artfully draped point appliqué lace adorned the delicate sleeves and the scandalously low décolletage.

She looked at Mr. Malik. He was watching her closely. "Did you make this?"

"I did," he said. "Quite recently."

"But not for me?"

"No. It wouldn't suit you."

She inwardly flinched. It was a fact, not an insult. The evening dress was made for a fairy princess of a woman. A lady who was slim and fragile—and who didn't have auburn hair. Mr. Malik's words nevertheless left Evelyn feeling vaguely unworthy. Just as she'd felt ever since leaving the park.

Seeing Stephen had bruised her confidence. And she needed her confidence now, more than ever.

"I expect not," she said, managing a smile. "I have it on good authority that pale blue is *not* my color."

Some of the tension left Mr. Malik's face. "No, it isn't. I envision you in something rather different."

"You envision me in a ball gown?"

"I do," he said. "One of mine."

She hesitated for an instant, caught by the intensity in his obsidian eyes. This was important to him, that much was plain. Whatever *this* was. "I didn't realize you made anything for ladies other than riding habits."

"Not for society ladies, no. But I had planned to this season." A shadow passed over his countenance. "That is, I had a commission from a titled lady. The dress you see here, and two others like it. She's since decided she doesn't want them."

"I can't imagine why. I've never seen anything so beautiful." Evelyn carefully folded the evening dress back into its box. "Did your dresses not suit her?"

"They suited her," he said. "Too well."

"Yet she refused them?"

"She's a lady of many moods."

Evelyn waited for him to elaborate, but he said nothing more. And there *was* more, she sensed it. Something had happened to make his expression so grave. To harden his jaw and cause his gaze to darken with intensity. As if the whole of his future hinged on this moment.

She gestured to the sofa. "Won't you have a seat?"

Mr. Malik remained standing, only sitting down after she took a seat in the armchair across from him.

She arranged her skirts, privately wishing she'd worn one of her new dresses. That she'd pinched her cheeks and used a pad to fill out her hair. Instead, she was as plainly clothed and coiffed as the first day she'd met him.

If he noticed, he gave no indication. He was looking at her face as intently as when he'd entered the room.

She folded her hands in her lap. "As I say, it's a very beautiful dress. But I don't know why you've brought it to me."

"Because," he said, "I wanted you to see what I'm capable of."

Her smile came easier this time. "I hope I already know. One need only look at the habit you made for me to appreciate your talent." Wearing it had been magical. Momentous. Indeed, up until the moment she'd laid eyes on Stephen Connaught, she'd almost imagined she *was* one of the Pretty Horsebreakers. "You should have seen me in the park today. I do believe every gentleman I passed stopped and stared. Your habit was a great success."

"I did see you," he said.

She gave him a startled look. "You were there?"

"I was. And you were . . ." He frowned, shaking his head.

Her smile froze on her lips. She instantly regretted her boast, however feeble. "What?"

"You were dazzling."

Heat infiltrated her veins, making her cheeks warm and her heartbeat quicken.

Dazzling.

No one in the world had ever described her so. Certainly not a handsome gentleman—one for whom she was growing rather too fond. Compliments in her life were rare enough as it was. But to receive such a compliment from him . . .

There was no disguising the effect it had on her. No pretending she was some sophisticated beauty who had heard it all before.

She exhaled an unsteady breath. "Do you really think so?"

"It's not a matter of opinion. You eclipsed every other lady in the park. I wouldn't be surprised if they wrote about your triumph in tomorrow's paper."

She tilted forward in her seat, fixing him with a hopeful gaze. "You're not just saying that?"

He looked steadily back at her. "I never just say things, Miss Maltravers."

"No. I don't suppose you do." Her smile broadened to a ridiculous degree. She felt the urge to laugh. "It was your habit that did the trick, you know. Your habit and my riding." She sank back in her chair. "Oh, but I do feel vindicated when things go according to plan! Would that all of life could be arranged so happily."

"Perhaps it can."

"Yes, well . . . it all depends on the eligible gentlemen I meet. Today wasn't a success in that regard, I'm afraid." In truth, Evelyn privately admitted to a distinct feeling of disappointment. The masculine prospects on display in Rotten Row had been nothing to make a young lady's heart beat faster.

Rather the reverse.

They'd left her cold and vaguely despairing, wondering what her future would be like as the wife of a mean-faced lord or an army captain with a gaggle of unruly children.

"But it was only my first foray," she said bracingly. "I shall go back again tomorrow and the day after that. There's bound to be a likely candidate at some point. And with the new habits you're designing for me—"

"What about the rest of your wardrobe?" Mr. Malik asked abruptly.

"What about it?"

"You do plan on attending evening entertainments?"

"Eventually." She was certain to be invited somewhere.

"And you *are* going to a ball?"

"More than one, I trust, once my season is officially under way. As for what I shall wear, Lady Arundell has insisted that, tomorrow, I accompany her daughter to Madame Elise's salon in Regent Street."

Mr. Malik's expression darkened.

Evelyn added quickly, "I know you object to her designs, but—"

"It isn't her designs I object to," he said. "It's the way she treats her seamstresses."

A question formed on Evelyn's lips. He answered before she could ask it.

"Did you never wonder how a fashionable London dressmaker can deliver a ball gown so quickly after it's been ordered? How—for an exorbitant sum—such orders can be expedited in mere days?"

"Certainly I haven't. I've never patronized such establishments in my life. A fact which should be abundantly plain to you. Even your employer, Mr. Doyle, noted how ill I was turned out when first he saw me."

"He's not my—" Mr. Malik broke off. He surged to his feet, briefly looming over her before walking to the fireplace. "The point is, dressmakers like Madame Elise don't care tuppence for the young girls they employ. She works them from dawn until dusk. As many as thirty of them, in small rooms with no ventilation. And then, when they're at last permitted to retire to bed—*if* they're permitted to retire at all—it's to rooms even smaller. Rooms with no air, where they sleep two and three to a bed, breathing in the same noxious fumes."

Evelyn stared up at him. She couldn't recall when Mr. Malik had ever said so much all at once, or with so much animation. "I'd no idea."

"Of course not." He ran a hand over his hair. The glossy black strands glistened in the gaslight, still slightly damp from the rain. "Forgive me. I get rather passionate on the subject."

"I don't blame you. If it's as horrid as you say—"

"It's worse. Every garment Madame Elise makes may as well have blood on it. If you go to her for your ball gown—"

"I won't," Evelyn said.

"Won't you?"

"Not now. How could I? After what you've told me, it would be unconscionable."

He looked both relieved and a little doubtful. "You may find that a conscience is a luxury in London. Especially when weighed against the demands of fashionable society."

She raised her chin. "Not *my* conscience."

His mouth ticked up at one corner. "You're very sure of yourself."

"I know my own mind. And as for my conscience . . ." She'd already sacrificed too many of her principles on this venture. "I won't burden it on Madame Elise's account, no matter how pretty her dresses."

"I'm glad to hear it."

She searched his face. "Is that why you came? To offer to make a ball gown for me?"

"No. At least, not only that." His expression sobered. He cleared his throat. "I came because . . . I have a proposition for you."

She blinked up at him. *A proposition?*

"Something that would benefit us both." He paused, looking more serious than Evelyn had ever seen him look before. "I'd like to offer myself to you as a dressmaker. Not only for your habits and eveningwear, but for your entire wardrobe this season."

Thirteen

※

Ahmad stood in front of the dwindling fire, every inch of his frame fraught with tension, waiting for Miss Maltravers's reply.

Coming to see her had been a gamble. And he didn't like to gamble with his future—or with Mira's. Had Lady Heatherton not rejected his work, he'd never have risked it. He hated making himself vulnerable. And in this taut moment, he *was* vulnerable. Indeed, offering himself to Evelyn Maltravers was akin to stepping off a cliff into a vast unknown.

What if she didn't want his services? Or worse: What if she couldn't afford them?

Her uncle's house in Russell Square was stately enough, to be sure, but there was nothing about it to indicate that he was a man of extraordinary wealth. Faded wealth, more like it. The drawing room was littered with worn carpets and old-fashioned furnishings.

Miss Maltravers appeared a little faded herself. Not only that, she seemed smaller somehow. He never noticed it so much as when he saw her directly after having watched her ride. She was majestic on a horse. Almost queenly. Another person entirely.

Standing at the rail in Rotten Row, Ahmad had been riveted by the sight of her. She'd ridden down the stretch of tan at a prancing trot, in company with a blond lady on a golden stallion, their two grooms following not far behind.

"Is that her?" Mira had whispered from her place beside him. *"On the bay?"*

"It is." Ahmad's chest had tightened painfully as Miss Maltravers trotted by. She'd looked more than beautiful. She'd looked formidable. A veritable goddess on horseback, drawing the eyes of everyone she passed.

"Are you sure she's not a courtesan?" Mira had asked.

Looking at Miss Maltravers now, seated in her chair, with an old cashmere shawl drooping around her shoulders and her spectacles slipping down her nose, he saw no resemblance to one. No trace of the powerful sensuality she exhibited when riding.

"My entire wardrobe?" she repeated in tones of disbelief.

"Yes," he said. "Excepting what you've already ordered from Madame Lorraine."

He had just enough left in his savings to cover the expenses for fabric and trimmings, and to hire seamstresses to assist him. It would deplete his resources until Miss Maltravers settled her bill, leaving him with no funds to take over Doyle's lease.

A gamble, indeed.

If it failed, he and Mira would be left with nothing at all.

"I haven't ordered much," Miss Maltravers said. "Not yet. I confess, I've been wholly focused on my habits."

"Understandably so. They're an important piece of your plan."

She gave him a faint smile. "You must think me silly to have contrived it. To come to you as I did, claiming I could rival the charms of Miss Walters and the other Pretty Horsebreakers. Considering their attributes—"

"You have attributes to surpass theirs."

"When I'm riding? Yes." A spark of that familiar determination lit her face. "As for the rest of the time . . . I'll endeavor to do my best, but I have no illusions."

"You believe you can't make a success of your season unless you're on horseback?"

"Not a success, no. Outside of riding, the best I can hope for is that I won't distinguish myself in some unfortunate way."

Ahmad's brows lowered. He refused to accept that she could give up so easily. Not her. Not the young lady who'd entered Doyle and Heppenstall's a week ago, all but demanding he make her a habit. The one who rode with such innate poise and skill. "You're either too modest, or—"

"I'm realistic."

"You're not."

"I hope I am, sir. One can't make a successful plan without assessing one's strengths and weaknesses. I've done both. And quite impartially, I might add."

"Very impartial. You've never had a season before. Never before even been to London, as far as I can tell. And yet you're convinced you have nothing to offer outside of Rotten Row."

Miss Maltravers stood suddenly. Tightening her shawl about her arms, she walked toward him, coming to a halt only a few feet away.

His heart thumped heavily. She was near enough he could reach out and touch her. And he wanted to touch her quite badly. To take her hand or to cradle her cheek. To reassure her somehow.

"I know myself, Mr. Malik," she said. "And while I should very much like to have a ball gown of yours, I can offer you no promises about how well it will be received if I'm the one wearing it."

He stared down at her, half of him irritated at her for underestimating herself, and the other half aroused by her proximity.

Which wouldn't do at all.

He wasn't here because he was attracted to her. He was here because she had possibilities. *Distinct* possibilities. The potential to make a success of her season, and to make a success of *him*. He was supposed to be persuading her, not romancing her.

"That's what you meant, isn't it?" she asked. "When you said that making gowns for me would benefit us both?" She pushed her spectacles further up on her nose. "It's obvious how it would benefit me. But I don't see how you would gain any advantage from it."

Ahmad didn't mince words. "In six months' time, I mean to open a dress salon. To do it, I need fashionable ladies to see my designs." He gave her a pointed look. "*You'll* be out in fashionable society."

"I will, but there are no guarantees."

"You're going to be introduced at a ball given by the Countess of Arundell, aren't you?"

Miss Maltravers fell quiet. Her gaze slid from his.

"Aren't you?" he asked again.

"Yes. Though, it's not the kind of ball you imagine." She exhaled heavily. "It's not the kind I imagined, either." Turning, she walked to the window. The drapes were drawn back to reveal the rain-streaked glass. Outside, the sky was as gray as damp slate. "It's some sort of annual function related to the society of spiritualists that Lady Arundell and my uncle belong to."

"Ah." He followed her to the window.

"So you see—"

"Spiritualism is quite popular of late."

"I've been told." She turned back to him. "But as to whether it can serve to put your designs in front of the right people . . . Who can say?"

"Fashionable society is fashionable society, especially where titled lords and ladies are concerned. If you wear my designs, the right sort of people will see them."

"Yes," she said grimly. "On me."

"You'll make an impression, I promise you."

"I don't know if I can." There was an edge of emotion to her voice. Bitterness, perhaps, or even wistfulness. "I haven't had much luck in a ballroom. Not even at the village assemblies in Combe Regis. I've always been better on four legs than on two."

He rested his shoulder against the window frame as he looked at her. Long seconds passed, the rain pattering steadily on the glass. "What is it about riding that gives you confidence?" he asked at last.

"That's easy. It's because I'm not alone. I have Hephaestus as my partner."

"Only that?"

"Not only," she said. "I suppose it's because I understand the rules. I know what I must do to get the desired effect. The way to use my weight, and how much pressure to apply with my hands or my leg."

"You know all of this by instinct?"

She laughed. "Hardly. Some of it comes naturally, but the greater portion of my skill is derived from practice. Years and years of it."

"Practice with your partner."

"And the others that came before him. Experienced horses. They taught me far more than I taught them."

"And you never felt self-conscious when you were on them?"

"No. They were my partners then, just as Hephaestus is now."

"Perhaps that's what I'm proposing," he said. "A partnership."

❖

"With *you*?" The very notion was enough to make Evelyn's stomach quiver. Whether it was with excitement or apprehension, she couldn't tell.

"Why not?" Mr. Malik asked.

"Because . . ." She floundered, her mind temporarily drawing a blank. "Because it's not the same, that's why. For one thing, you wouldn't be with me at any of these hypothetical events."

"No," he said. "But my designs would."

"And they'd give me courage, is that it? Simply by wearing them?"

It wasn't as outlandish as it sounded. Not if she was honest with herself. His habit had been transformative. What would it be like to wear one of his evening gowns? A gown as radiant and revealing as the one in the box he'd brought her?

"You already have courage," he said. "In abundance. It's why you came to see me."

She folded her arms, wrapping herself tighter in her shawl. There was no reason to refuse his offer. His dresses would be beautiful, she knew. Her only doubt lay in herself. It was one thing to cut a figure on a horse. Cutting a figure in a ballroom was another thing entirely.

"If it's the cost that concerns you—"

"It's not the cost," she said. "Or rather . . . I do have to adhere to some kind of budget. But that isn't what makes me hesitate."

"What, then?" he asked.

She leaned back against the window frame, facing him. "Have you truly thought about this? About what it might mean for your future? Pinning all of your hopes on my making a success of things?"

"You *will* make a success of things."

"And if I don't? If I make a thorough hash of it all?"

He lifted one shoulder in the barest suggestion of a shrug. "I believe in you."

The words were uttered so casually. So completely offhand. They nevertheless wrapped themselves around Evelyn's heart. It was a lovely sentiment. Especially from him. But how could she accept it? Trust it?

"You don't know me," she said.

"I know enough."

"You don't. You've no idea what I'm like in company. At a dance or a dinner."

"Are you so very awkward?"

"Not that." She was self-assured enough in most situations. Rather too self-assured, in fact. Freely offering her opinions, even when those opinions were at odds with others in village society.

"Must you be so decided in your views, my dear?" Aunt Nora had asked her once as the two of them returned in the carriage from a disastrous Sunday dinner at the vicarage. "If you disagree with a gentleman, it's far better to say nothing than to make your displeasure known."

"But he was wrong," Evelyn had said. "He misquoted the entire passage. *And* he missed the point of it. What else was I to do but—"

"You might have chosen to remain silent. No one appreciates a know-all. Particularly one who happens to be female."

Evelyn had thought it monstrously unfair. She *still* did.

That was one of the benefits of being on horseback. There were no difficult conversations to navigate. No cause to agree or disagree with a long-winded gentleman. To laugh at his feeble jokes.

On a horse, she never had to do much more than offer a greeting to someone. If conversation existed at all, it was of the brief variety, and more than likely focused on equine matters.

But it wasn't only the conversation—or the lack of it—that appealed to her about riding. It was the strength she was permitted to exhibit. The one place she could do so without fear of censure. No one ever expected her to be quiet and obliging while on a stallion. She had to be strong and competent. Bold and brave. And so long as she looked minimally pretty while doing it, gentlemen would laud her for it. Admire her, even.

"It isn't awkwardness that plagues me," she said. "It's that I simply don't fit. I'm not a pattern card of femininity. Not like—"

"Not like your sister?" His words held a note of disapproval.

"Yes, if you must know. I'm . . . I'm *odd*. I'm going to try to be less so this season—to do whatever I must to secure a husband—but the chances of my being hailed as the most beautiful or the most fashionable are as slim as a blade of grass. It's my riding that will get me noticed, not anything that happens in a ballroom."

"That's where my gowns come in." He sounded so confident. So utterly sure of himself. "If you would but consent to wear them—"

"Of course I'll wear them," she said. "It would be an honor."

A flash of relief passed over his face. She was astonished to see it.

Goodness. Had he really thought she'd refuse? That she'd prefer Madame Lorraine, or some other dressmaker, to him?

"Thank you." He straightened from the window frame, and stepping forward, offered her his hand.

She took it without hesitation, even as she braced herself for the inevitable physical reaction. The jolt of heat and bone-deep awareness. The way gooseflesh rose on her arms and her heart squeezed in her breast.

Their eyes locked for a breathless moment.

And before she knew it—before she could clamp her teeth to stop the words from escaping—she heard herself saying, "There's something else that might pose a difficulty."

Mr. Malik stilled, his hand clasping hers. His grip tightened for a moment before he released her. Any sign of relief was gone from his face, replaced by an expression as solemn as the grave.

She registered the change in him, even as her words continued to tumble out, unchecked. "The thing is, I like you."

What?

She felt a vague sense of horror. It was the truth, but—good lord! There was plain speaking and there was plain speaking. This was . . .

Exposing herself entirely.

A stupid notion. As if he didn't already recognize her feelings. Even if their brief kiss could be passed off as purely accidental, there was still their chance meeting at Hatchards. He'd marked her reaction to him then. Had noted how flustered she became in his presence. She recalled how he'd smiled at her, seeming to be amused by her obvious attraction to him.

He wasn't smiling now.

He merely continued to look at her, his gaze even more intent than it had been before.

She forged ahead. "What happened between us at Doyle and Heppenstall's . . . When I . . . When we . . ." Oh, why couldn't she simply spit it out! "What I'm trying to say is that, whenever I'm with you, I feel something. A sort of connection. I don't know what to call it. But if we're to work together with any frequency—and I imagine we must if you make all of my gowns this season—then it's better we're honest with each other about these things. We neither of us would wish a recurrence of what happened last time."

Still, he said nothing. She began to fear she'd rendered him speechless.

Heat rose in her cheeks. "I daresay it's only me. No doubt you've been on the receiving end of countless—"

"It isn't only you," he said gruffly.

"I know *that*. It's what I was trying to say. That countless ladies must feel this way in your presence—"

"No," he interrupted. "That's not what I—" He took a step forward, coming to an abrupt halt in front of her. He gazed down at her face. "It isn't only you who feels it. I've felt it, too."

Evelyn was glad she had the window frame at her back. Without it, she might have swooned into a heap on the drawing room floor. "Felt it," she said. "Past tense?"

Mr. Malik gave her a fleeting smile. "I feel it every time I'm near you." An endless pause. "I'm feeling it now."

Her breath dammed up so tight in her chest, she could barely manage a whisper. "I've never experienced this before. Not with anyone."

"Nor have I," he admitted.

"What do you suppose it is? Some form of particularly strong attraction? Something chemical, or what have you?" She thought it must be. Something primitive and elemental. What else? She'd met handsome men before and had never responded to them the way she responded to him.

"I don't know," he said. "All I know is that you inspire me. That when I look at you, I feel something here." He touched his chest.

"Do you?" Her question was a mere thread of sound. So soft, she was astonished it wasn't drowned out by the mad hammering of her heartbeat.

"Every time I see you," he said. "It stands to reason that others will, too."

Her heart stopped. "You're talking about your designs?"

He inclined his head in silent acknowledgment. "We *will* have to work together with some frequency in the coming weeks, but you have nothing to fear from me. This thing between us—the connection you describe—I've heard of it happening on occasion in the creative world. If an artist is very lucky, he sometimes meets his muse. The day you walked into Doyle and Heppenstall's, I believe I met mine."

She swallowed. How was it possible to feel at once so moved and yet so disappointed? She inspired him. That wasn't nothing.

But it wasn't a romance.

"An artistic connection," she said. "I, ah, never considered it."

"It's a rare occurrence. One that, I hope, will allow us each to obtain the thing we want most."

"A fashionable dress shop for you," she said.

"And a wealthy husband for you," he replied.

She pushed up her spectacles. He was right. This wasn't a romance. It couldn't be. Their goals, and their positions in society, were diametrically opposed. What this was, was a partnership. A *business* partnership. One that could ultimately benefit them both. "Very well," she said. "When do we start?"

Fourteen

❖

The following morning, alone in her uncle's breakfast room, Evelyn perused the society page as she ate her toast and jam. Mr. Malik had said she might be in the paper, and this was the very latest edition. Her gaze drifted over the small black print.

Despite all the attention she'd garnered as she rode, she didn't truly expect to see any mention of her debut on Rotten Row. When it appeared, her heart fairly leapt into her throat. It was tucked at the bottom of the page, sandwiched between a report on French millinery and a write-up on mourning fashions:

THE PRETTY HORSEBREAKERS

> Our fair Anonyma has, it is said, gone to America, leaving many creditors to lament her departure, but another horse-breaker has appeared in her place. From whence came this titian-haired enchantress? Anonyma's abandoned admirers demand to know.

A titian-haired enchantress? Evelyn's hair wasn't titian. Auburn, possibly, when the light hit it just right. But not red.

Perhaps the article was referencing someone else?

She suggested that very possibility to Lady Anne when she arrived later that morning to collect Evelyn for their shopping excursion.

"It's definitely you," Lady Anne said as Evelyn welcomed her into the drawing room. "I nearly choked on my tea when I read it."

"Is it vey shocking?"

"It's a triumph. To be mentioned in the gossip columns so soon after your arrival. And in company with Miss Walters, too. One wonders if she's truly gone to America."

"It would explain why we haven't seen her." Evelyn gestured for Lady Anne to have a seat.

"We haven't much time to spare. Madame Elise's shop is best visited before noon."

"About that . . ." Evelyn offered a hasty explanation as to why she couldn't accompany her.

Lady Anne sank onto the sofa. She was wearing a black carriage dress with a white collar and crisp white undersleeves, her golden hair confined in a silk net. "Good lord," she said as she arranged her voluminous skirts. "Don't say you're a social reformer?"

Evelyn sat down across from her. "Must one be interested in reform to object to such outrageous conditions? It's a human issue, surely."

"I agree wholeheartedly. But others aren't likely to be so sympathetic. Madame Elise counts the wives and daughters of many a duke, marquess, and earl as her customers. Few of them would be willing to give up their pretty party dresses for the sake of a common girl forced to work and sleep in such conditions."

"I can only answer for myself," Evelyn said. "And *I* shan't be patronizing her salon, no matter how pretty her frocks."

"Nor I," Anne replied in solidarity. "Have you another dressmaker in mind? I warn you, there are none to rival Madame Elise. Not unless you manage a jaunt to Paris to buy one of Mr. Worth's creations."

"Not Mr. Worth," Evelyn said. "Someone better."

Lady's Anne's brows shot up. "Better than Worth? You intrigue me. Who is this person?"

"The gentleman who designs my riding habits."

"Your tailor in Conduit Street?"

Evelyn nodded. "He's a dressmaker, too, and has consented to make the rest of my wardrobe this season. He's selecting the fabrics and trimmings for my ball gown as we speak."

"Gracious. That *is* an inconvenience."

Evelyn felt a flicker of guilt. "I daresay I should have sent a note round to you, but I didn't think." She offered an apologetic smile. "I was so looking forward to your company."

"And I yours. I'd hoped today would be the first of many shopping excursions. My mother never permits me out of her sight unless I'm riding. Not unless she's preapproved the outing. And she seems inclined to approve of all my outings with you."

"Because she's friends with my uncle?"

"Because," Lady Anne said, "Mama prides herself on her ability to read people. She recognized right away that you were trustworthy— or so she claims. I suspect it's because you wear spectacles. It would never occur to her that a bluestocking could be dangerous."

Evelyn couldn't stop herself from bristling. "I'm not a bluestocking."

"Don't be offended. I count myself as a bluestocking, too." Lady Anne paused. "Bluestocking adjacent, anyway."

Evelyn had cause to doubt it. With her flawless alabaster face and enviable figure, Lady Anne appeared the polar opposite of a bluestocking. She was too poised. Too elegant. A perfect English lady.

"Mama will be expecting us to leave soon," she said.

Evelyn cast a glance at the door. "Your mother is here?"

"She went straight from the carriage to your uncle's study. The pair of them are in rhapsodies over a new report from Birmingham. Some boy claiming he's received a message from Prince Albert. If it's true—"

"You think it might be?"

"I'm not a believer myself. But who knows? 'There are more things in heaven and earth, Horatio,' and all that."

Evelyn recognized the quote from *Hamlet*. Among the books remaining in her family's modest library was a tattered copy of *The Collected Works of William Shakespeare*. As a girl, she'd read it from cover to cover, equally enamored of the romantic plays and thrilled by the gruesome ones. "If Prince Albert had a message to send from the great beyond, wouldn't it make more sense for him to send it directly to Buckingham Palace?"

"Rather. Unless Birmingham is more convenient for some reason."

"Why would it be?"

"Because of the boy. Mama says he must have a powerful spiritual antenna. Like a telegraph pole."

Evelyn's lips quivered.

Lady Anne's eyes glimmered with answering humor. "You may laugh, Miss Maltravers. But *I* have to live with this flummery."

"Oh, do call me Evie."

"And you must call me Anne. I never use my honorific if I can help it. Not with my friends."

Evelyn smiled. A friend. Her first one in London, and she hoped not her last.

Anne stood suddenly. "Would you like to do something else?"

Evelyn rose from her chair. "Instead of shopping?"

"Mama expects us to go somewhere. We may as well do so. The coachman won't tattle on us, nor will the footman. We can direct them where we will."

"And where is that?"

"Why, to call on Julia Wychwood, of course."

❦

Twenty minutes later, the Countess of Arundell's black lacquered carriage came to a stop in front of the Wychwoods' residence in Belgrave Square. The windows of the grand white stuccoed house were covered with cloth and the door knocker had been removed. The place looked all but abandoned.

"Are you certain they're at home?" Evelyn asked as the footman handed her down from the carriage.

Anne climbed out after her. She shook her skirts. "Pay no attention to its outward appearance. The Wychwoods are always battling some sickness or another. Julia's father, Sir Eustace, has even been known to put straw on the steps on occasion, when he feared the end was near."

Evelyn eyed the town house warily. "What kind of sickness?"

"Biliousness, apoplexy, green fever, megrims, palsy, the ague. Any number of unfortunate conditions, and even more of them undiagnosed." Anne climbed the stone steps to the front door. "Julia's parents keep half of the physicians in London in business."

"So long as it's not anything contagious." Evelyn couldn't afford to become ill. Not at this stage of her plan.

"Heavens, no. You'll never catch so much as a cold from the Wychwoods." Curling her gloved hand into a fist, Anne rapped sharply on the door.

It was opened by a balding footman in canary-yellow livery.

"Good morning, Jenkins," Anne said. "We've come to see Miss Wychwood. She's in her room, I take it?"

"Yes, my lady." He stood back to allow them entry. "The doctor has just been."

"That bad, is it?" Anne removed her black silk hat and stripped off her gloves, handing them to the footman.

Evelyn followed suit. Her gaze drifted over the entry hall. It was too dark to properly make out the wall coverings or furnishings. Not only that, the interior of the house was distinctly over warm.

A shiver of uneasiness went through her.

Mama's sickroom had been just the same. Dark and close in the aftermath of giving birth to baby Isobel. Evelyn could still recall the coppery smell of blood. There had been so much of it.

The memory only served to drive home the urgency of her mission. Her sisters were depending on her. She had to marry well for their sakes. For Gussie, Caro, Bette, and Izzy. Each of them was due a chance at happiness and security. A chance for love. And if Evelyn had to marry without it in order to give them that chance, then by God, she'd do it.

And why shouldn't she be the one to make the sacrifice? She was the most unsentimental of them all.

At least, she *had* been until she'd met Mr. Malik.

But those feelings would pass, surely. The way butterflies fluttered in her stomach whenever she saw him. The way her breath caught and her pulse quickened. Soon she'd meet someone else. Someone suitable. Life would go on, and if she never felt those exquisite palpitations again—

Well.

She'd forget she ever had, wouldn't she? She'd be precisely as she was when she'd first arrived in London. Sensible and pragmatic. Decidedly unromantic.

"Sir Eustace is beside himself," Jenkins confided in low tones. "He's taken to his bed."

"What a shame." Anne headed for the curving oak staircase. "No need to accompany us. I know the way."

Evelyn ascended the steps after her. "It sounds as though Miss Wychwood may be too ill for company."

Anne gave a very unladylike snort. "Julia has the constitution of a horse."

"But—"

"You'll see." Anne led Evelyn down a carpeted hallway to a large, wood-paneled door. She knocked on it twice.

There was a frantic rustling from within. At length, a weak voice answered: "Come in."

Anne flashed Evelyn a speaking glance as she opened the door.

Miss Wychwood's chamber was as dark and warm as the rest of the house. Velvet curtains were drawn shut over the windows, and a dying fire crackled in the grate. At the center of the room stood a carved four-poster bed draped in blue damask. Julia Wychwood lay inside of it, tucked deep beneath her bedcovers, her head resting on a stack of feather pillows. She turned her face to the door as they entered. Her countenance was pale as wax.

"You sound as though you're about to cross through the veil," Anne said dryly.

"Anne!" Miss Wychwood struggled to a sitting position. Her blankets slid down to her waist, revealing her ruffled white nightgown. "Thank goodness you've come. And is that Miss Maltravers?"

"It is," Anne said. "Shut the door, won't you, Evie?"

Evelyn closed it behind her. She approached the bed. "I didn't know you were ill, Miss Wychwood. I hope you're feeling a little better?"

"Enormously better now," Miss Wychwood said. "Fancy your calling on me. Mind you, I *did* wonder when we might meet again. Though I never thought it would be in such circumstances as these." Her cheeks pinkened. "Forgive my state of undress."

Evelyn smiled. "Not at all. I'm pleased to see you again, in any state."

"For goodness' sake, Julia. How can you bear this stifling heat?" Anne crossed the room. "We must open a window."

"Yes, do. But only a little. If Papa were to see—"

"He won't," Anne replied. "Jenkins says he's taken to his bed."

"Has he? Well, that's a relief." Miss Wychwood gestured to the spoon-back chair beside her bed. "Pray sit down, Miss Maltravers." And then to Anne: "With Mama gone to Bath, he's been hovering over me like an old mother hen."

Anne struggled with the window, at last managing to raise it a few inches. She drew the drapes shut again. "You're not helping in that regard, dear. Not if you will insist on playacting that you're at death's door."

Evelyn sat down, arranging her skirts all about her.

"Not quite at death's door," Miss Wychwood said. "And it's not playacting. I haven't felt at all the thing these past three days."

Anne returned to the bed. "You haven't felt the thing these past three seasons." She sank down on the edge of the mattress. "I thought, at the very minimum, you'd be out to exercise Cossack. But I haven't seen you. Nor has Evie. Don't say you're having your groom to do it?"

Miss Wychwood gave her friend a sheepish look. "I meant to ride him this morning, but Papa swore I had a fever."

"This house is enough to give anyone a fever," Anne said.

"Papa's ordered all the fires lit. He claims to have a chill in his lungs." Miss Wychwood drew back her blanket, uncovering a half-eaten box of chocolates and a blue cloth-bound book with gold lettering on the spine. "Would you like some candy?" She proffered the box to Evelyn.

"Oh yes, thank you." Evelyn selected a chocolate.

"Anne?" Miss Wychwood held out the box. "Take as many as you like."

Anne helped herself to several. She popped the first one into her mouth. Her eyes fell shut as she chewed and swallowed.

"Lady Arundell doesn't allow Anne to have sweets," Miss Wychwood explained to Evelyn. "She's awfully strict about food."

"She is," Anne admitted. "But I won't be distracted." She fixed Miss Wychwood with a stern glare. "You're hiding again."

"Can you blame me?"

"No, indeed. If I had chocolates and a novel to keep me company, I might withdraw to my bed, too. But that's no excuse. We must all face the season, like it or not."

"Is it truly so terrible?" Evelyn asked, taking a bite of her chocolate.

Miss Wychwood's bosom rose and fell on a sigh. "It is when you've had several seasons before, none of which resulted in a single offer of marriage."

"That isn't the reason." Anne ate another chocolate. "It's because Mr. Hartford and his asinine japes have made our time in London a misery. We can't set foot out of doors together without someone making a remark."

"He *is* unpleasant," Miss Wychwood acknowledged. "But worse than that—"

"What can be worse?"

"Being overlooked. Passed over like a jar of preserves that have expired on the shelf."

Anne frowned. "Preserves don't expire. Do they?"

"Not in three years' time they don't," Evelyn said. "Not if they're unopened."

"Well, there you are," Anne said in a bracing tone. "An unopened jar of preserves. You've plenty still to offer. We all of us do, if anyone would trouble to look."

"I'd rather remain unmarried," Miss Wychwood said under her breath.

"The devil you would," Anne retorted. "You, more than anyone, must find a way to get out from under your parents' thumbs. Much more of those doctors bleeding you and you'll have no blood left. You already look half dead."

"I'm perfectly well. Except for the heat and being obliged to hide my novel under the covers whenever Papa enters."

Evelyn leaned forward in her seat to examine the spine of Miss Wychwood's book. "What are you reading?"

"The third volume of *Lady Audley's Secret*. It's wonderfully thrilling. A favorite of mine. It's about a beautiful young lady who—"

"Don't spoil it," Anne warned.

"That's all right," Evelyn said. "I've already read it." On its release earlier that year, the circulating library in Combe Regis had managed to procure the entire three-volume set for their collection. It had proved hugely popular with the local young ladies, Evelyn and her sisters chief among them. "It *is* rather gripping, isn't it?"

"Oh yes," Miss Wychwood said. "Lady Audley is my favorite character."

Anne chuckled. "The villainess, naturally."

"She *is* the villain of the piece, to be sure," Miss Wychwood said. "But one must admire her a little. Imagine being so devious—so deliciously diabolical—as to change one's name and create a whole new life for oneself."

Evelyn had never thought of it that way, but she supposed Miss Wychwood had a point. There was a lot to be said for a lady who knew what she wanted and didn't hesitate to take it. "If only she could have refrained from committing bigamy and attempting to murder people in the process."

"Yes," Anne agreed, finishing off her chocolates. "That *was* taking things a bit too far."

"Bigamy won't be an issue where I'm concerned," Miss Wychwood said. "I can scarcely hope to find one husband, let alone two." She settled back against her pillows. "I wish I could go someplace where no one knew me. Someplace I could reinvent myself and start afresh. Like Lady Audley, but without the violent bits."

Anne withdrew a handkerchief from her wide pagoda sleeve and wiped the melted chocolate from her fingertips. "Yes, but wherever you go, one thing will remain the same."

"What?" Miss Wychwood asked.

"You, of course. A person can never truly change who they are."

"Not at the core, no," Evelyn said. "But outwardly, certainly. With the right clothing and in the right setting."

Both Anne and Miss Wychwood looked at her.

Evelyn hesitated an instant before confessing, "*I* mean to do so."

Miss Wychwood's pale face brightened. "Do you? How exciting!"

"You're the only one of us who could," Anne said. "You're a blank slate. No one knows you in town, except for that gentleman who was watching you in the park yesterday. Who did you say he was? Stephen something?"

"Connaught." The mere mention of his name was enough to depress Evelyn's spirits.

It had been less than twenty-four hours since she'd seen him in Rotten Row. And yet, in that short time, his presence in town had become akin to her own personal sword of Damocles. She didn't know what he might do or when he might do it. All she knew was that her plan may very well be in danger.

Miss Wychwood's gaze flicked between them. "Who is he?"

"A neighbor of mine in Sussex. He and I used to go riding together. For a time, I thought he might propose."

Anne tucked away her handkerchief. "He didn't, I gather."

"No," Evelyn said. "In truth, we're not even friends anymore. It's been a long while since we were."

"What happened?" Miss Wychwood asked.

Before Evelyn could answer, there was a rap at the door.

Miss Wychwood responded to the sound with comical efficiency. Quick as a flash, she was back underneath her blankets, her head resting on her pillow, and her novel and box of chocolates well hidden. "Come in," she called out in a faint voice.

The door cracked open. A young lady poked her head in. She was wearing a wool cloak, the hood drawn up over her hair. "It's only me."

"Stella!" Anne leapt from the bed to greet her. The two of them clasped hands and kissed each other's cheeks.

Evelyn stood. This must be Miss Hobhouse, the third of the three Furies. She was a strangely pretty girl, with large, luminous blue eyes of a shade so pale it might pass for silver. Evelyn had never seen such a color before. There was something about it that was almost otherworldly.

"When did you get back?" Anne asked.

"Last night after dinner. I'd thought to see you riding in the park this morning. I was there at eight."

"I'm riding this afternoon, and Julia isn't riding at all today unless we can persuade her to get out of bed." Anne pulled Miss Hobhouse into the room. "Here. Come and meet Miss Maltravers. She's newly arrived from Sussex. Evie? This is Stella Hobhouse, the best rider among us."

Miss Hobhouse smiled. "She only says that because I ride so often. And that owes more to my horse's nervous temperament than to my skill." She extended her hand to Evelyn. "I'm pleased to meet you."

Evelyn shook it. "And I you."

"Miss Maltravers has a bay Spanish stallion," Miss Wychwood said. "When first I saw her, she was riding him in nothing but a snaffle."

"Oh? He must be very well trained." Miss Hobhouse pushed back her hood.

Evelyn's eyes widened. Stella Hobhouse's hair was twisted back in a series of plaits, rolled and pinned within an inch of its life. It was glossy and shining with good health. It was also completely gray.

She caught Evelyn's gaze. Her mouth hitched at one corner. "Don't be alarmed. It's been this color since I was sixteen."

"My mother suspects it has something to do with the spirit world," Anne said.

"And that's exactly what I shall tell any gentleman who asks me this season." Miss Hobhouse sat down on the edge of the mattress. "The trouble is, they never do ask. They only gape at me in horror."

Anne perched next to Miss Wychwood at the top of the bed. "Evie is here for the season, too."

"Her first season," Miss Wychwood said.

"Only your first?" Miss Hobhouse gave Evelyn a curious glance. "You're not fresh out of the schoolroom?"

"No, indeed." Evelyn resumed her seat. "I'm three and twenty."

Miss Wychwood gasped. "That old?"

"Really, Julia," Anne said. And then to Evelyn: "Ignore her. We none of us are much younger."

"Yes," Miss Wychwood countered, "but you and I are already on our third season, and Stella's on her second. Miss Maltravers is just getting started."

Miss Hobhouse's brow furrowed. "Maltravers. I feel I've heard the name before. You don't have a sister, do you?"

"Several. Four of them younger than me." Evelyn steeled herself before adding, "And one of them older."

"That must be it," Miss Hobhouse said. "There was some incident attached to her, wasn't there?"

Evelyn exchanged a glance with Anne. She was the only one of them who knew. And if she didn't, her mother certainly did. Not because Evelyn had confided in her, but because Uncle Harris had. Goodness only knew how many of the details he'd shared.

"It was years ago," Anne said. "Long past and best forgotten."

"Was there a scandal?" Miss Wychwood asked.

"A scandal." Miss Hobhouse's eyes lit up. "Now I remember. She ran off, didn't she? With a baronet's son or—" She stopped short, her cheeks reddening. "Oh, I *am* sorry. It must be painful to recall it. And here I am running on."

"Not painful," Evelyn said. "Inconvenient."

"I can understand how it would be." Miss Hobhouse gave her a sympathetic grimace. "I apologize again, Miss Maltravers."

Evelyn believed she meant it. None of the ladies seemed cruel or malicious. Indeed, they appeared to be exactly what Evelyn was herself—ladies who didn't quite fit. "Please," she said. "I wish you would all call me by my given name. Or Evie, if you prefer. It seems silly to stand on ceremony."

Miss Hobhouse promptly agreed. "I'd be honored if you would address me as Stella."

Miss Wychwood nodded. "And you must call me Julia."

"Now that we've dispensed with the niceties," Anne said, "perhaps we can focus on the week ahead? My mother's ball is next Friday, after which our seasons will have officially begun. That leaves us eight whole days of freedom—not a single one of which can be wasted in bed."

A notch formed between Julia's brows. "But, Anne—"

"I propose we ride tomorrow. We can meet at dawn, if you like, to avoid the crush." Anne gave Julia a pointed look. "There's to be no more retreating to your bed. It will only make things worse when you finally have to emerge."

Stella took Julia's hand. "You'll feel better afterward. A good gallop always sets everything to rights."

"I agree," Evelyn said. "I'm never so clearheaded as after a ride. It puts the entirety of life in perspective."

Julia sat up straighter in her bed. "I suppose I might come. If we ride early enough. And if we're all together."

Anne slipped her arm around Julia's shoulders. "Of course we will be."

Fifteen

—✦—

*D*isembarking from the crowded omnibus, Ahmad crossed Commercial Road, ducking through traffic, to enter the East End slums he'd once called home. There hadn't been much cause to return since leaving Mrs. Pritchard's employ. No reason to tread the familiar streets or to revisit the shops he'd patronized as a boy.

Until now.

An image of Evelyn Maltravers sprang into his mind. The elegant turn of her countenance, enlivened by the stubborn tilt of her chin and the determined twinkle in her velvet-soft eyes.

"The thing is," she'd said, *"I like you."*

His blood warmed to recall it.

She was rarely out of his thoughts of late.

Understandable, he supposed. She was his muse, after all. The motivating force for his coming here today.

He wondered what she'd make of this place—the neighborhood where he'd spent thirteen years of his life. Would she be repulsed? Disgusted? She might be a sensible country girl, but she was still a lady. An Englishwoman, gently born and bred, and sheltered from the worst of society.

He couldn't imagine her ever setting foot here.

As he strode up one narrow lane and down another, a waft of fetid air rolled in from the East India Docks. With it came a flood of memories.

Nothing had changed.

Even the people looked the same.

Which wasn't surprising. There was precious little opportunity for anyone to leave. Rare chance to advance in society—either in their own sphere or in the greater world around them. Those who hadn't expired from drink or despair were still pushing the same carts and peddling the same wares; still lingering outside the same public houses, and propping themselves up in the same doorways. Dirty-faced ruffians and gin-soaked women vied for space with raggedly dressed children, faded prostitutes, and broken-down seamen.

Among them, Ahmad saw the occasional Indian face. Lascars—Bengali and Yemeni sailors—on leave from British ships. Either that or discharged completely. Left to fend for themselves in a strange land, far away from home.

It wasn't uncommon.

During Ahmad's early years at Mrs. Pritchard's, he'd been aware of a small community of Muslim Indians living nearby. They were known to gather regularly for worship. He might have joined them if he'd been willing to accept their faith. He'd certainly been tempted.

But no.

His aunt had raised him and Mira with only the semblance of religion—a faint imitation of the Christianity practiced by the colonials. It was yet another affectation of Englishness. A product of their being half-white—this constant desire to behave as the British did. To *be* British. As if denying the Indian part of them would somehow make them more palatable to the sahibs and memsahibs who ruled their country.

It never had. Not in Ahmad's experience.

No amount of posturing could make him and Mira fit into a world where they didn't belong. It was why he'd been intrigued by the presence of other Indians in the East End. Why he'd briefly considered joining them, despite his lack of faith. As a lad, it had meant something to see others like him, even if they had nothing else in common. Even if they were strangers.

That was one thing that could be said for the docklands: they may not have been particularly desirable to live in, but they boasted a diversity sorely lacking in Mayfair.

Pulling his hat down over his brow, Ahmad continued walking until he came to the corner of Lost Hope Yard. It was marked by a crooked wooden building, teetering precariously on its foundation. Two large, grease-streaked windows faced the front, giving the sinister structure the appearance of a sightless man staring blindly out at the deserted square.

A rag-and-bone shop occupied the downstairs premises. The same one that had been there in Ahmad's youth. On the floor above were two small apartments: one for the shop's proprietor, Mrs. McCordle, and another—no bigger than a closet—for Becky Rawlins. It was the closest thing to respectable lodgings she'd been able to find after leaving Mrs. Pritchard's establishment.

The brass bell above the door jangled as Ahmad entered. He was met by the stench of mildewed linens and rotting wood.

Mrs. McCordle was seated at the bottom of the stairs, sorting through a bin of old clothes. She peered up at him. "Who's there?"

Ahmad saw no need to identify himself. "Is Miss Rawlins in?"

"Aye, she's up there. But I'll have no messing about. This ain't that kind of establishment."

"I'll wait here if you'll fetch her," Ahmad said.

Mrs. McCordle scowled. "You expect me to go up them stairs? And me with my rheumatism playing up?" She resumed sorting through her rags. "Fetch her down yourself. And be double-quick about it, or I'll know what you're up to."

Ahmad climbed the rickety steps. They creaked and groaned under his weight. An ominous sound. The short hallway above was no less unstable, with sagging floorboards and a ceiling with a dark water stain seeping out to its edges. It smelled fetid and damp. Rotten to the core.

He rapped on one of the two doors.

"Give me a minute!" a high-pitched voice called out. Several seconds passed before the door was cracked open to the length of its chain latch, revealing Becky's careworn face.

She was young. Younger than Mira, though one wouldn't know it to look at her. Fine lines etched the corners of her eyes, and her back was bent from too many hours of needlework. She was free and independent now, which was no small thing, but her life hadn't been easy since leaving Mrs. Pritchard's.

"Ahmad Malik! Is that you?" She unlatched the door. "What are you doing here?"

"I've come to take you for a walk," he said. "Fetch your shawl."

Becky's brows raised, but she asked no questions. She disappeared back inside for an instant. When she emerged again, she had a knitted wool shawl draped around her shoulders and an old stuff bonnet in her hand. She tugged it on over her dull blond hair and tied it under her chin. "I could do with a breath of fresh air."

"Not fresh enough for my taste," Ahmad said as the two of them descended the stairs.

"Oh, it's not a patch on the air you have in Mayfair. But I'll take it any hour over what I have to breathe in that room of mine. Some days, seems I never leave it." Becky shouted to Mrs. McCordle as they passed her: "Going out, Mrs. McCordle!"

"You behave yourself, my girl," Mrs. McCordle called back. "I don't rent lodgings to them who gets themselves in trouble."

Ahmad pushed the door open for Becky. The bell jangled again, announcing their exit. "How are you getting on?"

"With the piecework?" She stepped out into the yard. "Keeps me busy enough. Good thing, too. Every time work picks up, Mrs. McCordle raises the rent."

Ahmad followed after her, letting the door slam shut behind him. The two of them walked side by side down the lane. "She hasn't any right to. Not for that rathole."

Becky's room was little more than an attic garret. And its location had even less to recommend it. While some impoverished streets in the neighborhood still retained a certain dignity beneath their shabbiness, Lost Hope Yard was as bleak and desperate as its name suggested.

Standing in the shadow of chimney stacks, the street ahead was empty save for a ragged girl shepherding a herd of equally ragged children. Dirty faces peered up at Ahmad as they passed—curiosity warring with suspicion.

"What ho, Becky," the older girl said.

"What ho, Lizzy." Becky flashed the girl a smile before returning her attention to Ahmad. "A rathole you call it?"

"On its best day."

"It's good enough for some," she replied, indignant. "We can't all become lady's maids and manservants to the gentry."

"The Finchleys are hardly gentry. And I'm not their manservant any longer."

She shot him a concerned glance. "Out of a job, are you?"

"No. I'm finally doing what I've always wanted to do."

"Don't say you're making ladies' gowns?"

"I am."

Her face spread into a grin, revealing a missing tooth. "Lord, look at you! A proper dressmaker."

"It's why I've come to see you," he said. "I have a commission. One I can't hope to complete on time, not even with Mira's assistance."

She folded her arms. "Go on."

"I require another pair of hands. Someone who knows how to sew according to my requirements, and who can work with a variety of trimmings. Glass beads, swansdown, and so forth."

He'd sketched out a half dozen ideas last night after leaving Russell Square. Designs for ball gowns, and evening and day dresses. Garments that would showcase the wealth of Miss Maltravers's charms. That would make the fashionable elite stand up and take notice. That would make them see her as he did.

"Where's this work to take place?" Becky asked. "You haven't got a shop, have you?"

"Not of my own. Not yet. But I often work out of a tailor's shop in Conduit Street. If I can convince the proprietor to allow it, I propose that you, Mira, and I use the workroom there. Otherwise—"

"I could do the work in my room," she offered. "Like my piecework."

They walked past the drooping door of a lodging house. A blowsy woman with a drink-reddened face leaned out of the second-floor window to shout at one of her neighbors across the way.

"You could," Ahmad said. "Either that, or at my lodgings. They're larger than what you have here. *And* better ventilated."

"Where are you living at?" she asked.

"In King William Street."

"And Mira would be there?"

"Most days, yes."

"What about you?"

"I'll continue to work at the tailor's shop. It's more convenient. And that way, you wouldn't have to be on your own with me."

She gave a derisive snort. "You're the last man in the world I'd worry about trying anything. After what you did for me—"

"It's *your* reputation I'm concerned with."

"*My* reputation?" She laughed. "Only you would say so. To everyone else, I'm just a whore."

Ahmad frowned. He briefly took her arm to guide her around a puddle of filth in the road. "You're not a whore. You're a seamstress."

"It doesn't matter how I earn my living now. Once you've earned it on your back, you can't ever wash the stain away."

"Rubbish." He didn't like to hear her talk that way, as if there was no coming back from a life at Mrs. Pritchard's. No chance for a happy life once one had been ruined in the eyes of society.

His mother had believed that.

She'd been unable to face the scorn of her community. Had chosen to give up rather than live with the shame. As a result, Ahmad had been left in the care of his aunt. Growing up in their small village, he'd been surrounded by women who had been used and discarded by men. Strong women—survivors. Just like most of the women he'd met at Mrs. Pritchard's.

"Mark my words," Becky said. "I'll be in that room above Mrs. McCordle's 'til the day I die—and that's if I'm lucky. There's nothing else I'm fit for now. And don't say marriage. I shan't ever be getting married or having a family. No good man would have me."

"If they don't want you because of your past, then they aren't good men. Not as far as I'm concerned."

She pushed against him with her shoulder. "Fool. You've been among women like me too long. A proper English gent wouldn't be offering a job to the likes of me."

"I've never aspired to be a proper English gent." He looked down at her. "What do you say? Do you have the time to spare?"

She shrugged a shoulder. "I might do. Will you pay me the same as I make on my piecework?"

"I expect I'll pay you more."

"More?"

"With an added benefit."

She laughed. "As if the money ain't enough!"

"In addition to the money, you'll have the satisfaction of having helped to secure my future. All of our futures if things go according to plan."

"What's that mean?" she asked. "All of our futures?"

"If enough people see my designs—see them and want to order gowns of their own . . . By the end of the season, I'll be in a position to open my own shop."

Her weary eyes lit with understanding. "You'll be needing good seamstresses."

He smiled. "That I will."

❖

The next day, as dawn broke over the city, Evelyn entered the park on Hephaestus, Lewis not far behind her. Fog billowed over the rolling landscape, swirling about the shrubbery and clinging to the branches of the trees. It was cold and damp, but the grayness was fading quickly, burned away by shafts of brilliant sunlight piercing through the clouds above.

Evelyn glanced up at the brightening sky with a feeling of relief. There was no trace of the scattered thundershowers that had prevented her from riding the previous afternoon.

She prayed the rain wouldn't return. She couldn't afford to lose any more days of riding. Not when her entire plan depended on her making a showing during the fashionable hour.

Hephaestus pranced beneath her, chomping on his bit. "Easy, boy," she murmured, reaching to scratch his neck.

"He's full of himself this morning," Lewis remarked. "Take care he don't try nothing, what with a mare nearby."

"What mare?"

"That one," Lewis said.

Evelyn followed his gaze.

Across the grass, Stella Hobhouse came into view, perched atop an imposing silvery-white mare. Despite her size, the mare's features were refined, with an elegantly dished face and wide-set eyes. She arched her neck and tail in the manner of a highly strung Arabian.

Stella managed the spirited creature beautifully, her hands quiet and her seat impeccable, even as the mare danced and shied.

Evelyn couldn't help but be impressed. Keeping a firm grip on Hephaestus's reins, she rode toward her. "Good morning."

"Good morning," Stella said. "Are we the first ones here?"

"It appears that way." Evelyn held Hephaestus to a walk. "I hope Julia is equal to riding this morning."

"She will be." Stella brought her mare alongside Hephaestus. A gentle wind ruffled the veil on her riding hat. Made of black net, it all but covered her gray hair. "Anne went to fetch her herself."

"In that case," Evelyn said, "shall we go ahead to Rotten Row?"

"I think we'd better. Locket can't think straight until she's had a good gallop."

"Locket? Is that what you call her?" It seemed a sweet name for a sweetly beautiful horse. "Anne said she was a Thoroughbred cross."

Stella nodded. "She's by Stockwell."

Evelyn was familiar with the name. Stockwell was one of England's leading Thoroughbred sires. "And her dam?"

"A crossbreed mare. Half-Arab and half-who-knows-what. Apparently, the mare's owner thought it would result in a mount with greater endurance. Instead, all he got was a horse so skittish she was bound for the knackers when I found her."

Evelyn was incredulous. "But if Stockwell is her sire—"

"Quite so. She might still have been used as a broodmare. Unfortunately, she nearly killed her last rider, the silly beast. The son of an earl, too. He believed himself to be something of a horseman." Stella smiled wryly. "I'm afraid the experience rather bruised his tender masculine feelings."

"It's fortunate you came along."

"Exceedingly fortunate. Locket was being led to a stockyard outside my village when I first saw her. I bought her from the man on the spot. Quite irresponsible of him, really, selling her to a young lady. Or so my older brother claimed. He was fairly up in arms." Stella paused, explaining, "He's my guardian, and a very strict one. He only approves of my riding because he considers it a wholesome pursuit. One his congregation can't object to."

"Your brother is a clergyman?"

"He is. A very severe one." A troubled frown passed over Stella's face. It was gone in an instant, replaced by a look of droll humor. "You can imagine what my first season was like under his watchful eye."

"Was it very hard?"

"It was miserable. I was teased awfully over my gray hair. One gentleman even composed a rude verse about it. People were giggling at it for months."

"How dreadful."

"It was, frankly." Stella adjusted her reins. "The only good thing to come out of last year was meeting Anne and Julia. It was they who convinced me to come back for a second season. If not for them—and for Locket—I fear I'd lose my nerve."

"You ride her very well," Evelyn said as they entered Rotten Row.

"I *know* her very well. She wants tiring out, that's all. Her energy and mischief get the better of her otherwise." At that, Stella kicked Locket into a canter. "Shall we?"

Hephaestus snorted and shook his heavy black mane. He knew how to behave himself around mares, but he was still a stallion. His muscles were coiled tight and there was an added spring in his step. It wouldn't take much for him to bolt.

Evelyn made sure her seat was firm and her hands steady on the reins as she urged him forward, first into an extended canter and then into a thundering gallop.

Wind whipped at her face and whistled in her ears, the skirts of her dark green habit flying behind her. She felt as if she were riding in a horse race. The St. Leger or the Newmarket Stakes.

Hephaestus was bigger and more powerful, but Locket had a longer stride. Each time he surged ahead of her, she swiftly caught him up, her ears flattened and her velvet-gray nose outstretched as if seeking an imaginary finish line.

"She's determined no stallion will ever master her," Stella said, laughing, as she brought Locket back down to a canter. "Even a handsome devil like yours."

Evelyn kept pace with her, their two horses matching each other stride for stride. "It must be her racehorse blood."

"I daresay. She always wants to run—and to win. Pity she has a reputation for being so difficult. She might have had a brilliant career."

"Don't say you've already exhausted the pair of them?" a lady's voice called out.

It was Anne, riding toward them on Saffron. Julia trotted along next to her, mounted on her large black hunter. Two liveried grooms rode a distance behind them.

"Don't be absurd," Stella said. "I could run her all day and she'd still have another gallop in her."

"I'm sorry we're late," Julia said.

Anne made a face. "It was my fault. I was very nearly out the door when my mother waylaid me. She's been up all hours fretting. Apparently, she overheard Lady Heatherton saying that the annual Arundell ball has lost its luster."

A breeze ruffled the feathers on Julia's high-crowned riding hat. "It isn't true."

"Certainly not this year," Anne said. "Mama has spared no expense. She's even bringing in that fellow who writes the astrological almanac. He's going to tell fortunes. Mama's been giddy with anticipation over it. If not for Lady Heatherton—"

"I wouldn't bother listening to Lady Heatherton on any subject," Stella said. "She's a spiteful cat who uses her claws indiscriminately."

"True," Anne replied. "But she can be counted on to set the fashion. Her words carry weight, however spiteful."

"Who is Lady Heatherton?" Evelyn asked.

"The wife of Viscount Heatherton," Julia said. "She's very rich and very beautiful."

"And her husband is very old," Stella added.

Julia nodded. "*Very* old."

"Which is why she's constantly on the prowl." Anne adjusted the folds of her riding habit. "We'd all do well to steer clear of her this season. Age hasn't improved her disposition. If anything, it's made her more unpleasant."

Stella made a soft sound of disbelief. "*That* hardly seems possible."

"I feel sorry for her," Julia said.

"I'd as soon feel sorry for a cobra," Stella retorted.

"I expect she'll avoid the three of us," Anne said. "It's one benefit to having been colossal failures on the marriage mart." She shot a pointed look at Evelyn. "It's you she'll perceive as a threat."

"Me?" Evelyn echoed in surprise. "Why should she?"

"Lady Heatherton likes to sharpen her teeth on young ladies making their debut," Stella said. "And you're something new—something different."

Anne exchanged a glance with Evelyn. "Stella's right. Your ride Wednesday afternoon has already stirred people's interest."

Excitement flickered in Evelyn's breast. She knew she'd made a provoking picture as she'd passaged Hephaestus down Rotten Row. She'd seen people's reactions firsthand. But staring at a lady and being interested enough to actually talk about her were two different things.

"How do you know?" she asked.

"I have eyes," Anne said. "And not only that, Mr. Fillgrave dined with Mama yesterday evening. It was under the guise of business for the Antiquarian Society, but he made a point of asking me about my 'fetching equestrienne friend.'"

"Mr. Fillgrave." Evelyn's excitement dimmed as she recalled the gentleman with the profuse pair of side-whiskers. "The one with the Spanish mares?"

"The very same." Anne clucked to Saffron, urging him forward. "He's coming to the ball, you know."

"Is he the best we're to expect this season?" Stella asked.

Julia looked horrified at the thought. "I pray he's not!"

"I don't know," Anne said. "Prince Albert's death has cast a definite pall. I don't suppose as many people will travel to London this year, and if they do, it won't be until June or July."

"So long as they come," Evelyn said.

Julia guided Cossack up alongside Hephaestus. "Don't despair. There's always next season."

Evelyn's fingers tightened reflexively on her reins. "Not for me there isn't."

Sixteen

—◆◆—

L ater that day, Evelyn sat atop the wooden horse in the fitting room at Doyle and Heppenstall's as Mr. Malik pinned the hem of her second riding habit. Made of lustrous black superfine, it was fashioned with a basque bodice that extended down past her waist in the back. In the front, the bodice was cut short, with wide lapels, known as revers, that opened to reveal a stylish vest underneath. The full skirts were gored, the sleeves cut close to her arms, and at her throat, she sported a claret-colored silk necktie.

Evelyn was so taken with the fashionable ensemble she almost didn't notice Mr. Malik kneeling beneath her skirts.

Almost.

His head was bent as he worked, his black hair gleaming. He was in his shirtsleeves, just as he always was when he was pinning and marking her garments. It lent an intimacy to his actions that she felt to her core.

As if things weren't intimate enough.

Good lord. The last time she'd seen him she'd told him that she *liked* him. That she was attracted to him. And he'd said he felt the same.

Everything should be different between them now, shouldn't it? The two of them alone again in the fitting room, however briefly, while Agnes collected Evelyn's order from the glovemaker.

"You've finished this one quickly," she said.

"I had help," Mr. Malik replied without raising his head.

"Oh?"

"I've employed two seamstresses to assist me. I expect you'll meet them eventually."

"They're not here now?"

Mr. Malik shook his head. "Doyle refuses to allow women in the workroom." He inserted another pin to mark her hem. "Until he relents, Mira and Becky will be working out of my lodgings."

Mira and Becky.

Evelyn wondered if they were young and pretty. If they conversed with Mr. Malik on equal terms. She suspected they did. And now they were at his lodgings, privileged to see a side of him that Evelyn never would. "Do you live nearby?"

"I have rooms above a tea dealer's shop in King William Street. Pity we can't do your fittings there. I'll need an extra pair of hands for your ball gown."

"You could come to Russell Square," she suggested. "My uncle wouldn't object. Not when your dressmaking is to his benefit."

Mr. Malik flashed her a questioning look.

"The sooner I make a match, the sooner Uncle Harris will be free of me," she explained.

A frown darkened Mr. Malik's brow. He seemed to hesitate for an instant. "Very well. We might as well make the most of Mira's and Becky's services while we have them."

"You're not employing them permanently?"

"Mira is my cousin. She helps whenever she can."

His cousin.

Evelyn felt a distinct flicker of relief. "And Becky? Is she another relation of yours?"

"No. She's someone I knew long ago. A competent seamstress in need of work. Her employment depends on what happens this season. On how many more orders I receive."

"In other words," she said, "it depends on me."

His fingers stilled on her hem. He glanced up at her again. "Nervous?"

"A little." Her mouth curved in a bleak smile. "More than a little."

He stood. "I have something that might help." He exited the fitting room, only to return seconds later with yards of luminous creamy white silk draped over his arm.

Evelyn sat up taller. "Is that my ball gown?"

"Part of it." He brought it closer to her. The delicate pearl hue of the fabric was as softly seductive as moonlight.

She ran her fingers over it. Anne and Lady Arundell were likely wearing black to the ball, but Evelyn had no restrictions on the color of her own costume. She'd left the selection of it completely up to Mr. Malik.

"Do you see how it complements your complexion?" His head was bent close to hers as he showed the fabric to her, their shoulders almost touching. "It will look even better in the ballroom. Mira is embroidering the upper skirt with glass beads—just enough to catch the gaslight as you dance."

"Goodness," she murmured.

"Embroidery is her particular gift. No one at the ball will have anything to compare."

"It sounds as if it will be very grand. I pray I'm equal to it."

"You are," he said. "Trust me."

She lifted her gaze. Their eyes met and held.

A tremor of longing went through her.

They'd been facing each other in just such a way when her lips had brushed against his. Was he thinking of it, too? Remembering how it had felt to almost kiss her?

Or perhaps he didn't view it as a kiss. Perhaps, to a man of his vast experience, it was nothing more than an awkward fumble. The intimate equivalent of someone accidentally bumping into him in a crowd.

A lowering thought!

"I do trust you," she said. "I know you'll make me look my best. That doesn't stop me from worrying about every detail."

He nodded once, seeming to comprehend her fears. "When we meet for your next fitting, I'll bring my sketches. Will that help?"

Her shoulders relaxed. She hadn't realized how much tension she was carrying in them. "Yes. Thank you."

"Not at all." He moved to set the bolt of silk on the fitting room table. "I should have brought them today. You could have seen what I have in mind."

"That's all right. We only made our agreement two days ago. I don't expect you've had time yet to think of very many designs for me."

He looked at her from across the fitting room. There was a brooding glint in his dark eyes. The same expression that had often put her in mind of a fallen angel. "You're all I've been thinking of."

Evelyn's pulse beat heavy at her throat. He didn't mean it. Not in the way she imagined. It was about fashion, that was all. It was nothing personal. Certainly nothing romantic. Even so, she couldn't help but stare at him.

An ironic smile edged his lips. "I told you that you were my muse. You've been keeping me up at night." Returning to her, he smoothed the line of her sleeve. It might almost have been a caress. "The trouble won't be that I don't have enough ideas for you, it will be that I have too many."

Ahmad spent the next several days cutting and sewing Miss Maltravers's ball gown. There were early mornings and late nights. Moments when he feared his vision may have outpaced his skill. Never in his life had he made something that meant so much to so many people.

Hunched over his worktable, he unpicked stitches and reworked seams, constantly checking what he was creating against his design.

His rough sketches depicted a silk dress with a formidable set of skirts. The lower skirt was edged in box pleats, while the upper skirt was made of embroidered gauze, drawn up on both sides with ribbon bows. The same delicate gauze framed the dramatic neckline of the bodice. Cut low both at the front and back, it was made to expose a daring expanse of bare skin.

And not just anyone's bare skin.

Evelyn Maltravers was in his mind constantly as he worked, never leaving his thoughts for even a moment. This was her dress as much as it was his, all the way to the hidden pocket he placed at the seam of the skirts.

"You're exhausted," Mira said as he accompanied her back to Half Moon Street on the evening before Miss Maltravers's final fitting. Unlike Becky, who slipped away from his lodgings early in order to make it back to the East End before nightfall, Mira always waited for him to escort her home, no matter how late the hour.

"And you're not?" He cast her a distracted glance. She was seated across from him in the hired hackney cab. The carriage lamp shone a weak light over her face. "You have shadows under your eyes, *bahan*."

"It will be worth it in the end," she said. "I only wish I could be there to see her wear it."

"You'll see it tomorrow." He was expected at Russell Square in the morning. Mira was set to accompany him. As for Becky, she'd be turning her attentions to some of the other dresses Ahmad had in mind for Miss Maltravers.

There was work enough to keep the three of them busy for weeks. Sketches for day dresses, evening dresses, and carriage gowns. Colorful skirts and Garibaldi shirts. The fashionable garments of a young lady making her debut, all of them informed by his taste for elegant lines and sensual silhouettes, and by Evelyn Maltravers herself.

"It's not the same as seeing it in a ballroom," Mira said, "when the candles are lit and the gasoliers are glowing. She'll shine like a star when she's waltzing. Like a moonbeam."

Ahmad expected to feel a sense of satisfaction at the thought. It was his dress, after all. His design. But imagining Miss Maltravers waltzing in the arms of some nameless, faceless Englishman brought him no pleasure at all. Not even if she was shining as brilliantly as a star. Not even if she glowed so brightly that every lady in London came calling at Doyle and Heppenstall's, demanding that he make them a gown just like hers.

His timing was execrable. These feelings he was having for her. His muse. His auburn-haired equestrienne.

He wanted her for himself.

<hr/>

The next morning, he and Mira set out together for Russell Square, the pieces of Miss Maltravers's ball gown boxed up in their arms. On applying at the kitchen door, they were shown up the servants' stairs to the morning room. The drapes were open, and the fire alight.

Miss Maltravers stood by the window, sunlight gleaming in her hair. A smile suffused her face as she came forward to greet them, shining first in her eyes before spreading to the soft curve of her mouth. "Mr. Malik. How do you do?"

His chest tightened as she approached.

This damned physical reaction!

And they hadn't even touched yet.

He'd done nothing more than look at her. Nothing more than register the gentle sway of her skirts and the way an auburn curl had fallen loose from her chignon to brush the elegant curve of her cheek. His fingers itched to tuck it back again.

A lover's prerogative. Or that of a husband.

He reminded himself that he was neither, and that no amount of intimacy between them—no measuring and pinning of her garments—would make him so.

"Miss Maltravers." He bowed. "May I present my cousin, Mira?"

Smiling warmly, Miss Maltravers extended her hand.

Mira gave it a wary look before taking it.

"I'm so very pleased to meet you," Miss Maltravers said. "I understand you've been embroidering my ball gown."

"Yes, miss." Mira withdrew her hand.

"I can't wait to see it." She ushered them further inside. "My uncle's housekeeper, Mrs. Quick, has given this room over for my use. I hope it will suit our purposes?"

He set the boxes down on a tufted chair. There was a silk-printed trifold screen in the corner, and a low tapestry footstool nearby, just the right height for alterations. "It will."

Miss Maltravers summoned her lady's maid, Agnes, to help her change. Mira disappeared behind the screen with the two of them, and after much whispering and rustling of fabric, Miss Maltravers at last emerged in her ball gown.

It was a shimmering jewel of a dress, with a magnificent set of double skirts, gored to form a slight train behind. The bodice was cut close to her figure, shaped with darts and skillfully curved seams to hug her midriff and provide a sensual frame for the voluptuous swell of her breasts. Short ruffled sleeves left her arms bare, and a silk ribbon belt served to emphasize the narrowness of her waist.

Ahmad stepped back to look at her, solemn and silent, even as his heart threatened to beat out of his chest.

Good God.

She was all the fanciful, overly romantic things Mira had predicted she'd be. Starshine and moonbeams. A vision of luminous beauty. All creamy ivory skin and fiery auburn hair falling from its pins.

He swallowed hard.

Now wasn't the time to lose his focus. The dress was unfinished and needed his attention. As for the lady in the dress . . .

"I haven't a looking glass," Miss Maltravers said. "And judging by your faces I must be grateful I don't. I might cry otherwise, to see myself in something so beautiful."

"Oh, miss," Agnes murmured under her breath. "It's ever so fine."

Mira arranged the delicate gauze upper skirt. It was caught up with ribbons to reveal the box-pleated hem of the silk skirt below. Sunshine glinted over the delicate embroidery, making the glass beads twinkle like tiny stars. "You must take care not to rend the gauze when you reach through to use your pocket."

Miss Maltravers's eyes widened behind her spectacles. She looked down at her skirts. "A pocket? What pocket?"

"Here." Ahmad came to stand in front of her.

He was painfully conscious of her low neckline. Though he'd designed the bodice to be revealing, he hadn't fully prepared himself for the lushness of this particular view.

Heat crept up the back of his neck as he gently took her hand and drew it to the secret, on-seam pocket he'd made in the silk lower skirt. "It's for your spectacles. You said you didn't need them for distance. Now you can tuck them away when you're not using them."

There was an odd glisten in her eyes. The same unsettling sheen that had appeared when she'd first seen herself in one of his riding habits. "I never asked you to do this."

"You didn't have to ask. It's my job to take such things into account."

Her hand slid into her pocket and then out again. "You've solved a problem I didn't realize I had."

"I can solve it in all of your dresses if you like."

"Can you?"

"Of course."

"And it won't spoil your designs?"

"A dress can be functional as well as beautiful," he said. "And they're my designs. I can do what I like with them."

"This dress isn't functional," Agnes remarked, running a fingertip over the embroidery. "It's as light as gossamer, it is. Like fairy wings."

"Be careful where you put your fingers," Mira said sharply. "The gauze is very fine."

Ahmad exchanged a look with Miss Maltravers. Her hazel eyes were shining soft as velvet. Soft as the smile edging her lips.

And he knew in that moment she was more than pleased with what he'd made for her.

She was pleased with *him*.

Satisfaction came at last. Not because of the dress or how she looked in it. But because he'd been of use to her. He'd made her feel seen—taken care of.

It would be no small thing to take care of Evelyn Maltravers. To look after her as his own.

As quickly as the sugar-spun thought arose, it was dispelled by brutal reality.

He was in no position to become entangled with anyone, least of all a gently bred English lady. He had nothing to offer her. Not now. And even if he did—*when* he did—the two of them could still never hope to be anything more to each other than what they were in this moment: a man and a woman divided by wealth, rank, and the entire history of British colonial rule.

"Where would you like me to stand?" she asked.

"Here, if you please." Taking her hand, he helped her up onto the footstool. "Mira will work on your skirts while I see to the bodice. If that's agreeable?"

"Perfectly agreeable."

For the next half hour, Ahmad forced himself to think of nothing but silk, gauze, and trimmings. Of needles, pins, and invisible stitches. Anything but Miss Maltravers herself.

It was easier than it might have been in the fitting room at Doyle and Heppenstall's.

Here—with Mira assisting him and Agnes hovering nearby— there were no opportunities for any long looks or private conversations. No illusion of intimacy. Instead, Miss Maltravers had been relegated to the role of marble statue.

"Will it be ready in time?" she asked when another quarter of an hour had passed. Mira knelt on the floor below her, re-pinning one of the box pleats on the silk lower skirt.

"It will be." Ahmad secured a fold of sparkling gauze along her neckline with another pin. His knuckles brushed briefly against the silky-warm curve of her bosom. He tried to ignore it, just as he was trying to ignore every other necessary intimacy between them. "I'll have Becky deliver it tomorrow evening. She can stay to help you into it."

Agnes gave an audible sniff of protest at this encroachment on her territory.

"You'll want a seamstress," he said, "in case you require any last-minute alterations."

"Yes, of course." There was a wash of color over Miss Maltravers's bosom and throat—the beginnings of a blush creeping its way to her face. "I'd be glad of the help."

"The ball is at nine?" he asked.

Her answer was forestalled by the arrival of Mrs. Quick.

The housekeeper materialized in the doorway, seeming to appear all at once. An unsettling skill, and one that Ahmad observed was possessed by only the most efficient of servants.

"I beg your pardon, miss," she said. "You have a caller. A gentleman by the name of Mr. Stephen Connaught."

The name had a startling effect on Miss Maltravers.

Her face paled and her knees wobbled. For a single horrified second, it looked as though she might topple to the floor in a heap of silk and embroidered gauze.

Ahmad's arm shot around her waist to steady her. "Are you all right?"

She turned to him blindly, blinking behind her spectacles as if to refocus her vision. "What? Oh . . . yes. A little light-headed, that's all. I haven't eaten enough today."

Rubbish.

She'd been steady enough until the housekeeper had announced her visitor.

"You've gone white as parchment." He helped her down. "You had better sit."

Agnes hurried to her side. "Shall I fetch the smelling salts, miss?"

"I'm fine." Miss Maltravers met Ahmad's gaze. "Truly." Her hand closed briefly over his forearm in silent reassurance.

He understood her. She didn't want anyone to fuss. Neither did she wish to be treated as a swooning female.

Comprehending her feelings didn't make it any easier to let her go. He slid his arm free from her waist.

"Where is he, Mrs. Quick?" she asked.

"I've put him in the drawing room, miss," Mrs. Quick replied. "Shall I bring tea?"

"No need," Miss Maltravers said. "His visit won't be one of long duration."

The housekeeper withdrew.

Miss Maltravers turned to Agnes and Mira. "Will the two of you please help me out of this?" And then to Ahmad: "I'm afraid I must cut our fitting short today."

He inclined his head.

And he reminded himself that he was just her dressmaker, not her brother or her father.

Certainly not her lover.

He had no right to question her—and no privacy to do so, either.

As she disappeared behind the screen with Mira and Agnes, he could do nothing. Nothing except pace and worry and wonder.

Who in the hell was Stephen Connaught?

Seventeen

✦

In no time at all, Evelyn was back in her plain woolen day dress and ascending the stairs to the drawing room. She made a concerted effort to compose herself. She'd never been a swooning sort of female.

And besides, there was no reason to panic.

She'd known Stephen Connaught would pop his head up again eventually. Indeed, she'd been expecting him to reappear ever since their encounter in Rotten Row.

All that remained now was to determine how best to deal with him.

On entering the drawing room, she found him standing in front of the cold fireplace, one arm draped across the mantelpiece. His unbuttoned frock coat gaped open to reveal a garishly patterned, double-breasted waistcoat.

It was no doubt fashionable, but when compared to the quiet elegance of Mr. Malik's black three-piece suits, it made Stephen look the veriest peacock.

In truth, there was nothing about his appearance that measured up to that of the broodingly handsome habit-maker she'd left behind in the morning room.

Where Mr. Malik was dark, Stephen was fair. Where Mr. Malik

was tall and muscular, Stephen was shorter and thinner, with a boyish face that—rather than being chiseled from granite—appeared to have been shaped by a disinterested artist working from a mold used countless times before.

There was nothing special about him, she realized. Nothing unique or different.

And it was the differences in a person that gave rise to true beauty. Isn't that what Mr. Malik had told her?

Sameness was comfortable, but it didn't move the soul.

Looking at Stephen now, she felt profoundly unmoved. No butterflies or blushes. Nothing except irritation at the inconvenience he was posing to her.

"Miss Maltravers," he said, bowing.

Her expression tightened.

Once he had called her Evelyn. Apparently, she was no longer worthy of being addressed by her given name.

"Mr. Connaught." She returned his formality like for like. "What are you doing here?"

He motioned toward a chair. His manner was commanding, but at only four and twenty, he lacked the innate authority possessed by a man of Mr. Malik's years. "Will you not sit down?"

She didn't move. "What are you doing here?" she asked again.

His lips thinned. "I have news of your sister."

Evelyn drew back as if he'd struck her.

Of all the things he might have said, this was the last she expected.

She braced one hand on the back of the scroll-armed sofa. "You've heard something from Fenny and your brother?"

"Indeed." He straightened from the mantel. "I have reason to believe the two of them are in town."

Evelyn sank onto the sofa's damask-cushioned seat. Better that than have her knees give way beneath her. "In London?" She could scarcely credit it. "Have you seen them?"

"I have not." He sat down in the chair across from her. "Anthony wrote to my father, proposing a reconciliation. He didn't say where he and your sister were staying, only that they were here in London. He requested my father reply care of Hoare's Bank. And he's done so, but not to Anthony's satisfaction. That's why father has sent me. I'm to find my brother and talk some sense into him. Pray God he hasn't already returned to France."

Evelyn was stunned. "Is that where they've been all this time?"

"That surprises you?"

"We suspected they'd crossed the Channel, but we had no proof of it."

"Nor did we, until my brother wrote from Paris, begging permission to marry your sister. Naturally, my father refused out of hand."

"When did this happen?"

"Two years ago, or thereabouts."

She stared at him in disbelief. "Do you mean to say . . . your family has been in correspondence with them all this time?"

"With my brother, yes. Though one can hardly term it correspondence. He writes from various locations abroad when he requires money. My father wires it to him, care of whichever bank Anthony specifies—so long as Anthony hasn't married without his blessing."

A tide of outrage rose in Evelyn's breast. All these years of waiting and worrying, and all the while, the Connaughts had known where Fenny and Anthony were? "Why on earth did you never say anything?"

"We presumed you knew. It's why I've come. To tell you that if you receive word from your sister, you must let me know immediately."

It was all Evelyn could do to keep from raising her voice. "My family hasn't heard from Fenny in three years!"

His eyes narrowed. "Then why are you in London?"

"Not on Fenny's account."

"Why else? You've never shown any interest in visiting town. Only a sense of familial obligation could have prompted you to do so. If not your sister—"

"I had no idea where Fenny was. She's never written so much as a word to any of us."

The truth of her assertion seemed to finally sink into Stephen's brain.

"Well," he said at last, "if that's the case, then I can't say I'm shocked. Your sister was never the most sensible of girls."

"Is that all you have to say for yourself?" She could no longer hold her temper. "Good lord, Stephen, we didn't know if Fenny was alive or dead!"

"Your sister was in no danger. Women of her stripe always land on their feet. It's my brother who—"

"I *beg* your pardon?"

"Anthony is my father's heir. He can't marry without father's permission, and he comes into no money of his own until his next birthday. If your sister thinks to keep him on the hook for another year—"

"Your brother *ruined* my sister."

Stephen gave a derisive snort.

"And his actions have very nearly ruined my family. Why couldn't he leave Fenny alone?"

"Don't try to pin this on my brother."

"It's not all my sister's fault."

"Your sister was a *flirt*." He imbued the single, scathing word with a wealth of evil implication.

Evelyn shot up from the sofa.

Just because she and Aunt Nora criticized Fenny didn't mean she would countenance hearing criticism of her from anyone else.

"Is that why your father still objects to them marrying? Because Fenny smiled too much and laughed too much? Because she used to enjoy a bit of fun?"

Stephen rose from his seat. "Don't be absurd. He objects for the same reasons he's always objected."

"Because of my family's lack of fortune and pedigree?" Evelyn scorned to say it. "Those concerns can hardly matter in the face of such a scandal.

"You think not?" Stephen's eyes were hard as flint. "Do you suppose my father relishes the idea of the baronetcy one day falling to a grandchild who's half Maltravers? *My father*, who can trace our lineage back to the Tudors?"

She refrained from pointing out that Sir William had seemed to have no objections where his second son was concerned. If he had, she'd never have dared hope that Stephen might one day propose. But the rules had always been different where Anthony was concerned.

"There's nothing wrong with a grandchild who's half Maltravers," she said. "And shame on you for saying so."

Stephen was unrepentant. "Your sister's lack of breeding isn't my father's only objection."

"What else?"

"If you must know, he refuses to sanction my brother tying himself to a woman who's lived with a man outside the bounds of matrimony."

"The man she's living with *is* your brother!"

"A fine way for the future Lady Connaught to behave." Stephen straightened his waistcoat. "I'm determined to run the two of them to earth. With luck, I can persuade Anthony to come home. He's always listened more to me than to Father."

"And Fenny? If you find them, what will happen to her?"

"Your aunt must do with her what she will." His lips pursed in a moue of distaste. "I regret her conduct has tarnished your reputation, and that of your sisters. You are to be pitied."

Evelyn didn't want his pity. She didn't want anything from him save his silence. "Fenny's conduct is hers alone. My reputation—and that of my younger sisters—is unblemished. So long as you don't go about stirring the scandal up again."

"What can it matter now?"

"It matters. News of Fenny's disgrace could very well harm my prospects. I would ask that you exercise discretion when speaking of it."

"*Your* prospects?" His fair brows elevated nearly to his hairline. "Is that why you're here? Making a spectacle of yourself riding in the park?"

"I'm here for the season. What I do during that time is no business of yours, sir."

"Quite so. But if you'd like my advice—"

"I would not." Evelyn walked to the tasseled bellpull that hung near the fireplace and gave it a firm tug. "Now, unless you have any more intelligence to pass on, I will bid you good day."

Stephen glowered. He never could stomach being refused the last word. His mouth opened to say something, only to shut again at the prompt arrival of Mrs. Quick.

"Mr. Connaught is leaving," Evelyn informed the housekeeper.

"Very good, miss." Mrs. Quick gestured to the door. "This way, sir, if you please."

"Miss Maltravers." Stephen bowed stiffly. "If you chance to hear from your sister, you may send a message to me at Brown's Hotel."

Evelyn watched him leave, her outrage only increasing as he disappeared from view.

How dare he come here and spoil her plans!

He'd been happy enough to ignore her for three years—to pretend she didn't exist. What on earth did he mean by turning up now? Telling her that Fenny was here in London, of all places.

Evelyn didn't know what to do with this information.

The only thing she knew with any degree of certainty was that she must write to Aunt Nora immediately. She'd have to tell Uncle Harris, too. And even Lady Arundell. The last thing any of them wanted was Fenny springing up from out of nowhere and damaging Evelyn's prospects beyond all hope of recovery.

With that in mind, she descended the stairs, making her way toward Uncle Harris's study.

Her thoughts were in turmoil. As she passed the morning room, she almost didn't notice the man inside. She might have walked right by if he hadn't stepped into the doorway to hail her.

"Miss Maltravers?"

Her footsteps were arrested by the familiar deep voice. "Mr. Malik!" The sunlight from the morning room's windows shone at his back, temporarily dazzling her. "You and your cousin haven't been waiting for me?"

"I sent Mira back to King William Street with your ball gown."

Her brows knit. "But you're still here." She searched his face. With his broad shoulders spanning the door frame, Ahmad Malik was all at once more imposing—altogether more formidable—than any other gentleman of her acquaintance.

The effect he had on her was equally powerful.

Her temperature rose and her insides trembled.

Good gracious, only a short time ago she'd been holding her breath while he pinned gauze trimming to the low neckline of her bodice. Suppressing hot blushes every time his fingers brushed the swell of her bosom. If not for the brisk efficiency with which he worked—the stoic professionalism that allowed him to handle her without giving offense—she might very well have burst into flames.

No doubt she shouldn't think of such things outside of her fittings. But looking at him now, it was impossible not to.

"I was concerned about you," he said.

"You shouldn't have been."

"You nearly fainted."

She folded her arms, feeling a trifle defensive. "I told you, I was light-headed, that's all."

"From not eating."

"That's right." It wasn't entirely a lie. Lady Arundell's ball was tomorrow evening and nerves were just beginning to set in. Evelyn's stomach had been in knots all morning. She'd scarcely had anything at breakfast. "I've been so busy—"

"Who is Stephen Connaught?" he asked.

Her gaze jerked to his.

It was an impertinent question. One a tradesman had no business asking a lady customer.

But Mr. Malik was no longer strictly her habit-maker, nor even her dressmaker. He was her partner.

That had been their agreement, hadn't it?

If her reputation was at risk, then his was, too. He had a right to an explanation.

"He's someone from my village," she said. "It's rather complicated."

A smile curved Mr. Malik's mouth. There was no trace of humor in it. "Isn't everything?"

"Yes. Quite." She fell silent for a moment. "Do you truly want to know? I warn you, it's a long, unhappy story. And worse."

His brows lifted.

"There's a romance at the heart of it," she said.

Something flickered in his gaze. An emotion that was difficult to read. "*Your* romance?"

"No. Not mine." She and Stephen had never had a romance. She realized that now. "Would you like to accompany me for a walk in the garden? We can speak freely there. Though I daresay you haven't the time—*or* the inclination. I wouldn't blame you on either account."

"On the contrary," he said. "I'm completely at your service."

<hr />

Ahmad waited while Miss Maltravers dashed back upstairs to fetch her shawl. Upon returning, she led him into the back garden.

Accessed through a set of doors at the rear of the house, it was a thoroughly ramshackle scrap of acreage, in desperate need of a proper gardener. Trees grew at odd angles, and roses and shrubbery ran wild, encroaching over the path and hanging from the garden gates that opened out to the mews.

It was private, Ahmad allowed that much. And that was all that mattered to him.

Hands clasped at his back, he strolled along the uneven garden path at Evelyn Maltravers's side as she relayed to him the origins of her sister's disgrace.

"Near to my family's cottage in Combe Regis is a great estate called Babbington Heath. It's the property of Sir William Connaught—a baronet. His two sons, Anthony and Stephen, are practically the same age as my sister Fenny and myself. We all but grew up together."

"You were childhood friends?"

They walked beneath an arch of branches. Sunlight shone through the leaves to dapple Miss Maltravers's face.

"More than that," she said. "From an early age, Anthony and Fenny behaved as sweethearts. Nothing could come of it. Anthony was just a lad. But as the years passed, he continued to exhibit a preference for my sister. A boyhood fancy, my aunt Nora called it. She didn't believe it anything serious. Certainly nothing to prevent Fenny from making her come-out in London."

"This was three years ago?"

Miss Maltravers gave a grim nod. "We'd just come out of mourning for my father and it was past time Fenny made her debut. She was the most beautiful of all of us. The most beautiful of all the girls in Sussex. My family anticipated she'd make a grand marriage. Indeed, she appeared poised to do so. But she hadn't been in town above two months before Anthony followed after her."

Ahmad cast her a frowning glance. "To what end?"

"I've asked myself that question countless times. He wanted her, that much is plain. And he refused to give her up to another. But if Anthony marries without his father's consent, he's left all but a pauper. And his father will never consent to him marrying my sister."

"Why not?"

"Because Sir William is terribly high in the instep. The daughter of an untitled country gentleman isn't good enough for his heir. He's made that fact plain from the beginning. It's put Anthony in an impossible situation. He has no money of his own until he turns twenty-six—and only then if he's refrained from marrying without permission. So you see, he couldn't have wed Fenny even if he'd wanted to."

"He could have done," Ahmad said. "Quite easily."

She gave him a doubtful look. A breeze through the trees ruffled a curl of her hair. The same vexing auburn lock he'd longed to smooth back earlier. "And how would he have supported her?"

"He might have worked."

"He's a gentleman," she said.

Gentleman.

How Ahmad hated the word. It was imbued with more rank masculine privilege than nearly any other appellation he'd ever encountered.

Any, perhaps, save *Englishman.*

"And that excuses it?" he asked.

"No," she admitted, "but it explains it."

Not to his satisfaction.

He recognized the gentry's aversion to honest labor, but he didn't accept it.

There was nothing shameful about doing whatever was necessary to look after one's family. Those gentlemen who refused to do so— who shrank from work and instead chose to let their estates and their families fall into ruin—deserved his scorn, not his pity. And certainly not his understanding.

Miss Maltravers tightened her shawl around her shoulders. "One day, when I returned from riding, I found my aunt weeping over a letter she'd received from Fenny's chaperone in London. It said that Fenny had run off with Anthony, to the Continent, she feared. Aunt Nora spent the next several months writing to all of her friends in search of news. She pleaded with Sir William for his assistance." A frown passed over her face. "He was too angry to oblige her. Angry at Fenny. Angry at Aunt Nora. Even at me. Relations between our two families rapidly broke down."

"He blamed your family rather than his own son?"

"Oh yes. He claimed that Fenny had cast out lures to Anthony. That she'd beguiled and entrapped him, all with a view to one day becoming Lady Connaught. As if Fenny had the wits to enact such a plan. But Sir William could not be told."

"Where does Stephen Connaught come into this?"

She exhaled a heavy breath. "He was my riding companion and, I believed, my friend. But he soon came round to his father's way of thinking. He never spoke to me again."

"Until today?"

"Until today." She fell quiet for several seconds before continuing. "It seems that my sister and his brother were never truly lost. Indeed, the Connaughts have heard from Anthony several times these past years, and have sent him money care of various banks on the Continent. All while my own family has been kept in the dark. And now Stephen says that Fenny and Anthony are here in London."

"Married?"

"No," she said. "It doesn't appear so. For if Anthony had wed my sister, Sir William would never have agreed to send money for his support."

"They might have married in secret," Ahmad suggested.

"Perhaps." She didn't sound as if she had much faith in the possibility. "Stephen intends to find them. To convince his brother to abandon my sister and return home. In doing so, I fear he may remind society of what it has so far forgot."

"And hurt your prospects in the process." A surge of bitterness took Ahmad off his guard. "Is it so important to you that you marry a fortune?"

She stopped on the path. "Is *that* what you think?"

"I'm not judging you. It's the whole purpose of the season, is it not? For ladies like you."

Twin spots of color rose in her cheeks as she faced him. "Ladies like me," she repeated in a voice of perilous calm.

"Gentlewomen," he said. "Englishwomen."

"You don't approve of either, it seems."

He shrugged. "I told you, I make no judgments."

"But you do. I can see that you do. You can't possibly understand—"

"Because I'm not an Englishman."

"Because you're a man! You don't know what it's like to be a woman. To have all of the burdens of life, but none of the power. My sisters and I depended on Fenny to marry well, so that we could have our chance at happiness and security. Whom do you think my sisters are depending on now?"

Ahmad stared down at her in dawning realization. "You're doing this for them."

"Of course I am." She resumed walking.

He caught up with her. "Making a sacrifice of yourself."

"That implies I'm selfless. Which I'm not. I have my own interests to look after."

"Such as?"

"Seeing that I'm clothed and fed. My uncle's generosity has limits. And my aunt isn't made of money. At some point, her funds will run out, and we girls will have to shift for ourselves. What shall we do then if we haven't any husbands?"

"You could seek employment." He expected her to scoff at the prospect. She was a lady, after all.

Miss Maltravers didn't bat an eye. "Even if we did—if *I* did—it wouldn't be enough. Not for my purposes."

The overgrown path ahead of them came to an end at the garden gate.

She stopped there, resting her hand on the latch. Seeming to come to a decision, she opened the gate and stepped out. "Come and see for yourself."

He followed after her to the mews and into the stable where her uncle housed his carriage horses. It was empty at the moment, no grooms or stable boys at hand to witness Ahmad in company with Miss Maltravers. No one about except the horses—and one horse in particular.

She approached a loose box in the corner. Her giant blood bay stallion stood inside, munching a serving of sweetly scented clover hay. He greeted her with a soft nicker, swinging his head over the door. Sticks of hay hung from his mouth.

"Here," she murmured, taking his muzzle in her hands. She pressed a kiss to his nose. "This is my reason."

Ahmad came to stand beside her. Before now, he'd only seen her stallion at a distance, in the park when she was riding. The great bay beast had looked formidable enough under saddle. Here, he looked even larger and more powerful. He was easily over sixteen hands in height, with a broad, muscular build, a Roman nose, and an abundant black mane and tail. His liquid brown eyes gleamed with intelligence.

"May I?" Ahmad asked.

"Of course. He's quite gentle."

Reaching out, Ahmad ran a hand over the stallion's glossy neck. It was as solid as velvet-covered marble.

"My father was an adventurer," Miss Maltravers said. "After my mother's death, he spent the rest of his days traveling. It was during his time in Southern Spain that he bought Hephaestus. He intended to train him in the Spanish fashion, and then send him home to England to be put out to stud." She scratched the stallion's long-whiskered chin. "Instead, my father died in Spain after a prolonged fever. His groom brought Hephaestus back to England with the rest of his effects."

"I'm sorry."

"Don't be. I didn't know my father half as well as I should, and he didn't know me at all—save one small detail. He knew I was a rider. On his deathbed, he scrawled a note, leaving Hephaestus to me. 'For my daughter, Evie,' it said, 'God willing she can make something of him.'"

Evie.

Ahmad added the affectionate diminutive to the private list of things he'd already learned about Evelyn Maltravers. It was a list that was growing by the minute, each new fact registered and cataloged for him to revisit during his long hours in the workroom, or at night when he lay awake, restless and wanting, in his bed. "You trained him yourself?"

"Not right away. Hephaestus was just a two-year-old at the time. Still a baby. He and I spent the whole of that first year getting acquainted. After that, yes, I did train him, with Lewis's help. He knows the basics of the haute école from traveling with my father, and assisted me on the ground with long lines. But it was I who broke Hephaestus to the saddle and bridle. I who taught him how to listen to my seat and legs and hands. He's only ever known one rider. If I were forced to sell him—"

"Your family has suggested it?"

"No. They wouldn't dream of it. But how selfish would I be not to consider it myself? Saddle horses are expensive, and Hephaestus is more valuable still. Were I a man, I'd do as my father wished and offer Hephaestus at stud. But I'm not a man. I'm an unmarried lady in a house full of other unmarried young ladies. Such a scheme would make us notorious."

"Have you no other alternative?"

"None. Not when all of my family knows that Hephaestus could be sold for a hefty sum." She dropped her hand from the stallion's muzzle. "We haven't sunk that far yet, thank God. But there will come a time when I'll no longer be able to justify keeping him. Not with the rest of us sliding rapidly toward ruin. When that day arrives, it will break my heart."

"Does riding mean so much to you?"

"It's means *everything* to me. It's the only thing I'm truly good at. The only thing I love. I can't envision my life without him in it." Moving away from the loose box, she removed her spectacles, giving Ahmad her back. "Perhaps you feel the same about dressmaking."

Ahmad didn't know that he did.

He was passionate about his designs, certainly. He felt a sense of fulfillment in his work, and in seeing his creations worn by someone like Miss Maltravers. But he'd learned from a young age that there was very little in a man's life he couldn't do without.

"It doesn't compare," he said. "The fabric I work with isn't a living creature. I wouldn't be heartbroken if it was taken from me."

She wiped at her face. "But you'd be disappointed to lose an opportunity for your designs, wouldn't you? It would distress you if your plans all came to nothing?"

He couldn't tell if she was dashing away tears or merely clearing the stable dust from her eyes. He feared the former.

His chest constricted.

It was all he could do not to go to her. Not to grasp her arms and compel her to face him.

But he didn't go to her.

He remained where he was, his emotions under ruthless control. "Naturally I'd be disappointed."

"Which is why my sister's arrival in town is as much a danger to you as to me." She settled her spectacles back on her face. "After the Arundell ball, your reputation will be inextricably linked with mine. And if I'm disgraced—"

"You won't be," he said. "You've done nothing to merit censure."

She turned back to him. "When has that ever mattered? A woman is easily tainted by association."

"What do you propose to do about it?"

"I'll tell you what I'm *not* going to do. I'm not going to sit around, waiting for the roof to come crashing down on my head." Arms folded, she walked back to the loose box, the hem of her full skirts brushing the hay-strewn floor. "If I could discover them first, I might be able to persuade Fenny to go away from London before she does any further harm." A notch worked its way between her brows. "But how am I to find her? It seems impossible."

"It's not impossible. Not if one knows their way around the city."

"But I don't. And I haven't the means to hire an inquiry agent."

Ahmad rapidly weighed the various possible outcomes of the situation. None of them would be to the good. Not unless someone intervened on Miss Maltravers's behalf.

It took him but a moment longer to come to a decision.

"You don't need to hire anyone to find your sister," he said. "I'll do it."

She gazed up at him in surprise. "You?"

"Why not?" He'd helped locate the missing Earl of Castleton, hadn't he? And that search had covered a continent thirteen times the size of England. London was nothing in comparison.

She slowly shook her head. "I'm obliged to you for the offer, but . . . I can't accept it. Not in good conscience. You're already overwhelmed with making my gowns. I can't ask you to go haring off after my sister. For one thing, you haven't the time."

Ahmad privately conceded her point. "Very well. If not me, then someone else. I know of a solicitor who might help."

"I can't afford—"

"He wouldn't ask for payment." At least, Ahmad didn't think so. "Not for something that requires so little work. And this would be the work of a moment for a man like him."

Finchley wasn't motivated by money. He trafficked in information. A whispered word into the ear of one of his old contacts and an entire network of informants would spring into action.

"You know this person well?" she asked.

"He and his wife took me on when I left Mrs. Pritchard's establishment. Mira works for them still. They're good people, if a trifle eccentric."

A fleeting smile briefly softened her mouth. "I can't object to eccentricity."

"Do you object generally?"

"No. Not if you think it wise to approach this man."

He nodded once. "Leave it with me."

Some of the tension eased from her face. "Thank you."

"I haven't done anything yet."

"You have." Her voice was husky with sincerity. "You've offered to help me. And . . . you've listened to me. It's for that I'm grateful. For everything you've . . ."

Her words trailed away as he finally did what he'd been wanting to do all morning.

He brushed the stray curl from her cheek, tucking it gently behind the delicate curve of her ear. The action was as impulsive as the question that followed it. "May I call you Evelyn?"

Her eyes were riveted to his. She looked adorably flustered. "If you like."

His pulse thrummed.

Evelyn.

He hadn't intended to ask for the privilege. But he'd wanted to.

By God, how he'd wanted to.

He forced himself to drop his hand from her face. His fingers had lingered long enough. Any longer and he wouldn't be able to pass it off as a meaningless gesture. A simple adjustment to her coiffure—the sort of thing a dressmaker might do.

Any longer and it would be a caress. A touch that spoke more of tenderness than of fashion.

He'd no sooner withdrawn from her than her horse swung his head back over the door, coming between them as surely as any chaperone.

Evelyn cradled the great beast's nose, giving him an absent pet. "What shall I call you?"

"Anything you want," Ahmad said.

"I wish to use your Christian name."

His mouth hitched. "I can't vouch for its Christianness."

"You know what I mean. I wish—that is, I should very much like to call you Ahmad. If you don't object to—"

"I don't object."

She looked into his eyes, her gaze uncertain. He had the sense that she was as much out to sea as he was himself. "It doesn't have to mean anything," she said softly.

"No," he agreed. And yet . . .

He very much feared that it did.

Eighteen

—✦✦—

"Ahmad. Come in and have a seat." Tom Finchley stood from behind the barrier of his desk to welcome Ahmad into his office in Fleet Street. The walls behind him were lined with bookcases filled with neat rows of leather-bound law books, locked securely behind glass.

Ahmad availed himself of one of the upholstered chairs opposite the desk.

It wasn't his first time facing Finchley in this manner.

He'd been here before, in the aftermath of the incident at Mrs. Pritchard's. Then, Ahmad had been confronting the very real prospect of transportation. Finchley had saved him from such a fate. And then he'd saved him again by offering him employment as a manservant to his future wife, Jenny Holloway.

"That will be all, Poole," Finchley said, dismissing the weedy-looking clerk who had escorted Ahmad upstairs.

Bowing, the young man withdrew, shutting the door after him.

Finchley resumed his seat. His cravat and waistcoat were rumpled, and his hair was mussed as if he'd been pushing his fingers through it. He was plainly in the midst of one of his cases. Teetering stacks of paper littered the surface of his desk in company with heaps of rolled documents tied with ribbon. "I'd offer you tea, but I'm afraid I can spare you no more than ten minutes. I'm due in court."

"This won't take long."

"It's not about Mira, I hope?"

Ahmad frowned. "Why would it be?"

"She's seemed as though she's preoccupied with something."

"She *is* preoccupied. I've tasked her with a great deal of needle-work."

"And you're sure that's all? There isn't something else that's troubling her?"

Ahmad didn't think so.

Then again, he scarcely saw Mira from day to day. While she worked in King William Street with Becky, he was toiling from dawn until dusk in the back room of Doyle and Heppenstall's.

Was Mira still feeling isolated and alone? As if she didn't belong? Even now, with dresses to sew and Becky to keep her company while sewing them?

"Has she said something?" he asked.

"No, no. It's just a feeling I had." Finchley seemed to dismiss the concern as quickly as he mentioned it. "No doubt I'm reading her wrong. I've been somewhat distracted myself."

"The work is good for her," Ahmad said. "It gives her purpose."

"I don't dispute it. But this isn't about Mira, you said."

"No. It's about another lady." Ahmad swiftly explained his predicament. Or rather, Evelyn's predicament.

Finchley listened in silence, his brow creased and his keen blue eyes thoughtful.

"I hoped you might drop a word in the ear of one of your informants," Ahmad said when he'd finished. "If you still employ any of them."

Finchley's mouth hitched briefly. "*If.*"

The single word spoke volumes.

These past years, happily married and comfortable in his new-found domesticity, Finchley no longer worked on behalf of the more sinister elements of society. Instead, he directed his talents to worthier causes.

But knowledge was still power.

Ahmad couldn't imagine Finchley being eager to give up his means of acquiring it.

"You'll do it, then?" he asked.

"Of course," Finchley said. "But one thing puzzles me."

Ahmad regarded his former employer from across the desk. He knew that look, and he didn't like it. "Which is?"

"You told me that Miss Maltravers was just a young lady from Sussex. A customer who commissioned riding habits from you in the style you made for Catherine Walters."

"She is."

"And that's all?"

Ahmad didn't reply.

"She clearly means more to you than that," Finchley said. "If you're exerting yourself on her behalf—"

"Exerting myself. Is that what I'm doing? This from the man who followed the lady he cared for across France and Egypt, by ships, trains, and *dak* cart, all the way to the farthest reaches of India?"

A smile glimmered in Finchley's eyes. "It's like that, is it?"

Ahmad wished he could deny it. But he couldn't. Not if he was honest with Finchley—and with himself. "Yes," he admitted. "I suppose it is."

Evelyn stood staring into the shining surface of the full-length pier glass in her bedroom. Her reflection shone back at her in its entirety, from the top of her gracefully rolled coiffure to the toes of her silk dancing slippers.

It was the first time she'd seen herself dressed in all of her evening finery. The first time she'd fully appreciated the splendor of Ahmad's design.

She'd spent most of the day in the clutches of a relentless anxiety, imagining the many things that could go wrong tonight.

Foolish, really.

It was only a ball, not the Battle of Waterloo. She'd consoled herself that, though it was the first she'd been invited to, it wouldn't be the last.

Not unless she made a complete fool of herself.

The prospect seemed less likely now.

With its daring bodice, voluminous silk skirts, and overlay of sparkling embroidered gauze, the ball gown Ahmad had made for her was lovelier than any garment Evelyn had ever seen. More than any she'd ever been privileged to wear, certainly.

But it wasn't only how it looked that made her catch her breath. It was how she felt when wearing it. As if her body wasn't something to be squeezed, pinched, and pushed into a desirable shape, but something desirable in and of itself.

She felt beautiful. Powerful. Just as she did when she was cantering down Rotten Row in one of Ahmad's riding habits.

"How does he do it?" she wondered aloud.

"Don't rightly know, miss." Becky Rawlins adjusted the ball gown's silk belt at Evelyn's waist. She was a young woman with a world-weary quality that lent a hardness to her features. Her open thread case sat on the end of the bed behind her, alongside the now empty dress box. "Mr. Malik's got a rare gift."

"He has at that." Evelyn lifted a hand to smooth her hair. The rolls at the sides of her face were drawn back to culminate in an even larger roll at her nape. Agnes had secured it with jeweled combs, metal hairpins, and half an atomizerful of bandoline. "And you and Mira, too. You both helped."

"Aye. Mira's got talent. But me—" Becky made a scoffing noise. "I'm just an ordinary needlewoman. I wouldn't know how to do more than plain mending if Mr. Malik hadn't taught me."

Evelyn gave her a curious look. "He taught you how to sew dresses?"

"He did." Becky busied herself arranging the ball gown's upper skirt. She didn't appear disposed to chatter.

Her reluctance only piqued Evelyn's interest. "Have you known him long?"

"Since I first came to London. We worked at the same establishment for a time. He were always good to me."

Evelyn waited for her to elaborate, but Becky didn't volunteer anything more. Evelyn suspected she knew why. There was only one establishment where Ahmad had mentioned working. A house of ill repute, he'd said. A brothel.

Was Becky one of the women who had worked there with him? One in whom Ahmad had a particular interest?

Evelyn felt a sickening flicker of jealousy. "The two of you aren't . . . ?"

"Oh no." Becky laughed. "Not that all the girls wouldn't have jumped at the chance. He were the handsomest man we ever saw. I wouldn't have shrunk from him myself, but he were always more like a brother to me. Besides, Mr. Malik don't go in for that kind of thing."

"He didn't have anyone special?"

"Special?" Becky scrunched her nose. "Like a sweetheart, you mean?"

Evelyn nodded. She was ashamed of how keenly she wanted to know. She had no right to be jealous—or curious. Ahmad didn't belong to her. No matter that his lips had brushed against hers. That he'd touched her and held her and seen her in her knickers. It was artistic proximity, nothing more. The purview of a dressmaker. Just as it had been when he'd smoothed a lock of hair from her face.

"Not that I ever heard," Becky said.

"No?"

Becky shook her head. "He's a rare one, he is. Keeps himself to himself. But he respects women. He were always looking out for us. If not for him—" She stopped herself, seeming to realize she'd said too much.

"What?" Evelyn asked, meeting Becky's eyes in the glass.

Becky straightened the gauze trim on Evelyn's bodice. "There were a gent once. A right big brute. He lost his temper with me over a trifle. Might have killed me if Mr. Malik hadn't stepped in."

Evelyn listened with bated breath. "This happened at the place where you worked?"

A look of embarrassment briefly crossed Becky's face. "A sort of tavern, it were. Not the finest place you ever heard of, but Mr. Malik made it safe enough. If he hadn't broke that bloke's shoulder, he might be there still. Strange how things happen. I thought he'd be sent away for sure. Now he's making gowns for the likes of you."

"Yes. Very strange." Evelyn wasn't sure she entirely understood. Ahmad had rescued Becky from a violent man? He'd tossed the man out of the brothel and broken the fellow's shoulder in the process? "Forgive me . . . Do you mean to say Mr. Malik was in some kind of trouble for hurting this man?"

"I should say so. The gent were a baronet, weren't he? Wouldn't be satisfied 'til Mr. Malik was punished." Becky made one final adjustment to the ball gown. "There, that should do for you. And very fine, too." Satisfied, she went to her thread case, and after returning her needle and thimble, closed the lid with a snap. "Will you be needing anything else, miss?"

Yes, Evelyn wanted to say. *Tell me more about him. Tell me everything.*

But when Becky turned around again, her expression was shuttered.

Evelyn didn't have to be a mind reader to know that their conversation had come to an end.

⟡

Uncle Harris's carriage traveled at a sedate pace toward Lady Arundell's town house in Grosvenor Square. The wheels clattered over an uneven patch of road, jostling Evelyn in her seat. The hour was approaching nine o'clock. It was cold and damp; the starless sky black as pitch. One might expect people to be nestled warm in their houses.

But not in London.

And not during the season.

Here, gleaming coaches crowded the gaslit streets, the clip-clop of hooves echoing in company with the shouts of hansom cab drivers and the laughter of merrymakers strolling through the fog.

"You'll have a fine time tonight," Uncle Harris pronounced from his place beside Evelyn in the carriage. He was dressed in evening black, with an ebony cane in his hand and a jaunty satin-lined cape thrown over his shoulders. "Her ladyship has a seer in for the evening. A celebrated fellow, calls himself Zadkiel. Uses a crystal ball rumored to have been passed down from an Egyptian magician."

Evelyn recalled the fortune-teller that Anne had mentioned. "This isn't the gentleman who writes the astrological almanac?"

"The very same."

"Is he going to perform parlor tricks for us?"

Uncle Harris shot her a narrow look. "Crystallomancy is no trick, my girl. Not when practiced by someone proficient in the arts."

"And this Zadkiel gentleman is a proficient?"

Her uncle's expression turned somber. "The best there is. He's the chap who predicted the death of the Prince Consort."

She hadn't realized Prince Albert's death had been predicted by anyone, let alone a famous crystal gazer. "When did this happen?"

"Last year. Had people taken the man seriously, the Consort's death may have been prevented. Alas, these mysteries are greatly mis-understood."

She could imagine. It sounded like so much silliness to her. The same sort of aristocratic absurdity as Lady Arundell's familiar spirit. It was on the tip of her tongue to say as much, but Evelyn had no desire to be offensive. Settling back in her seat, she refrained from further comment.

Her uncle had hardly spoken to her at all since her arrival, and never on the topic of spiritualism. She didn't wish to quarrel with him. Goodness knew they'd have reason enough to argue once she informed him that Fenny might be in London.

She hadn't done so yet, nor had she written to Aunt Nora. After her discussion with Ahmad, Evelyn had thought it best to wait.

It felt natural to put her trust in him.

And a little strange, too.

She'd never had someone she could rely on absolutely. Someone to shoulder a burden for her. To solve a problem that needed solving. In the past, it had always come down to her own ingenuity.

But not this time.

Ahmad had said to leave it with him. And that's precisely what she was going to do.

He'd promised to get back to her soon. Until then, there was no point in upsetting her entire family. Not when there was a chance that she could solve the problem without their intervention.

The carriage came to a rolling halt. Drawing back the velvet curtain, Evelyn peered out the window. The magnificent stone facade of the Arundell's town house lay ahead. A long line of carriages was backed up from the door.

Uncle Harris craned his neck. "What's the delay?"

"The other guests, I assume. We might have to wait awhile."

"Nonsense." He tapped the head of his cane against the ceiling, summoning the footman. "We'll get out here."

It was a wise decision. The pair of them arrived at the front door of the town house before most of the other guests had disembarked from their carriages.

Lady Arundell was waiting to receive them in the marble-tiled entry hall. She was garbed in a black velvet gown, trimmed with heavy black lace at the bosom and sleeves. A large jet brooch encircled by a frame of plaited hair was pinned at her breast.

Anne stood behind her mother, partially obscured. Her glistening golden locks were caught up in a net of heavy black silk. It harmonized with her black silk ball gown, the only adornment of which was a subdued trim of thick black cord. It framed the modest décolletage, short sleeves, and hem. A dour dress, really. One more suited to a middle-aged lady in mourning.

"Fielding," Lady Arundell said. "Miss Maltravers." She pointed her black lace fan at Evelyn, motioning for her to turn around. "Come, girl. Let me have a look at you."

Evelyn slipped out of her cloak and passed it to a waiting footman. She executed a quick pirouette for Lady Arundell. The glow from the gasolier hanging above caught the glass beading on her upper skirt, making the intricate embroidery sparkle and flash.

Anne's eyes widened. "My word, you don't exaggerate, do you."

"What's that?" Lady Arundell demanded of her daughter.

"Miss Maltravers said that her dressmaker was better than Mr. Worth. It seems she was telling the truth."

Lady Arundell withdrew her lorgnette from her sleeve. She subjected Evelyn to a thorough inspection. "Extraordinary."

"It's by a new designer in Conduit Street," Evelyn said. "Mr. Ahmad Malik."

"An Indian? Hmm. I can't vouch for the color. Rather gay, don't you think, given the circumstances? But your dressmaker seems to have talent." She snapped her lorgnette closed. "God's truth, Fielding, I scarcely recognized the girl. There may be hope for her yet."

It was as close to an outright compliment as Evelyn expected she'd ever receive from her ladyship.

"Quite, quite," Uncle Harris acknowledged absently. "Has Zadkiel arrived?"

"A full hour ago," Lady Arundell said. "He's set up a table in the library. He requires complete silence to make contact."

As Uncle Harris and Lady Arundell fell into conversation, Anne slid her arm through Evelyn's and quietly guided her away from the busy entry hall.

"Aren't you needed to greet the rest of the guests?" Evelyn asked.

"Not any longer. Not now your uncle is here. He and Mama will see to it." Anne paused. "She's right, you know. You look exceedingly grand. You'll be the belle of the ball, I wager."

Evelyn felt a flush of self-consciousness. "Do you truly like it?"

"Like it? I'm positively green with envy." Anne led her down a wide corridor. Liveried footmen rushed by, hurrying to tend to the new arrivals. "Most ladies are wearing color tonight, but Mama has made me keep to my blacks as a sign of respect for Prince Albert. A black ball gown, I tell you. I look like some ancient nobleman's young widow."

"No, indeed," Evelyn objected. "The color flatters you."

"And there's so much of it. Black bodice, black skirts, black trimmings. If you can call these trimmings." Anne cast another glance at Evelyn's gown. "I wonder what your Mr. Malik could do, limited to only black fabric and a few scraps of black embellishment?"

Evelyn answered without hesitation. "He could do magic."

"Do you think so?"

"I know he can. He'd be honored to make a dress for you."

"I would have to convince Mama," Anne said. "She might allow it, so long as he adhered to her requirements."

"Black?"

"And more black. Mama claims that mourning clothes help to keep her close to the spirit world. And she's sporting all of her very best memento mori tonight—a jet brooch made with a piece of my father's hair, an onyx locket containing a postmortem portrait of my deceased aunt, and a black-lacquered hairpin, said to be formed from the finger bone of a sixteenth-century seer."

Evelyn recoiled. "A human bone?"

"Oh yes. It's all ridiculously gruesome. But Mama is committed to enacting her rituals."

"How committed?" Evelyn wondered. "Will you be permitted to dance?"

They passed through first one luxurious antechamber and then another. Wall sconces lined the way, gas jets illuminating lush, silk-papered walls covered edge to edge in heavily framed oil paintings of sleek horses, palatial country houses, and golden-haired Deveril ancestors.

"For any other lady dressed as I am, dancing would be considered dangerously eccentric," Anne said. "Indeed, were we truly in mourning, we'd cancel the ball altogether. But that's a bridge too far for my mother. After all, what's the fun of a performance without an audience?"

Evelyn detected an odd undercurrent in Anne's airy tone. "Does it make things very difficult for you?"

"That depends on your view of difficulty. I'm not poor, and I'm not suffering from illness or infirmity." Anne's mouth tilted in a smile. "I confess, my situation is rather trying at times, but one must have a sense of humor about these things."

"I expect you're right."

"I am right. And besides, I'm not alone. Stella, Julia, and I have all faced obstacles during our seasons." Anne pulled Evelyn along. "Let us go and find them."

The other ladies weren't in the next room they passed through. And they weren't in the rapidly filling ballroom, with its painted domed ceiling, trio of massive chandeliers, and orchestra members tuning their instruments on the dais.

Evelyn caught the barest glimpse of grandiosity—of ladies in shimmering full-skirted gowns and gentlemen in black-and-white eveningwear—before Anne drew her to the closed doors of a room at the back of the house.

"My late father's study," she said.

It was there they found Stella and Julia, seated beside each other on a leather-upholstered sofa. Julia was drinking from a cut-crystal glass held in her gloved hands.

"Don't sip it like a hummingbird," Stella advised. "Drink it all down in one go, like the vile medicine it is."

"Oh, if I must." Squeezing her eyes shut, Julia tipped back the glass and downed the remaining contents in one noisy gulp. She'd no sooner swallowed than she began coughing in great racking heaves. "Ugh! It's *awful*."

"What in the world are you doing?" Anne strode purposefully into the room, Evelyn following after her. "That's not my mother's scotch?"

"It's whatever was in that decanter on the drinks table," Stella said. "An amber-gold liquid. I suppose it may have been scotch."

"Does scotch burn like fire?" Julia asked, her eyes watering.

"All spirits do." Anne plucked the glass from Julia's hands and returned it to the mahogany table that held the silver drinks tray. "I thought you'd gone to the ballroom?"

"We *were* in the ballroom," Stella said.

Julia coughed again. "It's my fault. One minute I was standing with the other wallflowers, and the next there was a weight in my chest so heavy I couldn't breathe."

"Oh dear." Anne's expression softened. "You became anxious, did you?"

"It was worse this time," Julia said.

"Much worse," Stella agreed. "A gentleman approached her."

Anne gave Julia an alert look. "What gentleman?"

"He was tall and stern, with black hair and a weatherworn countenance." Julia moistened her lips. "A soldier, I think. He had the most terrible scar across his face."

"Captain Blunt?" Anne's mouth nearly fell open.

"He was in company with Lord Ridgeway," Stella said. "His lordship was attempting to make an introduction. He hadn't finished yet when Julia had her episode."

"Captain Blunt?" Anne repeated. "Hero of the Crimea?"

Evelyn had heard the name from Anne before. "Not the one with the brood of illegitimate children?"

"*And* the haunted estate in Yorkshire," Stella said. "His reputation precedes him. Everyone knows he's seeking a drudge he can take north with him."

Julia looked rather dazed. "He walked right up to me."

"What did he say?" Anne asked.

"I don't know," Julia replied numbly. "There was a roaring in my ears and I couldn't breathe. I thought I might faint."

Anne winced. "You didn't, did you?"

"Indeed, she did not." Stella rubbed Julia's arm in reassurance. "She walked out of the ballroom with her head held high. And she's much better now, aren't you, dear?"

Julia groaned. "You should have seen how he looked at me. He was disgusted, I know it."

"Soldiers don't approve of swooning ladies," Anne said. "Not unless the soldier is young and gallant."

"And Captain Blunt is neither." Stella rose from her seat beside Julia, allowing Anne to take her place.

"He caught you by surprise, that's all," Anne said. "I wonder what he was playing at?"

"Perhaps he was merely expressing an interest?" Evelyn suggested. "It wouldn't be surprising. You look very beautiful this evening."

It was the truth. Julia was wearing a cornflower crepe ball gown. Overflounced and overembellished, it was nothing to compare with Ahmad's design, but the color caught the brilliance of Julia's blue eyes, making them sparkle like polished sapphires.

"You do," Anne concurred. "But Captain Blunt, of all people? I can't like it."

"Nor I," Stella said. "He was with Lord Ridgeway, after all. And we know what Ridgeway's like."

Evelyn stood back from them, feeling out of her element.

Her three new friends had years of history with the gentlemen in question. If not by experience, then by reputation. They knew who was a fiend and who was a rake. Who was likely to abuse his horses, and who was in need of a drudge to look after his haunted house full of by-blows.

Meanwhile, all Evelyn knew was that, among those fiends, rakes, and libertines, she had to find a husband. And, as much as she wanted to remain with her new friends, she wasn't going to find one hiding in here.

Stella exchanged a glance with her. It appeared her thoughts were tending in the same direction. "We should return to the ballroom."

"Oh, I can't!" Julia cried. "Not yet."

"You and Evie can go," Anne said to Stella. "I'll sit with Julia awhile until she regains her courage."

Stella accompanied Evelyn out of the room, drawing the door shut behind them. "You must understand," she said, as they made their way back down the corridor, "Julia's shyness isn't only in her head. It manifests in her body like a sickness. A crowded ballroom is akin to torture for her."

"It was brave of her to come tonight."

"She hasn't any choice. Her parents expect her to exert herself this season. The only excuse they'll accept is one of ill health. It's why she takes to her bed when things become too much for her."

"The way she did last week?"

Stella nodded. "Pity she can't do so with more regularity. But pleading illness in the Wychwood household comes with dangers of its own. Her parents subscribe to all manner of quackery. Even worse, they're strong believers in bloodletting. It's the price Julia pays every time she pretends to be unwell."

A shiver traced down Evelyn's spine. She couldn't abide bloodletting. The village doctor in Combe Regis knew better than to even suggest it to her. "It sounds awful."

"It *is* awful. And quite a shame, really. Julia is so sweet and good-natured, but more and more, her condition defeats her. This crippling shyness and anxiety. Anne says it will take a special gentleman to break the spell."

A special gentleman.

The phrase swirled around in Evelyn's head, conjuring an image, not of some illusive unknown, but of a man who was very much recognizable. A man with black hair and broad shoulders, standing close—breathlessly close—as he drew his cloth measuring tape snugly around her midriff.

Stella gave a soft chuckle. "Yes, I know. Isn't that what we're all searching for?"

Evelyn couldn't summon the words to reply.

The truth of the matter struck her like a lightning bolt, stopping her breath and stilling her pulse. She was brought up short by the stark, inconvenient reality of it.

Good lord.

She didn't need to search for a special gentleman.

She'd already found him.

Nineteen

❖

$\mathscr{E}$velyn had no immediate opportunity to reflect on her epiphany about Ahmad Malik. On entering the ballroom, she was commandeered by Lady Arundell, who introduced her to first one aged aristocrat and then another.

Invitations to dance promptly followed.

It took all of Evelyn's faculties to remember the names of the gentlemen scribbled onto her dance card, and to recall the steps as those same gentlemen led her out onto the polished wood floor.

Anne had predicted Evelyn would be the belle of the ball, and as she joined hands to promenade with her fourth partner of the evening, Evelyn began to feel as though it might be true.

It was her dress. The way it sparkled in the candlelight, the gauze-trimmed bodice clinging to her bosom, and the double skirts floating about her legs. It made her look as voluptuous as a courtesan and as rich as a duchess. A fragrant hothouse flower just waiting to be plucked.

"Are all the young ladies in your village as charming as you are, Miss Maltravers?" Lord Trent asked as he moved with her down the center line in a spirited country dance. "You make me regret having never traveled to Sussex."

It was hollow banter, the same sort all the gentlemen had peppered her with this evening. Evelyn had no skill at bantering back. She didn't dare try. It would only encourage Lord Trent. And she had no wish to do so. Despite his efforts at flirtation, he was old enough to be her father.

"You're teasing me, my lord," she said.

"Do I look like I'm teasing you, my dear?"

Evelyn had no idea. She'd taken her spectacles off when she entered the ballroom, slipping them into the secret pocket of her gown. It had made it easier to see across the distance. To admire the painted ceiling and the long mirrored panels on walls that stood two stories high. Now, however, nose to nose with her dancing partner, she regretted having removed them. Lord Trent's face was a blur.

Not so her friends.

Stella and Julia were plainly visible, seated together at the opposite end of the ballroom. The wallflower section, Julia had called it. Anne wasn't with them. She was dancing with an ancient white-haired gentleman, further up the line from Evelyn.

The violin section of the orchestra swelled to a crescendo as the country dance came to an end.

Lord Trent released her and sketched a bow.

Evelyn responded with a curtsy. Upon rising, she retrieved her spectacles from her pocket and settled them back on her nose. His lordship's face shifted into focus.

Offering his arm, he escorted Evelyn back to where Uncle Harris and Lady Arundell stood at the edge of the floor. They were in company with several other ladies and gentlemen, all talking animatedly about the boy medium in Birmingham who had received otherworldly messages from Prince Albert.

"He's reported to possess a strong spiritual force," Lady Arundell was saying. "As powerful a natural gift as Zadkiel himself."

"No, no," Uncle Harris objected. "I won't believe it. An untutored boy can't compare with a trained crystallomancer."

Lord Trent eagerly joined in the conversation. "Is it true the boy's representatives are in communication with Her Majesty?"

People gasped and murmured, whispering among themselves with renewed vigor.

It was during all this that strong fingers closed over Evelyn's arm. She turned with a start, coming face-to-face with a tall, immaculately dressed stranger.

But not a stranger.

It was Mr. Hartford, the roguish gentleman Anne had pointed out in Hyde Park. The one who had addressed her with such cheerful mockery.

Evelyn hadn't realized he was in attendance.

"I beg your pardon, Miss Maltravers," he said. "This is my dance, I believe."

In other circumstances, she might have been flattered. Mr. Hartford cut a dashing figure. He was healthy and handsome, standing head and shoulders over most of the men in the ballroom.

He was also dangerous.

Evelyn would have recognized that even without Anne's warning. There was an air of calculation about him. A gleam in his eyes that spoke more of strategy than impulse.

If he was asking her to dance, it wasn't on a whim.

"I think not, sir." She opened the dance card that fluttered from a silken cord at her wrist, turning the page to the penciled entry for the waltz. "This dance belongs to Mr. Babcock."

"And Mr. Babcock has generously ceded it to me." Mr. Hartford extended his hand to her. "Shall we?"

Evelyn cast a swift glance over the ballroom. Mr. Babcock was standing a distance away—an older man, like all of the others she'd danced with thus far. He gave her an apologetic shrug.

Her temper flared. "If this is some kind of a prank—"

"Ah. Lady Anne has told you about me, I see. A word of advice. Where I'm concerned, you'd be wise to take everything she says with a quarry of salt." His hand remained outstretched. "It's just a waltz, ma'am, I promise you. No pranks, tricks, or otherwise."

The orchestra struck up the first notes. It was Strauss. A bold, heart-stirring composition. The music filled the air.

And Evelyn was still standing there. Not dancing, but facing off with a gentleman in what must appear to be an argument.

People were beginning to stare.

She reluctantly took Mr. Hartford's hand, permitting him to guide her the rest of the way onto the floor. She could no longer see where Anne was. Her absence provoked a distinct twinge of discomfort in Evelyn's midsection. She didn't wish to be thought disloyal.

Mr. Hartford slid an arm about her waist, leading her into the first turn.

A quiver of uncertainty nearly made her stumble.

The last time she'd waltzed had been in the safety of her family's cottage. Her little sisters had partnered her in turn while Aunt Nora pounded out music on the schoolroom pianoforte. Each of them helping, in their own way, to prepare Evelyn for the rigors of the season.

They were the reason she was doing this. All of it, from the new coiffure and corset to the elegantly designed riding habits and gowns. It was for her sisters that she must marry a wealthy husband. Her own feelings were supposed to come second. *Everything* was supposed to come second. And yet . . .

And yet, she couldn't stop thinking about Ahmad.

She wondered what it would be like to dance with him. To be held in his arms.

"Relax," Mr. Hartford said. "Don't overthink it."

She clutched at his shoulder for balance.

"Don't look down. Look at me."

She *was* looking at him. Or trying to anyway. Other couples whirled by them, dipping and turning to the music. It seemed that everyone was on the floor. There was scarcely room to navigate among all the spinning skirts billowing out over wide wire crinolines.

"It's very crowded," Evelyn remarked. "Perhaps we should—"

"Ignore the crowd." Mr. Hartford expertly waltzed her through the crush. "Let me lead you."

It went against her every instinct to obey him. Then again, he clearly knew what he was doing. She gradually relaxed, allowing him to guide her around the floor.

People watched them from the edge of the ballroom as they passed, gentlemen staring and ladies whispering behind their fans.

Evelyn's confidence rose.

She felt a glimmer of what she'd experienced when she'd made her debut in Rotten Row. That awesome sense of feminine power.

"That's it," Mr. Hartford said. "It's not so difficult, is it?"

"Not difficult, no. I'm merely out of practice."

"Have you no dancing in your village?"

"Of course we have. Combe Regis isn't Timbuktu."

"Quite so. But it's all your admirers can mention. Your humble origins."

"I don't know why," she said.

"Don't you? A small village lends an air of freshness to a pretty girl. Not so much to an unattractive one."

She gave him a suspicious glance. "Is this one of your compliments that doubles as an insult?"

His large hand tightened on her waist. "Another warning from Lady Anne?"

She didn't deny it.

He swept her into a final turn as the music swelled to a close. "Tell her something for me, will you?"

"What?" she asked, a little breathless.

His head bent to hers. "Tell her that no plant can flourish in the shadow of another."

She frowned up at him, wishing she could make out his expression. "I don't know if *that's* entirely true."

"Just tell her," he said. The music ceased. He promptly released her, offering a curt bow. "Miss Maltravers."

"Mr. Hartford." By the time she rose from her curtsy, he was gone in the crowd. She stared at his retreating back in bewilderment.

What a peculiar man!

Briefly lowering her spectacles so she could see over the top of her lenses, she set off across the ballroom in search of her friends. She wasn't engaged for the next set and could use a glass of lemonade. More than that, she was anxious to find Anne.

It wasn't difficult. In her black ball gown, Anne stood out like a sore thumb.

Evelyn caught up with her just as she was exiting the ballroom. "Where are you off to?"

Anne stopped in the corridor. "The ladies' retiring room. Lord Dawlish trod on my skirts. The trim needs to be reattached."

Evelyn glanced down. The black cord along Anne's hemline had been torn loose. "What a nuisance."

"Yes, it is," Anne said.

Silence stretched between them.

"Mr. Hartford asked me to waltz," Evelyn blurted out.

Anne's face was a studied blank. "So I saw."

"He wasn't on my dance card. He simply shouldered his way in. There was no way to refuse him without making a scene."

"Why should you refuse him?"

"Because you think him a swine." Evelyn paused before adding, "He asked me to give you a message."

Anne's sherry-colored eyes betrayed a flicker of interest. "Oh?"

"He said I'm to tell you that no plant can flourish in the shadow of another. Whatever that means."

Anne's expression tightened. "Did he, indeed." The interest in her gaze briefly gave way to glittering anger. She resumed walking. "I was right. He *is* a swine."

Evelyn followed. She waited for her friend to explain, but Anne said nothing more on the subject. "I saw you dancing earlier. Who—"

"The Earl of Gresham. He desperately wants a wife. Or rather, he desperately wants an heir. He's well past fifty."

"He didn't look very promising," Evelyn said.

"It could have been worse. Gresham narrowly cut out Mr. Fillgrave for the country dance."

"Mr. Fillgrave is here?"

"Unfortunately. He's already danced with Stella, the poor thing. I'd almost rather Hartford had partnered her than that condescending windbag."

"Why does your mother invite such men?" Evelyn asked.

"Mama invites everyone who expresses an interest in spiritualism. So long as they're rich and she believes them respectable. And if they're eligible—"

"Anne!" Lady Arundell's booming voice rang out behind them.

Anne jerked to an instant halt. She and Evelyn turned to find Lady Arundell bearing down on them like a black-masted ship in full sail.

"Where are you going?" she demanded.

"To the retiring room," Anne said. "My skirt needs mending."

"Never mind your skirt, girl. Zadkiel is ready for my reading. You must accompany me. Dmitri insists that family ties help to anchor the spirits."

"But—"

"I'll hear no objections." Lady Arundell glanced at Evelyn. "You, too, Miss Maltravers. Your uncle has been summoned as well. Your presence as a blood relation will assist in directing Zadkiel's energies." She continued purposefully down the hall. "At once, girls. Don't dawdle."

Anne obediently trailed after her mother.

Evelyn accompanied her. She chanced a look at her friend. "Is this—"

"A charade? Yes." Anne dropped her voice. "Zadkiel is no mystic.

He's an aged ex–navy lieutenant named Morrison who's somehow managed to convince all of London that he communes with the spirits. I daresay he believes it himself. No doubt he'll put on quite a good show for us."

"My uncle says he predicted the death of Prince Albert," Evelyn whispered back.

"He did." Anne looked distinctly unimpressed. "He also said that in January we'd suffer 'a great conflagration.' And that, last month, Lord Palmerston would receive 'a sudden blow.' Neither has happened."

They followed Lady Arundell into the library—a vast, wood-paneled room that smelled faintly of leather polish and pipe tobacco. Walls lined with bookcases loomed in the shadows, punctuated by heavily curtained windows. The gaslight was turned low, casting an ominous glow over the dark mahogany furnishings and rich Aubusson carpets that covered the floor.

A circular, black, baize-covered table had been placed at the end of the room. Two gentlemen were seated at it, their faces illuminated by a single taper candle.

One was Uncle Harris.

The other was an older man in a plain suit and neatly tied cravat. He was easily in his middle sixties, clean-shaven, with gray hair receding from a stern brow.

Zadkiel, Evelyn presumed.

He had a small crystal ball in front of him, less than five inches in diameter.

"Lady Arundell," he said, rising along with Uncle Harris.

Her ladyship motioned the gentlemen back to their chairs. "I've brought my daughter, Anne. And this is Fielding's niece, Miss Maltravers."

Zadkiel bowed before resuming his seat. "If you will take your place, my lady. And you, Miss Maltravers. I ask you all to remove your gloves."

Evelyn took the vacant chair next to Uncle Harris. Lady Arundell and Anne sat down beside each other. The four of them stripped off their evening gloves.

"Hands on the table, if you please," Zadkiel said. "Palms down, fingers open."

Evelyn and the others obeyed. The candle flame flickered and snapped, as if caught by an invisible wind.

Zadkiel looked at them each in turn, his manner portentous. "I sense there are doubters among us."

Lady Arundell harrumphed. "The young have no concept of life's mysteries."

"It is to be expected," Zadkiel said. "And yet, quite strange in the circumstances. I'm sensing a powerful energy among us."

"Eh?" Uncle Harris tilted forward in his seat. "It's not coming from my niece, is it?"

"It's Anne," Lady Arundell said. "It must be. Dmitri has always said that my daughter has potential."

"It is not Lady Anne." Zadkiel's gaze swung slowly to Evelyn. "It's emanating from you, ma'am."

Evelyn blinked. "Me? But . . . I'm not a believer."

"Spirits aren't fairies, to be animated by belief. They're souls who have passed beyond our understanding." Zadkiel's voice took on a hypnotic quality. He stared into his crystal ball. Its surface was flawed in several places, fracturing the light from the candle flame.

Anne was right. It *was* quite a good show. Though Evelyn knew there was nothing real about the endeavor, her heart nonetheless gave a kick of excitement when Zadkiel at last pronounced: "I see a man."

Lady Arundell sucked in a breath. "Is it the Prince Consort?"

Zadkiel's brow furrowed. "The clouds have not yet parted. His face is unclear. But the spirits are out in force tonight. We shall soon make contact." He bent his head to his crystal ball. "Ah! He begins to emerge. A guide, sent to lead us."

Uncle Harris strained to see for himself. "Can we speak with him?"

"Yes. We must talk to the fellow." Lady Arundell searched the surface of the crystal. "Let us question him."

"He's fading," Zadkiel said. "Please, my lady, I must have quiet."

Lady Arundell sat back in her chair with a look of chagrin.

Evelyn exchanged a glance with Anne.

Anne's mouth quirked.

"Quiet," Zadkiel said again. "All of you. He's attempting to reach out to us—to grant us a vision. We must make the conditions hospitable for him."

Lady Arundell and Uncle Harris obeyed. Along with Anne and Evelyn, they passed the next half hour in taut silence, gazing fixedly into the crystal ball, waiting for something—anything—to happen.

Evelyn's eyes grew weary. She almost began to imagine she saw movement in the surface of the crystal. A shadow of a figure. It was, indeed, a man. A handsome, dark-haired gentleman. The longer she looked the clearer he became.

She wasn't the only one who was imagining things.

"I see the remnants of a castle," Lady Arundell said. "A crumbling structure of red brick."

Uncle Harris nodded fervently. "I see it, too."

Anne stared into the crystal ball, frowning. She glanced at Evelyn, brows lifted in question.

Evelyn gave a subtle shake of her head. She didn't see any redbrick castle, crumbling or otherwise.

"There's a gatehouse," Uncle Harris exclaimed.

"And an ivy-covered tower," Lady Arundell said.

Uncle Harris's expression was rapt. "Can that be a moat?"

"It is, it is." A look of elation came over Lady Arundell's face. "Upon my word . . . it's Kirby Castle!"

Uncle Harris nearly leapt from his chair. "By Jove, you're right!"

"Is this castle significant to you, madam?" Zadkiel asked. "Sir?"

"Not of itself," Lady Arundell replied. "But given recent events in the spiritual realm, it's location must be critical."

"Kirby Castle is in Leicestershire," Uncle Harris said. "The boy medium was born in Leicestershire. It's a sign, surely."

Lady Arundell's formidable bosom expanded with satisfaction. "The boy's messages from the Prince Consort are legitimate. They must be." Her gaze came to rest on Evelyn. "And it was your energy that enabled us to see it."

"Mine?" Evelyn drew back. "I really don't think—"

"Her ladyship is right," Zadkiel said. "I feel it quite strongly. You have a gift."

Uncle Harris fixed Evelyn with an appraising stare. It was as if he was seeing her for the first time. "Well," he murmured. "This changes everything."

Twenty

—✦—

Zadkiel's pronouncement about Evelyn had a profound and immediate effect. It not only elevated her in her uncle's estimation, but in the rest of occult society as well. By Monday afternoon, she'd received nearly a dozen invitations to various functions, all of them related in some way to astrology, crystallomancy, and the spirit realm.

"There are worse things to be known for than having positive psychic energy," Anne said when she called at Russell Square later that day in company with Julia and Stella.

Seated in the drawing room, Evelyn poured them each a cup of tea. "It's certainly provoked my uncle to take an interest in me."

"But that's good, isn't it?" Stella asked.

Evelyn wasn't so sure. "I wouldn't mind the extra attention so much if what Zadkiel said was true. Instead, I feel like the veriest fraud."

"Why?" Anne wondered. "You aren't the one who claimed to have a gift."

"No, indeed." Evelyn passed her friends their tea.

"Perhaps it *is* true," Julia said from her seat on the scroll-armed sofa. "The human mind is full of mysteries."

Stella nodded her agreement, adding, "You might have powers you haven't accessed yet."

"I don't," Evelyn assured them.

Anne sipped her tea. "It hardly matters. Merely by suggesting it, Zadkiel has all but guaranteed you'll receive invitations to the best entertainments."

"And callers," Stella predicted. "Lots of callers."

She was right on that score.

Not long after Evelyn's friends took their leave, Lady Blackstone arrived. It was she who was hosting the ball at Cremorne Gardens next month. After her came Mrs. Holt-Simmons and her sister—two black-clad young widows with a strong belief in crystallomancy.

They'd no sooner gone than Mrs. Quick brought in the visiting card of Evelyn's next caller. A name was engraved upon it in elegant script.

Mildred Lacey, Viscountess Heatherton

Evelyn suppressed a flare of unease. Unlike her previous callers, whom she'd met at the Arundell ball, she had no prior acquaintance with Lady Heatherton. She knew nothing of her save what her friends had told her.

"Show her in, Mrs. Quick," she said at length. And then she waited, expecting the very worst.

But if her ladyship had claws, they were—for the moment—well sheathed.

She swept into the drawing room, a smile fixed on her perfect porcelain face. She was an extraordinarily beautiful woman—slim and delicate, her corseted waist cinched to mere inches. "Miss Mal-travers," she said, inclining her head in a regal bow.

Evelyn rose to return the greeting. "Lady Heatherton."

"You'll think me impertinent calling on you in this fashion. We haven't been properly introduced. I am, however, acquainted with your uncle."

Evelyn offered her a seat. "He's not here, I'm afraid."

"No matter. It's you I wanted to see." Sitting down on the sofa, Lady Heatherton occupied herself with arranging her skirts. It was no small task. Her silk afternoon dress was a marvel of tassels, fringe, flounces, and ribbon bows. A testament to her wealth. Only someone of means could afford so many elaborate trimmings. "I've come to assuage my curiosity."

Evelyn resumed her seat. "Oh?"

Lady Heatherton's mouth curved in a smile that didn't quite meet her eyes. "After the report in this morning's paper, I simply had to look at you for myself."

Evelyn had seen the brief write-up in the society page this morning. It hadn't referenced her by name. On the contrary, it had been framed as yet another report on the Pretty Horsebreakers:

> Rumor has it that our titian-haired horsebreaker is no common incognita, but a marriage-minded miss from the humble home counties. She was observed at Lady A——'s ball on Friday, and your correspondent can report that she was as ravishing off her stallion as on it.

Evelyn had been pleased to be mentioned, however obliquely, but the whole of it had failed to excite any deeper emotion. It was difficult to muster enthusiasm for a plan that no longer matched up with the desires of her heart.

"You must be thrilled to be garnering such praise so early in your season," Lady Heatherton said. "A girl like you, fresh up from the country."

"I don't know about thrilled," Evelyn replied, smiling. She was glad, at least, that the write-up might do Ahmad's business some good. The more acclaim she received, the more attention was brought to his designs.

If he became a great success, then perhaps . . .

Perhaps she might have a future with him.

A mercenary thought. And one she shouldn't be indulging.

She didn't even know if he felt the same way about her. Granted, he'd admitted to being inspired by her. To looking on her as a muse for his designs. But her own feelings had advanced beyond the realm of fashion. She'd recognized that at the ball.

"Come now," Lady Heatherton replied. "You can't pretend you don't crave notoriety. I've had no less than three friends mention the gown you wore to Lady Arundell's ball on Friday. According to them, it was a triumph."

"All the credit goes to my dressmaker."

"An Indian, people are saying."

Evelyn's smile dimmed. "I don't know what that signifies."

"As a point of interest, I find it fascinating." There was an edge to Lady Heatherton's voice, as sharp as a freshly stropped razor. "Who is this person?"

Evelyn felt a strange reluctance to tell her. For all her beauty, Lady Heatherton had a calculating, serpent-like quality to her expression that made her seem very much the cobra Stella had compared her to.

"You do know his name?" her ladyship pressed.

"Mr. Malik," Evelyn answered grudgingly. "He works out of Doyle and Heppenstall's in Conduit Street."

Lady Heatherton's eyes glittered. "He's made more than your ball gown." It wasn't a question.

"He's made several of my dresses," Evelyn admitted.

"And this dress you're wearing now? I suppose he made this for you, too?"

"Indeed, he did." Evelyn wore a day dress of deep golden-oak alpaca. It lacked the lush adornment of Lady Heatherton's dress, but it was impeccably fitted, the rich color flattering Evelyn's hair and complexion to an extraordinary degree. "He's very talented."

"And very handsome, I understand."

Evelyn didn't reply.

"A young lady can't be too careful," Lady Heatherton said. "To permit a man to make her dresses—"

"Mr. Worth is a man."

"An Englishman, trained in the French style. Where has Mr. Malik trained?"

Evelyn knew exactly where he'd learned his trade, but she had no intention of sharing that information with anyone, Lady Heatherton least of all. "I haven't inquired," she said. "It hardly seems relevant when a dressmaker exhibits such inherent skill."

Lady Heatherton's smile was as brittle as glass. "You are very young, aren't you. Or is it only that you're countrified? Girls from small villages know little of our London ways. You must permit me to advise you." Her gaze was as rigid as her smile. "Take care where you give your custom. A lady's reputation is a fragile commodity."

The fine hairs rose at the back of Evelyn's neck. Lady Heatherton's words sounded alarmingly close to a threat.

Did she know about Fenny? About the scandal that had erupted three years ago?

Surely her ladyship could have no interest in such things?

No. She was only sharpening her claws, as Stella had said. Asserting her dominance in some twisted effort to dampen Evelyn's nascent success.

Evelyn resolved to ignore it. When riding, one never prospered by stopping to focus on a horse's naughtiness. The only way one ironed out disobedience and intractability was to keep moving forward. Things invariably worked themselves out along the way.

"My reputation is in good order," she replied. "But I thank you for the advice."

Ahmad dropped the stack of dress boxes down onto the morning room sofa. The drapes were open and the fire lit. Sunshine streamed through the high windows, suspending dust motes in shafts of light. It was half past ten. Most ladies of fashion were still abed. Were it anyone else, he would have delayed his call.

But Evelyn Maltravers wasn't a typical London lady.

She was a country lass with country habits. He knew that much about her. She sometimes rode at dawn with her new equestrienne friends—Lady Arundell's daughter and two other young ladies, Miss Wychwood and Miss Hobhouse.

Ahmad had seen them in Hyde Park this morning. He'd been out walking at sunrise to clear his head, and there they were, the four of them talking and laughing as they trotted past.

Evelyn had been wearing her newest habit. The one of mink-brown Venetian cloth he'd made for her. It was a sumptuous love letter of a garment. Every stitch and seam contrived with sensual intention. Indeed, the rich fabric embraced her with all of the care and reverence he longed to embrace her with himself.

Worsted wool was a poor substitute for his arms. But in Miss Maltravers's case, it would have to do.

The alternative was nothing at all.

Soon, she'd meet someone and marry. It was inevitable. She was already garnering attention. He'd twice seen her mentioned in the society pages, the second time only yesterday. It had been in regard to her appearance at the Arundell ball.

Reading the report, Ahmad had felt a gnawing jealousy. He would have liked to have seen her at the ball for himself. He would have liked to have danced with her.

"Good morning." Miss Maltravers entered the room as though his thoughts had conjured her. Her hair was rolled back in an invisible net, her spectacles settled on her nose. She wore a day dress of pearl-colored poplin.

One of his designs.

It was trimmed with Solferino velvet, sewn in banded waves along the edge of the full skirt and up one side of it to form a bright purplish-pink velvet bow at the edge of her waist.

A sweetly feminine gown, with none of the fussiness of a typically fashionable day dress. There was no unnecessary bulk. No profusion of flounces, fringe, or ribbons. There was only *her*. The soft lines and the shape of her, honored rather than obscured.

"When Mrs. Quick told me you were here, I feared I'd forgotten one of our appointments," she said, smiling warmly. "We haven't one this morning, have we?"

"Not today, no."

Her attention was diverted by the stack of dress boxes. "Is this my latest order?"

"Part of it. The skirts and blouses, and several more of the day dresses."

Moving to the sofa, she lifted the lid from the first box. "How quickly you've finished them."

"Some designs are less time-consuming than others." Less still with Mira's and Becky's assistance, and with the aid of the sewing machine at Doyle and Heppenstall's. "The garments with more intricate trimmings and embroidery will take longer."

She gave him a curious glance. "You don't usually deliver them yourself."

No, he didn't. He hadn't the time. Not when there was so much work to be done.

But today was different.

"I needed an excuse to see you," he admitted.

She stilled. "You've had news of my sister?"

"I have. Finchley sent a note round less than an hour ago." Ahmad withdrew the folded sheet of paper from the inner pocket of his coat.

She returned to his side in an anxious rustle of petticoats and poplin skirts. "What does it say?"

He handed it to her. "It's an address near the docks. An inn."

"And Fenny's there? With Anthony?"

"It appears so."

Evelyn pressed a hand to her midriff. "Oh, thank God." She exhaled an unsteady breath. "I didn't dare believe it." Unfolding the paper, she read the address. "I must go to her."

Ahmad steeled himself. This was the tricky part. The moment he must overstep his role. She wasn't going to like it.

But there was nothing for it.

"You can't go there," he said.

"Of course I can," she replied. "I must."

"You can't," he said again. "It's not a safe place for you."

"Fenny's there. Surely it's safe enough."

"I can't speak for your sister's security, but I know that part of London. It isn't safe for a lady—not even in daylight. You run the risk of being murdered. Or worse."

She huffed. "What could possibly be worse than being murdered?"

He gave her a hard look.

Her cheeks colored in sudden comprehension.

He was relieved he didn't have to spell it out.

"I don't intend to stay there long," she said, a little defensively. "Only enough time to speak with Fenny. I shall be in and out in a flash."

"Do you think that matters? There are people there. Desperate people. Men who would as soon slit your throat as look at you. It wouldn't take above five minutes."

"I'm not afraid."

"You should be. And if you don't fear for your life, you must consider your reputation. How do you imagine it would look to be caught wandering about the dockland slums? Your honor would be forfeit. Your hopes of making a prosperous marriage damaged beyond repair."

Her lips compressed. Her features etched with a growing frustration. She slowly refolded the note. "What do you suggest?"

"Let me go. I'll speak to her on your behalf."

"Why would she listen? You're a stranger. She's not likely to even receive you." Evelyn shook her head. "No. It must be me. I can take Lewis with me, or—"

"Your aged groom? Good God, Evie, this isn't your village in Sussex."

Her gaze flew to his.

He belatedly realized that he'd not only used her given name, he'd used the affectionate diminutive reserved for those closest to her. An intimacy upon an intimacy.

Damn and blast.

"Forgive me," he said. "I didn't—"

"It's fine. I don't mind it. It's just—"

"You're worried about your sister. I understand." He raked a hand through his hair. "If you insist upon going there—"

"I do insist."

"—you'll need an escort who knows what he's about. Who isn't going to blunder into the place and get you both hurt."

"An escort." She looked at him steadily. "Do you mean . . . yourself?"

Bloody hell.

He supposed he did.

She wasn't his responsibility. Not by any means. He was her dressmaker, not her protector. Having delivered his note, he should back away and be done with it. He *knew* that.

But he couldn't trust her safety to anyone else.

"It would have to be at night," he said. "Under cover of darkness. Otherwise, you run the risk of us being seen together."

A defiant flush bloomed in her face. "I'm not ashamed of being seen with you."

An answering warmth threatened in his own. He ruthlessly suppressed it. "It's not about that. It's about the fact that being caught with me outside of the tailor's shop will cause as much damage to your reputation as your being seen in a dockside inn."

She didn't argue the point.

He was grateful for that much. Determination she had in abundance, but she was no fool.

"After dark, then," she said. "But let it be soon." A weighted pause. "Let it be tonight."

Ahmad stared down at her in silence, his heart thudding an unmistakable warning.

He had the sense they were breaching some unspoken barrier. A wall they'd been gradually chipping away at. It had stood between them from the first moment they'd met. The same impenetrable barrier that separated every man and woman of different races, different classes. One forged long ago, fortified with centuries of fear, resentment, and mistrust.

He didn't know what lay beyond it. But once crossed, there would be no going back.

He nodded once. "Tonight."

Twenty-One

❈

Ahmad helped Evelyn into the dark interior of the hired coach. Her face and figure were shrouded by the drape of a drab wool cloak. The cab rocked as he climbed in after her. Closing the door, he sank down at her side. A brougham only seated two. It was a tight fit. They were shoulder to shoulder, her full skirts bunched against his leg. He angled himself to give them more room.

And not only that.

He wanted to see her face.

As the brougham sprang into motion, the single interior lamp bounced in time with the clip-clop of the horse's hooves echoing on the cobblestones. It cast a shifting light over Evelyn's countenance.

Behind them, the back entrance to her uncle's town house receded into the billowing fog.

"Did you have any trouble getting away?" he asked.

She pushed back the hood of her cloak. Her hair was arranged in a neat coil of plaits, bound in a simple chignon at her nape. "I had to tell Agnes I was leaving. She'd have raised the alarm otherwise. And I suspect Mrs. Quick knows. She knows everything that happens in my uncle's house."

"Will she tell him?"

"I doubt it."

It was half past ten. Still early by the standards of London high society, but late enough for their purposes. Darkness had settled over the city, broken only by a scattering of gas street lamps and the lights of passing vehicles.

"I've never ridden in a brougham before," she said. "Did you hire it for the evening?"

He nodded. It was less cumbersome than a two-horse carriage, and more private than a hansom. Unlike the latter, the brougham's cab was fully enclosed. "Where we're going, we'll need to move quickly. And you won't wish to be seen."

"You must tell me how much I owe you for the expense," she said.

"It doesn't signify."

"Yes, it does. I won't have you out of pocket on my account."

A prickle of irritation took him unawares.

Stupid.

He should be thankful she took note of such things. Lord knew he couldn't afford to squander his funds. And Evelyn didn't seem inclined to allow him to. Not on her behalf.

She'd already settled several of her dressmaking bills. A rarity among fashionable ladies, to be so prompt in paying for what one had ordered.

It had been a reminder that their relationship was purely transactional.

A reminder he hadn't liked. Hadn't wanted.

After paying Mira's and Becky's wages, he'd taken the rest of the money and folded it back into his business. Using it to buy the fabric and trimmings for her next ball gown, and for the evening dresses she'd soon require.

He needed her custom. But taking payment for it hadn't seemed right. Not given the way he felt about her.

"We can settle afterward if we must," he said stiffly.

She didn't press the matter. Straightening her skirts, she made herself more comfortable in the cab.

Several minutes passed, the brougham rattling steadily through the streets of London. The silence between them grew larger and more oppressive.

Evelyn attempted to fill it. "I haven't told you about Lady Arundell's ball."

He gave her a dark look. The last thing he wanted to think about at the moment was her dancing with an endless queue of well-to-do Englishmen. "You were a great success, I assume."

"Not in the way you might imagine," she said. "Your dress was widely admired, of course. Many ladies inquired after its design. But my own triumph wasn't in the ballroom." The corner of her mouth tipped up. "It's a rather amusing story, actually."

His brows lifted.

"Lady Arundell invited a famous crystal gazer to the ball," she explained. "A man called Zadkiel. Lady Anne and I were obliged to be present during the performance he gave for Lady Arundell and my uncle."

Ahmad listened as Evelyn told him about her experience with the crystal gazer. About how this Zadkiel character had claimed she had extraordinarily strong psychic energy.

"As a result, Lady Arundell expects me to attend even more of her spiritualist functions. I've already accepted invitations to a dance and fireworks at Cremorne Garden, a dinner with the Antiquarian Society, and several other functions besides."

The brougham bounced over a pothole, jostling them against each other. Ahmad braced his arm across the back of the seat.

"Not only that," Evelyn went on. "Lady Arundell is trying to arrange a visit with this boy in Birmingham. The one who claims to have received messages from Prince Albert. She and my uncle want to test his veracity, and they believe I might be capable of helping them to do it."

"Because of your gift," he said dryly.

"Don't laugh."

"I'm not laughing."

"Had you been there, you'd have seen how earnest they were. They truly seemed to believe they'd seen something in the crystal ball."

"Did you?" he asked.

Her gaze slid from his. She smoothed her gloves.

His interest was instantly aroused. "You saw something?"

"Not to speak of." She hesitated. "That is . . . I might have done." Another pause. "After a time staring into the crystal, I thought I saw the face of . . . of someone I know."

"Of course you did."

She flashed him a sharp glance. "That doesn't surprise you?"

"Not at all."

"I don't have a gift," she informed him.

"A gift isn't required to see things in a crystal. No more than it is when one is performing automatic writing. The visions and words that materialize have nothing to do with the spirits. They come from the practitioner's own mind."

The brougham jolted them close again. Her knees briefly bumped his through the countless layers of her petticoats and crinoline. "You're saying that it's all a deception?"

"Not in the way you mean." He was silent a moment. "When I was a boy, there was a man in my village who used to stare into a bowl of water. It was a form of meditation. Something to clear his thoughts and focus his mind. It helped him to make decisions. To ascertain what it was he truly wanted."

"You're speaking of water divination."

"Call it what you will," Ahmad said. "Crystal gazing is no different. The longer one stares, the more chance there is that one's own thoughts and feelings will manifest. Images of long-lost loved ones and the like."

"But it isn't only the dead who manifest."

"No. People are as likely to see their deepest desires. The dark and the light. An enemy on whom they wish ill. Or a person for whom they cherish a regard."

"In other words, the visions are all in their head."

He shrugged. "People see what they wish to see. Staring into something like a crystal or a candle flame merely helps to reveal what it is they truly want."

She was noticeably quiet.

He wondered if he'd offended her. "I don't discount the presence of other forces. If you believe in spirits—"

"I don't believe in them. What you've said makes perfect sense." She tugged at the thumb of her glove, her expression preoccupied. "I wonder why Zadkiel would tell my uncle that I had a powerful energy."

Ahmad didn't have to guess. "These charlatans make their fortunes on being at the forefront of fashionable society."

"But I'm not at the forefront."

"Not yet. But you're beautiful and fascinating. And you're dressed like no other lady in London. He'd have to be blind not to see it. Your star is ascending."

She turned in her seat, bumping against his outstretched arm. He set his hand on her shoulder to steady her. An instinctive movement. He meant nothing untoward by it.

It nevertheless ratcheted the intimacy of the moment up by several degrees.

Good lord.

His arm was around her. It was practically an embrace. And . . . it didn't feel wrong.

Quite the reverse. It felt profoundly, unsettlingly, gloriously right.

His throat spasmed on a swallow.

This was getting ridiculous. This ungodly connection between them, taut as a wire stretched to its breaking point.

"Do you really believe all of that?" she asked.

He managed a wry smile. "Obviously. I've latched onto you myself, haven't I?"

A frown shadowed her brow. "It's not the same at all."

His smiled faded. He couldn't maintain a pretense of humor. Not about this. Not about her. "No," he said. "I don't suppose it is."

The brougham slowed. Noise rose from outside its curtained windows—the swell of coarse voices, inebriated revelry, and a hornpipe playing a raucous tune. It was the music of the docks. An all-too-familiar sound.

Ahmad's muscles tensed. He removed his arm from the back of the seat. "Draw up your hood. We're nearly there."

◆━◆

Evelyn pulled the hood of her cloak over her head, shrouding her face and hair, as the brougham came to a clattering halt.

Beside her, Ahmad attended to his own clothing, drawing up the collar of his coat and settling his hat low over his brow. He was dressed in unrelieved black—tall, commanding, and capable of vanishing into the shadows at a moment's notice. A fallen angel, indeed.

She felt a frisson of nervous excitement as he opened the door of the brougham. She wasn't afraid. Not when he was with her.

His large gloved hand held tight to hers as he helped her down.

She was at once assailed by the unmistakable stench of the Thames. It was an unpleasant fragrance at the best of times, but here—so close to the water—it was positively overpowering.

And it didn't exist in isolation.

It was accompanied by the perfume of tobacco and rum, mingled with the pungent black smoke emitted from the neighborhood's tall chimneys.

The docks were at once both awake and asleep. Warehouses stood silent, while the streets teemed with life, filled with swaggering men of every stripe. She felt them looking at her with varying levels of interest. They were sailors, most of them.

At least, Evelyn thought they must be.

Among the ruddy-faced Englishmen were figures of every ethnicity and description.

A group of fair-haired men chattered loudly together in German. A Chinese gentleman leaned against the wall of a storage building, smoking a long pipe. And a black sailor, with a brightly colored hand-kerchief knotted at his neck, walked arm in arm with a woman in a cheap satin dress.

The woman gave Ahmad a lewd wink as they passed.

Evelyn stiffened. "Do you know that person?"

"No."

"She seemed to know you."

"It's her business to know men."

"Oh!" Evelyn glanced back over her shoulder. The only courtesans she'd ever seen were the Pretty Horsebreakers. This female was of another class entirely, heavily rouged and powdered, with false hair arranged in a disordered pile.

A working woman, isn't that the phrase Ahmad had used once? There had been no judgment in it.

He tucked Evelyn's hand in his arm as he led her across the busy street to the entrance of the inn. It was a weather-beaten building, the wooden slats buckled and faded from salt and wind. A battered sign hung over the door, proclaiming the establishment's name: *The Jolly Tar*.

Evelyn concealed a wince.

Oh, Fenny. How far you've fallen.

"Keep your head down," Ahmad said. "And let me do the talking."

She didn't argue. He'd already explained that she must do nothing to make herself memorable. It was why she'd slipped her spectacles into her pocket.

On entering the inn, they were greeted by a blaze of oil lamps. Every table in the smoke-filled dining room appeared to be full. Loud conversation was punctuated by cackles of laughter and the clink of heavy glasses and tankards of ale.

A grizzled man stood behind the wooden counter, filling a row of dirty glasses from an equally dirty bottle. He flicked a glance from Ahmad to Evelyn and back again as they approached. His thick mouth curled into a leer. "Looking for a room?"

"For a guest staying here." Ahmad withdrew a half crown from his pocket. He set it down on the bar. "A lady and a gentleman of quality."

The barman took the coin without hesitation. He resumed pouring his drinks. "Upstairs. Third room on the right."

Evelyn exhaled a breath. "That was easier than I anticipated," she murmured as she accompanied Ahmad up the narrow staircase at the back of the bar.

She didn't know what she'd been expecting. More danger, perhaps. A threat of fisticuffs—or worse.

No doubt things would have transpired differently had she been alone. She was exceedingly grateful she wasn't.

"We may yet have some excitement," Ahmad said. "Stay on your guard."

"I will," she promised.

He stopped outside the door of the third room on the right of the corridor. "I'll wait here."

"You needn't—"

"This is between you and your sister," he said.

He was right. Fenny wasn't likely to listen if Ahmad was present. Gathering her courage, Evelyn knocked softly on the door.

There was no answer.

She was just raising her hand to strike again when a woman called out sharply from inside: "Who's there?"

It was Fenny's voice.

At the sound of it, Evelyn's eyes burned with unexpected moisture. Bowing her head, she rested her brow against the paneled wood of the door, her own voice sinking to a whisper. "Fenny? It's Evie."

"Evie?" Seconds later, the door was flung open. Fenny stood there, her dark hair loose about her shoulders and her rosebud mouth parted in horrified surprise. The bodice of her dress strained over her swollen belly. "By all the saints. What in heaven are *you* doing here?"

Twenty-Two

——✦——

$\mathcal{E}$velyn folded her hands in her lap to stop their trembling. Seated in a shabby armchair situated beside an equally shabby wash-stand, she watched her heavily pregnant sister pace the confines of her rented room. Fenny was clad in faded linen, wearing neither corset nor stockings. Her bare feet padded silently on the ash-singed carpet.

She looked older than when Evelyn had last seen her.

And not only in years.

There were lines on Fenny's face that spoke of hardship and dis-solute living.

"How far along are you?" Evelyn asked.

"Six months," Fenny said.

"Is that why you came back?"

Fenny's expression tightened. "Anthony was convinced his father would finally give permission for us to marry. But Sir William won't budge an inch. His pride won't allow it. He still can't forgive Anthony for defying him and chasing after me to London."

"Does Sir William know you're with child?"

"He doesn't care. He says that many gentlemen sire children on their mistresses, but it doesn't mean they're obliged to wed them."

Evelyn winced. "When did he say that?"

"He wrote it in reply to Anthony's letter. Anthony was furious. He said we'd return to France straightaway, but we don't have enough money for our passage. We had expenses. Food and lodgings at this wretched place. Sir William made us wait over a week on his reply. He must have known that lingering here would leave us short of funds."

The rough voices of inebriated sailors and dockworkers drifted up from the dining room below. An unsettling sound. Evelyn was grateful that Ahmad was standing guard at the door.

"What will you do?" she asked.

Fenny shrugged. "Find the money somehow. That's where Anthony is now. Trying to win our passage in a card game with some sailors he met on the steamer from France."

Evelyn didn't like the sound of that. It seemed reckless—and dangerous. "Surely gambling isn't the answer?"

"How do you suppose we manage to make Sir William's quarterly allowance last so long? If not for Anthony's prowess at the gaming tables, I shudder to think where we'd be."

"I didn't even know Sir William was in contact with you," Evelyn said. "Not until Stephen told me. You can imagine how I felt, learning that you were alive and well and here in London."

Fenny ceased pacing. Her mouth flattened into a mulish line. She didn't apologize. Didn't ask after Aunt Nora or inquire about their sisters. She just stood there, glaring.

Evelyn recognized that look from their childhood. Fenny had been willful even then. Stubborn and selfish. It was one of the reasons she and Evelyn had never been as close as Evelyn was with her younger sisters.

It didn't mean Evelyn didn't care for her. As difficult as Fenny had been over the years, there had still been moments of sisterly affection between them.

"Why didn't you write to us?" Evelyn asked.

"And tell you what?"

"You might have explained."

"After Aunt Nora had spent all of her savings on my debut? And you and all our sisters counting on me? There was nothing I could say."

"You could have told us where you were. Aunt Nora has worried herself sick over you. I have, too."

"You? I thought you'd be glad to see the back of me. You were always so disapproving of my having fun."

Evelyn frowned. Is that how her sister had perceived her? It wasn't the truth. Not anywhere near it. "I'm sorry if I seemed that way," she said. "Our lives were so different. You with your friends and parties—"

"And you with your horse. Off riding without a care in the world."

"I had as many cares as you did."

Fenny snorted. "You weren't expected to be the savior of us all. To give up your happiness—your very future—for the sake of the family."

Evelyn's stomach knotted.

It might not have been expected of her then, but it was certainly expected of her now.

When she'd set out for London, it had seemed a worthy sacrifice. But not anymore. Not since her affections had been engaged.

And they *were* engaged.

Indeed, driving here tonight with Ahmad, the two of them pressed against each other inside the brougham, everything had seemed to fall into focus.

He was the one for her. The *only* one. There could be no other.

In just a few short weeks, he'd become essential to her happiness. Even now, when he was but a short distance away, all she could think of was seeing him again.

Is this what it was like to lose one's heart to a gentleman? This feeling that you'd risk everything—give up everything—just to be with him?

"It's why you're here, isn't it?" Fenny asked. "With me gone, you're the next in line to play sacrificial lamb. Take my advice and save yourself the trouble. Our sisters won't thank you for it. Not unless they've changed a great deal during the past three years."

"I don't know what you mean."

"Don't you?" Fenny's gaze flickered with sisterly condescension. "Gussie might be happy with a London season, but Caro? Bette? The last I saw of them, they were as eager to join the ranks of bluestockings as you were."

"I'm not—"

"You *are*."

Evelyn's posture went rigid. But she refused to be drawn into an argument. She'd come here to discuss Fenny's troubles, not her own. "I wish you'd written," she said. "I was afraid for you."

"You shouldn't have been."

"I feared you might have met the same fate as Mama."

Fenny's expression sobered. She'd been only sixteen when Mama had died in childbed, and had taken the loss very hard. "There was no chance of that. Up to now, I've managed to keep myself tidy. The French have ways of doing so, you know."

Evelyn gave her sister a blank look.

"Things to prevent a child from coming," Fenny said impatiently. "We thought them reliable. They weren't, obviously, which is how I find myself in this state. It's all very inconvenient."

Inconvenient.

That was one word for it.

Evelyn rose from the chair. She didn't have much time left. She'd promised Ahmad she would be quick. "You *do* intend to marry him?"

"The moment Anthony turns twenty-six, we'll be up before the parson. He'll have access to his mother's funds then. It's more than enough for us to live on."

"And until that happens?"

She shrugged. "So long as we don't wed without his permission, Sir William will keep sending Anthony an allowance. It will have to do for us."

"Where will you live?"

"In France, naturally. Steamers leave for Calais twice a week. We'll depart as soon as Anthony procures our passage. And then, I shall have my baby, and you can have your season. Though I suggest," Fenny added with some asperity, "if you're truly concerned about your reputation, you refrain from visiting places like this in future."

"I came here to see you."

"At night. In company with a man. Your dressmaker, of all people." Fenny laughed. "Wouldn't Aunt Nora be interested to know *that*."

"I don't see why either of us should burden Aunt Nora with any of this."

Fenny stilled. "You haven't told her about me?"

"Not yet."

"I don't expect she'd want to know anyway. Not after what I did."

Evelyn felt a stab of compassion for her sister. "Do you truly wish to go back to France? To have your baby so far from home?"

A shadow of a smile touched Fenny's lips. "I thought you wanted me to leave? The better for you and your marriage prospects."

"It *would* be best. But I'll not drive you away. Not when you're in this condition." Evelyn meant it. It wouldn't be easy for her sister to return to Combe Regis. Not for any of them. But it was plainly the best option for Fenny and her child. "You must come home."

"To Sussex? To live under Aunt Nora's thumb?" Fenny sat down on the unmade bed. The sheets were rumpled and the pillows askew, as if she'd only just risen moments earlier. "Combe Regis hasn't been my home for a long time."

"And France has?"

"Not France," Fenny said. "Anthony." She curved one arm around her belly. "You'll understand one day when you fall in love yourself. *If* you fall in love. Some ladies never do."

"Is this what love is?" Evelyn gestured at the dilapidated room. "Giving up everything for one man? Abdicating your responsibilities? Disappointing your family?"

Fenny's cheeks flushed. "It wasn't what either of us wanted."

"Then why—"

"Because there was no other way," Fenny said. "I had to choose."

Evelyn didn't want to believe it. Surely love wasn't an either-or proposition. It couldn't be. There must be a way to have it all. For a lady to both fulfill her obligations and to be with the man she cared for.

Just because Fenny hadn't found it didn't mean it didn't exist.

Evelyn was oddly quiet as Ahmad herded her back through the dining room of the Jolly Tar and out onto the darkened street. There wasn't time to inquire into her state of mind. On leaving the inn, Ahmad had registered a noticeable shift in the atmosphere. With every passing minute, the docklands became more dangerous. Emboldened by drink and the cover of night, the worst of the region's inhabitants were out looking for sport. Unsavory types who wouldn't blink at committing violence.

Ahmad guided Evelyn toward the waiting brougham. A group of sailors in the street watched them pass.

"Where you headed to, love?" one of the men called.

"Don't be shy," another said. "Let us see your face."

The men followed after them, moving as one.

Evelyn's hand tightened on Ahmad's arm.

"Ignore them," Ahmad said. Opening the door of the brougham, he quickly assisted her in.

The coachman had a horse pistol. They'd be safe enough. In the meanwhile, all that was needed was to make an example of one of the sailors.

Ahmad was more than ready to do so.

"Don't look back," he said to Evelyn.

"Ahmad—"

He shut the carriage door on her before she could object.

Turning, he faced the three ruffians. Fog from the river billowed about their legs as they advanced on him. Their faces were revealed in the light of the carriage lamps—not foreign faces from a distant land, but Englishmen. One of them grinned to see that Ahmad was Indian.

"That's a fine carriage for a chichi," he remarked.

"And a fine woman," the second sailor said. "How much for her company?"

The third and biggest of the three sailors stepped forward. "Let's have a look at her."

"I wouldn't," Ahmad advised.

The sailor only laughed. He reached to shove Ahmad out of the way.

Ahmad caught the man easily by his collar. Twisting the fabric in his hand, he hoisted the sailor up nearly off his feet. "Perhaps you didn't hear me."

The sailor struggled against Ahmad's grip, choking out a stream of oaths and threats.

His friends hastened to assist him.

They were none of them very worthy opponents. Their blows were imprecise, their balance affected by too much rum.

It was over in seconds.

The first two sailors limped away into the fog, supporting the third between them.

Ahmad climbed into the carriage, sinking down beside Evelyn. The coachman sprang the horse into a trot.

Evelyn looked horrified. "Did you fight them?"

"It wasn't a fight."

"You're bleeding!"

He touched the side of his mouth, surprised to find a trickle of moisture. "A trifling thing. It's no matter."

She withdrew a handkerchief from her sleeve. "Here. Let me." Leaning closer, she gently dabbed away the blood. "I don't know what you were thinking. They might have killed you."

"There was no chance of that."

"There were three of them."

"They were drunk."

"There were *three* of them." She blotted the side of his mouth with renewed vigor.

He caught her hand, stilling her ministrations. "I was in no danger. Dealing with situations like that . . . It was my job for nearly half of my life. It's nothing to me."

She stared into his eyes. "That's what you did at Mrs. Pritchard's? Fought men like that?"

"I told you. It's not fighting."

"What, then?"

"They were making a nuisance of themselves, so I dispatched them." His fingers curled around hers. "I didn't mean to scare you."

"It was those men who scared me. Shouting at me that way—and at you. What was that name they called you?"

Ahmad inwardly grimaced. "Nothing." He released her hand. "A stupid slur Englishmen like to call people who are part Indian."

Her brows knit. She looked as though she wanted to say more on the subject. To ask him what the slur meant, no doubt. But she didn't.

A fact for which he was grateful.

She folded her handkerchief before putting it away. "I'm sorry you must be subjected to such things on my account."

"I would endure a great deal more to keep you safe," he said.

Her gaze found his in the dim light of the carriage lamp. There was something inexplicable in her eyes.

His chest tightened. He wished he hadn't said anything.

"You're very good," she said. "To bring me here like this, and to deal with those men on my behalf."

"I fear all of this excitement has taken away from your reunion with your sister."

"Ah. That."

"Was your errand successful?"

"Did I persuade her to leave London, do you mean?" Evelyn sighed. "She wants to leave. But you must have seen her condition."

Ahmad *had* seen it. He'd not been surprised. To be sure, it was probably the least surprising aspect of this episode.

But he made no judgment. He only listened as Evelyn described her sister's dilemma.

He could muster little sympathy. Not when the whole situation could be resolved through the expedience of a quick marriage and steady employment.

"I wonder if I was right to bring you here," he said when Evelyn finished.

"Why would you say so?"

"Because it seems this visit has failed to set your mind at ease."

Indeed, she was wearing the same expression of worry she had when they'd entered the tavern. Worse still, she looked absorbed by her troubles to the point of distraction. As if, in the aftermath of seeing her sister, even more burdens had been laid at her door.

"It's not you," Evelyn said. "I appreciate your help, and I'm very grateful for your—" She broke off.

He wondered what she might have said if she'd continued. Your kindness? Your friendship? "What is it, then?" he asked.

"My own weakness of mind. I can't help but fixate on the unfairness of it all. If Anthony abandons Fenny and returns with his brother to Sussex, he'll be permitted to resume his life as if nothing had ever happened. He'll face no consequences at all for what he's done. Men never do. It's the ladies who must bear the burden, not only for their own misconduct but for the misconduct of gentlemen, too."

"You blame him."

"I blame them both. I blame the world we live in—a world that makes it impossible for a lady and a gentleman to marry where they will." Her voice thickened. "And I blame myself."

He frowned. "What had you to do with it?"

"These past years, I've been accustomed to think of Fenny as selfish. She was meant to marry to benefit us all. It was her duty, I thought. I gave no consideration to what she might have wanted. Whom she might have loved. It wasn't until I came to London that I began to understand the depth of her feelings for Anthony. I'd never felt them for myself, you see."

Ahmad's heart thumped hard. "And now you have?"

Once again, her gaze met his in the carriage light. "I believe so. An approximation of them, anyway."

He thought he knew what she meant. All the same, he was reluctant to give voice to it. "Because of this thing between us."

"Yes."

He searched her eyes. What he found there fairly stole his breath. "Evelyn . . ."

"You asked me if I saw something in the crystal ball, that night at Lady Arundell's. But you didn't ask me what."

"You said it was someone you knew."

"And *you* said," she reminded him, "that the images in the surface of the crystal are projections of a person's own mind. Of the thing they most desire. The thing they want most in all the world."

He shook his head. "Evie . . . don't say it."

"It was you I saw in the crystal," she whispered. "*Your* face. Because you're the one I'm meant to be with."

Twenty-Three

—◆—

$\mathcal{E}$velyn waited for him to reply, her heart in her hand. She hadn't planned to say anything to him. Not here. But after everything that had happened this evening, she couldn't manage to keep her feelings to herself. Not when they were alone together like this, side by side in the darkened brougham, her skirts spilling over his legs.

Tension crackled between them. It was a palpable presence. Even more so after she'd tended his wound, and he'd covered her hand with his.

He held her gaze. "You're mistaken. I'm not the man for you."

She looked steadily back at him. Her pulse was racing. She felt much as she did when she was galloping on Hephaestus. A thrilling sense of fear and excitement. The knowledge that she was risking life and limb.

"I believe you are," she said. "I know it to be true. The feelings we have for each other—"

"And where would such feelings take us if you gave them their head? Straight down the road to ruin. Right into the selfsame predicament that you find your sister in. Poor. Miserable. Exiled from polite society."

Evelyn shook her head. "It wouldn't be that way for us."

"No. With us it would be worse." He brought his hand to cradle her cheek. His touch made her breath stutter. He was gentle. Almost reverent. As if she were made of the finest French silk. "How would I keep you, Evie?" he asked. "How could I ever make you happy?"

"You do make me happy," she said.

He bent his head. They were already dangerously close. The small movement brought them closer still.

Her heartbeat accelerated. She knew he was going to kiss her an instant before his lips brushed hers.

It was a brief caress. Similar to the accidental kiss they'd shared in the fitting room at Doyle and Heppenstall's.

But no.

It was more than that—and different. This kiss was purposeful. A tender, searching inquiry. He was asking her permission.

She gave it readily. Arching up to him, her lips yielded beneath his in unspoken answer: *Yes, please.*

And he kissed her again, softly, gently.

It was achingly sweet. Quickening her pulse and warming her blood. And yet . . .

Evelyn recognized the feeling of leashed power. The way it coiled just beneath the surface. She knew it well enough from riding a stallion. But this wasn't only power restrained. This was something else. Something stronger and more hazardous still.

It was passion.

Ahmad's passion for *her.* And he was holding it back. Leashing it as though she needed protecting from it.

Her hand lifted to curl around his neck. Her fingers threaded in the thick hair at his nape. "You don't have to be careful with me."

His forehead came to rest against hers. "Yes. I do."

"If you truly want me—"

"I do want you," he admitted. "So much. But this . . . It can't happen."

Her heart dropped into her stomach. He was pulling away from her. Not physically, but in every other way that mattered.

She wanted to hold him tighter. To keep him from withdrawing.

A pathetic impulse.

Gathering her dignity, she dropped her hand from his neck. "Have I made a fool of myself?"

A troubled frown shadowed his brow. "No."

"But you're rejecting me."

He didn't deny it. His thumb moved over the slope of her cheek in a slow caress. "Because this can't work."

"Why not?" There was a sullen flavor to her words. She hated how it sounded. But good lord, this *hurt*.

"I can't give you what you want," he said.

She opened her mouth to object, but he forestalled her.

"You require a wealthy husband," he reminded her. "It's why you're here. You've told me so yourself."

"That was before."

His lips twisted in a humorless smile. "Before you saw my face in the crystal."

"I saw your face in the crystal because you were already on my mind. Every gentleman I met at the ball . . . I compared them all with you and found them wanting."

"That's very flattering, but—"

"Don't." She moved away from his touch. "Don't patronize me."

His hand fell from her cheek. "I'm not patronizing you. I only want you to see that being with me isn't part of your plan."

"Plans can change," she said. "Mine already have."

It was true. Her carefully calibrated blueprint for the season had gone out the window within the very first fortnight. It had been altered by Stephen's arrival, and Fenny's return. And by the fact that all of the balls and parties Evelyn would be attending were now in some way related to spiritualism.

And it had been altered by Ahmad. An alteration not only of her plans, but of herself. It had happened the moment she'd heard his voice behind the curtain at Doyle and Heppenstall's. The moment she'd seen him behind the counter.

"Is that what this is?" He searched her face. "Have you changed your mind? Decided to give this all up?"

"No, but—"

"No," he said. "You can't, can you? You have your sisters to think of." He paused, adding, "And your horse."

He may as well have dashed cold water in her face. It rather felt like he had.

"I *am* thinking of them," she said. "I never stop."

"Of course you don't. They're your first and best concern."

She couldn't deny it. "They are. That doesn't mean there's no room in my heart for anyone else."

"Evie . . ."

"There must be a way for us to be together. There *must* be. All it requires is a bit of ingenuity. If we improve our fortunes, and—"

"It isn't only the money," he said gruffly.

Her breath stopped. "What, then?"

"We're different, you and I. Your world . . . it isn't the world I live in."

"It looks similar enough to me," she said.

"Not from where I'm standing."

"Because you're Indian?" She frowned. "But you're English, too."

"I'm both," he said, "and neither. I don't belong to either world. I belong nowhere."

A lump formed in her throat. "Don't say that."

"It's the truth. That's the way it is in India for people like me. And it's the way it is here. If you were with me, that would be your life, too."

"You make it sound as though you're unhappy."

He didn't answer her.

She stared up at him, brows knit, wanting so much to understand.

To learn who he was and why he was. All those secret hidden pieces of himself that manifested in the beauty of his designs. *"Are you unhappy?"*

———❈———

Outside the brougham, the unruly noise of the docks drifted away, replaced by the sounds of respectable traffic—the clip-clop of hooves and the rattle of hansom cabs and carriages. Soon, they'd be back in Bloomsbury, and thence to Russell Square. Ahmad would deposit Evelyn at the garden gate and take his leave. And then . . .

And then, with luck, she'd forget any of this had ever happened.

He looked at her in the shadows, remembering the taste of her mouth. The feel of her lips, soft and voluptuous, half-parted beneath his. It stirred a helpless ache within him. An ache that only deepened as he recalled her words, spoken with such earnest intensity.

"There must be a way for us to be together."

His heart echoed the words back in frustrated silence.

Damn and blast it all to hell.

He'd known something like this might happen. It had been the risk of coming with her tonight. What he hadn't reckoned on was how deeply it would affect him. How difficult it would be for them to return to any semblance of normalcy.

Good lord.

They'd done more than breach the wall, they'd knocked it down completely. There would be no rebuilding it now.

"Are you?" she asked again. Her gloved hand lay on the seat between them, perilously close to his.

He couldn't help but take it. "I'm not unhappy."

"Yet you assume I would be, if we were together."

"The difference being that I'm accustomed to living life on the outside of society. But for a woman . . . for a lady . . ." He paused. "You don't know what it's like. How it affects people. My mother—" He stopped himself.

"What about your mother?"

He was quiet for several seconds. "Not long after I was born, she walked into the river and drowned herself."

Her hand tightened on his. "Oh, Ahmad. How dreadful."

It *was* dreadful, albeit something far outside the reaches of his memory. One of the benefits to losing her in the first days of his life. He couldn't remember the pain of it. She'd always been gone. Almost as though she never existed, except as some manner of morality play.

"Why did she do it?" Evelyn asked.

"Shame," he said.

She waited for him to explain.

"How much do you know about the British occupation in India?" he asked.

"Nothing at all, I'm afraid. Except what I read in the papers about the uprising. We've been there a long while, I gather."

We.

He could have done without the reminder.

But there was no avoiding it. They both were who they were. There could be no accepting it without first acknowledging it.

"A very long while," he said. "The British soldiers often take native women to wife. They have children. Entire families. Nowadays, the soldiers are encouraged to make such marriages legal, but in decades past, the arrangements were nothing more than unlawful conveniences, contrived for the man's comfort. When the soldiers returned to England, they frequently left their Indian families behind."

Understanding registered in her eyes. Compassion swiftly followed. "Is that what happened to you and your mother?"

He nodded. "She believed herself wed to a soldier, but when the opportunity arose for him to return home, the truth of their arrangement was revealed. They weren't married at all. Not legally. He left her behind, alone and with child. She couldn't return to her family. She'd been dishonored. She had nowhere to go. No one who was willing to help her except her younger sister."

Indeed, it was from his aunt that Ahmad had first heard the story. As a boy, it had been so much folklore to him.

"Many people believed it an accident, but my aunt knew the truth. My mother went into the water on purpose. Fortunately for me, she waited until after I was born to do it. My aunt claimed that my mother didn't wish to compound her sin. Who knows if that's true?"

"I'm sorry," Evelyn said. "I had no idea."

"It was a long time ago. Long before I can remember."

"She was still your mother."

"My aunt was the only mother I knew." His thumb moved absently over the curve of her palm. "She fell under the spell of a British soldier, too. It was difficult not to, the way we lived."

"What do you mean?" she asked. "How did you live?"

"On the outskirts," he said. "On the fringes of colonial society. My aunt was stuck there, raising me in the same village where many people lived who were of mixed Indian and English blood. It was a dubious privilege. We mimicked the British—their speech and customs. Their religion. But that's all it was. Mimicry. A bastardization of British life." He failed to keep the rough edge from his words. "No doubt my aunt thought she was delivering Mira and me our birthright. But we were never English, no more than we were Indian. We were nothing."

Evelyn's hand gripped his even tighter. So small and slender, yet strong enough to hold a stallion at bay. It was an unmistakable reproof. "You shouldn't say such things."

"I say them for *your* benefit. So you'll know what it's like to live that way. What it does to a person after a time. It's not for the faint of heart, Evie. Never fully belonging anywhere. Never having an identity that's your own. For a lady, it's an equation that rarely leads to happiness. Can you not understand that?"

"I do understand. But there's an error in your equation." Her chin lifted a notch. "You've mistaken me for a lady who's faint of heart."

His chest clenched on a rush of affection for her that was almost painful. Good God, she was right. He had the sudden, bitter urge to laugh. She was right, and it didn't make one whit of difference.

"No, you're not, are you." His voice deepened. "You'd gallop head-long through any obstacle, no matter the cost. But I'm telling you, this time the cost is too great."

"You're wrong," she said. "None of this is a headlong gallop. I'm not reckless like my sister. You should know that by now. I wouldn't give everything up, not even for someone I—" She stopped herself. "Someone I care about."

He heard her unspoken declaration as clearly as if she'd shouted it from the rooftops. Not just someone she cared about. Someone she loved.

It *was* love, wasn't it?

This soul-stirring attraction, underscored by unwavering admiration and respect. He felt it whenever they were together. And when they weren't together, too. A desire to move mountains for her. To make her path smooth, no matter the cost. It was becoming as much a part of him as breathing.

The two of them were falling in love.

Or perhaps they'd already fallen.

"I wouldn't let you give anything up," he said. "Not for me."

"There won't be any need. I'm certain I can come up with a plan. A way to honor my responsibilities and to—"

"On no account. You're not to risk anything for me. I mean it."

"Then what is it you're proposing we do?" she asked.

A leaden weight settled in his stomach. "The only thing we can. We must put this interlude behind us, difficult as that is. We must return to what we were before. Partners. Friends, I hope."

"And nothing more?" She gave him a look of consternation. "Despite the fact that you claim to want me as much as I want you?"

"I do," he said grimly, as the brougham rolled steadily back to Russell Square. "But I'm accustomed to not getting what I want."

Twenty-Four

❖

$\mathcal{E}$velyn had been waiting to talk to her uncle about Fenny for the better part of the day. After breakfast, she'd even attempted to beard him in his den. But Uncle Harris had already left the house. For where, Evelyn had no notion.

She didn't see him again until later that afternoon, and then very much by chance. He was returning home, crossing the hall at the selfsame moment she was descending the stairs in her dark green riding costume.

"Taking that horse of yours for an airing?" he asked.

"I am." Evelyn could muster little enough enthusiasm for it. After last night's events, the prospect of displaying herself in Rotten Row was about as palatable as the thought of attending another society ball or dinner. There seemed no point anymore. She'd found the gentleman she wanted.

Never mind that he'd rejected her.

Her spirits sank to recall it. But she didn't indulge the feeling. Hephaestus still needed exercising. And Ahmad's designs still needed showing off.

It was that which had got her out of bed this morning when she'd awakened, heartsick and tempted to wallow in her own misery.

She continued down the steps, one gloved hand trailing lightly on the curving bannister. "Where have you been today?"

"In conference with Lady Arundell." Uncle Harris removed his hat and coat and passed them to a waiting footman. "A few points have arisen about this boy medium in Birmingham. Indeed, you may be capable of rendering me some assistance."

"In what regard?"

Her uncle didn't answer, merely strode off down the hall.

She hesitated for an instant. She'd promised to meet Stella at the Hyde Park Corner end of Rotten Row at half past five on the dot. It wouldn't do to be late.

Then again, Evelyn must take her opportunities where she found them.

She quickly caught up with her uncle, following him into his study. It was in the same state of outrageous disarray as on every other occasion she'd visited. The one room in the house the servants weren't allowed to tidy.

Uncle Harris plopped down behind his cluttered desk. "A brief question or two on the subject of spiritual amplification."

"Spiritual *what*?"

He waved his hand in a vague swirling gesture. "This energy you possess. Her ladyship claims it amplifies the spirits' ability to make contact. Helps them to project a clear message."

Evelyn frowned. "How can she possibly know?"

"Her familiar spirit conveyed it to her only this morning. Dmitri, he calls himself. Dashed contradictory fellow, if you ask me. But he confirms Zadkiel's opinion about your gifts."

"With respect, sir, Zadkiel was spouting nonsense. And as for Dmitri, I don't believe—"

"Which brings me to my first question." Her uncle leaned across his desk, his gaze narrowing over the tops of his half-moon spectacles. "What does this energy feel like?"

Evelyn sighed. "I don't feel any particular energy. Certainly nothing of an otherworldly nature."

He clucked his tongue. "No strange sensations? Vibrations in your limbs or midsection?"

Her cheeks warmed. Last night, she *had* felt strange vibrations in both her limbs and her midsection. They'd been inspired by Ahmad's kisses.

But such feelings weren't supernatural. They were all too human. Emotional. Physical.

Deliciously physical.

Were ladies supposed to enjoy such activities? Evelyn wondered.

"No, sir," she said. "Nothing of the kind."

"What about messages?" he asked.

"Messages from whom?"

"Words of import from beyond the veil. Instructions sent to guide us."

A rogue thought occurred to her.

She took a step closer to her uncle's desk, choosing her next words with care. "I sometimes experience a very strong sense of things. An impression of something I must say to someone. I suppose you might call it a message."

Uncle Harris's face lit with excitement. "From the spirit realm?"

"I daresay it could be."

"Have you received any messages of this kind about me?" he asked.

"Yes," she replied. "Now you mention it."

"Well?" he prompted with growing impatience.

She cleared her throat. "I have the distinct feeling that . . . it's time you concerned yourself less with the dead and more with the living."

Uncle Harris gaped at her.

She felt a flicker of guilt.

Botheration.

It wasn't fair to mislead him. Not even in a good cause. Better to rely on the truth, however inconvenient.

"Fenny is in town, uncle," she said abruptly.

"Fenny?"

"Fenella. My older sister. The one who ran off with Anthony Connaught. The two of them are stranded at a dockside inn. They're in need of money to pay for their passage back to France."

A look of amazement passed over his face. "The spirits told you this?"

"No. This much I know for a fact. And if you wish to concern yourself with the living, you might start with them."

Uncle Harris seemed to consider this. And then he nodded. "How much do they require?"

"Obviously he still believed it was a message from beyond," Stella said, bringing Locket up alongside Hephaestus.

"I suspect he did." Evelyn shortened her reins, slowing Hephaestus so that she and Stella could ride abreast. "It was wrong of me to tease him."

"Bah. Stuffy old men need a bit of teasing," Stella said. "I tease my older brother with regularity."

"Your brother isn't an old man, surely?"

"He acts as though he is. He's sober and self-righteous. Dreadfully old-fashioned. He doesn't appreciate being nettled. Which is a sure sign that one must nettle him more."

The two of them walked their horses along Rotten Row, navigating through the fashionable crowd.

Evelyn had been surprised that Stella had agreed to ride with her at this hour. Anne had ceased doing so, preferring to ride in the mornings with Julia instead. Evelyn might have preferred it, too, if she hadn't a plan to enact.

Her plan.

Thus far it consisted of little more than a determination to keep Ahmad's designs at the forefront of society. As for the rest of it . . .

She felt a flash of frustration.

Perhaps Fenny was right. Perhaps the youngest three of their sisters didn't require London seasons and well-to-do matches.

Evelyn supposed it was possible.

It didn't lessen her obligation. She must still contrive a way to support them.

A daunting proposition given the changing circumstances.

At least Fenny's dilemma had been successfully dealt with. No sooner had Uncle Harris written out a check than Evelyn had tucked it into an envelope, along with the note she'd penned to her sister, and sent it off to the Jolly Tar in care of a footman.

Now all that was left was for Evelyn to resolve the remainder of her problems. It was no small feat. Not when Ahmad was ready to quit the field before the battle had even begun.

He was being noble. She recognized that much. It was why he'd told her about his mother and about the burdens Evelyn would face if she became part of his life. He was trying to shield her from pain. To prevent her from throwing everything away on his account.

Little did he know, his story of adversity had only made her admire him more.

"Will your sister truly go back to France now?" Stella asked.

"I believe so." Evelyn had confided a little about Fenny's predicament. Just enough to illustrate the danger presented by her remaining in town.

Stella had a way of inviting confidences. Perhaps it was because, like Evelyn, she came from relatively humble origins. Whereas Anne's and Julia's parents were wealthy, Stella had only enough funds from her clergyman brother to keep her horse and to purchase a modest wardrobe for the season.

Or perhaps it was the way Stella had of looking at one with such tender gravity. Her silver eyes steady, her gray hair lending her an air of uncommon solemnity.

Not that Evelyn could see her friend's hair at the moment. Whenever they were riding together, Stella concealed it with a hat, paired with a closely-woven silk hairnet.

"It seems, then," she said, "that the crisis has been averted."

Evelyn cast her a glance. "*This* crisis, anyway."

Stella laughed. "Have you so many others?"

"Several," Evelyn said. She guided Hephaestus around an open carriage. He was in fine form today, his thick neck arched and his ears pricked forward. Bristling with energy, he intermittently sprang into a lofty passage. It took most of Evelyn's attention to keep him to a walk.

She used her leg and her seat, along with the steadiness of her hands, encouraging him to engage his hindquarters. It was a delicate balance of weight and pressure. A conversation, of sorts, in a language Hephaestus could understand.

It was a language she spoke with fluency.

There was infinitely more to riding than simply kicking a horse to go faster or pulling on his mouth to slow him down. A fact that appeared to be unknown to many of the other riders out today. Lady Heatherton among them.

She trotted by on an elegant mare. She was glamorously clad and ruthlessly tight-laced, applying her whip to her horse's flank with no little force. Her gaze locked onto Evelyn as she rode past. "Miss Maltravers."

Evelyn inclined her head. "Lady Heatherton."

Her ladyship rode on, without so much as a word of greeting to Stella.

Stella didn't appear offended. "Thank goodness she didn't stop to converse with us."

"I don't think she likes me very much," Evelyn said.

"Indeed. She looked at you as though you were her rival."

"I'm certainly not." Before Evelyn could say anything more, another rider approached. She stiffened slightly in her sidesaddle.

"Miss Maltravers." Stephen Connaught tipped his hat. He was mounted on a rawboned bay.

Evelyn swiftly dispensed with the introductions.

Stella greeted him civilly, if not warmly.

Stephen didn't seem to notice. He was too busy admiring Hephaestus. "He's looking fit," he said. "How is he acclimating to town life?"

"Wonderfully," Evelyn said. "As am I."

Stephen's gaze drifted up over her figure before coming to rest on her face. "It suits you."

Once, the compliment might have meant something. But not anymore. "What about you?" she asked. "How long do you intend to remain in London?"

"Until my business is concluded," he said.

His business with Fenny and Anthony.

Evelyn prayed Stephen wouldn't find them. With luck, the moment Fenny received the check, she and Anthony would be on the next steamer back to France.

"We shan't keep you from it." Evelyn urged Hephaestus on, dismissing Stephen with a curt bow of her head. "Good day."

Stephen turned in his saddle to watch them as they passed.

"Does his remaining in London pose any difficulty for you?" Stella inquired when they were out of earshot.

"Not anymore," Evelyn said. "Not unless he's indiscreet about my sister."

"Would he be?"

"Only out of carelessness. He doesn't take the idea of my having a season very seriously." It was a lowering thought, but one Evelyn had come to accept. "He's never thought of me as a pretty girl who might appeal to a suitor."

"He's thinking of you that way now, I wager."

"He can think what he likes. I have no interest in him any longer."

"Truly? He's not unhandsome. He rather reminds me of those guileless, faired-haired young heroes in Julia's novels."

"Stephen is no hero. A hero doesn't abandon a lady when she's at her worst. And he doesn't humiliate her for three years by pretending she doesn't exist." Evelyn grimaced. "Enough about my tedious problems. What about you? Is there nothing you need sorting out this season?"

"Hmm. You could find me a respectable beau for starters. One of your young castoffs, perhaps?"

"I haven't any castoffs, young or otherwise. At the ball, nearly every man I danced with was in his dotage."

"You're faring better than I am. Only look at how the gentlemen stare at you. You're drawing all of their eyes. And *that* fellow isn't in his dotage. Nor is that one on the liver chestnut. Ugh. He's positively leering."

Evelyn registered the men's stares as surely as she always did when she entered the park. It made less of an impression now, especially in light of her feelings for Ahmad. "It's Hephaestus they're admiring— *and* my riding costume. When I commissioned it, I meant it to attract attention."

Stella smiled. "It's not your riding costume, you silly creature. It's you. No habit can make a lady desirable if she isn't already."

"Mr. Malik's habits can." Evelyn felt an odd tightness in her chest to mention him. The same oppressive weight that had been there ever since she and Ahmad had parted last night.

He hadn't even deigned to kiss her goodbye before she'd stepped out of the brougham. She feared he might never kiss her again.

But he'd squeezed her hand.

And his voice had deepened in that way of his, making heat pool low in her belly.

He *did* want her. He'd said so himself.

The rest was up to her.

"His designs bring out the very best in whoever wears them," she said. "It's a sort of magic he has."

"Perhaps I should commission one for myself," Stella said. "And one of his ball gowns, too, while I'm at it."

Evelyn brightened. "Oh, you should. He'll make something beautiful for you, I know it."

Stella's smile turned quizzical. "You have a great deal of faith in him."

"Not without cause." Evelyn was quiet for several seconds before admitting, "It means everything to me that his business should succeed."

Stella nudged Locket closer to Hephaestus. "Why should you care?"

Warmth infiltrated Evelyn's words, imbuing them with unspoken emotion. "Because," she said, "I think him the best gentleman in the world."

Stella was silent for a moment. "Well, then," she replied at last. "We must see what we can do for the fellow."

Twenty-Five

Ahmad was at his worktable in the back of Doyle and Heppenstall's, cutting a length of figured green grenadine barege, when Doyle poked his head into the room.

"A pair of ladies is here," he said in somber tones. "They're inquiring after your dresses."

Setting aside his scissors, Ahmad carefully folded away the thin gauzelike fabric he'd chosen for one of Evelyn's day dresses.

He'd been expecting new customers. After Evelyn's attendance at Lady Arundell's ball, they were all but inevitable. He nevertheless felt a glimmer of anticipation.

This was his goal. Not romance. Not falling in love. But building a fashionable clientele. It was past time he set his mind to it, instead of spending every waking hour brooding over Evelyn.

And he *had* been brooding.

Never mind that it had been only two days since he'd kissed her. Since he'd told her about his mother, and about his childhood in India. Secrets he'd never shared with anyone.

It was a sordid history. But it was *his* history. He didn't regret confiding it to her.

At the time, he'd meant it as a warning. It was only later, as the brougham had pulled away from the garden gate of her uncle's town house, leaving Evelyn safely behind, that Ahmad had realized how much he'd wanted her to know. Not just for her sake, but for his own.

Another infuriating part of this attraction he felt. This blasted desire to share every last piece of himself with her.

It was foolish. Dangerous.

If he wasn't careful, such impulses would ruin them both.

Rising from his worktable, he reached for his coat and pulled it on.

Seated nearby, Beamish and Pennyfeather cast him nervous glances as he strode past them to the curtained door. It was they who were responsible for filling Doyle's orders for gentlemen's suits at present. Orders that had lately been coming with decreasing frequency.

But that was none of Ahmad's concern at the moment.

He entered the sunlit showroom to find two young ladies standing at the counter. One was dressed entirely in black. The other—though she could be no older than her early twenties—had the most astonishing head of gray hair.

He recognized the pair of them. They were Evelyn's riding companions: Lady Anne Deveril and Miss Stella Hobhouse. They were accompanied by a smartly dressed lady's maid and a footman in Arundell livery. The footman's arms were filled with wrapped packages tied neatly with twine.

"Mr. Malik, I presume." Lady Anne's gaze swept over him. "You're Miss Maltravers's habit-maker?"

"I am," he said.

"And her dressmaker?" Miss Hobhouse asked.

"That, too."

The ladies exchanged a weighted glance.

Ahmad looked between the two of them with a growing sense of uneasiness.

Had Evelyn said something?

He doubted it. Not about their kiss, at any rate. But she might have said something else. Young ladies often shared confidences about men. Indeed, at Mrs. Pritchard's, Ahmad had frequently been the subject of secret glances and giggling whispers. He'd thought himself past the age of being embarrassed by such things.

But this was different.

This was Evelyn.

Heat rose beneath his collar.

"Can I help you, my lady?" he asked.

"I trust you can." Lady Anne set her gloved fingertips on the edge of the polished wood counter. "I require a black ball gown. Something with minimal trimmings—no flounces or frills. Miss Maltravers assures me you're the man for the job."

"Black," he repeated, frowning.

"Quite. And a black riding habit as well. The same style as the green one you made for Miss Maltravers."

"I, too, require a riding costume," Miss Hobhouse chimed in. "But one like Miss Maltravers's mink-colored habit."

"I can make something similar," he said, "but not identical. I don't duplicate designs. Whatever you order will be made for you alone."

"As to that . . ." A shadow of uncertainty crossed Miss Hobhouse's face. "Miss Maltravers did say you had an evening gown that another lady had returned. She said I might ask about having it made up for me as a ball gown at a discount."

His frowned deepened. "Did she, indeed."

"If the color suits me, that is," Miss Hobhouse added.

Ahmad thought of the ice-blue muslin gown, folded neatly in the storage chest at his lodgings. He'd resigned himself to taking a loss on it. It had been made so particularly for Lady Heatherton. But that shade of cool blue would also suit someone of Miss Hobhouse's complexion. In fact, with her gray hair and silver-blue eyes, it could—with a few minor adjustments—be quite stunning.

"Has Miss Maltravers any other message you wish to relay to me?" he asked.

Lady Anne smoothed her gloves. "I trust our dress orders are message enough."

They were, at that.

Evelyn hadn't forgotten him. Not only had she given his particulars to the ladies who had admired her dress at the Arundell ball, she was sending her friends to order gowns from him, too.

He was touched by the gesture.

Deeply touched.

And grateful. Business was business, after all.

Lady Anne and Miss Hobhouse weren't the leaders of the fashionable elite by any means, but they were moving in fashionable circles this season. Were they to wear his designs, it could only accrue to Ahmad's benefit.

He spent the next hour showing the young ladies some of his sketches and discussing fabrics and trimmings. By the time he finished taking their measurements, it was past one o'clock. He returned to the workroom, his head full of ideas for Lady Anne's ball gown.

Strange that that would be the order to catch his creative interest.

Black. It was unheard of. No lady in mourning would dare attend a ball. But Lady Anne wasn't in mourning, no more than her mother. Not in the strictest sense of the word. They were spiritualists, honoring the passing of Prince Albert. And black was a universal sign of respect for the dead.

He would have to approach the design as he did his riding costumes. Much like a lady's habit, mourning dress was distinguished by its lack of embellishment. If there was any style to be expressed, it was achieved through the luxury of the fabrics and the elegance of the cut.

This, Ahmad flattered himself, was where he excelled.

It was what the Pretty Horsebreakers had admired in his work. It was what Evelyn admired, too.

Fortunately for him, they weren't the only ones.

The next day, another lady called at Doyle and Heppenstall's, and then, the next day, three more ladies altogether. It set the pattern for the week that followed—a busy Monday and Tuesday, and an even busier Wednesday. When the last customer had gone, Ahmad once again retreated to the workroom to attend to his commissions. He was contemplating shades of claret velvet for a dowager's dinner dress when Doyle stepped in front of him, blocking his path.

"A great many ladies visiting the premises this week," he said. "They're beginning to outnumber the gentlemen."

Ahmad moved around him to get to his worktable. "That was the idea when we made our agreement."

Doyle followed after him. "Has it come to that already?"

"Near enough." Ahmad sat back on the edge of his worktable. "I'll need to hire another seamstress. Two, possibly."

Beamish and Pennyfeather paused at their work, looking up at Doyle and Ahmad with twin expressions of anxiety.

"And you wish to house them here?" Doyle asked.

"Naturally."

"What about Beamish and Pennyfeather? What's to become of them?"

"That depends," Ahmad said, "on whether or not they're willing to learn to make my designs."

Beamish was immediately on his feet. "Mr. Doyle, I heartily object. I won't be taught my trade by a . . . by a . . ." His face took on a ruddy hue. "By a *foreigner.*"

"I object, too, sir." Pennyfeather rose in solidarity with his fellow cutter. "Since Mr. Heppenstall's death, the tone of this establishment has lowered to such a degree I can no longer—"

"Then go," Ahmad said quietly. "You're not obliged to stay."

"I don't take my orders from you," Pennyfeather retorted, his voice wobbling. "I work for Mr. Doyle."

Doyle sighed. "You disappoint me, lads." Walking to Ahmad's worktable, the old tailor picked up a section of the now cut and basted grenadine barege. His gnarled thumb moved over the gauzy weave of the fabric, his expression contemplative. "Did neither of you ever ponder why so many of our customers request that Mr. Malik make their suits? Or why ladies call, demanding he design their riding habits?"

Beamish and Pennyfeather stood mute.

"Our customers recognize his talent," Doyle said. "And so would the two of you if you had an ounce of talent of your own." He dropped the fabric back on the table. "It's why I've agreed that he'll take over on my retirement."

"Mr. Doyle, no!" Beamish exclaimed.

Pennyfeather surged forward. "You're not really giving him Doyle and Heppenstall's?"

Doyle held up a hand. "Mr. Malik has said you can stay. I advise you to consider it. You might learn something of value. But if you can't bring yourself to work for him, I'll pay out your wages for the week and bid you good fortune."

Ahmad had no illusions about which path the two young cutters would choose. They'd never looked at him except with suspicion. Never shown any interest at all in his work. When they stiffly exited the room, he watched them go, unmoved.

"It's for the best," Doyle said wearily. "Suit orders have dried up. Perhaps if you—"

Ahmad slowly shook his head. "I have no interest in making gentlemen's suits anymore."

"No. Why would you when you can work with fabrics like that?" Doyle's rheumy gaze rested briefly on the folded grenadine. "Muslins and velvets and sheer silk weaves. It's a pleasant change from black and gray superfine."

Ahmad gave him a long look. He recalled all the times he'd caught Doyle examining his work. "Do you really believe that? What you said about my talent?"

Doyle's face was set in the same bleak lines as it always was. He showed not a glimmer of warmth. "I suppose I do," he admitted. "Why else would I have agreed to let you have my shop?"

Twenty-Six

❖

"A letter for you, miss," Mrs. Quick said, entering the breakfast room.

Evelyn looked up from the morning paper. She was alone at the table, the remnants of her breakfast arrayed in front of her—cold tea and a half-eaten serving of eggs, toast, and jam. "The post doesn't come this early, does it?"

"It didn't come with the post." Mrs. Quick gave Evelyn the letter. It was little more than a carelessly folded note, sealed with a crude blob of red wax. "A boy brought it round."

Evelyn was instantly alert. Setting aside the newspaper, she broke the seal of the letter, casting a grateful glance at the housekeeper as she did so. "Thank you, Mrs. Quick."

Mrs. Quick inclined her head. "I'll send in a fresh pot of tea," she said before withdrawing.

Evelyn scarcely heard her. The letter was from Fenny. A hastily written missive in her characteristic scrawl.

Dear Evie,

I should chastise you for interfering, but find I cannot. We were on the brink of despair when your note arrived. How in heaven did you manage to persuade our uncle to part with his money? However you did it, I thank you and Anthony thanks you.

He's booked us passage on the next steamer to France. By the time you receive this letter we'll have arrived in Calais and be well on our way to Paris. I've given the tavern owner strict instructions to hold delivery until Anthony and I are safely across the Channel. We can't be too careful with Stephen lurking about.

Once we're settled in our new lodgings, I'll send you our direction. Perhaps we might write to each other? It would be nice to have someone to tell when the babe arrives.

Faithfully, your sister,
Fenny

Relief coursed through Evelyn as she finished reading. Fenny was gone from London, safely on her way back to France, having done a minimum of damage to the Maltravers name in the process.

Evelyn privately wished her well. She couldn't condone the extremes Fenny had gone to in order to be with Anthony, but Evelyn understood her sister's motivations now better than she ever had.

When given the opportunity, what else could a lady do but follow her heart?

❦

The following Monday, Evelyn stood atop the elevated platform in the fitting room at Doyle and Heppenstall's as Ahmad pinned the bodice of her new green grenadine day dress. They hadn't been alone since the night they'd gone to the docks.

But they were alone now.

She'd seen to that. Only minutes ago, she'd sent Agnes off on an errand in Bond Street. It had been the veriest pretext and Ahmad knew it.

"You're determined to flout propriety," he said. His thick black hair was rumpled, the cuffs of his white linen shirt rolled up nearly to his elbows as he worked.

Evelyn's gaze lingered on his muscled forearms. She felt a familiar tightening in her belly. "You could have come to Russell Square. I'm amply chaperoned there."

"I'm too busy to leave the shop today." He sank a pin into the edge of her sleeve. "If I don't finish fitting your gowns this morning, I won't have time for the rest of the week."

Evelyn had three gowns waiting for their final fittings: the day dress she wore now, an afternoon dress, and a ball gown. The latter two garments were draped on the table in the corner, waiting their turn. All three were due to be delivered on Wednesday.

She had nothing else on order. No other dresses or riding habits were required. She was amply outfitted for the remainder of her time in London, and dared not test her uncle's generosity.

Besides, she wasn't really participating in the season any longer. Certainly not in the way she'd originally intended. Though she still went out with regularity—attending dinners, dances, and evening entertainments—it wasn't with the goal of finding a husband. Now she was merely displaying Ahmad's gowns. Praying that other ladies would admire them enough to order gowns from him of their own.

Given that, it would have felt dishonest to keep spending her uncle's money. As if she was taking advantage of him.

Thus far, he'd been fairly openhanded when it came to her wardrobe. More openhanded still now that he expected her to accompany him to some of his spiritualist events. But even he had his limits.

It meant no more visits to Doyle and Heppenstall's. No more chances to be alone with Ahmad.

She was painfully conscious of the fact.

"Work has been good?" she asked.

"It's been unending. Not to mention that the new seamstresses are settling in, and the workroom is in chaos."

"New seamstresses?" She was briefly diverted. "Are they more friends of yours, like Becky?"

"Not quite like Becky. But yes. I knew them before. They've been working for Madame Elise for the last year and were anxious for a change."

"Is that how you knew about the conditions at her shop?"

He nodded. "They thought they were bettering themselves, taking employment in Regent Street. Madame Elise soon disabused them of that notion."

"They're lucky you could take them on."

"I'm lucky to have them. I have more commissions than I can manage, even with Becky's and Mira's help. New customers are coming in nearly every day."

"They must be impatient for their orders," she said. "I don't mind waiting on my gowns if you need to finish theirs first."

He flashed her a dark glance. "*You* come first."

The words sparked a warm glow in her breast. She hadn't realized how much she needed to hear them.

All of last week, as she'd heard various society ladies remark on having placed orders with "that handsome Indian tailor in Conduit Street," Evelyn had been faced with a warring sense of triumph and misery. She'd pictured each of those ladies—many of them more beautiful than she was herself—standing just as she was now on the fitting room platform. She'd imagined Ahmad measuring them. Touching them and talking with them.

And worse.

Being inspired by them.

She'd feared it wouldn't take much for one of them to supplant her in his affections. She wasn't even certain of her own place there, not when he'd told her in no uncertain terms that this thing between them—this romance—couldn't work.

"My ball gown looks lovely," she said. The pale amber silk spilled over the edge of the fitting room table, revealing an overskirt of pale amber crepe and a bertha of lace and tulle. It would have fresh flower trimmings, too, on the night of the ball at Cremorne Gardens. Roses and frosted leaves to adorn the skirts and the bodice.

"You'll look lovely in it," he said. It was a compliment, to be sure, but one delivered in a state of distraction. He was entirely focused on finishing her dress.

Which was as it should be.

She nevertheless felt a flicker of frustration. "I didn't know what sort of dress was appropriate for an outdoor ball. I've never been anywhere like Cremorne Gardens."

He continued pinning. Either he hadn't heard her, or he was too consumed by what he was doing to render a reply.

She stood quiet for several minutes as he worked, letting the heavy silence unspool between them. Her frustration gradually transformed into a muted anguish, heavy as a boulder in her chest. Didn't he know this was their final moment together?

She made another effort at conversation. "Lady Anne tells me you're making wonderful progress on her ball gown."

"I am. I thank you for sending her to me."

"She and Miss Hobhouse were glad to come." Indeed, Evelyn's friends had been heaping praise on Ahmad for days. They thought him wondrously talented—and outrageously good-looking. "They're, ah, great admirers of your work."

Ahmad bent to adjust the seams of her bodice. "There have been other ladies, too."

"I'm aware."

"I thank you for that, as well."

"You don't need to thank me. All I've done is wear your clothes. I daresay they've helped me as much as I've helped you." She was possessed by the urge to rattle a response from him. A childish impulse—and a desperate one, too. But she couldn't seem to help herself. "It's what we intended when we formed our partnership, isn't it? The both of us getting what we want." Her airy tone was belied by the trembling in her stomach. "And now we have."

His hands stilled at her waist. "You've acquired a suitor?"

"Several," Evelyn said.

It wasn't a lie. Not if one counted the aged Lords Trent and Gresham, and the dreary Mr. Fillgrave. The latter had even called once in Russell Square. She'd spent a painful ten minutes with him in the drawing room, listening to him drone on about the bloodlines of his Spanish mares. An interesting enough subject to her mind, but Mr. Fillgrave never gave a woman room to speak. He'd talked *at* Evelyn rather than *to* her.

As for younger gentlemen, they seemed content to admire her from afar. Even Stephen Connaught. He'd been appearing in Rotten Row with regularity, always stopping to bid her good day.

"I'm pleased for you," Ahmad said.

But he was no longer pinning her gown.

He was looking at her and frowning, his shoulders visibly taut beneath the lines of his black cloth waistcoat.

"And I you. I hope your new customers . . . that all of them . . ." Evelyn trailed off. She didn't know what she hoped anymore. This was all so confusing.

"What?" he asked.

"Nothing." Her vision blurred. "Only . . . I wonder, what I am to you in all of this."

His brow creased. "Evie . . ."

"Just another customer?"

"I've told you what you are to me." His voice went gruff. "You're my muse."

"Yes. Well. That's splendid." She removed her spectacles. "But I suppose I want to be more than that."

"You *are*."

"Then tell me so," she whispered.

His jaw tightened. Taking her spectacles from her fingers, he withdrew a clean handkerchief from his waistcoat pocket and cleaned the tear-fogged lenses. "There's no point."

"Why not?"

"Because nothing can come of it."

She refused to accept it. "Just because you say that doesn't make it true. I believe—"

"What you believe is irrelevant." He settled her spectacles gently back onto her face. His fingers traced the thin metal earpieces over the curve of her ears. "I know how it is from actual experience."

And there was the rub. She hadn't any experiences to weigh against his. Only her heart and her determination. Proceeding from a position of strength, like her mother had taught her. It had to be enough.

But it wasn't.

Evelyn saw it plainly on his face. Despite how tenderly he touched her. Despite how his voice deepened and his body loomed so protectively over hers. Despite all of that, he'd set his mind against their being together.

Her throat squeezed with unexpected emotion. "I realize I don't know anything. Living in Combe Regis, the rest of the world feels very far away. I spent every day there worrying over my own family's troubles. There was precious little opportunity to think of anyone else's. No doubt it makes me seem small-minded and countrified, but I'm trying to do better. To listen and to learn. If you would but give me a chance—"

"You're not small-minded. You're innocent. You can't imagine what my life is like from day to day. The suspicious looks and the muttered remarks and innuendo. They come with such regularity I scarcely notice them anymore. But *you* would. You'd be hurt by them."

She felt a swell of frustration. He was trying to protect her. It was at once endearing and infuriating. "Ahmad—"

"You can't come here again without a chaperone," he said. "We can't be alone together like this anymore. It's too dangerous." He turned to walk away from her.

Evelyn placed a staying hand on his forearm. His bare skin was impossibly warm beneath her fingers. It sent a quiver of awareness through her.

He felt it, too, she could tell. He stilled at her touch, his expression transforming into something like a scowl.

It wasn't very encouraging.

Dropping her hand, she made one last attempt. "I'm stronger than you think."

He briefly averted his face. "Strength has nothing to do with it."

"But it does," she insisted. "I would endure anything for someone I cared about."

He glanced back at her, his eyes dark with frustrated longing. "I know you would," he said. "But I'd never ask you to."

Twenty-Seven

❧

For the purchase of fake flowers, foliage, and fruits, there was no better warehouse in London than Messrs. Valmar and Richardson in Cripplegate. It was a small establishment by most standards, but one packed full of lavishly exhibited stock.

Hands thrust into the pockets of his trousers, Ahmad strolled alongside Mira as she passed from one glass-fronted case to another. Inside were blossoms of every imaginable shade and size. Roses in all their forms—from humble dog roses to the most exquisite of French hybrids—kept company with orange blossoms, jasmine, and lush pink and white camellias.

"May I see this one, please?" Mira asked. "The pale pink?"

The warehouse clerk withdrew the tray of camellias from the case and set it down on the counter. "Is this for a hat, ma'am?"

"A lady's toilette." Tugging off her glove, Mira picked up one of the camellias with her bare fingers. The flower petals were nearly translucent.

"It's made of rice paper," the clerk explained. "With a flexible stem."

Mira glanced at Ahmad, her expectant face framed by a stylish little bonnet with an uptilted brim. The wide ribbons were knotted in a large bow beneath her chin. "What do you think?"

He shook his head.

Her lips thinned. She placed the rice-paper camellia back on the tray.

Ahmad wandered to the next case. He stopped to examine a garland of roses through the glass. It was exquisitely made, and uncannily lifelike, all the way down to the touch of brown on some of the leaves.

Mira caught up with him. "Is that more to your taste? It could do nicely for the skirts."

"No."

"You mentioned a garland."

"Of real flowers," he said. "Not fake ones." He walked to the next case. It contained a profusion of ivy interspersed with pieces of fruit.

"You haven't liked anything we've seen today," Mira said, following after him.

"I told you I wouldn't."

"Yes, because if you had your way, every gown you design would have the same amount of embellishment as on that black ball gown you made for Lady Anne. In other words, no embellishment at all." She exhaled a huff of breath. "What is your aversion to trimmings?"

He shrugged. "I don't like fuss."

"Fuss is in fashion. Mr. Worth's gowns—"

"I don't want to hear about Worth." Ahmad moved on to the next case.

Mira marched behind him. The swish of her skirts was beginning to take on an air of irritation. "I don't know why you agreed to come."

"I needed some fresh air. I thought I may as well accompany you as not."

"What *you* need is a good scolding." She drew him to a display case that stood unattended. Her voice lowered to a fierce whisper. "You're gloomy all the time now. And you're working too much. You don't even take five minutes to eat."

This was neither the time nor the place for such a conversation. It didn't stop Ahmad from responding in kind. "*Me*? What about *you*?"

She stiffened. "What about me?"

"You're as miserable as I am." He caught her bare right hand in his, turning it palm up between them. Her fingertips were discolored. "Ink stains," he said. "You've been writing a great many letters."

Mira jerked her hand away. "What of it?" She quickly slipped her glove back on. "Letter writing isn't a crime."

"Who are you writing to?"

"It's none of your concern."

"Who?" Ahmad demanded. He didn't like to play the tyrant. But Mira hadn't been herself lately. Even Finchley had remarked on it. She'd been preoccupied. Distracted by some private anxiety.

Adrift, she'd called it. Uncertain of her place in the world.

Ahmad had tried to anchor her. He'd offered her books to read in her leisure hours. And he'd offered her work. Work that she loved— sewing dresses and busying herself with embroidery designs and trimmings. It had filled her days, seeming to give her purpose.

But nothing, no matter how time-consuming, had yet served to take the cloud of worry from her brow.

She glowered at him. "Must you know all of my business?"

He didn't hesitate. "If it's something that's upsetting you, yes."

"I'm fine," she said. "I'm not the one who's pining. Who's losing weight from not eating."

"Don't change the subject."

"You're beginning to look like a feral wolf. It's scaring the customers."

He inwardly grimaced. "They can't be that scared. They're still coming, aren't they?" He'd taken on four new customers in the last week alone.

"Oh yes, the ladies keep coming to you," Mira said. "No doubt it gives them a thrill, just like it did the girls at Mrs. Pritchard's."

"You put our customers in the same class?"

"Why not? You do. You never saw any difference between those women and all the rest of them. They're one and the same to you.

Each just another figure for your designs." She folded her arms. "Until you met *her*."

Ahmad gave his cousin a bleak look.

"Why don't you go to her?" she asked.

His spirits sank even further. He hadn't thought it possible. He already felt as low as a man could get.

It had been two weeks since the day Evelyn had last come to Doyle and Heppenstall's. An entire fortnight since she'd stood in front of him, clothed in the basted pieces of the figured green grenadine barege day dress he'd made for her. Flutings of dark green ribbon had trimmed the bodice and skirt, and there had been a dark green ribbon belt at her narrow waist. She'd looked beautiful. Vibrant as the spring.

And he'd wanted her so much.

He still wanted her.

Much good it did him.

"I have nothing to offer her," he said.

Nothing save removing her from the society into which she'd been born. Making her an outcast. The same as any Englishwoman would be who yoked herself to a man of a different race.

And that was but the first obstacle standing in their way.

Even if they could clear it—somehow, some way—there would still be Ahmad's lack of fortune to contend with.

"Nothing to offer her?" Mira scoffed. "Within a year you'll be the most celebrated dressmaker in London!"

His mouth hitched. "You have a great deal of confidence in me, *bahan*."

"I speak as I find," she said. "Don't tell me you disagree?"

"Not in that respect." Despite everything, his faith in his work had never wavered. "But one year? Is that really your estimation?"

"If business continues at this rate, yes. Why? Is it not soon enough for you?"

It wasn't. Not for Evelyn's purposes. She needed a wealthy husband now, not twelve months from now. A respectable gentleman with the financial wherewithal to take care of her family, and to house and feed her horse. A man with financial security, not a newly minted dressmaker, dependent on the whims of London high society.

"A year is a very long way away," he said. "Too long."

Where would Evelyn be at such time? Married to someone else, probably. One of the many suitors who danced attendance on her—flirting with her at supper parties or sitting beside her at the theater. The society pages reported on them with regularity, speculating on which gentleman would ultimately win her hand.

The mere thought of it was another sharp knife in Ahmad's heart. He was beginning to feel as though he was bleeding internally.

Mira slipped her hand through his arm. "Let's get out of here."

"You don't want to look around upstairs?" The second floor of Valmar and Richardson's was dedicated solely to feathers. Ostrich, peacock, marabout. Any color and style of plumage a dressmaker or milliner could imagine, all displayed in the same neatly arranged glass-fronted cases as the floor below.

Ahmad had no appetite for any of it at the moment, but he wouldn't deny Mira the pleasure.

"Not today," she said. "Some other time when you're in a better mood." She pulled him toward the door. "Come. You'll feel better after you've eaten something."

❖

Evelyn entered Hatchards Bookshop, two clothbound volumes cradled in her arms. She dropped them down on the counter with a decided thump.

The clerk looked up with a start. It was the same older gentleman who had assisted her on her previous two visits. "May I help you, miss?"

"Yes, you may," she said. "I require a book on India."

His brows elevated. "Another one?"

"A better one. These aren't at all what I was looking for." She pushed the books toward him. She'd bought the first two weeks ago, and the second a week after that. On both occasions, she'd been disappointed. "I'd like to return them."

"On what grounds?" The clerk reached for one of the books. Opening the cover, he glanced at the elaborate frontispiece. "You asked for the history of India. There's none superior to Fletcher's writings on *England and Her Colonies*. And for local flavor, you can't do better than Captain Atkinson's reminiscences."

"So you said. But these books aren't written by the people who actually live in India."

"Captain Atkinson did indeed live in India, miss," the clerk replied. "As he describes in great detail."

"Yes, his descriptions are painfully detailed, but Captain Atkinson was not, in fact, an Indian."

"I see. You prefer a history written by a native."

"I do," she said firmly. "Haven't you anything of that sort?"

Outside the shop window, ladies and gentlemen bustled by in the bright midday sunshine. It was half past twelve. Evelyn hadn't much time to linger. She had to be back in Russell Square by one in order to make herself ready for any callers that might stop in during her receiving hours.

It was Agnes's half day. Blissfully on her own, Evelyn had taken the omnibus to Piccadilly Street, glad to be rid of the constraints of propriety, however briefly. For the past hour, she'd been as free as a tradesman's wife, making her way about town in virtual anonymity.

Well, perhaps not complete anonymity.

She was recognized by too many people now. Ladies and gentlemen who had met her at card parties, dances, and dinners, and who had seen her riding in Rotten Row. She was conscious of a few sidelong glances as she transacted her business at the counter.

Perhaps she shouldn't have ventured out alone?

But it was too late to second-guess herself.

"We may have something of that type," the clerk said. "But it wouldn't be anything I would call a reliable account. For that you'd do better to confine yourself to one of the military chronicles. The diary of Colonel Brough-Cholmondeley, perhaps?"

"No thank you," she said. "I've had quite enough of the tedious ruminations of ex-soldiers."

Behind her, a man cleared his throat.

Evelyn glanced back over her shoulder. And then she froze.

It was Captain Blunt, the infamous Hero of the Crimea.

She'd only seen him once, and had yet to be formally introduced, but his scarred visage was instantly recognizable. A gruesome slash ran from his right eye all the way down to his mouth. It gave his lips the appearance of a permanent sneer.

The impression wasn't helped by the rest of him. He was tall, dark, and dour, with a military bearing that put one in mind of a soldier on the battlefield. Indeed, he looked as if he could break her in half with his bare hands.

No wonder Julia had nearly fainted when he'd asked for an introduction.

"If you'll forgive the intrusion, ma'am," he said. "You're looking for an account of India written by a native Indian?"

"I am," she said.

"You might try *The Two Sisters* by Shahid Khan."

She blinked up at him. "Is that a history book?"

"It's a novel," he said. "A story about the importance of female education, recently translated from Urdu."

It was all Evelyn could do not to gape at the man. She didn't know what surprised her more, that he should know something about novels, about Indian writers, or about the education of women.

"We don't have that book," the clerk said.

"No doubt you can order it," Captain Blunt replied, "if the lady wishes."

"I do wish it," Evelyn said swiftly. "Thank you, sir."

The captain inclined his head to her. He was holding a brown clothbound book in his hand, waiting for her to finish her business so he could purchase it.

Evelyn chanced a glance at the gilt-embossed cover. Her eyes widened. Good lord. It was *The Woman in White* by Wilkie Collins.

Her gaze flicked to Captain Blunt's face. Never had she seen a gentleman who looked less sentimental. And yet . . . he read novels.

"I will make inquiries about Mr. Khan's book for you," the clerk said. He pushed her stack of books back across the counter. "But I can't accept these in return. You've already read them."

"I have," she said. "But—"

"This isn't a circulating library, miss."

Evelyn would have liked to argue, but not with a queue forming behind her. After leaving her direction for the clerk, she grudgingly collected her books, nodded a goodbye to Captain Blunt, and exited the shop.

Hansom cabs rolled by in the street, along with sporting gigs and carriages. Evelyn was walking briskly toward the omnibus stop when one of them stopped alongside her.

It was the Arundell carriage. Anne lowered the window. "Where are you going in such a rush?"

"Home to Russell Square," Evelyn said.

"Get in. I'll take you."

A liveried footman hopped down from his perch to open the door.

Evelyn murmured a thank-you to him as he assisted her inside. She sank down on the seat across from Anne as the door closed behind her. "I'm obliged to you."

"Not at all. I'm glad for the company."

"You're alone this morning?"

"For the moment. Mama is at a meeting with a representative of that boy medium from Birmingham. Such high drama! There will be a séance soon."

"With the boy in attendance?"

"Of a certainty. Mama is beside herself—far too distracted to mind me. She said I might use the carriage to do a little shopping. I've had an entire hour to myself." Anne arranged the skirts of her black silk dress as the carriage rolled back into traffic. "Did you just come from Hatchards?"

"I did. You'll never guess who I ran into." Evelyn described her encounter with Captain Blunt. "Do you suppose the man has hidden depths to him?" she asked when she'd finished.

"I suppose he might," Anne said. "But no amount of novel reading can blot out the fact that he has a brood of illegitimate children living with him. One child I could forgive. Even two, possibly. But an entire houseful?"

"A haunted houseful, if one believes Stella's description."

"Not only hers. I've heard tales of his haunted estate from others, too." Anne frowned. "No. Captain Blunt can't be considered a viable suitor for any of us. Julia least of all. She needs a mild, gentle sort of man."

"Do you have someone in mind?"

"Not yet. But I'm keeping my eyes and ears open." Anne leaned forward to examine Evelyn's books. "What did you buy?"

"These aren't new purchases. I was trying to return them."

"What's wrong with them?"

"They're bigoted rubbish," Evelyn said feelingly.

Anne picked up the topmost book. She read the title aloud. "*England and Her Colonies.*"

"Written by an overzealous colonizer, it turns out."

"Oh? And what about this one?" Anne lifted the second book. "*Curry & Rice, on Forty Plates: or, The Ingredients of Social Life at 'Our Station' in India.*"

"More rubbish." Evelyn had found the author's writing something worse than offensive. It had been contemptuous and condescending on the subject of native Indians and those of mixed Indian and English blood. Indeed, some of the passages had made her sick to her stomach.

"I'm sensing a theme." Anne cast her a sardonic glance. "If you want to learn about India, why don't you just ask him?"

Evelyn didn't need to inquire who *him* was. "It's not his responsibility to educate me. The ignorance is mine, and so must be the remedy for it."

"It would certainly be easier than exerting yourself over these." Anne flipped through the pages of the first book. "'The Hindoo and the Mahommedan readily acknowledge the superiority of the European,'" she read aloud, "'and are inclined to look toward him for instruction and protection.' Dear me. How dreadful it sounds." She snapped the book shut. "As dreadful in print, I suspect, as it is in practice."

"You disapprove of the British presence in India?"

"I disapprove of meddling, in all its forms. And we're a country of meddlers—often to disastrous effect. One can't help but condemn it."

"Not everyone is so enlightened," Evelyn said.

Anne lifted her shoulder in a shrug. "If I concerned myself with the opinions of other people, I would never leave my room." She dropped the offending book back onto the seat. "What will you do when you've finished all of your studying? Will you go to him?"

The notion tugged at Evelyn's heart. "No. I won't bother him at his shop anymore."

He'd told her not to come there without a chaperone. Had said they couldn't be alone together. And she wouldn't keep forcing herself on him. Heaven knew, she'd been reckless enough already where he was concerned.

"What, then?" Anne asked.

"I'll wait," Evelyn said. "If Mr. Malik wants to see me again, he'll have to seek me out for himself."

Twenty-Eight

———❈———

The following day, during her receiving hours, Evelyn was seated in the drawing room at Russell Square, sipping a cup of tea and reading the afternoon edition of her uncle's paper, when Mrs. Quick appeared in the doorway.

"Mr. Connaught, miss," she announced.

Stephen walked past the housekeeper into the room, still wearing his driving coat and gloves. His hat was in his hand. "Miss Maltravers," he said, bowing.

Evelyn experienced the faintest flicker of disquiet.

Between the hours of one and three, visitors dropped in regularly. She'd become used to welcoming them, everyone from Lord Gresham to Mr. Fillgrave. But Stephen was never among her callers. Indeed, since his acrimonious last visit, she hadn't done more than exchange passing pleasantries with him in Rotten Row.

"Mr. Connaught." Setting aside her teacup, she rose from the sofa. Her topaz-colored silk poplin skirt rustled softly over her petticoat and crinoline as she stood. Paired with a Garibaldi shirt of creamy white muslin, the ensemble was—thanks to Ahmad—as comfortable as it was beautiful.

She couldn't wear any of her clothes without thinking of him.

He'd been right to say they would give her confidence.

Indeed, though she hadn't seen him in weeks, he was always with her. There, in the seams that shaped her waist and the sleeves that skimmed her arms. In the low neckline of an evening dress and the elegantly gored fabric of her skirts. Making her feel strong. Beautiful.

Stephen's gaze swept over her in frank appreciation. "I bought a new gig," he said. "I've come to ask if you would accompany me for a drive."

She was taken aback by the invitation. "I'm not certain that's a good idea."

"It's an open carriage. There's nothing objectionable in you being seen with me in it."

"I don't doubt the propriety of it. I simply wonder if it's wise—"

He stepped forward, an expression of entreaty on his face. "I'd be grateful for the opportunity to speak with you in private."

She gave a sudden start. "It isn't about Fenny and your brother?"

"Yes," he said. "And, er, other matters."

Evelyn pressed a hand to her midsection. As far as she knew, her sister had safely returned to France. That didn't mean Fenny was free of danger. A pregnant woman was always at risk. Especially one living among strangers so far from home.

"Very well," she said. "Give me a moment to fetch my jacket and hat."

"I'll meet you in the square," Stephen said.

In short order, he was handing her up into his new gig. It was a smart vehicle, with a glossy black-painted body and bright yellow wheels. Two matching black horses danced in the traces.

"They're very elegant," she remarked as she slipped her spectacles into the pocket of her skirt.

"And priced accordingly." Hopping up onto the seat, Stephen gathered the reins and gave the horses the office to start. "I daresay I could have got the entire rig for less if I'd bought it in Sussex."

"Why didn't you?" she asked. "I thought you'd have returned there weeks ago."

He guided the horses from the square. Their steel-shod hooves clattered noisily on the cobblestones. "As did I."

Evelyn settled her wide-brimmed hat more firmly on her head. "Have you had news of them?"

"Of my brother? Yes. He's gone back to France if you can believe it. And your sister with him."

"Oh?" She made an effort to sound as if this was news to her. "It's for the best, I expect."

"For your sister, perhaps. For Anthony? I wonder. Sometimes I think he must be mad." He clucked to the horses, urging them into a trot. "You'll be glad, in any case."

"I *am* glad."

"Not for them. For yourself. You were concerned that your sister might harm your prospects." There was an undercurrent to his words, just shy of mockery.

She shot him a look.

"I didn't fully comprehend you at the time," he said. "But I've since come to understand."

"Have you?" She was doubtful. He didn't sound very understanding.

"I won't claim I wasn't surprised," he admitted. "A lack of imagination on my part."

That, Evelyn could well believe. "You never saw me as anything more than a comrade."

"A comrade. Yes. We were, weren't we?"

"I thought us friends," she said. "Until we weren't."

"You can't blame me for that. You know how my father is."

She did, but it was no excuse for Stephen's own behavior. "Your father wasn't anywhere near the village three years ago when you cut me dead in the street."

"Three years ago, I was a child."

"You were one and twenty. Nearly the same age as I was." She rested a hand on the side of the gig, gripping it to keep from being jostled against him. "There's no point in arguing over the past. What's done is done."

"Yes," he agreed. "Let's put that unpleasantness behind us. It makes no difference to our future."

"What do you mean our—" She broke off, turning sharply in her seat. "You're going in the wrong direction! Hyde Park is that way."

"We're not going to Hyde Park." He guided the horses through traffic. "There's something I want to show you on the other side of town. It's but fifteen minutes away. The drive will give us time to talk."

"What is it you want to show me?" she asked.

Stephen looked straight ahead as he drove. He didn't answer her. Not directly. "I had no inkling you were in London. The day I saw you riding in Rotten Row, I almost didn't recognize you. You've changed since coming here."

She watched the street flash by in growing apprehension. "Stephen—"

"I'm not criticizing you. You must know I find these changes appealing. It's part of the reason I've stayed in town. And we've always been comrades, as you say. Compatible in terms of interests and temperament."

Evelyn's blood ran cold.

Good lord.

He was going to propose to her.

All those years of waiting and hoping. Dreaming that he'd one day ask her to marry him. And now the moment was here, and all she wanted to do was leap out of the carriage and flee.

"Please don't say anything else," she said. "Truly. It's better if you—"

"I know you're upset that we've grown apart these past years. But that can't matter in the scheme of things. You must think of your place in the world. You'll want to be comfortable. And you'll want Hephaestus looked after. That much I can do for you."

"You're very generous, but I really don't—"

"I intend to be generous," Stephen said. He kept the horses at a quick clip. "Wait until you see the house I've found."

She stared at him, incredulous. "You've found a house for us?"

He nodded. "I was all over the city when I was looking for my brother. I scoured Mayfair to start, before moving on to Bloomsbury. From there I traveled east toward St. Paul's."

She listened to him describe his search in minute detail. Her alarm at the prospect of his proposal was gradually replaced by amazement at his rank stupidity. "Did it never occur to you to look near the docks?"

"At the logs of the steamers coming and going from France? I did. There was no trace of them."

"Not just at the ships' logs. At the inns and taverns nearby."

He snorted. "Anthony wouldn't be caught dead in such places. As for your sister, can you imagine her consenting to stay in a common inn?"

"Yes," she said dryly. "Only too well."

"Well, I can't. I thought it best to restrict my search to places where the pair of them might actually deign to stay. I got as far as Gracechurch Street. It was there I found the house I'm taking you to see."

Gracechurch Street?

"It's out of the way of fashionable society," he explained. "You wouldn't want to be always running into people you knew before."

A dawning suspicion awoke inside of her. "Just what is it you're proposing?"

"An arrangement," he said.

"An arrangement," she repeated. "Not a marriage?"

His gloved hands spasmed on the reins. The horses briefly broke into a canter. It took all of his attention to bring them back down to a trot.

"Not marriage, then," she said, "judging by your reaction." The carriage bounced along in silence for several uncomfortable seconds. It was a confirmation of Evelyn's worst fears. "I'll thank you to return me to my uncle's house."

"But what about—"

"I don't want to visit Gracechurch Street," she said. "I want to go back to Russell Square. Immediately, if you please."

He glanced at her. His color was high. "You can't honestly expect that I'd propose to you?"

Once, those words might have hurt her deeply. Now she felt only indignation. She didn't want him anymore. That didn't mean she'd countenance being insulted. "Why shouldn't you, if you care for me?"

"Because my father wouldn't approve. And because," he added, "you're not the kind of woman a gentleman would marry."

She stared at him.

"You must realize that," he said. "Why else are you here, parading about Hyde Park every afternoon in those riding habits of yours? You've all but put out your shingle."

"You think I'm setting myself up as a courtesan?" Evelyn sat back in her seat. She didn't know why she should be outraged at the suggestion. Ahmad had thought as much, too, when first she'd approached him about making her habits. But this was different. Ahmad respected women—*all* women. While Stephen meant to demean her. "And you thought you'd . . . what? Simply purchase my wares?"

"Don't be vulgar."

"The vulgarity is yours, not mine. What sort of gentleman suggests such an arrangement to a respectable lady? It's an insult."

"Respectable!" Stephen laughed. "Your family name will never be respectable. Your sister has lived with my brother outside of marriage. She's still living with him in an unmarried state. You're disgraced. You and all of your sisters. The sooner you face it—"

"Stop the carriage," she said.

"Indeed, I will not. You need to calm down and think about this rationally. The only path for you going forward is if I—"

"I said stop the carriage. Right now." When he didn't heed her, she moved as if to stand.

"For pity's sake!" He grabbed hold of her arm. "Do you want to kill yourself?"

"*Stop the carriage and let me out.*" Her voice was as hard as tempered steel.

At last, Stephen obeyed her. He pulled the gig alongside the edge of the street. "What do you mean to do, Evelyn? You don't even know where we are."

"I know exactly where I am," she lied. "And may I say, sir, before I take my leave, that I wouldn't marry you if you were the last man in the universe. You're right. You were a child three years ago, and you're still a child today. I suggest that, before you think about setting up a mistress, you consider *growing up*."

She didn't wait for him to assist her down. Taking her skirts up in one hand, she jumped out of the gig, landing hard on the dirty pavement.

Stephen cursed under his breath.

Ignoring him, she looked to her left and right, attempting to get her bearings. It wasn't a part of town she recognized. The street was lined with shops and warehouses, more commercial in nature than fashionable. Carts passed by, pulled by heavy draft horses, and a costermonger peddled his wares at the top of his lungs.

"You've made your point," Stephen said. "Don't be stupid."

"Goodbye, Stephen." She set off down the street at a purposeful walk.

"Wait, blast it. I can't chase you. I've no one to hold my horses. Evelyn. Evelyn!"

She kept walking, faster and faster, propelled more by anger than good sense. Stephen's voice faded behind her, lost amid the shouts of street hawkers and lorry drivers. He'd follow her in the gig, she had no doubt.

And she didn't wish to be followed.

At the first intersection, she turned right onto a street that was even busier than the one she'd just left. It was long, running as far as her eye could see. Wooden barrels cluttered the pavement. She maneuvered around them, ducking under the canvas awning of a shop. A brawny man was unloading a cart stopped in front of it.

He whistled at her as she passed. "Give us a smile, love."

A jolt of fear hastened Evelyn's step. She kept her eyes on the street, hoping to spot a hackney cab, or failing that, an omnibus.

Up ahead, two humbly dressed women with baskets over their arms examined the offerings at a fruit stall. One of them gave her an inquiring look.

Evelyn pasted on a smile. "I beg your pardon, ma'am. Is there an omnibus stop nearby?"

"Lost, are you?" the woman asked.

"I am," Evelyn confessed. "I don't even know the name of the street we're on."

The second woman laughed. "This is King William Street, miss."

"King William Street?" Evelyn caught her breath.

Great goodness. This was where Ahmad lived. He'd told her once that he had rooms above a tea dealer's shop here.

She glanced up at the painted shop signs in the distance, her pulse quickening. And sure enough, there it was, not more than a block away: *Tea Dealer*.

"There's an omnibus comes regular at the end of the street," the first woman said.

"Aye, every ten minutes most days," the second woman added.

Evelyn thanked them both before walking on. The tea dealer's shop drew closer with every step. She couldn't stop looking at the sign. Looking and wondering about Ahmad. So consumed was she with her daydreams that she didn't see the man himself striding toward her until the very last minute.

But he saw her.

He stopped where he stood, as if the sight of her had turned him to stone. *"Miss Maltravers?"*

Evelyn stopped, too, her heart thumping hard. She wasn't entirely certain she hadn't imagined him into existence. "Mr. Malik. Good afternoon."

All the noise of the busy street seemed to fade away, disappearing as if there were only the two of them.

Recovering himself, Ahmad advanced toward her. He was wearing a black three-piece suit, just as he always did, looking handsome beyond bearing. But there was something different in his appearance. He seemed thinner. As if he'd lately been ill.

And that wasn't the only change.

His countenance had lost some of that brooding artistic intensity she so admired. In its place was a stark sort of weariness. He looked tired and cross. Not wholly himself.

"What are you doing here?" he asked, coming to a halt in front of her.

"Trying to find an omnibus," she said.

"You didn't come to see me?"

"No. Not intentionally. I didn't realize where I was until five minutes ago. But now I'm here . . ." She'd promised herself that she wouldn't press him. That she'd wait for him to seek her out on his own. But this was different. She squared her shoulders. "Is there someplace we can talk? Someplace off the street?"

She waited for him to say no. For him to hurry her to the omnibus stop, or worse—to stride off, washing his hands of her completely.

But he only regarded her in silence. And then he nodded. "I have rooms upstairs. We can go there."

Twenty-Nine

‹✦›

$\mathcal{E}$velyn's astonishment at Ahmad inviting her to his rooms was quickly dispelled.

"Mira and Becky are here," he said.

"Oh?" Evelyn followed him up the creaking stairs at the back of the tea dealer's shop. She privately admitted to a feeling of disappointment. "They aren't working at Doyle and Heppenstall's?"

"Not regularly. There have been some disagreements with the other seamstresses."

"I'm sorry to hear it." The stairs led to a narrow corridor. There was an equally narrow door at the end of it.

"It's not unusual." He flashed her a glance as he retrieved a key from his pocket. "There's an art to managing seamstresses. One I haven't yet managed to perfect." He unlocked the door and opened it, standing back for her to enter.

She passed under his arm into what looked to be a sitting room. It was sparsely decorated, with a round wooden table in the corner and a worn sofa and chair arranged in front of an unlit coal fireplace.

It was also completely empty.

Ahmad followed after her, shutting the door behind him. "Mira? Becky?"

No one answered.

Evelyn waited, hands clasped tight in front of her, as he disappeared into the adjoining rooms. Her gaze drifted over the sitting room. The curtains and carpets were as faded as the furnishings, but the room was as neat as a pin. Neat and rather welcoming. The cushions on the sofa were plumped invitingly, and books, magazines, and sketch pads were piled on every available surface.

"They're not here," Ahmad said when he reemerged. "They must have gone out to get something to eat. There's a bakery in the next street."

"I suppose they'll be back soon?"

"At any moment, I expect. Perhaps we should . . ." But he didn't say what he thought they should do. He only looked at her, frowning, as if he'd lost his train of thought.

"There's no harm waiting, is there?" she asked. "So long as we're already here."

His frown deepened. He took a step toward her only to stop again. There was an expression in his eyes that was hard to read. "Why *are* you here? You said you didn't even know where you were—"

"I didn't."

"Then how—"

"I was out for a drive," she said. "With, ah, Stephen Connaught, actually." She considered how best to relate the incident that had brought her to King William Street. But there was no way to sugarcoat it. As usual, the truth would have to do.

As she told it to him, Ahmad's face darkened like a thundercloud. "He *what?*"

Evelyn took an unconscious step back. Her skirts brushed the wall behind her. "He's an idiot."

Ahmad closed the distance between them. "Why did you go with him?"

"He said he wanted to talk about Fenny and his brother. I thought he might have had news of them. I never expected him to make advances. I didn't even realize he thought of me in that way."

"He didn't hurt you?"

"No. It was only an insult. I'll soon recover. One day, I shall laugh about it."

He loomed over her. "You're trembling."

She was, rather. An unnerving sensation. Her back found the wall behind her, relying on it to hold her upright. "I—I didn't anticipate seeing you."

His brows lowered. "You haven't been to the shop in a fortnight."

"You told me not to come."

"I said not to come without a chaperone. I didn't tell you not to come at all."

"What excuse would I have? You've finished all of my dresses. And I haven't the funds to keep ordering more. Besides," she added, "I have my pride."

"What has pride to do with it?"

"If you don't want me—"

He muttered a blistering oath. "You think I don't want you?"

Before Evelyn could formulate a reply, he was upon her, his legs crushing her skirts between them. His large hands came to frame her face.

And she couldn't move. Couldn't breathe. She could only stare up at him, transfixed, her heart pounding like Hephaestus's hooves, thundering down the hard-packed surface of Rotten Row.

He bent his head to hers, his voice rough with barely suppressed emotion. "What I feel for you is so powerful, it would destroy us both, given the chance."

She thought he might kiss her then. She wanted him to. But in that fraught moment, it seemed more likely that he would let her go.

And she couldn't let him. Not yet.

Her fingers closed around his wrists. "How?"

———— ✦ ————

How?

Ahmad would have thought it obvious. "There could be talk. Just being seen with me. The mere hint of a scandal would ruin your chances on the marriage mart."

"Oh. That."

"Yes, that. The whole reason you're here." His thumbs moved over the curves of her cheeks. He couldn't seem to stop himself from touching her. She was so silken soft. So warm and sweet and pretty.

And she was his.

Every nerve in his body proclaimed it with unmistakable conviction.

Evelyn Maltravers was his.

He'd known it for weeks. Had been fighting against it with all of his might. But no more. She was here now. Had walked willingly into his lair. He hadn't the strength to deny himself any longer.

"I'm not concerned about that anymore," she said.

"Your suitors—"

"I haven't any suitors. I shouldn't have said that I did."

His heart clutched. No suitors? It didn't seem possible. Not when he'd spent the last two weeks envisioning them paying court to her.

"There are older gentlemen who flirt with me at dinners and dances," she said, "and who have come to call on me at my uncle's house, but it's nothing serious. Nothing you could call a courtship. The fact is, there aren't very many eligible young men in town, and among those that are, none of them are very impressive."

"Just because you haven't met someone yet doesn't mean—"

"I *have* met someone," she said. "I've met you."

Her words were a caress. As soothing to his soul as the touch of her fingertips resting on the throbbing pulse points of his wrists.

He swallowed hard.

"I've only continued going out in society so people might see me wearing your dresses. And because my uncle commands it." Her mouth softened in a slight smile. "He's made me attend a spiritualist card party and a spiritualist tea this week. Which isn't very different from a regular card party or tea, now I think of it, except that everyone was talking the entire time about this boy medium in Birmingham."

"Evie—"

"There will be a séance in the coming weeks. Lady Arundell hasn't yet confirmed where it will take place, but I'm certain to attend. Anne tells me that I'll need a black afternoon dress. So, you see, I will have to come back to you, if only for that."

"Evie, I can't—"

Her lips trembled. "Please don't reject me again."

He pressed closer to her. Drawn to her almost against his will. In that moment, she seemed very much a siren, and he no better than some poor mad sailor dashing himself upon the rocks. "Reject you? Good God. All I want—"

"It's what I want, too," she said.

The scent of her clouded his senses. Orange blossoms and starched linen, mixed with a fragrance that was unmistakably her. It was as potent as any aphrodisiac. He wanted to bury his face in her neck. To kiss her. To have her.

His voice thickened. "You have no idea what you're asking. You're an innocent."

Her hands fell from his wrists. Her chin ticked up. "I'm a woman. And I still care for you. If your feelings have changed—"

"My feelings are the same. But if we start something . . . I don't know if I'll be able to stop."

"Then don't stop," she whispered.

Warmth was already coursing through Evelyn's veins, just to look at him. To feel him cradling her face with such infinite care. It was utterly disarming that a man his size should be so gentle. But Ahmad was no run-of-the-mill gentleman to fumble roughly about with a lady. He was used to handling fine things. And in his hands, she felt like the very finest.

It was a heady sensation, to be the object of his undivided attention. And not for her clothing this time, but for herself.

Dropping one hand from her cheek, he bent his head closer to hers. He placed a kiss on her lips, as gentle as the last kiss they'd shared.

"I told you that you don't have to be careful with me," she murmured against his mouth.

"Impatient," he murmured back. "I'm just getting started."

"Forgive me. Do go on." She felt him smile. Was he laughing at her? But he didn't seem to be amused. He kissed her again. A sweet, clinging caress that stole her breath.

She sighed into it.

And this time there was no holding back. His arm came about her waist, and his mouth covered hers in a kiss so deep and passionate that the warmth in her veins ignited into a blazing conflagration.

Her eyes closed and she melted against him. A strange sensation—part victory, part surrender. She gave herself over to it for a moment.

And then she returned his kiss.

She had little enough experience. Only the kisses they'd shared in the fitting room and the brougham. But she prided herself on her ability to discern physical subtleties. She felt the pressure of his kiss change, his mouth seeking . . . something. Her lips parted in answer. Their breath mingled. And—

"*Oh*," she said. "Like that?"

"Just like that," he said huskily, drawing her closer.

"I never knew." No one had ever told her that a kiss could be so warm and intimate. That it could make one's limbs weaken into blancmange, even as it was inspiring a peculiar, tightening ache at one's center. She felt strange all over. Stranger still when he pressed hot, drugging kisses to her jaw, and to the secret, sensitive spot behind her ear.

When his mouth found the curve of her neck, her knees sagged. She clung to him as he surged against her.

His fingers tangled in her hair, loosing the pins Agnes had placed so carefully this morning. Some of them pinged to the floor. Evelyn glanced down at them, half-dazed. They'd fallen into the corner at the edge of the fireplace, alongside a folded piece of white paper. It had Ahmad's name written on it in black ink.

"What's that?" she asked.

He continued kissing her.

She clutched at his cravat. "It looks like a note."

At last he stilled. Raising his head from her neck, he followed her gaze.

A long moment passed before he eased away from her.

Evelyn stayed pressed to the wall, afraid to move. She had the sense that they'd been on the precipice of some further intimacy. She wasn't entirely ignorant of the act. But she certainly hadn't planned to indulge in it before marriage.

And she realized, suddenly, how little planning had to do with it.

When one was in the arms of a man, feeling hot and trembly and longing for him so much, all one wanted was more and more and more.

It was all *she* had wanted.

Distance helped to cool her wild yearnings, but not by much.

Ahmad knelt to retrieve the note. "It must have blown from the mantel when I opened the door."

Evelyn put on her spectacles. "Is it from Mira?"

"It is." He scanned the message inside. His expression hardened into an implacable mask.

Evelyn had never seen him look so forbidding. "What is it? Has something happened?"

"She and Becky have gone."

"Gone where?"

"Back to where we lived before. To the East End. To see a friend,

Mira says. They left at nine." He turned to Evelyn, all traces of passion gone from his face. "They should have been back by now."

Evelyn stood from the wall. There was nothing like a crisis to bring one back to reality. She went to him. "What will you do?"

"Go after them."

"I'll come with you."

"No," he said. "That place . . . I don't want you anywhere near there. I'm putting you in a cab and sending you home."

He looked so terribly bleak. So resolved to face everything on his own. Her heart swelled for him, even as her will rose up to challenge his.

"Indeed, you are not." She reached to cup his cheek, looking steadily into his eyes. There was reassurance in her touch. And something more, too. Something between them, as yet unexpressed. "I'm coming with you."

He said nothing. Didn't speak. Didn't move. How long had he been alone in the world? Feeling as if he must forge his way himself, without an ally to stand at his side?

She wanted to be that for him. She wanted them to face the future together. And if they must first face his past, then so be it.

He gazed down at her. And he seemed to see it. The way she felt for him. It wasn't some weak, ladylike infatuation. It was strong, just like she was. Strong and true and willing to risk anything.

When next he spoke, he didn't argue. "Very well."

Thirty

—✦✦—

The hired hackney coach ricocheted through the streets of London at a perilous pace. It was a converted brougham, the coat of arms of its prior owner still vaguely visible on the nearside door beneath layers of fading paint. Ahmad had promised the driver an extra half crown to get them to Commercial Road double quick. He hadn't accounted for how uncomfortable the speed would be. Evelyn was pressed tight to his side, from shoulder to knee, jostling against him as the vehicle clattered and bounced over every crack and pothole.

She handed him back the note after reading it. "Mira doesn't mention Mrs. Pritchard's."

"She didn't have to." Ahmad thrust the folded note into a pocket of his waistcoat. He knew of only two places Mira might have gone—either to Becky's lodgings or to Mrs. Pritchard's establishment. Given recent events, it was the latter that seemed more likely. "She's talked about writing to friends there," he said. "She knows I don't approve of her visiting them. When we left two years ago . . ."

"Becky told me there was some kind of dustup."

"That's one way of putting it." Leaning back in the seat of the hansom cab, he raked a hand through his hair.

"She said you broke a man's shoulder. A baronet who'd been violent with her."

He grimaced. "Did she."

"Is it true?"

"Unfortunately, yes." It was one of the rare occasions Ahmad had lost his temper. And to disastrous effect. "He roughed her up. Blacked her eye and knocked out one of her teeth. She was only a girl, fresh up from the country. And he was drunk. Belligerent and unrepentant: I hauled him out into the alley and tossed him against a wall."

"Oh dear."

"He broke his shoulder. Which was no less than he deserved."

"Becky said you saved her life."

He exhaled. "I don't know. Probably. But I didn't have to injure the man to such a degree in order to do it."

"He didn't take it well, I gather."

"No, he did not. Nor did Mrs. Pritchard." Ahmad recalled the weeks that followed. Weeks during which there was a very real possibility that he might be hanged or transported, leaving Mira all alone to fend for herself. "The baronet wanted me prosecuted, which I was. Luckily, it didn't come to anything. Mr. Finchley used to take on cases like mine. Matters of conscience, he called them. Once he took up my cause, there was no question of my being transported."

"Is that how you came to work for him?" she asked.

He nodded. "After Mrs. Pritchard gave me the sack, Finchley offered Mira and me positions with Miss Holloway—his future wife. She was going to India for several months and needed a manservant and maid."

"Thank God for that," Evelyn murmured.

Ahmad *had* been thankful. For a time, following his dismissal from Mrs. Pritchard's, he hadn't known what he would do with himself.

"Were you glad to see India again?" she asked.

"It was an experience. I hadn't been back since I was fifteen. Long before the uprising."

"I've been reading about the uprising," she said.

He frowned. "Why?"

"I've been reading about all of India. Trying to, anyway."

"Yes, but . . . why?" he asked again.

A flush of pink tinted her cheeks. "Because," she said, "I want to know everything about you."

Something fractured within him. A part of his innermost self, made hard by time and experience. He felt it give way inside of his chest. "Ah, Evie . . ."

She turned in her seat, her eyes earnest behind her spectacles. "There aren't very many books that give a clear perspective. Everything at Hatchards seems to be written from a British point of view."

His expression softened. She looked so serious sitting beside him. And so damnably beautiful. She was wearing a topaz-brown silk skirt he'd made for her, and the matching Zouave jacket with lashings of black braid. Its wide pagoda sleeves revealed the soft white muslin undersleeves and linen cuffs of the Garibaldi shirt she wore beneath.

All of it was his. Garments he'd designed for her. Had sewn with his own hands, taking into account every curve on the landscape of her body.

It gave him a feeling of possession to see her in his clothes. A sense that she belonged to him.

As if he needed further proof.

Less than half an hour ago, he'd been embracing her. Kissing her lips, her face, and her throat. His fingers had been in her hair, forcing the pins from her thick tresses. And she'd been clinging to him and kissing him back with warm, half-parted lips.

If not for the interruption, God only knew what else might have happened.

"You won't learn anything about me by reading books," he said. "The India I knew isn't the one people write about. And anyway . . . it's part of my past. When I went back, I was a stranger there. I didn't fit anywhere, no more than I do here."

"I'm beginning to think that fitting in isn't all it's made out to be. Everyone I've met since coming to London has been peculiar in some way. Nearly as peculiar as I am."

"You are peculiar, aren't you?" His voice deepened to a murmur. "The most wonderfully peculiar girl I've ever known."

She slipped her gloved hand into his. "I shall take that as a compliment."

"I hope you will. It's how I meant it."

There was more to be said, but neither of them said it. They didn't have time.

The hackney stopped with a jolt along the edge of Commercial Road.

Ahmad's body tensed at the familiar sights and smells. This was the second time in as many months that he'd been back here. But this visit was different.

This time, he wasn't alone.

◆───✖───◆

Mrs. Pritchard's gentlemen's establishment stood at the end of a narrow lane. A filthy, sagging building held together with layers of soot and grime and a haphazard coat of peeling white paint. Every chip and crack was illuminated in the unforgiving midday sun.

It had been two years since Ahmad had seen it, this place where he'd lived for nearly half of his life. His shoulders were set, his jaw tight as they approached. Though he looked straight ahead, he was aware of every movement around them. Every twitch of a curtain and every shadowed figure lurking in a doorway.

A mob of children in ragged clothing trailed after them for a few yards, only to be chased off by a man emptying a pail of refuse into the street. It was another foul note added to the already-pungent symphony of night soil, rotting food, and fetid river water.

Evelyn briefly covered her nose.

"It's worse when the sun's out," Ahmad said. "You get used to it."

She gave him a doubtful look. "Are you sure Mira's here?"

"No." He wasn't sure of anything. "But she said she was visiting an old friend. And these are the only friends she had."

The stairs at the front of the house were broken in the middle. He led Evelyn up along the edge of them to the warped wooden door. A rusted knocker hung there from one loosened nail. A useless implement. He bypassed it completely, pounding on the door with his fist.

It was opened by a hulking older man wearing an ill-fitting coat and a pair of worn trousers. His broad face broke into a smile. "Malik!"

Ahmad recognized the fellow. It would be difficult not to. Joe Tweed had previously worked at the public house on the corner, removing quarrelsome drunks from the premises. He was as big as an ox. "Tweed," Ahmad said. "You're working here now?"

"Aye. Since you left." Tweed directed his snaggled grin at Evelyn. "And who's this with you? A new girl for the missus?"

Ahmad stepped in front of Evelyn. A muscle twitched in his cheek. He felt the overpowering urge to punch his old acquaintance squarely in the face. "She's mine," he said. "I'll thank you to keep your eyes in your head."

Tweed held up a hand, laughing. "Easy, lad. I don't mean nothing. Just puzzling over why you're back, that's all."

"I'm looking for my cousin. Is she inside?"

"Little Mira?" Tweed appeared genuinely surprised.

"You haven't seen her?"

"Not since the pair of you left."

Ahmad's stomach tightened with apprehension.

His mind went immediately to the darkest possibility, imagining Mira out there somewhere, vulnerable and exposed, prey for any villain who crossed her path.

Evelyn squeezed his arm. "She has Becky with her."

He nodded grimly. Mira and Becky together was better than either of them wandering about alone. But it wasn't much of a defense against the local elements. If a ruffian was intent on meddling with them, two young women couldn't hope to defend themselves.

"You want me to fetch the missus?" Tweed asked.

"I'm here." A familiar female voice floated up from behind him. It was followed by the woman herself: Lily Pritchard. She wore a loose housedress, her gray-streaked hair twisted up on her head in a careless knot.

Ahmad inwardly recoiled at the sight of her.

For thirteen years she'd been his employer. She'd never hurt him. Had never forced him to her bed. But her interest had always been clear. She'd petted and handled him, knowing all the while that he must endure it or end up back on the streets, and his cousin along with him.

"Malik." She regarded him in much the same way Lady Heatherton had. "What's the meaning of this, banging on the door in broad daylight, as if you were the law? You know we don't entertain visitors until sundown."

"He's looking for Mira," Tweed said.

Mrs. Pritchard's bloodshot eyes became acquisitive. "Well, well." She lounged in the doorway. "Have you lost her at last? Your little ward?" Her gaze moved to Evelyn. "And who might you be?"

"A friend," Evelyn said, pushing up her spectacles. "I'm no concern of yours."

"Oh ho!" Mrs. Pritchard laughed. "What starch! Malik's got himself a little bluestocking."

Ahmad turned to leave, guiding Evelyn back down the stairs. There was nothing to be gained by conversing with Mrs. Pritchard.

"If she comes here, I shall welcome her back," she called after them. "There's always a place for pretty girls in my house—if they're willing to work. That goes for you, too, my fine lady."

Evelyn stiffened.

Ahmad drew her along with him down the street, putting as much distance between them and the brothel as possible. "Ignore her," he said.

"What a horrible woman."

"You don't know the half of it."

"Nor do I need to. You dislike her excessively. That's enough for me."

Some of the tension in his muscles eased. "Is it that obvious?"

"To me it is," she said. "Did she not treat you well? I know she dismissed you, but—"

"It's not only that." The two of them walked back down the lane. "She's a particular kind of woman. I've met many of her type since coming to England. They're unpleasant at the best of times, dangerous at the worst."

"Dangerous how?"

"If you cross them, they use all of their power to punish you. And they have a great deal of power."

"She didn't look very powerful."

"Because of her class? She's still an Englishwoman." Ahmad looked out at the intersection of the lane ahead. "If Mira didn't go to the brothel, I can think of only one other place she might be."

"Where?"

"Lost Hope Yard. Becky has lodgings there above a rag-and-bone shop." Tucking Evelyn's hand more firmly in his arm, he guided her down the lane and to the right.

"I thought Becky was living above Doyle and Heppenstall's now?"

"Not consistently. Her room at Mrs. McCordle's is paid through the end of the month. She still goes back there on occasion, when she's had enough of the other seamstresses."

They walked down one lane and up another, keeping a brisk pace so as not to invite interference from beggars or any of the people who lingered between buildings.

At last, they came to the corner of Lost Hope Yard and the crooked wooden structure that housed the rag-and-bone shop. Becky was pacing in front of it, arms crossed at her waist.

Relief tore through him. "Becky!"

She looked up with a start. Her face fell. "Bloody hell. What do you mean by coming here?" Her gaze flicked to Evelyn. "And why the devil did you bring *her*?"

Evelyn's hand fell from his arm as he strode forward.

"Where's Mira?" he demanded.

"She's upstairs, but— Wait!" Becky held her hands up to block his path as he moved to walk around her to the door of the shop. "She's visiting a friend."

"What friend?"

"Her old sweetheart."

"*What?*" For an instant he could only stare at her. Mira had never had a sweetheart. She'd never had any relationship with a man at all. She was far too shy.

"She knew you'd take it bad," Becky said. "What with you always treating her like a child."

Ahmad ignored that. "Who is it?"

"A sailor. He only came back yesterday. She thought he might have died at sea. Either that or forgotten her. She's been in a right state over it."

"So you just . . . let them use your room?" He moved Becky aside.

She chased after him. "It's not like that!"

Evelyn entered the shop along with them. The brass bell rang loud and long, announcing their arrivals, one after the other.

Mrs. McCordle looked up from her seat at the bottom of the stairs. "Oh no," she said. "There's one man up there already. This ain't no knocking shop."

"Wait here," Ahmad said to Evelyn and Becky. His tone left no room for argument.

He vaulted up the stairs. The wooden steps groaned beneath him in protest. Striding down the short hallway at the top, he was nearly at the door of Becky's room when it opened and a man emerged.

It was a dark-faced sailor in a woolen peacoat and trousers.

An Indian man, in fact.

Mira came out the door after him. "I'll walk you back," she was saying. And then she saw Ahmad. She froze where she stood, eyes widening.

Becky called out from the bottom of the stairs. "I told you not to leave that blasted note!"

"You must be Mira's cousin," the man said. He had a British accent with a Bengali lilt to it.

"And you are?" Ahmad asked in a voice of perilous quiet.

Mira hurried between them, as if in anticipation of a fight. "Ahmad, this is my friend Tariq Jones. Tariq, my cousin, Ahmad."

Ahmad's gaze narrowed. It appeared Mr. Jones was part English, like they were. "Your *friend*?"

"That's right." She lifted her chin in defiance. The subtle action reminded him of Evelyn.

It didn't disarm him. He was too angry for that. But it brought him up short. "You and I need to talk."

"If you want to have words with me," Mr. Jones replied, "I'm ready to hear them."

"Not you," Ahmad said.

"He means me." Mira gently pushed Mr. Jones's shoulder. "It's all right. You can go. Please. I'll write to you this evening."

Mr. Jones's reluctance to leave her raised Ahmad's estimation of the man by several degrees.

"Go," Ahmad said. "She's safe enough from me."

Mr. Jones dipped his head. Giving Mira a last look, he disappeared down the stairs.

Ahmad pointed to Becky's room. "Inside."

Mira went rigid at the autocratic command, even as she obeyed it.

"Becky?" Ahmad called down the stairs. "Look after Miss Maltravers."

"Miss Maltravers?" Mira was aghast. "You brought her here?"

Ahmad inwardly flinched. He hadn't even begun to grapple with the fact that he'd subjected Evelyn to all this wretchedness. But he wouldn't be distracted. "Miss Maltravers is the least of your concerns."

He followed his cousin into the small, dank room and closed the door behind him. He cast a glance at the bed. It was neatly made, the thin coverlet unrumpled.

"Nothing untoward happened," Mira said.

"You were alone with him in here, with the door shut."

"I needed to have private words with him." She smoothed her dress—an embroidered muslin, as neat and unrumpled as the bedcovers. "Why were you at your rooms at this time of day? You don't usually return to King William Street until after six."

He didn't. Not in the normal course of things. But today he'd been too restless to remain in the workroom at Doyle and Heppenstall's. He'd needed some fresh air—a moment to clear his head—and had thought he might as well check the progress on a few of the dresses Becky and Mira were working on.

"Lucky I did," he said. "Else I wouldn't have seen your note."

"You weren't meant to see it. I only left it as a precaution, in case something happened and I didn't return by evening." She seemed to realize immediately that this was the wrong thing to say to him. "Nothing would have happened," she added hastily. "I've been in no danger."

"No danger? Does any of this look safe to you?"

"Safe enough. You brought Miss Maltravers here, didn't you?"

"You'll leave her well out of this," he warned.

"Is she the reason you were at your rooms in the middle of the day?" Mira gave him a challenging look. "Perhaps you wanted a private moment with her just as I did with Mr. Jones."

"The difference being I thought you and Becky would be inside my rooms. I didn't intend to be alone with her." His voice rose in spite of himself. "And I didn't have a friend standing guard in the street lest I be discovered."

"Becky wasn't standing guard. She was waiting until I finished talking with Tariq." Mira's voice rose to match his. "And I *had* to talk to him. Until this morning, I thought him lost at sea."

Ahmad silently counted to ten. Nothing could be gained by arguing with her. "Enough of this bickering," he said. "You had better tell me all of it."

Her lips pursed. Folding her arms, she walked to the grime-steaked window opposite the bed. "I met him two years ago. Not long before Mrs. Pritchard turned us out."

"Where?"

"When I was walking back from the market one day. He helped me to carry my basket."

"How obliging of him," Ahmad remarked with razor-edged sarcasm.

She shot him a dark look. "Do you see why I didn't tell you?"

"Forgive me. Go on."

She inhaled a deep breath. "He was kind and respectful. And he made me laugh. He didn't mind that I lived at Mrs. Pritchard's or that—"

"What right has he to mind?"

"Must you keep interrupting? I'm trying to explain that we *liked* each other. He understands me. He's patient and kind—"

"You said that already."

"Well, he *is* kind. And he writes the most beautiful letters. But one day, six months ago, they stopped. I thought he'd forsaken me."

"Which is why you've been so miserable." Ahmad was beginning to understand.

"Yes. That evening when we talked at the Finchleys', I'd given up hope of ever seeing him again. It wasn't until you hired Becky that I learned his ship hadn't arrived back in port from its last voyage. It was presumed lost at sea. I wrote letters to everyone I could think of, but no one knew anything. I feared the very worst."

"You thought him dead."

"I did. Until today. When Becky came to King William Street

this morning, she told me that his ship came in last night. It had been becalmed, you see. And then the crew took ill and they had to stop for repairs. Tariq very nearly didn't make it back at all. But he's here now, and he's going to find work on the docks. If he—"

"Do you love him?" Ahmad asked abruptly.

She didn't hesitate. "Yes."

"Why didn't you tell me? If you'd said something about him, I might have—"

"Because he's not good enough for you," she said. "And because I knew you'd say he wasn't good enough for me."

He shook his head. "Mira—"

"I realize a sailor isn't as well-to-do as a tailor."

He gave her an ironic look. One may as well compare a skilled tradesman to a common laborer. A sailor couldn't even rely on having employment all the year round. And when he did work, it was work that took him far from home, often for months at a time. His family was left behind to subsist on his meager earnings.

"I don't mind being poor," Mira continued determinedly. "I can go without fine things if I have to, so long as I have someone of my own. I'm not content to be an outsider all my life. An observer like you."

He scowled. "What's that supposed to mean?"

"That's what you are. That's why nothing hurts you. You stand on the outside watching, not because you have to, but because you choose to. Because it's safe. But I never wanted that. I don't need to be protected anymore. I want to be part of this life, even if it can't all be perfect."

"I see." He regarded her for a long moment, wondering how he'd missed all of this. He'd been so consumed with his dress designs and with Evelyn, he hadn't troubled to delve deeper with Mira. Perhaps if he had, things might have proceeded differently.

Or perhaps not.

Mira wasn't a little girl of eight anymore, clinging to his coat and hiding her face against his sleeve. She was a woman grown. One possessed of talent, intelligence, and decided opinions.

He respected her judgment in matters of fashion. Was it too much for her to ask that he respect it in matters of the heart?

Ahmad already knew the answer.

"I want to meet him properly," he said.

An expression of relief passed over her face. "Of course."

He felt a faint twinge of regret. Had he been so unreasonably restrictive as her guardian? So demanding that she keep herself apart from ordinary people?

It was what she claimed he did with himself. Held himself apart from life—from love.

An observer, she'd called him.

He wondered if there was any truth in the charge.

❖

By the time the hired carriage rolled up to the back door of Evelyn's uncle's house in Russell Square, it was approaching six o'clock.

Ahmad had sent Becky and Mira home together in a separate cab. Evelyn had said she could return on her own, but he'd insisted on accompanying her himself. Not to talk. He hadn't said more than three words strung together since they'd left Mrs. McCordle's. He'd been still and quiet. Gazing out the window in silence as the dilapidated buildings of the East End docklands gave way to the fashionable houses of the West End.

She suspected he had regrets about taking her with him. Not because there had been any danger, but because she'd seen pieces of his life he preferred to keep hidden. Remnants of his not-so-distant past. The sagging brothel with its chipped paint and broken front steps, and the equally derelict rag-and-bone shop.

People lived in such places.

And not only the working women of Mrs. Pritchard's, but other people, too. Families and children. Friends and neighbors. Couples like Mira and Tariq, meeting and falling in love, and planning to settle down.

The obstacles to Evelyn's own happiness seemed small in comparison.

"When will I see you again?" she asked before she climbed out of the carriage.

"Soon," he said. "I'll need to fit you for your black afternoon dress."

"I didn't mean at the shop."

"No." He frowned. "I realize that."

She gathered up her skirts. On the last occasions they'd been together, she'd been uncertain of him. But not now. Not after the passionate embrace they'd shared in his rooms. And not after the words he'd uttered as they'd stood on the steps of Mrs. Pritchard's establishment.

"She's mine," he'd all but growled.

Evelyn had felt his declaration to her marrow. She was his. And he was hers. There could be no more pretense between them.

"If you want to see me again," she said, "you must come to me in some other way."

His face was half-shadowed in the dim interior of the cab. "You want me to call on you here? At your uncle's house?"

She imagined him applying at the front door instead of the tradesman's entrance. Joining her for tea in the drawing room. A proper courting call. "Yes," she said. "Or you can seek me out at one of the events I attend."

He gave her a dark look. "I'm hardly likely to be invited to a spiritualist ball, Evie."

Her mouth tilted. "Who said anything about an invitation?"

Thirty-One

❈❈

$\mathcal{E}$velyn had often read about Cremorne Gardens in the newspaper and in ladies' magazines. Descriptions of grand events featuring tightrope walkers, balloon ascents, and military exhibitions. It had made Cremorne seem an exciting place. A true pleasure garden, where one might enjoy music, dancing, and spectacles under a starlit sky.

Reality was no less magical.

Indeed, as she crossed the grounds with her friends, Evelyn was unprepared for the beauty of the vast illuminated landscape—twelve glorious acres of it sprawling along the northern bank of the Thames. It was studded with fountains and statuary, and tables were tucked into every available nook and cranny to accommodate the fashionable crowds.

But it was still a garden. One edged by ancient trees and boasting private walks, hidden corners, and many a dark place for a secret assignation.

"Take care," Anne warned. "It can get rowdy after dark." Her alabaster décolletage shimmered in the moonlight. She was wearing the black ball gown Ahmad had made for her. A sumptuous confection of watered silk, it boasted a daring neckline, cut low across her bosom and shoulders, and a gored skirt that drifted to the back in a luxurious swell of fabric.

Julia traipsed along at her side, the flounced skirts of her own silk-and-lace ball gown held in her hands. "Only if one wanders away from the music and dancing."

The orchestra pavilion loomed ahead—a majestic Chinese pagoda illuminated by hundreds of colored lamps. It was surrounded by a circular wooden dancing platform.

"I've read that it can accommodate as many as four thousand dancers," Stella said.

"Oh," Julia moaned. "I get sick to even think of that many people."

Evelyn gazed up at the brilliantly lit pagoda in unvarnished wonder. Cool evening air kissed her bare chest and shoulders, and orchestra music hummed in her veins.

Her own ball gown was made of a shade of amber silk and crepe so delicately pale it resembled the glow of gaslight. Becky had come by Russell Square this evening to affix gold roses and frosted leaves on the skirts and bodice and in the stylish waterfall rolls of Evelyn's coiffure.

"Lady Blackstone has reserved half of it for us," Anne said. "Though it will be difficult to keep the two sides from mingling. One never can at these sorts of events, even with screens."

"Why does she not use her own ballroom?" Evelyn asked.

"She prefers to host her entertainments out of doors." Anne gave Evelyn a wry look. "A medium once told her that there should be nothing between her and the stars. And if there's a full moon, all the better."

"And yet," Stella remarked, "she still keeps a roof over her head when she's not entertaining."

"I prefer this to a ballroom," Julia said. "It's less stifling."

Evelyn nodded. "It reminds me of riding. All this fresh air and excitement. I can feel it in my blood."

"I agree," Stella said, straightening the fall of lace at her bodice and sleeves. She, too, wore one of Ahmad's dresses. The ice-blue muslin enhanced the silver of her hair and eyes and lent an ethereal glow to her complexion. No one would ever guess that it was a gown originally made for another lady. "Providing we can all find partners."

"We will," Anne said.

Stella smiled. "You're very confident."

"Why shouldn't I be? Nearly everyone Lady Blackstone invited is a spiritualist. And we four have much to recommend us in that regard. Me because of my mother, you because of your gray hair, Evie because of her purported psychic energy, and Julia—"

"I have nothing to recommend me," Julia said morosely. "Not even my ball gown."

"Why did you not go to Mr. Malik and order something new?" Evelyn asked.

"Because," Julia answered, "his gowns make the wearers look beautiful. And I have no wish to draw attention to myself. Too much attention and I go all to pieces."

"Oh, Julia." Anne sighed. "Don't you long to wear something pretty for once?"

"The only garment I long for is a cloak of invisibility." Julia looked out at the dancing platform. Couples were slowing as the final notes of a spirited polka came to a close. "That doesn't mean I don't wish to dance on occasion."

"I'll dance with you," Stella said.

Julia brightened. "Oh, would you?"

"Of course. But I must lead."

The orchestra struck up a country dance.

Stella and Julia burst out laughing, and then, arm in arm, bounded onto the dancing platform. They swiftly disappeared into the crowd.

"Good lord," Anne said. "Is it any wonder they can't find husbands?"

Evelyn smiled. "They're having fun."

"The season isn't meant to be fun."

"Don't you enjoy it?"

"I suppose, on occasion. I enjoy riding, certainly. And I do like my

new dress." Anne smiled. "I never knew that black could look so alluring."

"You'll dance every dance, I wager," Evelyn said.

She wasn't wrong. Their dance cards quickly filled, and by the
time the orchestra struck up the next piece, all four of them were on
the floor and in the arms of a gentleman.

Granted, they weren't the gentlemen any of them would wish.

But Evelyn wasn't going to allow that to ruin her evening.

It was the dancing that gave her pleasure, not the men. There was
a giddiness that came from being in the open air, surrounded by music and all of the colorful lights. It wasn't romantic. That part of her
was reserved for someone else. But she enjoyed it immensely, just as
she did any athletic endeavor. And the exuberant polkas, reels, and
country dances were nothing if not athletic.

As it grew closer to eleven, the hour allotted for the grand fireworks display, she took a break with Anne alongside the platform.
The two of them sipped champagne as they caught their breath.

"I hopped so much during that Scotch reel," Anne said, "I almost
fell out of my bodice."

Evelyn choked on a laugh. "You did not."

"It was a very near thing." Anne touched her low neckline with
her fingertips. "I've never exposed so much of my bosom in my life.
Just look at it!" She giggled along with Evelyn. "No wonder I've had
so many partners."

A man uttered a not-so-discreet cough from behind them.

Evelyn and Anne turned to find Mr. Hartford standing there in
company with Captain Blunt. Mr. Hartford looked as though he was
trying very hard not to laugh.

"My lady. Miss Maltravers." He bowed. "May I present Captain
Blunt as a very worthy partner?"

Unlike Mr. Hartford, Captain Blunt didn't appear as though he
found the situation at all amusing. Indeed, he looked far too grim for

such a jolly setting as Cremorne. He offered them a stiff, militaristic bow.

Anne's throat and bosom suffused with a blush, but her eyes glinted pure fire. "Upon my word, Mr. Hartford. Must you creep up on a person?"

"I beg your pardon," he said. "Was I creeping? I only meant to ask you to waltz with me."

As the two of them spoke, Evelyn looked to Captain Blunt. She'd initially thought him old, but in fact, if not for his scarred face, he might have appeared no older than his middle thirties. And it wasn't only his scar that aged him. It was his eyes. They had a world-weariness about them. A certain coldness, as if he'd rather be anywhere but here.

He must need a wife very badly to endure the rigors of the season. Evelyn could imagine no man less suited to it.

"Miss Maltravers," he said. "May I have the privilege?"

"You may." Evelyn set her hand on his proffered arm and allowed him to guide her out onto the dancing platform. She glanced back over her shoulder.

Anne appeared to be giving Mr. Hartford a piece of her mind. He no longer looked as though he was on the verge of laughing. He stood there, absorbing whatever Anne was saying, as solemn as a vicar on Sunday.

Evelyn saw no sign of Stella or Julia. No sign of Lady Arundell or Uncle Harris, either. Shortly after arriving, the two of them had ensconced themselves with a group of other spiritualists, talking and drinking champagne. They'd still been there when Evelyn had last seen them. In truth, their chaperonage left a lot to be desired.

Not that she could complain.

Captain Blunt's hand settled at her back as he led her into the first steps of a lively polka.

She smiled. Not because she liked him, or because he was a particularly good dancer, but because the music was swelling and the night was alive around her. It gave her a strange feeling of euphoria.

They danced for a long while before Captain Blunt finally deigned to speak.

"Your friend isn't here this evening, I see," he said.

"My friend? What friend?"

"Miss Wychwood."

Evelyn gave him an alert glance. She debated telling him that Julia was, indeed, here, only stopped by the fact that Julia would likely swoon at the very sight of the man. "You take a special interest in Miss Wychwood?"

He didn't reply. Not directly. "Tell me, does she never speak?"

"With great animation," Evelyn said. "But not, I fear, in a ball-room."

His gaze sharpened with raptor-like intensity. "Where?"

"Why do you wish to know?"

His mouth curved in a cold smile. The action pulled on his scar, making his face look positively menacing. "Chalk it up to my detest-able curiosity."

Evelyn stared at him. She wondered if he was as dangerous as he looked. He'd been a hero in the war, hadn't he? And he read novels. That must count for something. "Miss Wychwood is more comfort-able when she's riding."

"Ah."

"Do you ride, sir?" she asked.

His smile vanished. "I was a cavalry officer, ma'am."

"In the Crimea, I'm told."

He inclined his head.

They finished their dance in silence. When the music ended, he led her back to the edge of the platform. She was just about to step down when she caught sight of someone standing outside the iron arch that led to the pagoda.

A familiar someone, illuminated in the radiance of the colorful lamplight.

Her heart took flight.

"Do you know that person?" Captain Blunt asked.

She dropped her hand from his arm. "Yes. I know him very well."

It was Ahmad.

Dressed in elegantly cut black-and-white eveningwear, he looked more broodingly handsome than on any other occasion she'd seen him. Truly a fallen angel come to earth. Not reluctantly this time, but purposefully.

He'd come for her.

Ahmad hadn't taken the decision to come to Cremorne Gardens lightly. It was a public garden, to be sure, but there were plenty of obstacles to his making an appearance there. Although any stranger might wander among Lady Blackstone's guests, it was still a private party. His presence would be noted by those in attendance.

No matter how discreetly he approached Evelyn, there would be talk.

Even in the moonlight, people would see he wasn't entirely English. Some would even recognize him as a tradesman. Their tailor or dressmaker, in fact. His appearance would be seen as a declaration of equality—not just of race, but of class. A clear statement of his romantic intentions toward Evelyn.

Such things didn't matter to him for his own sake. They mattered because of her. He wouldn't allow her to be embarrassed or humiliated on his account.

But when Evelyn saw him, she didn't appear to be anything other than pleased. Her soft mouth curved in a smile, and her eyes lit with an expression of unfiltered joy.

She scarcely seemed to notice the dour gentleman who had partnered her in the polka, leaving him behind as she floated down from the platform in her rose-festooned amber silk-and-crepe skirts to the iron gate where Ahmad stood waiting.

"You're here," she said breathlessly.

"As you see." He couldn't keep the gruffness from his voice. "Who was that?"

"Captain Blunt. Would you like to meet him?"

"No."

Her smile ticked up still further. "How long have you been here?"

"Not long. I came straight to the pavilion."

"Did you?"

"I thought you might be here," he said. "And . . . here you are."

They stared at each other for a taut moment.

"I've dreamed of this," Evelyn said. "You coming up to me at a ball, and seeing me in one of your gowns." She stepped back. "What do you think?"

He devoured her with his gaze. She was resplendent in the light of the colored lamps hanging from the pavilion. Burnished roses shimmered in her thick auburn hair, and her creamy ivory bosom and shoulders were framed by an artfully placed swathe of shimmering amber tulle and lace.

A silk belt circled her midsection, adorned with a small gold buckle. It gave way to a graceful swell of silk skirts overlaid by a layer of fine crepe. The whole of it emphasized her every curve—from her neckline to her waist and hips, beckoning a man to take her in his arms.

"You're frowning," she said. "Have I not placed the roses correctly? Becky said they were meant to be draped—"

"It's not the roses."

The orchestra struck up a waltz.

Evelyn looked at him in anticipation.

He offered her his hand. It was a portentous moment. As she took his hand, he was keenly aware of the ladies and gentlemen around them, some of whom were already stealing curious glances. One of the ladies whispered loudly behind her fan.

And . . . he didn't care.

He'd come here to declare himself, and that's exactly what he was going to do.

He led her out onto the crowded dancing platform. It was packed with couples, already spinning and dipping to the strains of the waltz. His arm came around Evelyn's waist, his grip on her hand firm as he swept her into a turn.

She laughed in appreciation. "Where did you learn—?"

He smiled. "At Mrs. Pritchard's, if you can believe it."

The women there had all used him as a partner at one time or another. He hadn't enjoyed it much in his younger days. Dancing—especially with a girl one didn't fancy—wasn't much fun for a surly lad of fifteen.

But this was different.

Evelyn was his friend. His muse. And more than that. Much, much more.

He fancied her like mad.

"People are staring," he warned her.

"Let them stare," she said. "They don't matter."

Waltzing her around the pagoda, he began to believe it. Violins sang out, in company with flutes, oboes, and the deep soul-stirring vibrations of the cello. As they looked into each other's eyes, the rest of the world seemed to melt away. It was only the two of them, alone with the colored lights and the orchestra, waltzing beneath the stars.

For that suspended moment, she was right. It didn't matter what the rest of society thought. All that mattered was that she was here, in his arms.

He had no intention of letting her go.

As the music came to a close, he kept his hand at her waist, guiding her from the floor. Behind them, the orchestra struck up the music for the next dance—an energetic harmony of flutes, fiddles, and reverberating horns. Stomping feet thumped heavily on the wooden platform as hundreds of couples commenced the galop.

"Can we go somewhere a little quieter?" he asked.

She took his arm. "I'd like that."

They turned away from the platform—from the dancers and the clusters of fashionable people seated at tables nearby. Ahmad wondered if any of them would intervene. A chaperone of some sort. Evelyn's uncle or Lady Arundell, perhaps.

But no one stopped them.

Evelyn strolled at his side unimpeded, away from the pavilion. They crossed the lawn toward one of the wide, tree-lined avenues that Cremorne was known for. Lamps hanging in the branches lit the way, flickering in the darkness. It was already approaching eleven o'clock. A full moon hung, luminous, in the star-scattered sky above.

"Have you been here before?" she asked.

"Many times, when I was younger. Whenever the weather was fair and I had a few extra shillings in my pocket, I would bring Mira to see the exhibitions." He cast her a glance. "Why? Do I look out of my element?"

Her hand tightened around his arm. "You look perfect. I've never seen you in evening clothes."

"There's not much cause to wear them." He noticed a faint blush rising in her cheeks. His pulse quickened in response to it. "Do you approve?"

"I could hardly fail to," she said. "When I saw you standing there, I felt as though everyone else disappeared. It seemed there was just the two of us."

"A romantic thought."

She didn't reply.

He feared he'd embarrassed her. "Evie—"

"Why did you come here tonight?" she asked.

Ahead of them, a dense, tree-shrouded path led off the main thoroughfare. It was a dark walk. A famous feature in London's pleasure gardens, particularly for couples seeking a bit of privacy. He led Evelyn down it, and then down yet another, turning to an even darker path, illuminated by a single lantern hanging from an elm tree.

He stopped beneath the light to face her. "Why did I come here?" he repeated. "I thought it was obvious."

"You came because I told you to."

"You never said to come to Cremorne Gardens."

"Not expressly, but I said you must seek me out at one of the events I was attending. And this is the only place that doesn't require an invitation." Her brows drew together. "I hope you didn't take it as an ultimatum?"

"No. And I didn't come here because you told me to. I came because . . ." He shook his head.

Designing her clothing was one thing. He could put his heart and his soul into every stitch. Expressing himself with words was something else altogether. He'd never felt less articulate.

Her expression became uncertain. "Was it my gown?"

"What?"

Moonlight glimmered on the silver frames of her spectacles. "Because you wanted to see me in it? Dancing and so forth?"

"I don't care about your ball gown."

She drew back. "Then why—"

His hands closed around her upper arms, silencing her. "I care about *you*, Evie. That's why I came. I'm here because I care about *you*."

She stared up at him, lips half parted in tremulous hope.

"These past weeks, I have thought and thought about our predicament. I've weighed the judgment of society and the limitations of my bank balance. I've considered your sisters and my cousin. I've even deliberated over the upkeep of your horse. And I've come to one conclusion."

Her glistening hazel eyes were riveted to his. "What conclusion?"

"That I can't live without you." He bowed his head to hers, his voice dropping to a husky undertone. "You were right. You *are* more than my muse. You're my love."

A soft breath shuddered out of her. "Ahmad—"

"I've fallen in love with you. But it isn't—"

"I don't believe anything is impossible," she said in a rush. "Not if people care for each other, and are willing to work and to try as hard as they can."

He rested his forehead against hers.

And he felt, all at once, the full responsibility of loving her. It meant more than mere affection. More than passion or desire. It meant taking care of her.

A solemn obligation. As serious as any he'd ever undertaken.

"I wasn't going to say it's impossible. I was going to say that it isn't going to be easy." He couldn't offer her the life of a society wife. A grand house with a fleet of servants and a stable full of carriages and four. He could only offer her himself. A modest life to start, with a chance at brilliance. A future they might reach for together.

She set her silk-gloved hands flat on his chest. They smoothed over his waistcoat with infinite tenderness. Small hands, but strong ones. Strong enough to hold for a lifetime.

"I don't want you to have false expectations," he said. "Business is beginning to go well, but there are no guarantees. My fortunes could turn in the blink of an eye. It's going to take time. And if I fail—"

"You won't fail."

"If I do . . ." He was insistent. She had to know the risks, no matter how much it hurt his pride. "To say our life would be humble is an understatement. You may soon regret ever joining your fate to mine."

"Never." She slid one hand to curve around his neck. "I have faith in you." She tugged him closer, her lips a whisper breath away from his. "And I do love you, so very much."

He closed his eyes for a moment. Her feelings were no surprise. She'd alluded to them several times before. Her words, nevertheless, crashed over him like a tidal wave. "*Evie.*"

The privacy they had was an illusion. They weren't in a brougham or in his rooms above the tea dealer's shop. They were on a dark walk at Cremorne Gardens. Not the best place for intimacy between a respectable young lady and her beau.

In that moment, he hardly cared.

His mouth found hers in the moonlight. And he kissed her softly, deeply.

Her body listed against his, pushing her full skirts out behind her.

His arms encircled her waist, holding her close as his mouth moved on hers. She was warm and pliant. A voluptuous armful.

"I wanted to tell you for so long," she murmured.

He kissed her again, feeling foolish and besotted. Like a green lad with his first young lady. "How long?"

"Since we went to the Jolly Tar."

"Did you love me then, sweetheart?"

"Yes, though I dared not admit it, even to myself." Her arms twined around his neck. "I thought I was too sensible for love. That I didn't need it in my life."

"And now?"

"Now I know better." She stretched up to kiss him. Her lips shaped to his in a sweet, clinging caress.

Above them, the first of the eleven o'clock fireworks exploded, lighting the night sky in a fiery fall of color.

Evelyn gasped. She stared up at the heavens as another firework boomed and then another.

Holding her in his arms, Ahmad stared right along with her. He felt the full marvel of the spectacle, as if seeing it for the first time.

When the display finally ended, she looked at him and smiled. "What happens next?"

"An excellent question." Lady Heatherton's voice sounded from the end of the path. "I'm quite curious to find out myself."

Thirty-Two

$\mathcal{E}$velyn's arms fell from Ahmad's neck. She would have stepped away from him, but he made that impossible. He kept one hand firmly around her waist. A sign of his support and protection.

She appreciated it, but she didn't need it. She wasn't afraid of Viscountess Heatherton. "Lady Heatherton," she said. "Is there something we can do for you?"

It was a cool question, under the circumstances, delivered with creditable calm. Evelyn was rather proud of herself.

But Lady Heatherton didn't even seem to hear her.

Her gaze was fixed on Ahmad, her coldly beautiful face half-shadowed in the light of the lamp that dangled from the branches above. A cerulean silk evening gown, trimmed with acres of lace and satin piping, hugged her slight curves. "So much for refusing to dally with your customers," she said. "I thought you lacking in scruples in your personal life, but it seems even your business principles are writ on water."

Evelyn gave Ahmad an uncertain look. His jaw was set, and banked flames burned in his eyes. Not flames of passion, but of rage.

Good gracious. *He knew her.*

And suddenly Lady Heatherton's visit to Russell Square made sense. All those questions about Ahmad she'd asked, and the warning she'd issued.

"You've mistaken the situation," Ahmad said. "A common failing of yours."

Lady Heatherton's eyes flashed. "Our situation? Or *this* situation? You and your little Sussex horsewoman?"

"That's enough," he said.

"What's the matter, darling? Don't want to provoke a scandal?" Lady Heatherton laughed. "That ship sailed the minute the pair of you left the pavilion."

"Did you follow us here?" Evelyn asked.

Lady Heatherton flicked her a glance. "Don't be absurd."

"Then how did you—"

"You're not the only one of Lady Blackstone's guests having a stroll on the avenue. There are plenty of others here, too." Lady Heatherton shot her another acid look. "Best hurry back to your chaperone before your reputation is ruined beyond repair."

Ahmad's hand tightened on Evelyn's waist. "She's not going anywhere."

"I told you," Evelyn said to Lady Heatherton. "My reputation is in good order."

"Not for long, my dear. As for *your* reputation—" Lady Heatherton turned on Ahmad. "How dare you give my evening gown to that odious gray-haired creature?"

"I *beg* your pardon," Evelyn said.

"It wasn't your gown," Ahmad said at the same time. "You returned it."

Evelyn's indignation on Stella's behalf dissipated as understanding set in.

So, this was what had prompted Ahmad to come to Russell Square that evening, asking if Evelyn would agree to a partnership. He'd lost Lady Heatherton as his customer and needed another lady to wear his gowns in her place.

Evelyn supposed she should be grateful to Lady Heatherton for withdrawing her custom. If she hadn't, Ahmad would never have come. But Evelyn didn't feel particularly grateful at the moment.

A burgeoning anxiety was building within her. She'd been caught with a man in the gardens, unchaperoned, on a dark walk. If word got out . . .

And it would.

Lady Heatherton would never be persuaded to keep her silence.

Evelyn's throat closed with frustration. All this time spent worrying over whether Fenny's presence would harm her, and here Evelyn was, fully responsible for her own ruination.

"We should go back to the pavilion," she said softly.

"Yes. We should." Taking her hand, Ahmad guided her around Lady Heatherton in the direction of the main avenue. They'd gone no more than a few steps when Lady Arundell appeared, blocking their way.

She wasn't alone.

Anne was with her, and so were Stella and Julia.

Evelyn's heart plummeted. Good lord. Had everyone followed after them?

Her three friends ran ahead to meet her.

"I tried to stop her," Anne said under her breath.

"She insisted on coming," Stella whispered.

Julia added, "Your uncle nearly did, too."

Evelyn winced. Uncle Harris knew about this?

"Miss Maltravers." Lady Arundell's tone was so frosty and authoritative it made Evelyn's pulse jump. "Lady Heatherton. And you, sir?"

"This is Mr. Malik, ma'am," Evelyn said.

Lady Arundell didn't seem interested in his name. "Watching the fireworks, were you? They are, indeed, better the further one gets from the pagoda. All this darkness, I expect."

Lady Heatherton cast a withering glance at Stella's ice-blue gown before turning her wrath on Lady Arundell. "They weren't watching fireworks. If I hadn't arrived when I did—"

"Nonsense. Miss Maltravers is a sensible girl." Lady Arundell advanced on Lady Heatherton. "I'm more concerned with you, Mildred. Your husband wouldn't like to hear you've been wandering the dark walks alone. Pray he doesn't learn of it."

Lady Heatherton's eyes narrowed. "Are you threatening me?"

"I'm reminding you," Lady Arundell said. "Gossip works both ways. I'll not see a girl in my charge ruined because you failed to hold your tongue."

The two of them stood facing each other for an interminable moment. If Lady Heatherton was an elegant cobra, then Lady Arundell was a mongoose in black mourning silk. She not only outranked her opponent, she outmatched her in terms of size and aggression. Indeed, in that instant, she seemed quite fierce.

A proud smile edged Anne's mouth.

"Your charge is in no danger from me," Lady Heatherton said at last. "I have no quarrel with her."

"I'm delighted to hear it." Lady Arundell gestured to the end of the path. "I bid you good evening."

Lady Heatherton's expression tightened. Casting one last cold look in Ahmad's direction, she stalked away.

Only when she was gone did Evelyn take a breath. It was the briefest respite before Lady Arundell turned on her.

"I'm disappointed in you, Miss Maltravers. Don't you realize what people will think? And you, poised to make something of yourself in society!"

"It's my fault," Ahmad said.

"Too right, sir," Lady Arundell shot back. "But you're not my responsibility. That honor belongs to you, madam. I'll not have you risking your good name by wandering off with a stranger."

"Mr. Malik isn't a stranger," Evelyn said.

"Yes, I know," Lady Arundell replied impatiently. "He's your dressmaker. You've mentioned him often enough. But this isn't Bond Street or wherever it is he plies his trade. You can't be alone with a man in these circumstances. Not unless he's your husband or your betrothed."

Evelyn caught Ahmad's gaze.

And he looked at her.

How he looked at her.

There was no anger in his eyes any longer. There was only tender concern. Affection, and a glimmer of rueful apology.

"Perhaps we should have stayed for the galop," he said.

She smiled. "I'm glad we didn't."

He didn't return her smile. His face was solemn with resolve. "I shall call on your uncle tomorrow, if that's acceptable to you."

Her heart thumped swiftly. "Yes."

He gave a final press to her hand before relinquishing it, and then, at Lady Arundell's urging, he took his leave.

Her ladyship watched him go with a look of exasperation. "Your Indian dressmaker!"

"I love him," Evelyn said. And he loved her, too. He'd said so himself. And now he was going to call on her uncle. There could only be one reason for such a visit. She felt a flush of wild antici-pation.

"Love!" Lady Arundell scoffed. "How can that possibly be?"

"He sewed pockets in all of her skirts," Anne said.

"Pockets." Julia sighed. "Imagine."

"And she didn't even have to ask him to do it," Stella said.

"Pockets?" Lady Arundell frowned as she shepherded them back to the pavilion. "This is all very vexing," she said. "Yes, quite vexing, indeed. I shall have to consult Dmitri on the matter."

◆━◆

"He means to call on *me*?" Uncle Harris eyed Evelyn from across the dim interior of the carriage. His evening clothes were rumpled and his cheeks flushed from too much champagne.

They'd left Cremorne as soon as Lady Arundell had delivered

Evelyn back to the pavilion. It was nearing midnight. Still early by the standards of the season. Uncle Harris appeared a trifle irritated to have his evening cut short.

"What have I to do with it?" he asked. "It's Nora who must give her approval, not I."

Evelyn's brow furrowed. "You want him to apply to Aunt Nora?"

"She's your guardian."

"Not formally. But if you'd prefer Mr. Malik go to Sussex—"

"Malik," Uncle Harris repeated with a snort. "Don't know which is worse. That he's an Indian or that he's a tradesman."

She stiffened. "He's a brilliant dressmaker. And he's as much English as he is Indian."

"You think that mitigates the matter? A hint of Indian blood is as damning as a surfeit of it. A touch of the tar brush, people call it." Uncle Harris gave her a narrow look. "Don't suppose he can pass for English?"

Her lips compressed. She was very close to losing her temper. "Really, uncle."

"It's a fair question."

"It's an offensive question. Mr. Malik isn't ashamed of who he is. If his being part Indian makes people uncomfortable, that's their problem, not his."

"It will be your problem soon enough if you wed the fellow."

Evelyn didn't need reminding. She was clear-eyed about her future. There would be plenty of obstacles. But she and Ahmad would face them together. "People may say what they like. I'm not afraid of the opinions of strangers."

"Not only strangers, my girl. You'll lose friends."

"Not true friends," she said. "Not people who matter."

"You'll never know, will you, until it comes to the point. You might well lose everything. Is it worth it for the sake of such a man?"

Evelyn recalled how Ahmad had waltzed with her around the pavilion. How he'd held her and kissed her as fireworks exploded in the evening sky above them. Warmth bloomed in her breast. "He's worth it," she said. "And a great deal more, besides."

The carriage rolled steadily through the fog. Gaslight from the lamps that lined the streets shimmered through the gaps in the velvet curtains that covered the carriage windows, intermittently illuminating Uncle Harris's face.

He shook his head in disappointment. "Nora said you were the sensible one. And here you are, going the same way as your sister."

"It's not the same at all," Evelyn said.

Fenny had abdicated all of her responsibilities to run away with Anthony. She'd chosen love over duty. Evelyn refused to make the same stark choice. She had no intention of throwing her hat over the windmill. There was Hephaestus to consider. And her little sisters, too. They were more than obligations; they were as essential to Evelyn's happiness as Ahmad was himself. She wouldn't forsake one to have the other.

What she needed was a new plan.

It was already beginning to take shape in her head. Only half-formed at present—and not entirely guaranteed to succeed—but a plan, all the same.

"I have half a mind to send you home," Uncle Harris said.

She drew her wrap more firmly about her bare shoulders. "I might go anyway."

"You what?"

"If Mr. Malik is obliged to travel there to ask permission from Aunt Nora, I'd like to be there, too. I could leave as soon as next week."

Her uncle's brows lowered over his half-moon spectacles "You'll do nothing of the sort."

She frowned. "But you just said—"

"I know what I said," he snapped. "The séance is next week. I've promised Lady Arundell and the others you'll be in attendance."

"My presence is hardly necessary. We both know I haven't any talent in that regard."

"What of the message you received? Telling me it was high time I turned my eyes to the living instead of the dead?"

She flushed. "That was my own opinion."

"Rubbish. It was the wisdom of the ages."

"It was common sense."

"It was guidance from beyond. And prescient, too. If I hadn't been concerned with your temporal whereabouts, Lady Arundell would never have gone looking for you. And then where would you be?"

Evelyn blinked. "*You* sent Lady Arundell after me?"

"Quite so." Uncle Harris settled back in his seat. "One never prospers by ignoring advice from the spirit realm."

Thirty-Three

✦

A hmad woke the next morning before dawn, just as he always did. He lay awake in his bed for a moment staring up at the shadows playing over the ceiling. The previous evening's events seemed so much a dream.

Had he really appeared at Cremorne Gardens and waltzed with Evelyn Maltravers in front of the entire fashionable world? Had he really told her that he loved her?"

And he did love her.

He rested one bare arm behind his head, a smile curling his lips.

It was then he remembered what else he'd done at Cremorne. Not only danced with Evelyn and declared himself but compromised her, too.

His smile vanished.

Good God. What had he been thinking? To lead her onto the dark walk where they might be discovered by any passing busybody?

And they *had* been discovered. First by Lady Heatherton and then by Lady Arundell.

Word would get out. It was inevitable.

This afternoon, he would go to Russell Square and formally ask Evelyn's uncle for her hand in marriage. With luck, Ahmad's proposal would ameliorate any damage he'd done to her reputation.

Though, he was fully aware, it would create a whole new scandal in and of itself.

But that was to be expected.

He and Evelyn both knew the consequences of forming an attachment. They both accepted them. He could only pray she wouldn't come to regret her decision.

Rising from his bed, he washed and dressed and made his way downstairs to the street. He bought a paper from a newsboy at the corner before hailing a hackney to take him to Conduit Street.

He always spent a few hours alone in the workroom at Doyle and Heppenstall's before going to fetch Mira from the Finchleys'. With the seamstresses now in residence, it was the only time of day Ahmad had any quiet.

As the hackney rolled through the streets, he opened the paper. He turned to the society page, a pit forming in his stomach at the prospect of finding something there about Evelyn's conduct at Cremorne.

Lady Heatherton had made it clear that Ahmad was her enemy. As a leader of fashionable society, she need only drop a word to one of her contacts at the paper and Evelyn would be ruined. It was no comfort that Lady Heatherton had promised to hold her tongue. Ahmad no more trusted the word of his former patroness than he would trust a viper.

But as he scanned the society page, he realized that Lady Heatherton had, in fact, kept her word. The article, when he found it, made no mention of Evelyn at all.

It was about him.

A POOR LADY'S DRESSMAKER

Our correspondent's discerning eye has lately noticed a trend among the fair ladies of London: a distinct lack of embellishment in their fashionable toilettes. On close in-

spection, we can find none of the rich trimmings that grace
the gowns of our city's Parisian sisters. Instead, the gowns
of the exotic Mr. M—— are marked by a noted nothing-
ness. Does he cater to ladies in straitened circumstances?
Or is he himself impoverished? We leave it to you to judge.

A chill crept into Ahmad's veins as he read it, turning his blood
to ice.

He understood what the damning words meant for his career as a
fashionable dressmaker. They were akin to a death blow. But in that
moment, he wasn't thinking of what it would mean to lose his business. All he could think of was losing Evelyn.

———◆———

Ahmad arrived in Russell Square at half past ten. He bounded up the
steps of the town house, presenting himself at the front door like a
proper suitor. The housekeeper welcomed him in, her face inscrutable
as she showed him into the drawing room. Evelyn joined him there
directly. They'd scarcely greeted each other before he thrust the paper
into her hands.

She sat down on the sofa to read it, the full skirts of her cuir-
colored cambric morning robe pooling around her in an elegant spill
of golden-brown fabric. "What is it that they're implying?"

Ahmad ran a hand over his hair. "At worst? That the ladies who
wear my designs are too poor to afford the trimmings."

She looked up at him. Morning sunlight filtered through the curtains, casting a glare on the glass lenses of her spectacles. "No one
would ever believe that, surely. All they need do is use their eyes. Any
fool can see how beautiful your dresses are."

"It isn't only about beauty. It's about proclaiming one's wealth and
status." Ahmad sank down beside her on the sofa. "A skirt weighted
down with flounces and fringe may be unflattering to some, but it
shows that its wearer can afford the expense of it."

She folded the paper and set it aside. "I'm sorry."

"So am I," he said. "Sorry to come here so early, and for such a reason. I shouldn't be burdening you with this."

"You have nothing to apologize for. I would have seen it myself soon enough." She angled herself on the sofa to face him. "I usually read the paper at breakfast, but after last night, I feared the society page would contain something awful about me."

"We can thank Lady Heatherton for that much, at least."

"Was this her doing?"

"I suspect so. Although . . . I suppose it might have been Madame Elise. I've taken some of her customers."

"And two of her seamstresses," Evelyn reminded him.

He smiled wryly. "Yes. And that."

She gave him a searching look. "What happened between you and Lady Heatherton?"

The question shouldn't have startled him, but it did. He hesitated before answering it. "Nothing happened."

"It didn't look that way. Indeed, she seemed to be rather angry with you."

"She is angry," he said. "*Because* nothing happened." He was reluctant to explain the sordid matter in any detail. But there was no avoiding it. "That's why she sent back her dress. I rejected her advances."

An expression of dawning understanding came over Evelyn's face. It was followed by a blush. "I see."

He began to feel a little like blushing himself. This wasn't the conversation he'd envisioned having with her this morning. Or ever, if he was honest.

"Does this kind of thing happen often?" she asked.

He rubbed the back of his neck. "Sometimes. With certain women."

"Who?"

"Shall I make a list?"

She looked both fascinated and appalled. "Have there been so many?"

"A few," he admitted.

"And . . . do you always reject them?"

"Always. I don't mix business with pleasure." As soon as he said it, he could see the wheels turning in her head. The conclusions she must be drawing.

"How do you account for me?" she asked.

"You were different. Unexpected. The way you came into the shop that evening. How you spoke to me and shook my hand. You took me by surprise."

"Undoubtedly," she said. "You must have been horrified when I kissed you that day in the fitting room."

He was startled into a husky laugh. "Hardly. I kissed you back, didn't I?"

"Did you? I've never been certain."

"I did," he assured her. "And very nearly said something stupid."

Her mouth tilted up at one corner. "What?"

"Something about how beautiful you are, probably." He took her hand and held it warmly in his, bare skin to bare skin. The same jolt of connection crackled between them as on the day they'd first met, warming his blood and quickening his pulse. "Or about how much I admire you. Something that would have put us both to the blush."

"Shocking," she murmured.

"Terribly shocking," he agreed.

Her fingers threaded through his. "Will the article harm your business?"

He answered without equivocation. "Yes."

"You're that certain?"

"If fashionable ladies begin to equate lack of embellishment with pauperism, they'll turn away from my designs."

"Your designs are admired by everyone who sees them," Evelyn said. "People will soon forget whatever nonsense was printed in the papers."

"Possibly," he said.

But he wasn't counting on it.

He had a sinking feeling that this was but the beginning of the end of his brief blaze of popularity as a dressmaker. And if his fortunes sank, then any chance of a future with Evelyn sank right along with them.

He drew her hand onto his knee. "Evie . . . There's another reason I came today."

Her color heightened. "You wish to speak with my uncle."

"I did intend to, but—"

"I'm afraid it's impossible. For one thing, he's gone to his club. And for another, he says it's not to him you must apply, but to my aunt Nora. Which means . . . if you have a particular question to ask, you must go to Sussex."

"Ah. That might be a bit tricky."

Her gaze softened. "Yes, I know. You're very busy. You needn't go immediately."

Ahmad felt a stab of bitter regret. He could no more go to Sussex to ask permission for Evelyn's hand than he could approach her uncle. He had to wait and see how this all affected his business. If everything fell to rack and ruin over the next weeks, he would be in no position to take a wife.

But he wouldn't burden Evelyn with that possibility. Not today. He couldn't bear to see the disappointment in her eyes.

"No, indeed," he said. He brought her hand to his lips and brushed a kiss to her knuckles. "I still have your black afternoon dress to finish."

❖

Evelyn cantered down the length of Rotten Row on Hephaestus, in company with her three friends. Anne's older stallion, Saffron, kept a lazy pace, sometimes falling behind. Stella intermittently surged ahead on Locket. And Julia cantered steadily on Cossack, the great black gelding's gait never changing.

It was half past five and the rest of London society was out in force. Ladies riding their expensive horses, gentlemen driving stylish sporting gigs, and stately dowagers parading in lavish open carriages.

Evelyn and her three friends cantered until they were out of the way of most of the traffic before slowing to a trot, and then to a walk. Their grooms followed several yards behind them.

"I needed that," Anne said. "I've been cloistered inside all morning with Mama and her spiritualist friends."

"More preparations for meeting the boy medium?" Stella asked.

"Endless preparations," Anne said.

"I've never been to the West Midlands," Evelyn said. "It will be an adventure."

Anne gave her an amused look. "I wouldn't go that far. We'll probably have more fun on the railway journey than we will in the city itself."

"Where will you be staying?" Stella asked. "With the boy's family?"

"No, indeed. We've booked rooms at a hotel for two nights." Anne straightened the skirts of her habit. "The séance will be at the boy's house. Mama says it's where he's best able to commune with his spirit guide."

"He has a familiar spirit, too?" Evelyn had thought only Lady Arundell was gifted with one of those.

"Oh yes," Anne replied. "Most mediums do. It's quite fashionable."

"Not according to my brother," Stella informed them. "He thinks spiritualism is the work of the devil, and spirit guides nothing more than demons leading ladies and gentlemen into sin."

"If only it were that exciting," Anne said. "The truth is, Dmitri is worse than any maiden aunt. He's always giving Mama new edicts about my behavior. At least . . . she claims they come from him."

Julia giggled. It set the rest of them off.

Two well-to-do ladies driving by in a barouche gave them a quelling glare. It was considered ill-bred to show undue emotion in public.

Evelyn's laughter faded.

Julia rode up alongside her. "I like it better here in the morning. One can ride without censure."

"There's always going to be people watching and judging," Anne replied, coming up on the other side of Julia. "The secret is not to mind it."

Stella leaned forward in her sidesaddle to stroke Locket's silvery neck. "Not all of us have the privilege of ignoring society's opinions."

"Why shouldn't we ignore them?" Evelyn wondered. "If they're wrong."

Her three friends exchanged knowing glances. They weren't subtle about it.

"I agree," Anne said. "One must defer to one's own conscience."

"And one's own heart," Julia added.

"Speaking of hearts . . ." Stella looked to Evelyn. "Has Mr. Malik called on your uncle?"

Evelyn was silent. It had been two days since Ahmad's visit to Russell Square. Then, he'd come not to see her uncle, but to see her. She'd sensed a reluctance in him. Not exactly a change of heart, but something else.

It was that dratted article.

No doubt Ahmad thought it would be the end of everything. Not just of his business, but of their future together, too.

"It's complicated," she said.

Julia's ebony brows notched. "But . . . you do love him, don't you?"

"I do," Evelyn said. "Unfortunately, there are other obstacles."

Anne met her gaze. "Insurmountable obstacles?"

"Of course not," Evelyn said.

"You have a plan, I suppose," Stella said. "A glorious plan."

"I don't know about glorious . . . But yes," Evelyn admitted. "I do have the first few legs of a plan in mind."

Up ahead, Mr. Fillgrave appeared around the bend, riding toward them on his glossy chestnut gelding.

"Oh no," Julia whispered.

"Pray, no one look at him," Anne said. "He won't engage us if we don't make eye contact."

On any other occasion, Evelyn would have been the first to take her friend's advice. But not today. As Mr. Fillgrave approached, she looked him straight in the eye.

"Oh, Evie, no," Stella said under her breath. "What have you done?"

"Ride on," Evelyn told her friends. "I must have a private word with him."

"One of the legs of your plan, I gather," Anne said.

"Precisely." Giving Hephaestus a kick, Evelyn rode to meet Mr. Fillgrave, while behind her, her three friends rode at speed in the opposite direction.

"Miss Maltravers," Mr. Fillgrave said. "A pleasant afternoon to you." His pale eyes swept over Hephaestus. "Such an impressive beast. On every occasion I see him, I'm struck anew. Did I perchance tell you, during my last call, about the Spanish stallion I encountered on the Continent during my grand tour . . . ?"

Evelyn listened to him in silence for several minutes. Mr. Fillgrave rarely stopped to draw breath. It was his habit to overwhelm his conversational counterparts with an impenetrable wall of words.

In Evelyn's experience, the only way to combat such an overbearing technique was to construct a rival wall. Eventually one of the parties would have to relent and stop building.

She didn't intend it to be her.

"As to that," she said, talking over him. "I do wonder about the quality of these Spanish horses you describe. And the diversity of them, too. The majority are gray, aren't they? And many of the stallions are no bigger than fifteen and a half hands, with short necks and equally short leg action. I daresay many view this style as baroque, but I ask you, how can any of these qualities benefit our English horses? A cross would only serve to impart shorter legs and greater bulk to our Thoroughbreds. And as for riding horses, we would gain none of the Andalusian's more famous qualities. The smoothness of stride and the elegance of appearance—that particular regal beauty. On the other hand, if you had a stallion like Hephaestus—"

"Yes, yes," Mr. Fillgrave replied, at last curtailing his own speech. "Just so. I've thought the same myself from the moment I first saw him. A bay of his size, with his leg action and extension—"

"There's no finer Andalusian stallion outside of Spain," Evelyn vowed. "And none with a sweeter temperament."

Mr. Fillgrave rode closer. His muttonchop whiskers trembled with excitement. "You would consider selling him?"

The mere thought—however remote—was enough to make Evelyn recoil from the man. Her fingers tightened on the reins. Hephaestus stamped restlessly beneath her. She easily brought him back under control.

"No," she said firmly. "He's not for sale. But I am planning to put him out to stud at the end of the summer."

Mr. Fillgrave reddened. "Miss Maltravers. I beg your pardon, but—"

"It's what my father wished for him."

"Your father was a gentleman. That is to say, a man. A lady shouldn't speak—"

"Of putting a stallion out to stud? Why not? The Queen has a Royal Stud. I'm sure she's aware of the goings-on there. And it isn't as though I'd be handling the particulars of the actual servicing."

Mr. Fillgrave made a choked noise.

"My groom will see to that, of course," she said. "The financial arrangements, however, will be entirely in my hands."

"If I may make bold to say, ma'am, this is a matter for men to arrange. You are a young lady. An unmarried lady."

"But not, in either case, an ignorant one," she said.

She wished she felt as confident as she sounded.

The fact was, Mr. Fillgrave was right, to an extent. The Maltravers family was already on thin social ice as it was. Evelyn wasn't going to help matters by doing something as eccentric as this. Indeed, she'd never even dared consider it before.

But things were different now.

She was no longer seeking acceptance by fashionable society. She was fighting for love. For her very future.

"I take it you're interested? You've mentioned your Spanish mares on several occasions."

"Quite so. Quite so. I can't deny it." Mr. Fillgrave rode alongside her down the row, his bewhiskered face the color of a Sussex tomato. "Have you a fee in mind?"

Her palms were damp beneath her gloves. "As a matter of fact, I have."

Thirty-Four

*A*hmad finished Evelyn's dress for the séance the following week. When the final stitches were placed in the hem, and the last silk-covered button affixed to the back of the bodice, he delivered it to her in Russell Square himself.

There was precious little else to occupy him.

Since the publication of the article, orders for new dresses had decreased nearly by half. Not only that, several ladies who had already commissioned ball gowns had canceled their orders.

A man didn't have to be a member of the spiritualist society to see the direction things were headed.

Ahmad steeled himself as he followed the housekeeper into the morning room. Evelyn was already there. She was seated at a walnut secretary desk in the corner, engaged in writing a letter. Her quill pen quivered as the steel nib moved swiftly over the page.

"Mr. Malik, miss," the housekeeper said.

Evelyn looked up with a start. Her expression softened. "Thank you, Mrs. Quick. That will be all."

The housekeeper withdrew, leaving Ahmad alone with Evelyn.

She crossed the room to greet him, one hand outstretched.

He took it, engulfing it in his. In that moment, it seemed rather like a lifeline. "Who are you writing to?"

"My aunt Nora," she said. "After so many days of silence, I owe her a long letter."

"You write her every day?"

"I try to. And to my little sisters, too. It's a treat for them to receive something in the post." She slipped her hand from his so she could take the dress box. "You didn't have to bring it yourself."

"I had time." An understatement. It wasn't work that had kept him away from Evelyn these past days. It was his own sense of impending disaster. He'd known, when next he saw her, they would have to discuss their future.

If they still had a future.

"And now you've finished making my dress, you shall have even more." Her face lit with guarded hope. "Will you go to Sussex this week?"

Ahmad regarded her from across the short distance, a raw ache in his chest.

He could think of nothing to say. Nothing that wouldn't put an end to their relationship before he was ready.

"You won't have to brave it alone," she said "I intend to go, too."

That startled him. "When?"

"The day after the séance." She put the dress box down in a chair. "I should have told you. Lewis is taking Hephaestus back to Combe Regis this week. I want to be there for him."

Ahmad was instantly at her side. "Has something happened? He's not ill or—"

"No, no," she said quickly. "Nothing like that. It's something else. A business decision I've recently come to."

He listened in growing astonishment as she explained her plan for putting her stallion out to stud.

"What can you be thinking?" he asked when she'd finished.

"I'm thinking of the future," she said. "Trying to be pragmatic."

He was incredulous. "You told me once that involving yourself in such things would make your family notorious."

"Yes," she admitted reluctantly. "But only by the standards of fashionable society."

"Society's standards are the ones that matter."

"Do they?" she wondered. "All of these rules that tell women how to think and how to behave, restricting our lives to the confines of a certain neighborhood and the approval of a certain kind of people. We're supposed to pretend that the world outside doesn't exist. That there aren't wider concerns than whether a lady rides an omnibus unchaperoned or forgets to wear her gloves during an afternoon call."

He could understand her frustration. That didn't make the reality of her situation any less precarious. "You're right," he said. "But your good name is more than a philosophical argument. The rules may be tedious, but—"

"They're unfair is what they are. And hypocritical, too, given what most English gentlemen get up to on a regular basis. You must recognize that."

He sighed. What she was describing wasn't new to him. He grappled with the ramifications of unfairness and inequality every day. "I do recognize it," he said. "But it's not the sum total of life. Rules still matter. Reputation still matters, especially for a young lady like yourself."

Her hazel eyes took on a martial glint behind the lenses of her spectacles. "It's lately seemed to me that we ladies are dropped into a churning sea and forbidden from revealing that we know how to swim. But I *do* know how, and I'm not too delicate minded to do it. Not anymore. I refuse to believe that it's more respectable to drown than to save myself."

"Evelyn . . ."

"Besides," she said. "I've done nothing to tarnish my reputation, not by rational standards. Putting Hephaestus out to stud is sensible. Indeed, one might argue that failing to make the most of his bloodlines is the greater sin. Not to mention the financial aspect of the business. If arranged efficiently, the fees would pay for his upkeep, and leave a tidy sum left over besides."

Ahmad had grown up in the city. Saddle horses were a luxury. He knew precious little about their upkeep, and even less about the fees attached to their breeding arrangements. "Whatever the sum, it can't be enough to justify endangering your good name."

"Fifteen pounds."

"Fifteen pounds?" It was nearly as much as Ahmad charged for one of his habits. The difference being that he didn't earn the sum outright. He had to deduct the not insubstantial cost of fabric and trimmings.

"You think it too steep? I assure you, it isn't. Indeed, I've discounted the fee to ten pounds for the first year, as an incentive. Quite a bargain, I thought."

"By what measure?"

"By any measure. One need only look at the sporting pages. Champion studs are advertised for a similar amount. And when one considers I have the best horse in the world—"

"Evie . . . who in their right mind would pay such a fee?"

"Lots of gentlemen," she said. "Lewis has already taken five bookings, including two from Mr. Fillgrave for his Spanish mares."

Ahmad stared at her, dumbstruck. Five bookings? That was fifty pounds.

He felt the sudden urge to laugh.

It was offset by a grimmer impulse.

He knew why she was doing this. It was because his business was in danger of failing. She was trying to alleviate some of the burden.

By God, he admired her for it.

At the same time, he hated that she was obliged to even think of such things. A man looked after the woman he loved. He didn't take from her. And he didn't permit her to risk her good name on his account.

"That's why I must go back to Combe Regis for a time," she said. "I want to see Hephaestus settled, and to visit my sisters while I'm there. It would be the perfect opportunity for you to call on my aunt."

"How long do you intend to stay?"

"A few days"

"Is that all?"

Her brows knit in an uncertain frown. "You suggest I stay longer?"

Last week, when the two of them parted at Cremorne Gardens, he wouldn't have dreamed of suggesting any such thing. But the landscape of his life had changed dramatically since then. He was no longer certain about anything.

"I do," he said.

Evelyn stared at him. His words were so entirely at odds with his attentive manner, she didn't know how to receive them. "What is this?" she asked softly. "What are you trying to say to me?"

"Only that I wonder if, given the circumstances, it might not be best if we took some time apart."

She stopped breathing. "What circumstances?" A terrible thought struck her. "I haven't scandalized you with my plans for Hephaestus, have I?"

"No. It's not that. It has to do with my own situation."

Her eyes searched his. "Is this about that ridiculous item in the paper?"

"In part." He paced to the window, giving her his back. His shoulders were taut beneath his coat. "I've lately been compelled to face reality."

She didn't move. Couldn't move. Only stood there, waiting for him to elaborate.

When next he spoke, it appeared as though he was explaining things as much to himself as to her. "A dressmaker needn't be famous in order to marry. Even a moderately successful tailor can afford a wife. But if his business should fail entirely—"

"Yours won't," she said.

"If it does . . ." He turned, looking at her as if it pained him to do so. "I'll not bind you to me at the very moment my fortunes crumble."

She felt a rush of compassion for him. Goodness, is that what he feared?

"I see," she said.

And she did.

That didn't mean she had to agree with him.

Her footsteps were silent on the drawing room carpet as she crossed the room to join him. "What's to be gained by our taking time apart?"

"It will give you a chance to think about things."

That sounded ominous. "By *things* you mean us, I suppose."

"Us. Our future. Whatever you want to call it."

"Can't I think about our future while I'm here in London?"

"Not properly," he said. "In Sussex, you'll be free from my influence, and from this damnable attraction we have for each other. You'll be able to assess your feelings clearly. If they should alter—"

"They won't."

"But if they should—"

"What about *your* feelings?" she asked.

His jaw hardened. "My feelings for you won't change. I'm bound to you. But *you'll* be free. If after a month you're still committed to this course—"

"A month!" She blinked up at him. "I might consent to stay a fortnight. But I won't spend a month there on the slim chance I'll stop loving you. I'm not some changeable milk-and-water miss."

He loomed over her. "And I'm not some rogue who would coerce a young lady into marrying me against her better interests."

"You presume I don't know what's in my own best interests."

"You're young."

Her chin ticked up. "I'm three and twenty."

"Yes. Young. All of this is new to you. And none of it is what you wanted when you came here. Is it so out of the question that I ask you to take some time to think things over?" His large hand curved around her corseted waist. The gentleness of his touch tempered his words. He tugged her closer until her wide skirts bunched against his legs. "I'm trying to do the honorable thing, Evie."

Evelyn realized that. His reasoning was abundantly plain.

He wasn't only worried about his dressmaking business. He was afraid he was taking advantage of her. That proximity had made her love him. All those sessions in the fitting room at Doyle and Heppenstall's. The sensual familiarity as he'd fitted her habits, day dresses, and ball gowns.

Many young ladies would have had their heads turned by such intimacies.

Evelyn certainly had. But it had never been only about that. There had always been something more. Respect. Admiration. Friendship and mutual support. He'd believed in her almost from the first. And she believed in him, too.

"I know you are," she said. "Which is why I'll do as you ask."

Relief flashed in his gaze. "Will you?"

"Yes." She set her hands on his chest. "But at the end of a fortnight . . . I expect you in Sussex."

Thirty-Five

❖

The small brick house in Birmingham was nothing very remarkable. It was built in a block of identical houses, back-to-back around a communal yard. Evelyn stood next to Anne in the modest dining room. The heavy curtains were drawn shut, blocking out the dusky light of the setting sun. Walls covered in faded blue paper appeared almost black in the dim glow of a brass gasolier that hung over the large round table.

On the opposite side of the room, Uncle Harris, Lady Arundell, and six other black-clad figures conversed in soft tones. Among them was Robert James Lees, the Birmingham boy who had, of late, inspired so much excitement in the world of spiritualism.

Evelyn could find nothing extraordinary about him. Indeed, he looked like any other boy of twelve or thirteen, albeit one decked out in his Sunday best. He wore a plain black suit, and his dark hair was combed into meticulous order, aided by a liberal application of Macassar oil.

He stood in front of a heavy mahogany sideboard, flanked by a gentleman. Not his father, Evelyn guessed, but his spiritualist representative.

Anne looked at the boy with an expression of vague disappointment.

Evelyn couldn't blame her. After an hours-long rail journey to the West Midlands and a night spent in a loud and keenly uncomfortable Birmingham hotel, their first sight of the much-vaunted boy medium was somewhat deflating.

"He's spotty," Anne remarked under her breath.

"He's just a child," Evelyn said. "I wonder if he knows what he's doing?"

"I expect he does," Anne replied cynically, "in one way or another."

"Anne? Miss Maltravers?" Lady Arundell beckoned them closer. "Come and meet Mr. Lees."

Evelyn and Anne joined the crowd of spiritualists. Lady Arundell introduced them first to Mr. Lees, and then to the others. There was Mrs. Inkpen, an elderly woman wearing several strands of jet beads, and Mr. Vance, a short fellow with a diabolical mustache. Next was an elegant blond lady by the name of Mrs. Brown, and two bewhiskered gentlemen of middle years, Mr. Popplewell and Mr. Burns.

Mr. Burns was the editor of a weekly spiritualist journal. "I'll be taking notes of the proceedings for my next issue," he explained. "My readers are fascinated by reports of your gifts, Mr. Lees."

Mr. Lees didn't say a word. He seemed quite stoic for a boy of his years.

"You will find that Miss Maltravers's presence renders a benefit to your work," Lady Arundell told him. "Zadkiel himself has called her a person of significant energy."

The rest of the company murmured in varying tones of awe and approval.

"Are you a medium, ma'am?" Mr. Popplewell asked Evelyn.

Evelyn swiftly disabused him of the notion. "I have no talent in that regard whatsoever."

"And you?" Mr. Popplewell asked Anne.

"I'm merely an interested observer," Anne said.

Mrs. Brown smiled. There was a touch of irony in her expression. "As are we all in the face of such a talent."

Mr. Popplewell motioned them to the cloth-draped table. "Shall we begin?"

Evelyn and the others took their seats. While they removed their gloves, Mr. Popplewell lit the candles on the table and turned down the gaslight. When he'd finished, he sat down in the chair beside Mr. Lees.

There was no crystal ball. No cards or other implements of fortune-telling. There were only the candles and a few pieces of note-paper and a pencil set between them.

"Join hands please," Mr. Popplewell said.

Evelyn reached out to her neighbors. Anne was on her right side and Mrs. Brown on her left. The three of them clasped hands. All the while, Evelyn watched Mr. Lees for signs of deception. His young age made him no less suspicious to her. Children weren't guileless, in her experience. Many were as adept at dishonesty as adults.

Was Mr. Lees such a boy?

He gave no indication of fraud or malice. He sat straight in his chair, eyes closed, mouth pressed shut.

Mrs. Brown was watching him as intently as Evelyn.

"He must prepare himself," Mr. Popplewell said.

Silence grew heavy throughout the room. The candle flames flickered and cracked. Suddenly, a sharp knock rent the air.

Evelyn jumped. She caught Anne's gaze, brows lifting in question.

Anne gave her a reassuring smile, whispering, "It often happens at a séance."

"Shh!" Mrs. Inkpen hissed.

"Quiet, ladies," Mr. Popplewell intoned. "We must all focus our minds."

Another period of silence stretched between them.

"The veil is thin this evening," Mr. Lees said at last, his eyes still closed. "I will attempt to walk into the ether to find my spirit guide."

Anne squeezed Evelyn's hand.

Evelyn bit her tongue. She refused to laugh. This was a serious matter, if not for her and Anne, then for Lady Arundell and Uncle Harris. The two of them were tilted forward in their chairs, riveted by Mr. Lees's performance.

The boy's breathing became more pronounced. His lips moved silently. Suddenly, his body swayed, first to the left and then to the right. All at once, he stiffened straight up like a poker. His mouth fell open on a rattling sigh.

"Whom do you seek?" he asked. But the voice wasn't his. It was the voice of someone older, with a distinct Scottish accent.

"A highlander," Mr. Vance murmured. "Astounding."

"We would like to speak to the late Prince Consort," Mr. Popplewell said loudly. "Is he there with you, sir?"

"Prince Albert is here," Mr. Lees said in the same Scottish burr. "He awaits your questions."

Mr. Popplewell addressed the rest of the table. "One at a time, if you please. I can make no promises for how long his trance will last."

Evelyn hadn't thought of anything to ask herself, which was just as well. There was no opportunity to do so. For the next five minutes, the rest of the table peppered Mr. Lees with questions on everything from Prince Albert's opinions on the afterlife to his views on matters of state.

Only Mrs. Brown refrained. She continued to watch Mr. Lees. "I have a question," she asked at last, her polished voice breaking through the din.

"Who is that?" Mr. Lees asked. "Is that you, Lady Seymour?"

Lady Arundell and Uncle Harris turned sharply to look at Mrs. Brown.

Mrs. Brown's face was void of expression. "It is I."

Lady Arundell gasped. "Upon my word. One of the Queen's ladies-in-waiting!"

Evelyn's pulse raced. She exchanged a wide-eyed glance with Anne. The Queen had sent a secret representative! And Mr. Lees had identified her!

Uncle Harris couldn't conceal his excitement. "Does this mean that Her Majesty believes—"

"Silence, please," Mr. Popplewell said. "Mr. Lees cannot maintain the connection if he's distracted by the mortal world."

"What is your question, Lady Seymour?" Mr. Lees asked.

Mrs. Brown—or rather, Lady Seymour—cleared her throat. "Her Majesty wants a name."

"What name?" Mr. Lees asked.

"The secret name used by the Prince Consort to address her in their private correspondence. You're to write it down on a slip of paper for Her Majesty's personal verification."

Mr. Lees went still. A shuddering breath came out of him. At the end of it, he slumped in his chair.

"We must break the circle," Mr. Popplewell said. "The spirit has gone." Letting go of Mr. Lees's hand, Mr. Popplewell gave him pencil and paper.

Rousing himself, Mr. Lees wrote something down. When he'd finished, he folded the paper in half and handed it to Mr. Popplewell.

Mr. Popplewell conveyed it to Lady Seymour.

She took it without looking at it and thrust it into the mouth of her black silk-fringed reticule. She snapped the drawstring closure tight. "I thank you for your compliance."

Everyone at the table stared at Lady Seymour, expecting Evelyn knew not what. A royal proclamation, perhaps. Some edict passed down from the Queen.

But when Lady Seymour next spoke, the subject had nothing to do with royalty. "Is there someplace I might wash my hands?"

"There is, my lady," Mr. Popplewell said. "It's at the back of the house. I can show you—"

"Miss Maltravers can accompany me." She rose from her chair. "If you will?"

"Yes, of course." Evelyn stood to follow her, aware of the rest of the company staring after them.

"One must never wander about strange places alone," Lady Seymour said. "And never in company with an unfamiliar gentleman."

"No, indeed," Evelyn agreed.

Lady Seymour led the way through a dark sitting room shadowed with heavy furnishings. As they passed through to the hall, a young maid in an ill-fitting stuff dress appeared. She wobbled a curtsy.

"The lavatory?" Lady Seymour inquired.

"This way, madam." The maid escorted them to a small room off the kitchen. Inside was a basin, tub, and little else. "The necessary is outside."

"This will suffice." Dismissing the maid, Lady Seymour went to the basin and turned on the tap. Water came out with a sputter. "Was this your first séance, Miss Maltravers?"

"How could you tell?" Evelyn asked.

Lady Seymour cast her a glance. "You were gripping my hand rather hard."

Evelyn smiled a little sheepishly. It had been difficult not to be overcome by the atmosphere once the séance got underway. "Mr. Lees's gyrations did startle me a little."

"Do you think his gift legitimate?" Lady Seymour asked as she washed her hands.

"I'm not inclined to believe," Evelyn said. "Then again, he *was* able to identify you."

"Anyone might have done. I'm staying at an inn nearby. One can never be entirely incognito when traveling with servants."

"What about your question? He appeared to answer it."

"He did, didn't he? And yet . . . the Prince Consort had no secret name for the Queen."

Evelyn's smile broadened. "You tricked him?"

Lady Seymour's mouth curled into a smug smile of her own. "I tested him."

"And now? Do you think him a fraud?"

"It's not for me to decide," Lady Seymour said. "That must be left to Her Majesty's judgment."

"Do you not wonder what he wrote down?"

"Not in the least."

Evelyn smoothed her skirts as she waited for Lady Seymour to finish freshening up. The action caught Lady Seymour's gaze. After drying her hands, she came closer to inspect Evelyn's gown.

"I noticed this garment the moment you arrived with Lady Arundell," she said. "It's a stunning creation."

Evelyn couldn't disagree.

Made of black French grenadine laid over black silk, the afternoon dress was cut and sewn to perfection. It did more than flatter Evelyn's curves; it worshipped them, giving her the illusion of a near-perfect hourglass figure.

Full skirts swelled out from a close-fitting bodice, long sleeves skimmed her arms, and a row of delicate, silk-covered buttons traced the length of her spine.

It hadn't much in the way of trimmings, save a little black lace and near-invisible pleating at the hem, but the gown was by no means plain. On the contrary. It was a masterpiece of artfully placed stitches, darts, and seams.

"You must have recently visited France," Lady Seymour observed.

"No, indeed. I've never been out of England in my life."

"It was made here?" Lady Seymour's brows lifted. "You astonish me."

"It was designed by a gentleman in London," Evelyn said. "A brilliant dressmaker."

"He must be. I've never seen a gown manage to do so much for one's figure while still preserving the dignity of mourning. May I?"

"If you like."

Lady Seymour reached to touch Evelyn's skirts. "We're all in mourning these days. The entire court. It can be quite dreary. All one sees is crepe and more crepe." She examined Evelyn's sleeve and bodice. "You must give me the name of this dressmaker of yours."

"Of course." Evelyn smiled to herself as she reached for her reticule. "I just happen to have his card."

※

They departed Birmingham the following morning. On arriving at the railway station in London, Evelyn was obliged to switch trains in order to continue her journey home to Sussex. Her uncle waited as she hugged Anne goodbye.

"It's only for a fortnight," Evelyn said. The sound of a whistle nearly drowned out her voice. It was punctuated by the hiss of steam and the ungodly screech of metal as another train rolled into the station.

"Yes, I know," Anne replied loudly. "You'll be back before you know it. In the meanwhile, you must write to me."

"I will," Evelyn promised.

Passengers emptied from the compartments of the newly arrived train. They rushed past, some shouting to porters and others calling out to friends awaiting them on the platform. Everyone seemed to be in a spectacular hurry.

"Really, Fielding," Lady Arundell said. "Have you no maid to send with the girl?"

"I thank you, my lady," Evelyn said, "but I don't require a maid. I'm an old hand at rail travel by now." She'd made the journey up to London from Sussex alone. It would be no more difficult to make the journey back.

Uncle Harris summoned a porter to take Evelyn's luggage to the baggage car. "A lot of to-do," he grumbled as he escorted her to the correct platform. "All so you can return in two weeks' time."

She took his arm, walking with him through the clouds of smoke and steam. "I'm sorry for the inconvenience."

He gave an absent pat to her hand. "I won't say there haven't been compensations. Spiritual amplification and so forth. But a man of my age grows accustomed to his peace and quiet."

"Yes, I know. My presence in the house has been rather disruptive, I fear."

"Quite so. That business at Cremorne. I blame myself. When the other girls come to stay, I shall insist Nora accompany them."

Evelyn glanced at him, frowning. She hadn't been fully listening. Perhaps she'd misheard? "What other girls?"

"The next younger girl. What do you call her? Augusta? And the three younger ones after that. Can't recall their names."

"Caroline, Elizabeth, and Isobel." Evelyn stared at him. "I'm sorry. Are you saying that . . . you'll give each of my sisters a season?"

Uncle Harris had never committed to any such thing before. He was too eccentric. Too unwilling to disrupt his life. He'd only hosted Evelyn on sufferance. To presume anything more had never been an option.

"Seems little enough expense, providing Nora keeps them out of trouble." He scowled at her. "Pity she didn't accompany you."

A smile spread over Evelyn's face. Impulsively, she stretched up to press a kiss to her uncle's cheek. "Concerning yourself with the living," she said. "I heartily approve."

Thirty-Six

❦

When she was a girl, Evelyn's summers in Combe Regis had been lazy and long, stretching out, seemingly forever, beneath the sunshine sky as she rode down the tree-lined lanes or walked and rambled with her sisters. As a woman grown, however, time proceeded at a much different rate of speed.

A week, for example, passed with uncommon swiftness. And the week that followed that was gone in the blink of an eye.

Before she knew it, an entire fortnight had elapsed, with no word from Ahmad. No letters. No telegraph. No surprise visit to ask for her hand in marriage.

Tightening her fingers on the reins, she deepened her seat in her sidesaddle, bringing Hephaestus to a halt atop the rise. The village of Combe Regis was spread out below—all thatched roofs and stone chimneys, humble country people going about their day.

She gazed out over the burnished landscape, squinting her eyes against the midday sun.

He hadn't promised to write to her. His intention had been to give her time away from his influence. Evelyn had nevertheless expected . . . something.

In her worst moments, she'd begun to think that the black afternoon dress he'd made for her had been his parting gift. A gown to outshine all the others, as eloquent in its beauty as in its subtlety. A mourning dress, to mark the end of their romance.

He was an honorable gentleman, already facing qualms about removing her from her sphere of life. If his business were to fail on top of that . . .

Well.

Evelyn knew what he might think. What he might do.

Turning Hephaestus, she tightened her leg, urging him into a trot and then into a canter. The skirts of her green habit floated behind her as she guided him along the lane that would take them back home.

By the time she returned to the stables, she was perspiring, and some of her hair had fallen loose from her hairnet to curl about her face.

Lewis emerged from the old wooden barn.

"Will you take him?" she asked, moving to swing her leg over the pommel of her sidesaddle.

And then she froze.

Ahmad walked out behind Lewis. He was in his shirtsleeves, his frock coat flung over his shoulder in a concession to the heat.

Her heart lurched.

It had only been a fortnight. She hadn't forgotten how handsome he was. How the sight of him made her insides quiver. But memory didn't do the sensations justice. Feeling them now, she wondered if she would be able to dismount without making an utter fool of herself.

She didn't have to worry.

Tossing aside his coat, Ahmad came to her aid. He reached out to grasp her waist. "Allow me."

His touch sent a minor earthquake through her. As he lifted her down from the saddle, setting her booted feet firmly onto the ground, she was keenly conscious of her disheveled state.

If he noticed, he didn't seem to mind it. His gaze drifted over her face, drinking her in, as though he'd been missing her as keenly as she'd been missing him.

"You came," she whispered.

"As promised." He released her waist, but he didn't move away from her. He remained there, close enough to touch her, as Lewis fetched Hephaestus and led him back to the stables.

"Did you just arrive from the railway station?" she asked. "You must be wanting some refreshment." She turned. "I'll take you to the house."

He gently caught her wrist, arresting her movement. "I've been to the house."

Evelyn's breath stopped. "You've seen Aunt Nora?"

"And met your little sisters, too. They fed me tea and seedcake." The barest hint of a smile edged his mouth. "They seemed to know all about me."

A blush threatened. "I might have mentioned you."

He looked at her steadily, an emotion in his eyes that was hard to read. "Your aunt said there was a grove of trees on the other side of the garden. Someplace we could be private. Shall we walk there?"

She nodded numbly.

Good gracious.

Good lord and all the saints above.

This was the moment. It was truly happening.

She brushed her hair back from her face with an unsteady hand, fervently wishing she'd had a minute to tidy herself. To change into a pretty summer frock and to dab orange blossom perfume behind her ears.

Instead, she was still in her riding habit—windblown and rumpled and probably smelling of horse.

But it was Ahmad's riding habit, too. The first one he'd made for her.

It seemed fitting somehow.

He walked alongside her away from the stables. An overgrown path led down to the gate at the edge of the property. "I understand you've been well occupied with your new business venture."

Evelyn draped the long skirts of her habit over her arm. "Did my aunt tell you what's happened?"

"Not a word," he said. "She blushed to mention the subject."

Poor Aunt Nora. She wasn't at all comfortable with the particulars of putting Hephaestus out to stud. The business *was* a trifle shocking for a household of unmarried ladies. Evelyn nevertheless felt proud of herself for contriving it. "We've received five more bookings for Hephaestus. That makes ten altogether."

"Impressive."

"I thought so." It meant that Hephaestus would be able to pay his own way. That he wouldn't be a burden, either to Aunt Nora or to Evelyn's future husband.

Ahmad opened the crooked wooden gate, waiting as she walked through it ahead of him. "I have some news as well."

"Good news?"

He shut the gate behind them. "Quite good." The two of them continued on down the path. "I must thank you for it."

"What have I to do with it?"

"A great deal," he said. "Ten days ago, a lady visited Doyle and Heppenstall's. A very elegant lady, inquiring after a mourning dress."

Evelyn shot him an alert glance. "Lady Seymour?"

"You sent her to me."

"I gave her your card. I didn't know—"

"Didn't you?"

"I hoped," Evelyn admitted. "Did you make her a dress?"

"Two of them." He gave her a wry look. "But that isn't the good news."

"Something more happened?"

The grove of trees lay ahead—old oaks with their branches tangled in places, making a canopy against the sun.

"It did," he said. "Not many days after Lady Seymour's order was delivered, a footman in royal livery came into the shop. He brought a summons from the palace."

The significance of Ahmad's words stopped Evelyn where she stood. She looked up at him in amazement. "To make mourning clothes for the Queen?"

His gaze softened with warmth. "Maybe one day. For now, it's only a few members of her court."

"*Only*," she repeated. And then she smiled, so filled with pride for him she could burst. "Oh, Ahmad."

"It seems I have a talent for mourning clothes. Something about my designs being beautiful without being ostentatious."

"Like your riding habits."

"Indeed," he said. "Do you know what this means?"

She beamed up at him. "That one day you shall have a Royal Warrant on the door of your shop?"

The Royal Warrant of Appointment was a coveted designation, signifying that a tradesman had earned royal patronage. Those who received the honor displayed it on their premises with pride.

"Perhaps." Ahmad didn't appear at all interested in the possibility. His attention was wholly focused on her. "Do you know what else it means?"

Evelyn's smile faltered. She felt all at once very young and very uncertain. Not because she didn't want him, but because she wanted him too much. It was dangerous to want something this badly. A challenge to the universe to take it away. And she'd already lost too much in her life.

But wonderful things didn't happen because one was cautious. They happened because one dared.

And she was ready to dare anything to be with him, even if it meant risking her own pride.

"It means that your prospects have improved," she said, "and that you've come to ask me if my feelings have changed. They haven't, by the way." She paused, her courage wavering. "And if yours have . . . you had better tell me quick before I say something stupid."

❦

Ahmad felt a rush of tenderness for her. As bold and brave as she was, these were uncharted waters. Not just for her but for him.

He'd been both eager and anxious the entire way from London.

His nerves hadn't relented on meeting with Evelyn's aunt and sisters. They were charming, all of them, but he'd felt very large and very male seated in the dainty parlor of their cottage, sipping tea from a little porcelain cup as they regarded him with rapt feminine attention.

Part of him had anticipated a chill reception—well-bred disdain for his being a tradesman, accompanied by veiled contempt on account of his mixed race. He'd been prepared to ignore it, just as he always did, even as he'd dreaded it for Evelyn's sake.

But her family had shown him nothing but the wide-eyed curiosity ladies might be expected to show toward a man in their midst, come to court one of their kinswomen.

He'd received permission for his suit from Evelyn's aunt, and encouragement from her younger sisters. All that had been left was to wait for Evelyn to return from her ride.

When he'd seen her trotting into the stable yard, he'd felt a profound sense of certainty.

This was right. This was how it was all meant to be.

"My feelings haven't changed," he said. "I told you they wouldn't."

Evelyn's eyes glimmered with relief. And something else. Something that made him weaken at the knees. A smile played at her lips as she continued down the path, leading him further through the trees.

A siren. *His* siren.

He was powerless not to follow her. "There are things we must discuss first."

"Haven't we already discussed them?"

"You don't know what I'm going to say."

"I do." She brought him beneath the branches into the cool shadow of the leaves. "You were going to tell me the same thing you did at Cremorne Gardens. That it's not going to be easy."

"It won't be. There will be no avoiding some of the talk. I may not be able to shield you from the worst of it."

"I don't require a shield." She backed against the curving trunk of the oak as he came to stand over her. There was a soft flush in her cheeks and a determined tip-tilt to her chin. "What I want—what I've always wanted—is what you proposed the evening you came to Russell Square. A partnership."

His blood simmered. "Ah. But that was a business partnership." He set a hand on the trunk beside her, half caging her with his arm. "What I'm proposing now is something different."

She looked up at him in trembling anticipation.

"I'll be your partner, Evie," he said. "Your shield, your support, your champion. I only ask for one thing in exchange." His voice deepened. "I ask that you be my wife."

She bit her lip. Tears welled in her eyes.

"I love you." Emotion constricted his chest. "I love you," he repeated. "And you needn't marry me to have me as your partner—your friend and champion. It's not a condition of my esteem. But I would be honored if—"

"Yes," she said. "*Yes.*"

In the next instant, she was in his arms.

Satisfaction surged through him. He enfolded her in a powerful embrace, lifting her straight up off her feet. She clung to him fiercely. And he gloried in it, the sensation of her arms twined so tight around his neck. She was strong, his siren. Strong and singular and beautiful.

He buried his face in the curve of her neck.

Her fingers twined in his hair. "I've imagined this moment a thousand times since we parted, every day, down to the smallest detail. But real life is so rarely how one plans it." Her lips brushed his ear, her words an intimate whisper. "It's better. So much better."

"Evie," he murmured.

"I love you, Ahmad."

His eyes shut tight. He felt the soft declaration as much as heard it. The same precious words she'd uttered to him at Cremorne Gardens. They resonated within him, now just as they had then, sweetly, tenderly, a balm over the sharp edges of his soul. "Tell me again, sweetheart."

"I love you," she said. "And I shall be your shield and support, too. Your friend. Your partner. And more."

He drew back to look at her. "More?"

Her damp cheeks were rosy with blushes.

His arms still around her, he set her feet gently down on the ground. "There will be more," he promised. And bending his head, he captured her mouth with his in a kiss that said far more than he could ever express with words.

She was right. Life rarely went according to plan. It veered off the path in unexpected and extraordinary ways. His had done so. Bringing him from India to England, from the East End to Mayfair, and eventually all the way to Sussex—here into the arms of the woman he loved.

His muse. His auburn-haired equestrienne.

Her fingers curled in the rumpled cloth of his cravat. "I don't know all the particulars of that side of things," she confessed.

He smiled against her mouth. "My love, you must put yourself entirely in my hands."

Her lips curved in answer, remembering. "You know," she said, kissing him again, "I do believe I shall."

Epilogue

❦

LONDON, ENGLAND
SEPTEMBER 1863

*E*velyn stepped back to admire the placement of the Royal Warrant of Appointment on the wall of her husband's shop. It had arrived only today, issued by the Lord Chamberlain's Office at the palace. She'd hung it up herself, affixing it just above the polished mahogany counter, beneath a gas wall sconce. The glow of the gas jet illuminated the royal coat of arms and swirling script below:

These are to certify that by command of
the Queen
I have appointed
Mr. Ahmad Malik
into the place and quality of
Dressmaker
to Her Majesty, the Queen

Ahmad's arm settled around Evelyn's waist. He was in his shirtsleeves, a measuring tape still draped around his neck from his last fitting of the day. "Is it everything you imagined?"

She leaned into his embrace. She knew he'd never aspired to royal patronage. When first they'd met, all he'd wanted was the acclaim of fashionable society.

But things had changed since then.

His elegantly sewn mourning dresses were now as much admired as his smartly tailored riding habits. Not only were his designs worn by several of the ladies at court, this past summer, he'd finally been called upon to create a mourning gown for the Queen.

"It is," Evelyn said, beaming up at him. "I'm so very proud of you, my darling."

He pressed a kiss to the top of her head. It was half seven in the evening and they were alone in the shop. "The credit is all yours, my love. If you hadn't attended that séance—"

"Rubbish." Covering his arm with hers, she gave him a little shake. "It was your designs that made the difference. The rest was so much happenstance."

"You can't deny you've brought me a great deal of luck."

"I'm the one who's lucky," she replied softly.

After marrying last year, she'd embarked with him into a great unknown. Though certain of each other, neither had been entirely certain about anything else.

Would they be rejected by society? Obliged to live on the outskirts? To struggle for every shilling?

Evelyn needn't have worried.

Things had progressed beautifully in their new marriage, starting with a wondrously romantic wedding night spent at Claridge's Hotel. The memory of it still brought a blaze of warmth to her cheeks.

There was a great deal to be said for a man who was familiar with the topography of a woman's body. A man who honored every peak and valley. Who could be both patient and passionate.

He'd taught her much about that side of marriage. She flattered herself that she'd taught him even more. She mightn't have been as familiar with the male form as he was with the female, but she was bold and adventurous and—with the proper incentive—quite a quick learner.

Indeed, there was nothing more satisfying than driving her new husband to distraction. She loved every part of it, from the kisses and the intimate embraces to those drowsy moments in the sun-filtered morning when she woke, warm and languorous, in his arms and realized anew that this was her life now. A life where she was safe, protected, and supported. Where she was adored, body and soul.

Predictably, not everyone approved of them. But the world was bigger than Mayfair.

Ahmad had found them an old farmhouse near Hampstead. It wasn't Upper Belgrave Street or Grosvenor Square. For them, it was better. Close enough to Ahmad's dress shop, while still retaining the feeling of a rambling country property, with plenty of wide-open spaces nearby to tempt Evelyn on her morning rides.

When Anne, Julia, and Stella were in town, they often joined Evelyn for a gallop on the heath, followed by tea and iced lemon cakes served in the farmhouse's old-fashioned sitting room.

There were other visitors, too. Mira and Tariq. Uncle Harris and Lady Arundell. Even the Finchleys. Evelyn and Ahmad were blessed with a wealth of family and friends, and their home was open to all of them. A warm and welcoming place, with no aristocratic pretensions about it.

Evelyn was happy there.

Hephaestus was happy, too, settled in his own small stable at the back—his expenses defrayed by his successful career at stud.

And every day brought more happiness for all of them.

There was the news that Fenny had been delivered of a healthy baby boy.

The announcement that Mira and Tariq had finally set a date for their wedding.

The rapturous letter from Aunt Nora proclaiming that Uncle Harris was, indeed, subsidizing Gussie's London season next spring.

And there was the day the sign outside the dress shop had been replaced. When the words *Messrs. Doyle and Heppenstall, Tailors* had at last given way to a placard that proclaimed: *Mr. Ahmad Malik, Dressmaker.*

And now this.

Royal patronage.

Evelyn turned in Ahmad's arms, encircling his neck. "We must do something to celebrate."

Heat flickered in his gaze. "I know what I'd like to do."

"You have only to name it."

He bowed his head to hers, smiling. His deep voice was a husky invitation. "Let's go home, Evie."

An answering smile shone in her eyes. "Home," she murmured. "I like the sound of that."

Author's Note

❖

*T*he *Siren of Sussex* was inspired by several real-life people and
events from the Victorian era, including the Pretty Horsebreakers, famed courtesan Catherine Walters, fashion designer
Charles Frederick Worth, court dressmaker Madame Elise, the astrologer Zadkiel, and the child medium Robert James Lees. In the
aftermath of Prince Albert's death in December 1861, many of these
elements converged. I set Ahmad and Evelyn's love story during this
period, attempting to adhere as much to the actual historical timeline
as possible.

It wasn't always possible. In some instances (such as the precise
month Catherine Walters left England or the exact date that Robert
James Lees claimed to have contacted Prince Albert), I had to mas-
sage the dates a bit to make them match the timeline of my story. For
more info on these historical figures, see my notes below.

The Pretty Horsebreakers

The Pretty Horsebreakers were courtesans of the 1860s, famous as
much for their formfitting riding habits as for the equestrian skill
they exhibited in Hyde Park's Rotten Row. The most celebrated
among them was Catherine Walters. Newspapers of the day referred

to her as "Anonyma" or "Incognita," but to many in society, she was known simply as "Skittles"—a reference to the bowling alley where she worked in her youth. Through her successful career, she was, at various times, under the protection of dukes, marquesses, and even (it was rumored) members of the royal family.

In 1862, Catherine Walters briefly departed London for America. The newspapers reported that she left "many creditors to lament her departure." Her reputation for stiffing creditors followed her through the years. In 1872, Messrs. Creed and Evans—tailors and habit-makers in Conduit Street—sued her for an order of riding habits valued at £334 3s. This case served as the inspiration for both the location of Ahmad Malik's shop and Miss Walters's unpaid bill for £100.

Victorian Spiritualism

Richard James Morrison—popularly known as Zadkiel—was a Victorian era astrologer and crystal gazer. For a time, he was in possession of a small crystal globe reported to have once belonged to an Egyptian magician. Zadkiel exhibited this globe among the nobility, many of whom claimed to see visions in its fractured surface.

After retiring from the Royal Navy, Zadkiel made a name for himself writing astrological almanacs. It was in his 1861 almanac that he predicted the death of Prince Albert. The Victorians already had a morbid interest in séances, fortune-telling, and crystal gazing, but after the Prince's death, spiritualism became even more popular. It was rumored that Queen Victoria herself engaged in efforts to reach her deceased husband. One of the most persistent of these rumors involves the boy medium Robert James Lees.

In the years following Prince Albert's death (sometime in 1862 or 1863, depending on reports), the teenage Lees claimed to have made contact with the prince. On hearing of this, the Queen is rumored to have sent two court officials in disguise to Lees's next séance. With the aid of his familiar spirit, Lees successfully identified both of them. As further proof of his authenticity, the court officials asked Lees for the secret name that Prince Albert used in correspondence with his wife. Lees is said to have provided it.

According to some sources, Lees later went on to correspond with Queen Victoria and even to perform séances for her at court.

Are any of these stories about Lees true? The answers is yes—up to a point. Robert James Lees was a known spiritualist and medium, but though he did claim to have contacted Prince Albert, there is no actual evidence that his claims ever resulted in any interaction with the Queen or the royal court.

Victorian Fashion

During the 1850s and 1860s, the prevailing style of fashionable women's dress owed much to the influence of Empress Eugénie, wife of Napoléon III. She was the undisputed arbiter of fashion in mid-nineteenth-century France. It was her preference for enormous skirts that set off the crinoline craze, and her patronage of Paris designer Charles Frederick Worth that helped to make his dresses as coveted as they were costly.

By 1860, women's skirts had reached their largest size of the century, with hemlines sometimes as much as fifteen feet in circumference. Trimmings were no less daunting. Following Worth's lead, the most fashionable gowns were made in luxurious fabrics adorned with acres of lace, ruffles, flounces, fringe, and ribbon bows.

London modistes, like Madame Elise of Regent Street, employed fleets of seamstresses to sew gowns of this size and style. She was known to work her employees literally to death, forcing them to sew for endless hours and housing them in cramped, unventilated rooms. In 1863, one of Madame Elise's seamstresses, Mary Walkley, was found dead in her bed. The resulting scandal prompted a swell of public outrage.

Fortunately for some, the silhouette of women's dresses was gradually beginning to change.

Skirts began to be gored at the sides, which had the effect of flattening the front and pushing some of the fullness to the back. As the years progressed and women became more active, additional gores were added, making the fullness at the back even more pronounced. This would eventually lead to the bustle silhouette of the 1870s and 1880s.

I imagined Ahmad to be at the forefront of this evolution. The dresses he designs are slightly gored so that the skirts drift to the back in an approximation of a train. It's a subtle difference from the prevailing silhouette of the time, but a significant one, as it foreshadows the larger changes to come, both in terms of the bustle and in terms of women's burgeoning independence.

Ahmad's gowns are also notable for their lack of excessive embellishment. He brings a tailor's aesthetic to his designs. This is something he would have learned from his years making men's suits and women's riding habits. The very best riding habits of the day were made by tailors. These habits had no flounces or frills. Instead, they were distinguished by the quality of their fabric and the elegance of their cut. This tendency toward simplicity worked in Ahmad's favor as he began to make mourning gowns.

Indians in Victorian England

I've often written about Victorian era India in my romance novels, but the legacy of British colonialism isn't a romantic one. This is especially evident in nineteenth-century British books about India, like the ones Evelyn buys at Hatchards Bookshop. The writers of these histories had a tendency to either dehumanize, demonize, exoticize, or infantilize native Indians. The descriptions of half Indians were sometimes even worse.

In my story, I've interspersed references to real history books with those to fictional ones. The fictional books are either based on a single historic text or are an amalgam. For example, the quote Lady Anne reads aloud in Chapter Twenty-Seven—attributed to the fictional *England and Her Colonies*—is a paraphrased version of a passage in John Holloway's *Essays on the Indian Mutiny* (1865). Similarly, the fictional Urdu novel Captain Blunt recommends to Evelyn at Hatchards—*The Two Sisters* by Shahid Khan—is inspired by Nazir Ahmad's novel *Mirat-ul-Uroos* (1869).

To read some colonial texts, one might believe there were no happily-ever-afters for people in Ahmad's and Mira's circumstances. But nobody's story is ever entirely one of pain. It certainly wasn't for Indians in nineteenth-century London. Across the city, they worked, lived, worshipped, and loved, all while navigating the obstacles that came from being a person of color in Victorian England.

Among them, Ahmad and Mira faced challenges that were as much internal as external. In India, during the long period of British East India Company rule, there were many Englishmen who fathered children with Indian women. Those children were left in a difficult predicament—not quite Indian and not quite English. When writing *The Siren of Sussex*, I chose to focus more on that internal struggle for identity and sense of self. It's a struggle I'm personally familiar with.

Acknowledgments

————

*W*riting a book is a solitary task at the best of times. It's doubly so during a global pandemic. The isolation has made me even more grateful to everyone who helped me along the way. Here's a list of just a few of the people to whom I owe my heartfelt thanks:

To Deb, for feedback on the first chapter.

To Rachel, for encouraging me to give this process a chance.

To Flora, Dana, and Alissa, for beta reading the first draft.

To Jackie and Sandy, for help with translations.

To David and Christiane, for teaching me (and my horses) so much about dressage.

To my mom, who asked me, "How come the only people who look like you in your stories are the side characters?" prompting me to write something where Ahmad and Mira were front and center.

And to my dad, who supports my writing even though he's never read one of my novels.

Extra special thanks are also owed to my literary agent, Sarah Hershman. To my amazing editor at Berkley, Sarah Blumenstock. And to Farjana Yasmin, for the beautiful cover.

Last but not least, I'd like to thank my animal family for providing so much emotional support while I researched and wrote. To Stella, Tavi, and Bijou. And to Centelleo—my Andalusian dressage horse—who passed away from colic two weeks after I turned in my manuscript. He was my friend and companion for nearly twenty years. I hope this story can be a memorial to the strength of our partnership and to how much I loved him and will always love him.

The Siren of Sussex

❖

MIMI MATTHEWS

Discussion Questions

1. Evelyn and Ahmad are both a mixed-race couple and a cross-class couple. Once married, what challenges do you believe they'll face because of their differences? Which of these challenges do you think will prove most difficult for them to overcome?

2. Evelyn uses her skills as a horsewoman to make her mark in the fashionable world. How else might a Victorian lady distinguish herself in fashionable society? How far could she go before she sacrificed her respectability?

3. Evelyn takes umbrage at being labeled a bluestocking, despite the fact that she exhibits many of a bluestocking's stereotypical traits. Did labels like *bluestocking* help or hurt Victorian women in their quest for individuality and independence? Did it make them more or less likely to strive for what they truly wanted?

4. Ahmad began his dressmaking career by making gowns for the prostitutes at Mrs. Pritchard's gentlemen's establishment. Do you think this helped him become a better dressmaker? If so, how?

5. Both Evelyn and Ahmad use fashion as a means of self-expression. How did fashion help ladies of the Victorian era express their unique personalities? Do you think this form of expression was reserved for the rich?

6. Throughout the story, Ahmad is shown to have great respect for women. How much do you think being raised by his unwed aunt shaped his views? How did the tragedy of his mother's death influence his conduct with Evelyn?

7. Ahmad mentions having to negotiate an uneasy peace with himself in order to live and work among English people. How does he use his dressmaking to symbolically reclaim the spoils of colonialism? Do you believe this is an effective strategy?

8. In order to secure her younger sisters' future, Evelyn embarks on a London season. Is her quest to find a wealthy husband misguided? Would it have been better to let her sisters fend for themselves?

9. Spiritualism was all the rage in the Victorian era. What do you think fueled society's passion for all things occult? How do you think fashionable people used séances and crystal gazing to further their own social agendas?

10. Ahmad makes the decision not to sue Lady Heatherton for her unpaid dressmaking bills. Was this decision truly the right one for his business or do you think he should have taken her to court?

11. Becky Rawlins does "piecework" (freelance sewing paid on a piece-by-piece basis) in her rented room above the rag and bone shop. Was this sort of work better or worse than working in the workroom of a fashionable shop, sewing for dressmakers like Madame Elise? Did it help women to gain a measure of independence or do you think it was exploitive?

12. In the Epilogue, it is revealed that Ahmad has been engaged to make mourning clothes for the Queen. Given England's history with India, do you feel this is a moral conflict of interest? Should Ahmad have refrained from doing business with the Queen and her court?

Keep reading for a preview of

The Belle of
Belgrave Square

Available now!

LONDON, ENGLAND
JUNE 1862

Julia Wychwood was alone in Rotten Row, and that was exactly the way she liked it.

Well, not quite alone.

There was her groom, Luke Six. And there were some humbly clad men and women tarrying along the viewing rail. But otherwise . . .

Yes. Alone.

It was often the case at this time of morning—those early moments after break of dawn, when the air was misty cool and the rising sun was shining brightly to burn away the fog. Some ladies and gentlemen chose to ride at this time of day, but not many. Certainly not as many as during the fashionable hour. Then, all of society was out in force.

Which was precisely why Julia preferred riding in the morning. There were less stares and whispers. Less judgment.

With a squeeze of her leg, she urged Cossack into a canter. It was the big ebony gelding's best gait—a steady, even stride, with a sway to it like a rocking chair. She relaxed into it. When cantering, Cossack required nothing more of her than that she maintain a light contact on the double reins. He did the rest, which left her ample time to daydream.

Or to fret.

She wasn't only alone in Rotten Row. She was alone in London. Her three best friends were all out of town until Sunday. That left four days for her to get through on her own. Four excruciating days, and on every one of them, an equally excruciating society event.

Julia was tempted to take to her bed. She'd done it before to get out of attending a ball or a dinner. But she'd never done it for more than two days at a time. Even then, her parents insisted on summoning the doctor—an odious man who always came with his lancet and bleeding bowl in hand.

She shuddered to think of it.

No. Faking an illness wouldn't work this time. Maybe for one day, but not for all of them.

Somehow, she was going to have to get through it.

Cossack tossed his head at something in the distance.

Julia's gloved hands tightened reflexively on the reins. She squinted down the length of the Row at the rider coming toward them. "Easy," she murmured to Cossack. "It's just another horse."

An enormous horse. Bigger and blacker than Cossack himself.

But it wasn't the horse that made Julia tense in her sidesaddle. It was the gentleman astride him: a stern-faced, battle-scarred ex-military man.

Captain Blunt, the Hero of the Crimea.

Her mouth went dry as he approached. She was half-tempted to bolt. But there was no escaping him. She brought Cossack down to a trot and then to a walk.

She'd met the captain once before. It had been at Lady Arundell's spring ball. A meddling acquaintance had introduced him to Julia as a worthy partner. In other circumstances, the interaction might have been the veriest commonplace—a few polite words exchanged and a turn about the polished-wood dance floor.

Instead, Julia had gawped at Captain Blunt like a stricken nitwit. Her breath had stopped and her pulse had roared in her ears. Afraid she might faint, she'd fled the ballroom before the introduction had been completed, leaving Captain Blunt standing there, his granite-hewn features frozen in a mask of displeasure.

It had been one of the most mortifying experiences of Julia's life.

And that was saying something.

For a lady prone to panicking in company, mortifications were a daily occurrence. At the advanced age of two-and-twenty, she'd nearly grown accustomed to them. But even for her, the incident at Lady Arundell's ball had marked a new low.

No doubt Captain Blunt thought her actions had had something to do with his appearance.

He was powerfully made. Tall, strong, and impossibly broad-shouldered. Already a physically intimidating gentleman, he was made even more so by the scar on his face. The deep, gruesome slash bisected his right eyebrow and ran all the way down to his mouth, notching into the flesh of his lip. It gave the impression of a permanent sneer.

Rather ironic that he was hailed as a hero. In looks, there seemed nothing heroic about him. Indeed, he appeared in every way a villain.

"Miss Wychwood." He removed his beaver hat, inclining his head in a bow. His hair was a lustrous raven black. Cut short to his collar, it was complemented by a pair of similarly short sideburns edging the harsh lines of his jaw. "Good morning."

She scarcely dared look him in the face. "Good morning."

He didn't reply. Not immediately. He was studying her. She could feel the weight of his stare. It set off a storm of butterflies in her stomach.

Ride on, she wanted to say. *Please, ride on.*

He didn't ride on. He seemed intent on making her squirm.

She suspected she knew why. She'd never apologized to him for her behavior at the ball. There'd been no opportunity.

Perhaps he wanted her to suffer for embarrassing him?

If that was the case, Julia was resigned to take her medicine. Heaven knew she deserved it.

She forced herself to meet his gaze. The butterflies in her stomach threatened to revolt. Goodness. His eyes were the color of hoarfrost— a gray so cold and stark it sent an icy shiver tracing down the curve of her spine. Every feminine instinct within her rose up in warning. *Run*, it said. *Flee.*

But this wasn't Lady Arundell's ballroom.

This was Hyde Park. Here in the open air, mounted on Cossack, she wasn't the same person she was at a ball or a dinner dance. For one thing, she wasn't alone. She had a partner—and an imposing one, at that. Cossack lent her his strength and his stature. Made her feel nearly as formidable as he was. It's why she was more confident on horseback.

At least, she'd always been so before.

"How do you do?" she asked.

"Very well." His voice was deep and commanding, with a growl at the edge of it. A soldier's voice. The kind that, when necessary, could be heard across a battlefield. "And yourself?"

"I'm enjoying our spell of fine weather," she said. "It's excellent for riding."

He flicked a glance over her habit. Made of faded black wool, it did nothing to emphasize the contours of her figure. Rather the opposite. It obscured her shape, much as the net veil on her short-brimmed riding hat obscured her face. His black brows notched into a frown.

She suppressed a flicker of self-consciousness. Her clothing wasn't meant to attract attention. It was meant to render her invisible. But it hadn't—not to him.

The way he looked at her . . . Hades might have regarded Persephone thus before dragging her down to hell to be his unwilling bride.

And everyone knew that Captain Blunt was looking for a wife.

If one believed the prevailing rumors, it was the sole reason he'd come to town. He was on the hunt for a vulnerable heiress he could spirit back to his isolated Yorkshire estate. An estate that was said to be haunted.

"You ride often at this time of day?" he asked.

"Whenever I can," she said. "Cossack is glad for the exercise."

"You handle him well."

Some of the tightness in her chest eased at the compliment. "It's not difficult." She stroked Cossack's neck. "He may look imposing, but he's a lamb underneath. The biggest creatures often are in my experience."

Captain Blunt's own mount stamped his gigantic hooves as if in objection to her statement.

She gave the great beast an interested look. He was built like a medieval warhorse, with a broad chest, heavy fetlocks, and a thickly waving mane and tail. "What do you call him?"

"Quintus."

"And is he—"

"A brute through and through," Captain Blunt said. "Sometimes, Miss Wychwood, what you see is precisely what you get."

Julia wondered if that was true in the captain's own case. Could he really be as menacing as he appeared? She didn't know to a certainty. All she knew was that, according to society gossip, he was positively dangerous—especially to marriageable young ladies.

It didn't excuse how she'd behaved toward him at the ball.

She moistened her lips. "I believe I owe you an apology."

He looked steadily back at her.

"When Lord Ridgeway was introducing you to me at Lady Arundell's ball . . ." She faltered. "Perhaps you don't remember—"

"I remember," he said gruffly.

Heat rose in her cheeks. "Yes, well . . . I'm sorry to have run off like that. I fear I'm not at my best when meeting strangers."

"Do you often run off during introductions?"

"Not generally, no. Not unless I suspect I'm going to swoon." Her mouth ticked up at one corner in a rueful smile. "You wouldn't have appreciated having to catch me."

Something flickered behind his icy gaze. An emotion impossible to read. "You don't know me very well, ma'am."

Were it any other gentleman, Julia might have suspected him of flirting with her. But not Captain Blunt. His scarred countenance was as coldly serious as his tone.

Her smile faded. "No, indeed." She tightened her fingers on the reins. "But I apologize all the same." She inclined her head to him as she urged Cossack on in the opposite direction. "Good day, Captain Blunt."

He didn't return her farewell. He didn't say anything. He only sat there atop his horse, watching her ride away.

Julia felt the burning impression of his stare at her back. And this time, she didn't will herself to be brave. She did what she'd wanted to do since she'd first laid eyes on him.

She pressed her heel into Cossack's side and she fled.

***

Jasper was half tempted to ride after her, no matter that she'd just dismissed him.

But no.

He held Quintus to a standstill as Miss Wychwood rode away. She kept to a walk for several strides before kicking her horse into a lofty, ground-covering canter. Her seat was impeccable, her gloved hands light on her reins. She had a reputation for being a good rider. And she must be one to handle a horse so obviously too big for her.

Good God. She couldn't be more than five feet and two inches in height. A petite lady, with a gentle way about her. Had she no one to choose her a more suitable mount?

Jasper suspected not.

Her parents were well-known invalids, prone to all manner of fancies. Their elegant townhouse in Belgrave Square played host to an endless stream of doctors, chemists, and an ever-changing roster of servants.

Even Miss Wychwood's groom was of a recent vintage—a different fellow from the one who had accompanied her three days ago. He cantered a length behind her, the pair of them disappearing into the distance.

Jasper's frown deepened.

He'd learned many things about Miss Wychwood in the past several weeks, enough to know that marrying her and whisking her away to Yorkshire was going to be anything but simple.

Damn Viscount Ridgeway for suggesting it.

Exiting the park, Jasper returned to Ridgeway's house in Half Moon Street. It was a fashionable address, if not an ostentatious one, tucked between the house of a rich old widow on one side and that of a well-to-do solicitor on the other. After settling Quintus in the mews with his groom, Jasper made his way up the front steps to the door.

Ridgeway's grizzled butler, Skipforth, admitted him into the black-and-white tiled hall. "His lordship has requested your presence in his chamber," he said as he took Jasper's hat and gloves. "He's breakfasting there."

Of course he was.

Ridgeway rarely emerged from his room before ten, and then only on sufferance.

Jasper felt a flare of irritation. Not for the first time, he regretted accepting Ridgeway's invitation to stay.

"Shall I take you to him, sir?" Skipforth asked.

"No need." Jasper bounded up the curving staircase to the third floor. He rapped once on Ridgeway's door before entering.

The heavy curtains were drawn back from the windows and sunlight streamed through the glass, revealing an expansive bedchamber decorated in shades of rich crimson and gold. On the far side of it, opposite his unmade four-poster bed and the silver tea tray containing the remains of his breakfast, sat Nathan Grainger, Viscount Ridgeway.

He was sprawled in a wooden chair in front of his inlaid mahogany dressing table, eyes closed as his valet trimmed his side-whiskers.

"That you, Blunt?" He squinted open one eye. "Back so soon?"

"As you see. Skipforth said you had need of me?"

"So I do. And excellent timing, too. Fennel's just finished shearing me." Ridgeway dismissed his valet with a wave of his hand.

Fennel, a weedy old man with a shifty expression, promptly withdrew into the dressing room, shutting the door behind him with a click.

"I require your opinion on a horse I've been eyeing at Tattersalls," Ridgeway said. "Unless you have other plans today?"

"Nothing that can't be changed. When are you leaving?"

"Presently." Ridgeway sat forward in his chair, examining his freshly trimmed side whiskers in the glass. "What do you think?"

Jasper could detect no difference from the way Ridgeway usually looked. "I suppose they're shorter."

"Indeed. I despaired of them growing too full. A man wants to appear dignified, but after all, one doesn't wish to look like the Prime Minister."

"No chance of that." Jasper crossed the floor to take a seat in a velvet-upholstered wingchair near the fire.

Ridgeway kept only enough servants to support a bachelor establishment. His house was, nevertheless, comfortable and well-tended—a definite improvement from the hotel Jasper had been staying at when he'd first arrived in town.

Not that he'd had much choice in lodgings at the time.

He had no family in London to impose upon. No real friends on whom he could inflict his company.

Even his connection with Ridgeway was tenuous at best.

They'd met six years ago in Constantinople—both men at their lowest ebb. Ridgeway had come to Scutari Hospital to collect the body of his younger brother, killed in the skirmish that had taken the lives of the rest of Jasper's men.

Jasper had been at Scutari, too; not on an errand, but as a gravely injured patient—the sole survivor of the skirmish, rendered all but unrecognizable by the severe wounds on his face.

Ridgeway had spoken to him, attempting to rally his spirits. A futile task. Jasper had been in no mood to speak to anyone. But later, upon his release from hospital, when Ridgeway had written to him, Jasper had grudgingly replied.

An occasional correspondence had followed.

It wasn't a friendship. Not anywhere near it. Jasper hadn't any friends. And unless he was mistaken, neither had Ridgeway. They were merely two men brought together by circumstance. Cordial acquaintances—and sometimes, not even that.

Indeed, since coming to stay with him, Jasper had found Ridgeway's cold-bloodedness increasingly repellant.

"Why so glum?" Ridgeway cast him a glance. "No luck with Miss Wychwood?"

"Luck has nothing to do with it."

"You did see her?"

"I did," Jasper said. Despite the fact that she clearly didn't want to be seen.

Given the drab, ill-fitting clothing that shrouded her figure and the riding veil that concealed her face, one might think she had reason to hide. That her face and body were something to be ashamed of.

It wasn't true.

Julia Wychwood was beautiful.

He'd realized that from the first moment he'd set eyes on her.

In another time—another life—he might have been in grave danger of losing his heart.

Ridgeway continued admiring his reflection. "What's the problem, then?"

"The problem," Jasper said, "is that this business is becoming quite a bit more mercenary than I'd intended."

"Courtship *is* mercenary. And marriage is positively cutthroat. If you don't have the stones for it, you may as well resign yourself to a permanent state of bachelorhood." Ridgeway smoothed his hand over his side-whiskers. "Which isn't so bad, now I think on it. So long as you can afford it."

"Which I can't," Jasper reminded him.

Ridgeway shrugged. "There you are, then."

"Yes," Jasper said. "Here I am. And there you are, being absolutely useless, per usual."

"I say. That's unfair. Didn't I introduce you to her?" Ridgeway met Jasper's eyes in the glass. "She's an heiress. A sickly heiress, too. Take my advice and marry the chit. She won't overburden you for long."

Jasper's jaw tightened on a surge of anger. Mercenary he may be, but he hadn't yet sunk to marrying an invalid and praying for her early demise. "You're very sure of yourself."

Ridgeway shrugged. "She took to her bed last month for several days. I hear that the doctor was called in to bleed her. She's already a pasty thing. How much more blood do you suppose she has left to offer?"

"She's stronger than she looks."

"You can't know that. You've only seen her a handful of times."

"I've seen enough. I've seen her ride. She's not yet at death's door." Jasper paused, adding, "And she's not pasty."

"No? What would you call her complexion? It's not marble or alabaster. Not like her friend, Lady Anne." Ridgeway again looked at Jasper in the glass. "By the by, if you take my advice, you'll make the most of that lady's absence from town. You might have noticed, whenever she's here, she guards her little protégé like a hydrophobic mastiff."

"Lady Anne has left London?" That *was* news. "For how long?"

Another shrug. "A few days. She and her mother have hared off to Birmingham to look in on that child medium everyone's talking about. The one who claims to have contacted Prince Albert."

Jasper's lips compressed. He'd heard of the boy. When one was out in fashionable society, it was impossible not to. Jasper put no stock in such tales. No more than he put in spiritualism as a whole. It was all so much nonsense. Ghosts and spirits and proclamations from beyond the veil.

As if he hadn't enough of that to deal with in Yorkshire.

"I wonder that Miss Wychwood didn't accompany them," he said.

"The Wychwoods don't involve themselves in such things. They've enough trouble on this side of the grave, what with their rapidly failing health." Ridgeway stood abruptly. "Speaking of which, Fennel tells me that Miss Wychwood will be attending Lady Camden's musicale this evening. Good thing you didn't refuse the invitation."

Jasper sighed. A musicale meant a crowded room filled with the cream of London society. It meant him, sitting shoulder-to-shoulder with eligible young misses and their overbearing mamas.

"Having second thoughts?" Ridgeway asked.

Yes. And third ones, too.

But Jasper wasn't going to confide all of his doubts in Ridgeway. The man already knew too much. "There must be someone else who will suit."

"What?" Ridgeway gave him a narrow glance. "Another heiress, do you mean?"

"Yes," Jasper said. "Exactly that. Someone who . . ."

Someone who didn't nearly faint at the sight of him. Who wasn't afraid to look him in the face.

From anyone else, he could have tolerated well-bred disgust. It was a frequent enough reaction to his appearance. But he couldn't accept it from *her.*

"Blast it," he muttered under his breath. "This shouldn't be so complicated."

"It isn't." Ridgeway reached for his coat and tugged it on. "You require an heiress with no family or connections—no one to ask questions about you or to come snooping to Yorkshire. The only heiress who fits the bill is Julia Wychwood. If not her, then you may as well let the bailiffs take your estate."

Jasper ran a hand through his hair in frustration. The bailiffs. Bloody hell. It wasn't going to come to that, was it? Not after everything he'd already risked to forge a new life for himself.

Ridgeway laughed. "The look on your face. One would think you were too high-minded to follow through with it."

An image of Miss Wychwood materialized in Jasper's mind, her sapphire blue eyes shining vividly from behind her black net riding veil.

"I believe I owe you an apology."

She'd taken him completely off of his guard. Had puzzled and disarmed him.

Was she really who she appeared to be? A sickly wallflower heiress, ripe for the plucking?

He was beginning to have his doubts. "I might be."

"Bah," Ridgeway scoffed. "That's not the man my brother wrote to me about during the war. The cruel, ruthless, bloodthirsty Captain Blunt who had all of his men shivering in their boots. Surely you remember him?"

"Only too well," Jasper said grimly.

"Do you? Because it sometimes seems to me that you're not that man at all."

The accusation turned Jasper's blood to ice. His gaze jerked to Ridgeway's face. There seemed to be no ulterior meaning in his words. No hint of a threat. "I may well have been ruthless," he replied, "but never with women. And never outside times of war."

"My dear fellow, this *is* a war," Ridgeway said. "It's the London season."

He just wanted a decent book to read ...

Not too much to ask, is it? It was in 1935 when Allen Lane, Managing
Director of Bodley Head Publishers, stood on a platform at Exeter railway
station looking for something good to read on his journey back to London.
His choice was limited to popular magazines and poor-quality paperbacks –
the same choice faced every day by the vast majority of readers, few of
whom could afford hardbacks. Lane's disappointment and subsequent anger
at the range of books generally available led him to found a company – and
change the world.

*'We believed in the existence in this country of a vast reading public for intelligent
books at a low price, and staked everything on it'*
Sir Allen Lane, 1902–1970, founder of Penguin Books

The quality paperback had arrived – and not just in bookshops. Lane was
adamant that his Penguins should appear in chain stores and tobacconists,
and should cost no more than a packet of cigarettes.

Reading habits (and cigarette prices) have changed since 1935, but
Penguin still believes in publishing the best books for everybody to
enjoy. We still believe that good design costs no more than bad design,
and we still believe that quality books published passionately and responsibly
make the world a better place.

So wherever you see the little bird – whether it's on a piece of
prize-winning literary fiction or a celebrity autobiography, political tour
de force or historical masterpiece, a serial-killer thriller, reference book,
world classic or a piece of pure escapism – you can bet that it represents
the very best that the genre has to offer.

Whatever you like to read – trust Penguin.